The Empress Speaks...

"We *can*not and will not allow this insult to pass without a response. *Oni* will avenge us."

"You are playing with fire," her son said. "He is too much his own man. No one controls *Oni* — no one."

"I can. I can control any man . . ."

ONI

Also by Marc Olden...

GAIJIN

"Fast-paced, gritty . . . The intricate plot and rousing offbeat cast make this book difficult to put down."
— *Publishers Weekly*

"Top-notch thriller . . . providing one cliff-hanging chapter after another . . . a delicious entertainment!" — *Kirkus*

DAI-SHO

"Fast-paced action well-laced with guts, sex and hair-raising violence." — *San Diego Magazine*

"Nerve-wracking and tense . . . action-packed adventure!"
— *Desert Sentinel*

"Violent, exotic  . . ." — *Pensacola News*

MARC OLDEN

ONI

JOVE BOOKS, NEW YORK

In memory of
Salvatore T. Chiantia

ONI

A Jove Book/published by arrangement with
the author

PRINTING HISTORY
Jove edition/December 1988

ISBN: 0-515-09800-0

Jove Books are published by The Berkley Publishing Group,
200 Madison Avenue, New York, New York 10016.
The name "JOVE" and the "J" logo
are trademarks belonging to Jove Publications, Inc.

PRINTED IN THE UNITED STATES OF AMERICA

10 9 8 7 6 5 4 3 2 1

ONI Japanese for demon or evil spirit. In Buddhist legend it appears as a hideous monster with horns, large mouth, fangs, and possesses tremendous physical strength. Also refers to anything hidden or invisible that harms or kills humans.

He who makes the first false move is certain to lose the game.

Japanese

Twelve armed men cannot control the strife created by one elegant woman.

Chinese

1

France

August

VIKTOR POLTAVA CRAWLED from his hiding place before dawn. Six hours in total blackness had sharpened his night vision for his mission. He worked well in darkness.

He was on a horse farm in a green valley south of the seaside resort of Deauville. Trained to hide for long periods without moving, he had lain beneath the floorboards in a stable hayloft, hood covering his eyes, a rag in his mouth to muffle any sound while he slept. He ate food he carried in his pockets—cakes made from bleached rice, dried plums, and the softest part of the pine. He quenched his thirst by chewing sesame seeds.

Earlier he had listened to stable hands in the stalls below him as they tended brood mares and stallions and spoke to each other in French. It was a language he associated with Russia, where he and other foreigners had been taught terrorist tactics by the GRU, Soviet military intelligence. His closest friend among the trainees had been a French-speaking African from Zaire, a happy-go-lucky university student with excellent connections in Moscow's black market and a taste for teenage Russian girls.

Viktor Poltava had also acquired certain disciplines in the guerrilla training camps of Cuba, North Yemen, Lebanon and Libya. But his most valuable instruction had come from Asia, from the timeless ideas of Sun Tzu, the Chinese military strategist of 2500 years ago. The writings of Sun Tzu had taught him to be single-minded in his striving for supreme excellence in warfare, to do this by combining violence with deceit.

Poltava had always faced danger with a cold-blooded self-possession, but returning to France *now* was risky. An Interpol murder warrant for his arrest was still outstanding. And there was the two million franc reward offered by the Molsheim family for his capture and conviction.

Eight months ago he had assassinated Count Molsheim in the Tuileries Gardens, then murdered an informant who had attempted to betray him to the Paris police. The informant, a PLO member and former comrade, had wanted the reward and also wanted to win leniency for an imprisoned homosexual lover. Given the two reasons for the Palestinian's treachery, Poltava decided to kill him twice.

He nailed a *kaffiyeh,* an Arab headdress, to the informant's skull, using short nails to prolong the agony. Then he cuffed both hands behind the Palestinian's back, connected one end of a wire to the cuffs, and wrapped the other end around his testicles. Writhing in pain, the informant only tightened the wire. In minutes he had cut off his testicles.

Poltava's information on Deauville called it the northern St. Tropez, the most elegant resort of its kind in northern Europe, a playground for the continent's rich and famous. From their castles and penthouses they came here to enjoy a racing season which attracted top jockeys and trainers from around the world. They also came for the yearling sales, extravagant parties, polo matches, and casino gambling. Not Poltava's sort of place at all. To him it was nothing more than a bauble for grown-up children.

He had stared at a long, balustraded white casino and at Deauville's huge marina where dozens of yachts were berthed and remembered when this show of privilege would have left him enraged. That reaction belonged to his Marxist days. Now he held no social feelings of any kind. No more blind obedience to words of political or moral command. He no longer lived within a circle traced for him by others.

Face hidden behind the tinted visor of a crash helmet, he had smiled at Deauville's luxury hotels, tennis courts, and mile-long boardwalk, feeling neither revulsion nor attachment, feeling only indifference. Then he had kick-started his motorbike and ridden out of town across a stone bridge built by Viking raiders a thousand years ago, heading for the horse farm and reminding himself that with the exception of Sun Tzu, all philosophies were nonsense.

He had come to France to kidnap a Japanese woman who had run away from her husband. For this, she and the man who had helped her were to be punished. Punished in a way that would be memorable. Her name was Hanako, and she was young and beautiful. Six months ago she had fled Taiwan while on a business trip with her husband and now felt herself to be safe. Stupid woman. The sort who sees a finger pointing at the moon and looks at the finger.

There were special tactics for special situations, Sun Tzu had written. When possible, gain victory by imposing your will on the enemy or by breaking his spirit. Do not place a premium on killing. Attack the enemy's mind. Destroy his will to resist.

Destroy Hanako's will to resist.

She was sixty yards from the stables, in a fourteenth-century French manor house ringed by tall hedges and set between two small man-made lakes. The house, however, was protected by a perimeter alarm guarding doors and ground floor windows. It was also protected by two men with Uzis and Dobermans. Two additional guards and a single Doberman patrolled outside the stable where Poltava was hiding.

He could have concealed himself in either of two empty stables on the property. But the stable with the horses was closest to the manor house. And to the generator.

The horse farm belonged to Serge Coutain, a forty-four-year-old wealthy Frenchman who owned the country's largest computer store chain and was the majority stockholder in a company that built American-style shopping malls in Asia. He had installed tight security to protect a collection of antique tapestries and a prized foal. The colt had been carried by a mare that had won the Epsom Derby and sired by an Irish stallion, a champion thoroughbred that had retired with ten million dollars in race winnings. Coutain was determined that his colt not suffer the fate of the Aga Khan's *Shergar,* a derby winner who had been kidnapped in 1983 and never seen again.

Hanako was now Coutain's mistress. Yesterday the two had left his Paris town house for Deauville, where they were to attend a dinner at the luxurious Normandy Hotel tomorrow night in honor of an American jockey now riding in France. The jockey had one hundred wins on French tracks so far this season and was well on his way to breaking the nation's record. Coutain also hoped to talk the jockey into appearing in advertisements for his stores.

Daytime, Poltava knew, had many distractions. He had used them to enter the stable unseen. But there were fewer distractions at night, when the guards would also be more alert. A warm wind blowing in from the Atlantic Ocean to the west was the greatest danger, for it could carry his scent to the Dobermans. Inside the stable, his scent was hidden by that of the horses.

Viktor Poltava was thirty, a barrel-chested, broad-shouldered man with dyed black hair combed forward to hide plastic surgery scars on his temples and forehead. He was the son of a Russian father and a Japanese mother, and had been born with an animal ferocity which he had made no attempt to eliminate. Instead he had allowed it to direct his conduct in the world. He was an expert with weapons, explosives and in unarmed combat. But it was Sun Tzu's strategy of maneuvering, movement, combat, and espionage that had made Poltava an assassin spoken of in quiet, frightened whispers.

Kidnapping the Japanese woman was only the first step in a mission that was to take him to England and America, then back to Asia. Since the mission was both complex and risky, he had demanded and received a full payment of five million dollars in advance.

He had no cause or good name to protect. Therefore he could concentrate his total energy on his sole commitment, the art of killing. And because he had learned that today's friend is tomorrow's enemy, he trusted no one. He worked alone.

Poltava was invisible in the darkened hayloft. He blended in with the night by wearing reddish-black clothing: jacket, trousers, and a hood that covered his face with two slits for his eyes. Black sneakers cushioned with cotton padding allowed him to walk silently. He carried his supplies in a black shoulder bag and in the pockets of his trousers and jacket.

Crouched near his hiding place, he took a pair of black leather gloves from his shoulder bag and put them on.

Then he listened.

Listened with his ears and mind.

He heard an owl hooting in the barley field behind the manor house, and the wind rustling in oak trees lining the driveway, and a guard whistling as he urinated against the stable door. And he heard static from the radio of a second guard who had paused near a one-room stone cottage attached to the back of the stable. The cottage held stud records and served as the manager's office. It was also fifteen feet away from the generator that supplied the farm's electrical power.

Beneath the hayloft a massive Percheron draft house leaned against the side of its stall, causing the boards to creak. The noise sent a rat scurrying away from the grain bin. And in the stall across from Poltava, the newborn foal struggled to stand on uncertain legs.

Fashion your tactics until they are like water, Sun Tzu had written, for as water runs from high places and races downward, so must a fighter avoid his opponent's strength and strike at his weakness. That fighter is invincible who shapes his tactics to the enemy.

Poltava walked to the edge of the hayloft, then climbed down a wooden ladder to the stalls. His night vision was astonishing; the stable was in complete blackness, but he could see well enough to read the smallest print in a book or letter.

He crossed a manure-smelling earthen floor to the stall with the foal and its mother, where he stopped and stroked the hinges on the stall door. Then he removed a small, flat can from his bag, held it to the hinges and squeezed. When the hinges were oiled, he returned the can to his bag and opened the door. The hinges were silent.

He looked for the mare and found her sleeping on her right side, rear end facing him. The spindly legged colt, however, sat on its haunches near its mother and stared at Poltava. The killer took a single step into the stall, then hunkered down on his heels

Marc Olden

in the straw and froze, his breathing shallow and silent. He locked eyes with the foal. Rather a pathetic creature, Poltava thought. More like a tall, thin dog with white ankles and a white streak on its forehead. Trusting, too. It craned its long neck closer to the killer.

Poltava remained motionless. No sense disturbing the mother. Not just yet.

He listened to the mare's exhausted breathing. She had been in poor health while carrying the foal and had then suffered through a difficult delivery. Pity.

Poltava slowly brought up his right hand, reached into a jacket pocket, and removed a lump of sugar. He held it out to the foal.

The animal sniffed at the offering, then parted its lips and took the sweet from the killer's hand.

Poltava held out a second lump. No sniffing this time. The colt went for it directly and even allowed Poltava to stroke its nose. A third lump, with Poltava inching forward, and the animal was completely within reach.

The killer raised himself into a crouch and gently embraced the colt, putting both arms around its neck, feeling its warmth against him, feeling its bones press against his thigh, feeling the colt relax and trust him. Poltava's strength was immense. He inhaled, his large chest expanding, then suddenly he tightened his grip and snapped the colt's neck, killing it instantly.

The mare raised its head and looked around.

Grabbing the dead colt by an ankle, Poltava dragged it from the stall and locked the door. Then he picked it up in his arms and walked to the front of the stable. Behind him the mare rolled onto its knees, then pushed itself to its feet and charged, smashing its head against the stall door.

At the front of the stable, Poltava removed a bridle from a door peg, wrapped it securely around the colt's neck and hung the animal from the peg. Then he ran the length of the stable until he reached the connecting door to the office. The door was never locked. Nor did he have to worry about the hinges. The mare was acting as he knew it would. She slashed at the stall door with her hooves and made enough noise to wake the dead.

Poltava entered the darkened cottage, closed the door behind him, then dropped to his stomach on the bare wooden floor and crawled behind a desk before looking around.

The room was small, low-ceilinged, and lit only by a streak of moonlight coming through a single window. Furniture was sparse: two desks, wooden folding chairs, file cabinets and a battered refrigerator. The walls were hung with charts of stud records, along with black-and-white photographs of race horses with their owners, jockeys, trainers. Poltava inhaled the smell of gasoline used to power the generator kept in a nearby shack.

He pulled at his belt buckle; it came free and he was holding a knife with a three-inch blade of high-carbon stainless steel. Raising himself from the floor, he reached across the desk in front of him and cut telephone lines to the outside and main house. He crawled to the second desk, cut its lines, then lay down on the floor and rolled to the closet door.

He froze when he heard the second guard, this one near the window and adjusting the leash on his Doberman. Poltava could not wait until the guard moved on; he oiled the closet door hinges, then entered and closed the door behind him. Inside, he pushed aside the few clothes hanging in front of him—overalls, raincoat, workshirts—and reached for the fuse box. He opened it, removed the four fuses which furnished electricity to the stables and cottage, and placed them in a pocket of the raincoat.

Seconds later he was back in the manager's office, leaning against the closet door, attaching the knife to his belt.

And listening.

He heard the mare's stall door crack under her hooves, and the mare whinnied and then the stable door opened and a heartbeat later a man shrieked. A smiling Poltava thought: He sounds like a woman, this one. Hearing the shriek, the second guard ran from his post toward the front of the stable. In the excitement the Doberman, always a high-strung dog, began to bark. And because the bark immediately faded, Poltava knew that the second guard had taken the dog with him.

Poltava walked to the window, crouched, and stared across a well-tended lawn at the manor house. By crossing the lawn he could easily reach the house, but that meant traveling over open ground under a quarter moon. The safest way to the house was the oak-lined driveway behind the cottage and running alongside the front lawn.

His eyes went to the darkened ouline of the generator shack. Before trying for the house, he would have to destroy the generator. Without it the house would have no electricity. And without electricity the alarm system was useless.

Both guards could now be heard at the stable entrance. Poltava saw the faint outline of flashlight beams around the connecting door. Which meant the guards had tried the light switches and knew that the search for an intruder would now have to be conducted in darkness. They would have to proceed with caution.

Poltava could not understand a word they were saying, but he did understand that the two men were angry. Angry about working in darkness and about someone having gotten past them and done *this*.

Of course, the dead colt angered them most of all, as Poltava knew it would. And anger would arouse their pride, making their judgment the worse for it. Anger would make them foolish and this was confirmed when he saw the house Dobermans appear from behind the hedges and race across the lawn, two lean shadows speeding toward the stable. Both house guards immediately followed. The stable guards had radioed for help in hunting down the intruder, or intruders.

Because one man had allowed his mind to become crippled at the sight of a dead colt, the manor house was now unguarded.

Barking and slavering, the house Dobermans reached the cottage, then disappeared on their way to the stable. Seconds later the first guard, bearded and balding, his Uzi held shoulder high, followed the Dobermans. His partner, a small, dark Algerian, took longer to show. He ran on his heels, mouth open, finger on the trigger of his Uzi. When this one passed the cottage, Poltava acted. After counting five he stepped outside, closed the door behind him, and ran to the generator shack.

The shack was the size of a child's playhouse, made of fading pinewood, and its sole window was caked with dirt. A tin window box held freshly seeded earth; Poltava's gloved fingers probed the earth until he found the key. He used it to open a thick padlock on the front door, pocketed the key, and entered the shack, closing the door behind him.

He stepped into a humid darkness heavy with the odors of gasoline and oil. The generator stood in the middle of an oil-stained concrete floor. Hammers, screwdrivers, and a worn copy of the French *Playboy* rested on a wooden bench against the far wall. The door and other walls were mildewed and stained by rain.

The motor's noise not only filled the shack but sent vibrations through the concrete floor strong enough to rattle Poltava's teeth.

He moved to within inches of the generator, a type he had seen before. It was a simple one; the conductor was an open coil of wire rotating between the poles of a permanent magnet.

Destroy the coil and slip rings, and you destroyed the generator.

Poltava reached into his shoulder bag and removed a thick glass vial. He carefully unscrewed the top, leaned forward, and poured acid on the coil and slip rings. Smoke quickly rose from the generator, forcing him to step back. There was an acrid smell as glowing pieces of the saucer-shaped coil broke loose and fell into the machine. The slip rings disappeared immediately; they were made of thin metal strips and the acid liquefied them in seconds.

Eyes on the generator, Poltava edged toward the door. When the generator suddenly stopped, he leaped from the shack and threw the vial high in the air, toward the oak trees. Then he padlocked the door and raced toward the trees, running gracefully with his knees high and arms pumping rhythmically. At the trees he slowed his pace, turned right, and headed for the manor house. He ran from tree to tree, staying in the shadows and on the soft grass, avoiding the graveled driveway.

At the house he crouched behind a row of tall hedges, keeping the hedges between himself and the stable. He had given the guards enough to occupy them for the next few minutes. They would begin by searching the stable where the colt had been killed, then move on to the empty stables. They would awaken two full-time farm hands living in a cottage at the entrance to the driveway, and then everyone would search the storage shacks, an abandoned windmill, an apple orchard and the tack room, where saddles and bridles were stored. All of this should keep the guards and dogs away from the manor house long enough for Poltava to get in and out.

He looked at the manor house. It was a magnificent, two-story building, one of the better examples of Norman architecture in the area. Made of timber and limestone, it had a beauty spoiled only by a television antenna and an adjacent four-car garage. To

the right was a pool and patio ringed by white wooden furniture
and large colored umbrellas. Behind the house was more lawn, a
garden, and a shoulder-high field of barley. Beyond lay pasture
land leading to rolling hills and the jagged Atlantic coast.

Poltava jogged to the left side of the house, then stopped and
looked up at the second floor. The master bedroom was directly
above him, perhaps fourteen feet away. And two of its casement
windows were half open.

He reached into his bag and took out a pair of *tekagi,* metal
climbing devices used by feudal *ninja.* Each consisted of one
wide and one narrow metal band connected by a three-inch metal
strip. He slipped the narrow band over his hand and pushed it
down around his wrist. This left the wide band to fit around his
palm. Four spikes extended from the palm side.

He stepped forward, stretched his right arm overhead, and
clawed at the timbered wall. Pulling himself up, he reached
higher with his left hand, catching the wood and climbing toward
the window. He reached it in seconds, silently pushed it entirely
open, and peered into the darkened bedroom.

Six feet away a couple slept in a canopied bed. Fourteenth-
century paintings of minstrels, flowers, and jousting knights on
the walls and ceilings gave the large room a pleasant warmth. On
a table at the foot of the bed, two silver-gilt candelabra stood in
the middle of empty champagne bottles and the remains of a late
supper. Small model cannon flanked either side of a fireplace,
and a coat of arms hung above a heavy timbered bedroom door
bolted from the inside. The oak floor gleamed under moonlight.
Poltava, who appreciated fine art, briefly admired a pair of Au-
busson tapestry portières hanging from a far wall. They would
fetch a pretty penny. Theft, however, was not on his agenda.

He crawled across the window ledge on his stomach, brushing
over wires connected to the magnetic detectors at the top of the
window. The detectors were to have sent an electrical signal to
the control box in case of an intruder, and that would have started
horns blaring throughout the house.

Poltava sat facing the bed, his dew-wet shoes held inches off
the floor. Removing his shoes and the *tekagi,* he placed them in
his bag and stood up. He spent several seconds listening to Coutain and Hanako's breathing, and when he was satisfied that they

were truly in a deep sleep, he walked over to the bed in his stockinged feet.

The Frenchman was huddled close to the Japanese woman's bare back, their bodies covered from the waist down by black satin monogrammed sheets. Serge Coutain was short and thick-set, with thinning brown hair, moustache and a slight snore. Hanako was a small, sun-bronzed woman, with a full mouth and blue-black hair. No photograph could do justice to her hair, which was thick, glossy, and hung down to the small of her back. Coutain's face was partially hidden by the hair, as though he had tried to lose himself in it. Poltava also found her hair erotic.

He unzipped a pocket near his ankle, removed a thin black case, and took out a hypodermic needle. Then he walked around to Hanako's side of the bed. She was truly a beautiful woman. On an end table facing her were two small plastic vials; one was empty, while the other held a few grains of a white powder that Poltava knew was cocaine. He knew about her drug habits, just as he knew about her preference for American films, foreign sports cars, fast foods, and rich western men. She had wanted these things badly enough to leave her Japanese husband.

Poltava leaned over the bed and injected her high on the right arm, near a star-shaped mole. She moaned and attempted to open her eyes. The drug, however, took effect immediately. Her breathing became much slower, and she sank into an even deeper sleep.

Poltava dropped the hypodermic into his bag and took out a folded white handkerchief and a thumb-sized vial. He poured the vial's contents onto the handkerchief, then pulled a four-inch steel needle from the bag's shoulder strap and drew it across the damp handkerchief until it glistened. After walking around to Coutain's side of the bed, he leaned over the sleeping French-man, clamped his left hand over his mouth, and shoved the nee-dle into the base of his skull, into the hair which would hide the puncture mark.

Eyes bulging, Coutain woke up and lashed out with his arms, striking Hanako. Poltava climbed onto the bed, placed his right knee on Coutain's spine and held him in place, containing his struggle. Seconds later, it was over. Coutain relaxed and Poltava climbed off the bed. Then Coutain trembled violently for a few seconds, flopped over on his back, and clawed at the sheets before lying still to stare up at the canopy with sightless eyes. He wasn't dead. But he was in hell.

Poltava's training in *yagen,* pharmacy, had taught him to make various poisons, special powders, even curatives. The injection he'd given Coutain had been a compound made from the deadly blowfish, the powder of male rats, and the leaves of the *paulownia* tree. It had just destroyed the Frenchman's mind, turning him into a total and permanent human vegetable. He had been suitably punished.

Crushing a man like Coutain gave Poltava a sense of power. Simultaneously there was a terrible coldness in the killer which left him remarkably unaffected by what he had just done. On these occasions something inside him came to dominate his consciousness and make violence a necessity.

Hanako's injection had not been fatal. It had only rendered her unconscious, to be dealt with at another time, in another place. Poltava pulled back the sheet and looked down at her nude body. She was extremely still. Totally motionless. Almost as if she were dead. Poltava had always found a sensuality in death. Even now he felt the beginnings of an erection.

Her hair. . . .

It would have to be cut. It might easily knock over something while he was carrying her from the house. And his plan called for taking her to the sea a mile away, a journey to be made on foot. He would be traveling through woods and did not want to have Hanako's hair catch on a branch and break her neck. To deliver a corpse to those who had paid him was to have failed.

He pulled the buckle knife free, knelt on the bed beside the unconscious woman, and began to hack at her hair. Her motionless body aroused sensuous feelings in him, but he forced himself to ignore them. Instead he applied himself to the task at hand and when he finished, her hair had been chopped off at the base of her skull. The shorn hair, almost two feet of it, was dropped into his bag. He would make excellent use of it later on.

After checking Hanako's purse to be sure it contained her passport, he slung it over a shoulder and dressed her in a flowered housecoat. Then he draped her over the same shoulder, crossed the room, and slipped out of the house without making a sound. Outside, he walked through rows of roses that had been carefully trained to grow on wooden stakes until he reached a small flight of stone steps leading up to another iron gate.

He'd just closed the second gate behind him when he heard the dogs.

He stopped to glance over his shoulder, saw flashlight beams as men raced across the front lawn of the house, then smiled and turned his back to them. Looking straight ahead and past the barley field, Poltava's eyes went to the rolling hills in the distance. Then he looked up at the sky, marked the twin stars that were to be his guide, and raced forward, plunging into the shoulder-high field of golden grain and disappearing from sight, tightening his grip on the woman who was to be punished by *Oni*. The demon.

2

MRS. REIKO GENNAI stepped aside and allowed the three women to precede her into a small room of her hilltop Tokyo villa. She was the hostess for this afternoon's tea ceremony; tradition said she must be the last to enter the waiting room. Inside she lowered herself to the matted floor, closed the sliding paper door, then bowed to her guests. The gesture was a very formal one: Knees on the mat, then palms on the floor and a bow between the hands, head to within four inches of the mat.

When she sat back on her heels, she kept her body straight, with the big toes placed one on top of the other. She believed in the meticulous observance of etiquette, so she had performed the bow with aristocratic precision. As wife of the president of the *Mujin* group, Japan's largest multinational corporation, she was a person of very high rank, higher than that of the three young women now sitting on the floor in front of her. All three were married to major executives at *Mujin,* which did not give them the right to insult her, as they were doing.

The insults were meant to be subtle, but Reiko Gennai, quick to perceive and apprehend, missed nothing. For one thing, her bow was not returned. Yuriko, at twenty-seven the oldest of the three guests, politely said that bowing was obsolete. It belonged to Japan's dead past and not even her husband, who still clung to many of the old ways, could make her do it. Yuka and Oman, the other two, took their cue from Yuriko and also refused to bow. Mrs. Gennai could have told them there was nothing wrong with good manners, but she said nothing.

Nor did she comment on the fact that her guests had arrived late. Yuka and Oman had offered excuses. No apologies, merely excuses. Yuka said her regular chauffeur was ill and an inexperienced replacement had to be forced into service, while Oman claimed to have stopped off to pick up a favorite bracelet that was still being repaired upon her arrival at the jeweler's. Pitiful, pitiful lies.

Mrs. Gennai knew the truth. Yuka's tardiness was due to a prolonged telephone conversation she'd had with a man with whom she was about to begin an adulterous affair. And Oman was late because of a meeting with a *yakuza* loan shark over her gambling debts, a secret she wanted kept from her easily angered husband.

As for Yuriko, she arrived last, offering no excuse whatsoever, even refusing to give the maid her card to be presented to Mrs. Gennai. Yuriko was showing an increasing disrespect for Mrs. Gennai, which was not going unnoticed by other company wives. Lately the insolent Yuriko had begun to place too great a value on herself. It was time Mrs. Gennai let her know that she did not approve of this.

The four women had gathered in a room which looked out on the giant tulip trees of Ueno Park, Tokyo's largest and most popular park. Here guests relaxed before the actual tea ceremony, to be held in a tiny hut in Mrs. Gennai's walled garden. The room was bare, except for clean rice straw mats on the floor, a low cedar wood table, and a single shelf containing a dozen rare books on the tea ceremony. The *tokonoma*, a recessed alcove, was decorated with an *ikebana* arrangement of irises and a bare branch, along with a hanging scroll of calligraphy. The calligraphy, black ink on yellow silk, had been done in precise, beautiful brush strokes by Mrs. Gennai. Good manners called for guests to praise a host's calligraphy. The three young women, however, refused to do so.

Of the seven forms of tea ceremonies, Reiko Gennai had chosen *shogo no saji*, noon tea, named for the hour it was scheduled to begin. A powdered tea called *matcha* was served; it was so strong that it could not be taken on an empty stomach, therefore a meal was served in the waiting room thirty minutes before the formal tea party. The meal was always simple, in keeping with the purpose of the tea ceremony which was to instill in guests, whether high or low, the love of simplicity and tranquility. Above all, the goal of the tea ceremony was to teach humility.

In the past Reiko Gennai had invited *Mujin* wives to tea ceremonies, which served as occasions for pleasant conversation and conviviality. Today's ceremony, however, was special. When it ended she was certain that her three guests would have learned the value of humility and would be less impudent to her in the future. After today these three would no longer consider themselves exempt from authority.

The marriage of the three to *Mujin* executives had been arranged by Mrs. Gennai, who had arranged similar company marriages for suitable young women over the years. Unfortunately, the marriages of Yuriko, Oman, and Yuka were now threatened by their unacceptable conduct, something that could cause trouble for the company. Reiko Gennai had made *Mujin* her life; to protect it, she would have to curb the disobedient and unpredictable behavior of these three. For the good of the company and their own good as well, they would have to comply with her commands and instructions.

Reiko Gennai was in her late fifties, a thin woman who looked years younger and had flawless golden skin, sloe eyes, and jet black hair worn in a chignon. The chignon was held in place by three-hundred-year-old silver combs with inlaid designs, which were chosen for their craftsmanship and as a charm against evil. In the September heat she wore a summer kimono of gray cotton edged in black silk, with the Gennai family crest on the back and sleeves. Since she was not in western dress, she wore no jewelry. The buckle on the broad sash around her waist was made of lacquered wood, and she cooled herself with a fan of orange silk stretched over ivory ribs. She was the wife of a man whose company last year grossed over one hundred billion dollars.

Her husband, Yasuda Gennai, was president of the *Mujin* Group, which his family had founded five hundred years ago. Dwarfing any western multinational, *Mujin* was an empire stretching around the globe. Its confederation of four hundred companies dealt in businesses ranging from hotel chains to electronics. It had three million employees and offices in ninety countries which were linked by privately leased telephone and telex networks. *Mujin* was a kingdom which knew no borders.

While her husband was *Mujin*'s president, it was Reiko Gennai who ruled the company with an unconditional authority. She had no official status, but Yasuda Gennai had come to rely on her judgment, on the sharpness and clarity of her mind, on her strength. These traits, along with her aging husband's failing health, had allowed her to become *Mujin*'s shadow ruler. Like queens and concubines of the past, she had become the power behind the throne. And she had done it in a chauvinistic society where most women had power only in the home or among their families. To many she was known as "The Empress." She was not disturbed by the term.

She had conspired to become the wife of Yasuda Gennai and because she had an unbridled ambition for domination, she had connived to remain at his side. In her role as *Mujin*'s shadow ruler, there were secrets which she kept hidden as she would a physical defect. But this shrouded part of her life was now threatened by something so dangerous that it could put an end to the world she had so carefully built for herself.

The danger had begun with her husband's illness. He was twenty-three years older than she and seriously ailing from a series of strokes. Doctors had also recently discovered the presence of stomach cancer, which they pronounced incurable. The medical consensus was that his life could not be saved. Yasuda Gennai's immortality had been a delusion; he was neither eternal nor everlasting after all, a fact which surprised others more than it did Reiko Gennai. She believed that one's life was predestined. Nothing could change this. *Shini-gama,* god of death, had a book in which a date was written down for each person to die, and these death dates must be faithfully followed.

She knew for certain that the time of her husband's death was near. To her eyes his shadow had become faint. A dead man had no shadow; therefore, as the end approached, everyone's shadow became faint. Some called this a superstition, refusing to believe that approaching death brought any change whatsoever in a shadow. Reiko, however, knew it brought changes in one's attitude or manner. Her husband had lost his confidence and physical strength, things he had always prided himself on. He was also dependent on others, a trait he had always despised in anyone else, and he was more frightened than he had ever been in his life. Such changes, Reiko knew, meant the approach of *Shinigama*.

Before expiring, their love had ranged from intense sexuality to betrayal; in the end it had outwardly become a quiet companionship and away from the public eye, an uneasy alliance, for she had been the first to stop loving and thus the advantage was hers. He increasingly complied with her decisions concerning *Mujin*, because it was she who made certain that in the winter of his life his power continued to be used and that he remained feared and respected. They had ceased to be equal partners when she had learned the secret of their relationship; she was essential to his reign at *Mujin* because she was better fitted for the life of deception necessary in corporate affairs than he.

She also knew that his confidence in himself was shaken by her steeliness and that after their marriage he never quite trusted himself again. She alone knew that he welcomed death as an escape from her.

As her husband's health deteriorated, she watched the struggle begin to succeed him as company president. While she could influence those executives through those wives who were obligated to her, Reiko's future was no longer assured. She had made enemies of certain administrators, directors and division managers, men who could be influential in selecting the next president, men over whom she had little or no control. Meanwhile every day brought her husband closer to death and freed these executives from any fear of him and "The Empress." She would now have to defend herself against the ambitions of these men, some of whom would surely revenge themselves against her at the first opportunity.

Since the only passion of her life was power, she was determined to continue her role at *Mujin* at any cost. To do this she must choose the next president. He would have to be an outstanding leader, while submitting to her judgment and wishes. Her choice: Hanzo Gennai, her son and only child, and the president of *Mujin*'s worldwide banking division, which had shown a profit every year since he had taken it over.

He was forty-one, a beefy, thick-lipped man with close cropped graying hair and a withered left arm. At *Mujin,* he had begun as an office boy in the communications center, and because of a talent for finance he had worked his way up through the banking divisions in Europe, America, South Africa, Central America, and Japan. His success was not due to risk taking, but in adhering to a course of action without giving way. He saw his goals and aimed for them unswervingly. His mother had instilled in him an obsessive desire to win, while also teaching him to hide his true feelings and thoughts.

"One should not speak of secret matters even to the trees," she said to him.

She was extremely supportive and protective of Hanzo, loving him with an all enveloping and possessive love. Maternal cannibalism, her detractors called it. Nor did she hesitate to make unreasonable demands on him because of this love. As a result Hanzo was high-strung and edgy, particularly in an emergency, for he knew he dare not fail her, that she expected him to win at all costs. Which is why he became a man who saw everyone as a commodity to be exploited for his purposes.

He had little choice.

"There is no other way to survive in the cold-blooded world of business," his mother said. "You are involved in a war and there can be no substitute for victory, for success. As the son of *Mujin*'s president, your only goals are those of his company. The company's rewards are your rewards, and your obligation to it must never waver. Should *Mujin* fail, you will lose everything, for the company's disgrace and your father's disgrace will be your own. You will be destroyed; therefore you must fight for *Mujin* with the zeal of a samurai willing to die rather than face dishonor."

With Reiko Gennai lending Hanzo her experience, and with his extraordinary persistence, he attained the goals she had set for him. Thus she saw no reason why he should not make a successful *Mujin* president, as long as she was shadow ruler.

Her mind was fixed on Hanzo succeeding his father; the idea was a fire inside her and made Reiko incapable of having compassion for anyone who stood in her way.

Hanzo's chief rival, as she saw it, was Tetsu Okuhara, head of electronics, *Mujin*'s most successful division. He was in his early

fifties, a lean man with an austere face, intense gaze, and dark
hair parted in the middle. He was an outstanding executive, tact-
ful and intelligent, but totally lacking any sentimentality. Yasuda
Gennai had said little about a successor, but Reiko knew he favored Okuhara, his protégé and godson, over their child.

She feared Okuhara because she had never been able to control him. His only loyalty was to Yasuda Gennai, who had
brought him into the company directly from Tokyo University
where he had graduated at the top of his class. Reiko also feared
Okuhara because she had been attracted to the cold passion bor-
dering on sadism, which lay behind his quick eyes. She had
shown a rare weakness by falling in love with him and entering
into a love affair, confident that she alone would finally dominate
this one man whose strength appeared to match hers.

But she had failed, for he had been strong and too astute when
it came to understanding the motives behind her actions. In bed,
he had compelled her to submit to him, degrading and exciting
her at once, and when he had forced her to make him the focus of
her longing, he deliberately ended the affair. It was a humiliation
she would never forgive. For that reason and no other, she had
vowed he would never be president of *Mujin*.

But there was her husband's undeclared support of him as a
successor, and the backing from those executives who favored
Okuhara because of his cool insolence toward the woman he had
humbled in bed. His insolence had given them the courage to
defy her, albeit in little ways.

In the remorseless working of *karma*, fate, the approaching
death of Reiko's husband and the fight to succeed him had created a threat to her beyond that of losing her authority at *Mujin*.
Someone at the company, a damned Judas, was passing to people
in America and England the most private *Mujin* business secrets,
along with highly damaging information about the Gennai family
itself. Public exposure of this data would be extremely harmful,
particularly in America, *Mujin*'s largest and most lucrative overseas market. The American Congress, Justice Department, FBI,
and the American press would form a pack of howling jackals all
anxious to tear into *Mujin*. War criminal charges would again be
leveled at Yasuda Gennai and members of his family, while in
America an unsolved triple murder of forty years ago would be

reopened. The Empress herself would face a criminal trial and imprisonment.

Mujin's own Judas knew that major Japanese newspapers would never risk offending large advertisers with investigative reports of company wrongdoing. Such reports would mean a heavy loss of income for the newspaper, as well as government and social condemnation for having caused important businessmen to suffer a loss of face in front of the rest of the world. The Japanese were one tribe, a close-knit group which always protected its own against the outside world.

But once the most unflattering story appeared in western papers, any Japanese publication was then free to reprint whatever it wanted. That's why *Mujin*'s Judas was offering his information to people in America and Britain, while bypassing his own country. None of this data had been printed, but Reiko knew it was only a matter of time before this happened.

She had an idea who Judas might be, but it would take more, much more than that to bring him down. He was too important to approach in a haphazard manner. She had her own name for this man who wanted to end her role at *Mujin,* who wanted to prevent her son from becoming president, who wanted to reduce her to nonexistence. She called him *Aikuchi,* the short sword carried surreptitiously by gangsters. *Aikuchi* was the blade now being pressed against her throat.

To deal with him and his western allies, the Empress had called on *Oni.*

In the small anteroom of her villa, Reiko Gennai watched Yuka and Oman pick at vinegared rice, fish soup, and pickles on the low table before them. Yuriko refused to eat; she chain-smoked, spoke only when spoken to, and restlessly glanced at her watch. Reiko led the discussion on the tea ceremony, describing it as worship of purity and refinement, an adoration of the beautiful among the sordid facts of everyday existence. She attempted to get across to the young women that in this ancient ceremony the hosts and guests share a spirit of respect, gratitude, and friendship.

At no time did she comment on the breaches of etiquette committed by her guests. For example, there were small linen cushions on the floor and two of the women had made use of them before Reiko had done so. Yuka and Oman had slid cushions under their knees, while Yuriko had been even more insulting. She was sitting in front of the *tokonoma,* the seat of honor, which the hostess had not assigned to her or to anyone else. Yuriko also sat with her feet pointed sideways to relax her knees. It was improper to sit in such fashion before one of superior rank. Nor had Yuriko asked Reiko's permission to smoke.

Reiko alone wore the light, unlined summer kimono which was offered to all guests. The three young women, however, remained in western clothes that, while fashionable, struck Reiko as being in questionable taste. Oman wore a leather skirt which Reiko felt was a bit too short, while Yuka's silk skirt seemed a bit trampish with its tight fit and slit in the front. Yuriko wore baggy western jeans imported from France, along with a checkered tank top under which her nipples were clearly outlined. All three looked more like bold, brazen girls rather than the wives of respectable executives.

A few years of their husbands' money had allowed these women to fall under the amiable illusion that they now shaped their own lives and could afford to be indifferent to the Empress. Reiko knew what they were thinking: *We need curry favor only with ourselves and not with the Empress, who has given us everything.* Well, it was time she placed the halter of authority around the necks of these young colts. It was time all three learned to fear the Empress once more.

She continued to talk about the tea ceremony, the supposed reason for their getting together today. "One must remember that teaism is a warning against extravagance, that it is designed to instill in us a love of simplicity and serenity."

Silence.

Yuka and Oman poked their food with chopsticks, while Yuriko looked down at the silver-tipped fingernails of one hand.

Mrs. Gennai dipped her chopsticks slightly in her tea to cleanse them, then placed the chopsticks on her tray to show that she had finished eating. Fanning herself, she rose from the floor, walked to a paper window, and slid it open. Back to her guests, she stared into the walled garden at the tea house. It was small, two rooms and barely six feet tall, with roughly finished plaster walls, bamboo ceiling, and only two paper-covered windows. The tea house and the bamboo fence around it had a plain, stark appearance designed to give the suggestion of refined poverty called for by the tea ceremony.

Mrs. Gennai said, "Yuriko, do you know why the door to the tea house is called *nijiri-guchi,* the wriggling-in entrance?"

Yuriko blew smoke at the ceiling, then flicked a speck of ash from her jeans. "Please be kind enough to tell me." Her tone held a calm audacity.

Oman quickly looked at Yuriko and shook her head. Yuka closed her eyes.

The Empress said, "The entrance is quite small. Quite small. No more than three feet high, so one must bend low and crawl to enter the tea house. This communicates the true purpose of the tea ceremony. Humility. *Hai,* humility. King or a slave, you must creep into the house on your hands and knees. No matter who you are, you must learn humility."

Yuriko stared at the older woman's back. "Humility is one of my husband's favorite words. He insists that a wife is to be humble in her husband's presence at all times. He says that humility is a great aid in building character."

The Empress arched a single eyebrow. "And you disagree?"

Yuriko dropped an unfinished Marlboro into her untouched tea, then reached for her almost empty cigarette pack. "It has just occurred to me that perhaps the three of us have been invited here for reasons other than the tea ceremony. Could it be we are here because we are to be involved in the plan to make your son the next president of *Mujin?*"

She blew smoke through her nose. "Your son . . ." She left the sentence unfinished. But there was no mistaking the contempt in her voice.

The Empress turned to face her. The older woman was smiling, but her eyes were icy, unforgiving. "He isn't just my son. He is also your husband. Have you so little respect for him?"

Yuriko was Hanzo's second wife. They had been married for a year; he had chosen her for her beauty and voluptuous figure, but now she was more of a competitor than a companion, and he could no longer bend her to his will. She insisted on remaining childless, had begun taking drugs and socialized too often with westerners when her husband was away on business trips. Such a wife could shame a man who was president of *Mujin.* And such a wife should not be allowed to influence other company wives, particularly those whose minds were not possessed of wisdom.

Lust held Hanzo in its grasp; he was besotted with Yuriko and did not want to lose her. Reiko told him that after today Yuriko would obey his every wish and give him the children he never had with his first marriage and still wanted badly. Today Yuriko would be made to see right reason and to do what was needful for the good of her husband.

The Empress said, "The three of you were quite friendly with Hanako, were you not?"

Yuka and Oman exchanged sly grins, schoolgirls sharing a secret behind the teacher's back. Yuriko, elbow on the back of one hand, brought her cigarette to her mouth. Then she allowed the smoke to drift from her nostrils; it hid her face, forming a barrier between her and the Empress. And her words were delivered with a barely controlled impudence. "It has been six months since Hanako left her husband, the husband you chose for her, the one who smelled no matter how many times a day he bathed. The one she could not bear to have touch her."

"Then my assumptions are correct," Mrs. Gennai said. "The three of you are getting your courage from Hanako's rebellion. Strong in her strength, it would appear."

"She is living her own life now," Yuriko said. "We are all quite happy for her and wish her well."

"My son tells me you plan to seek a divorce. You realize, of course, that such a thing is totally out of the question, especially now."

"Hanako has shown us that anything is possible. If nothing else, I can simply walk away without waiting for a lawyer's approval. Or anyone else's approval, for that matter. Hanako has also shown us that you can't be pushed around when you are thousands of miles away from people who want to run your life."

"Did you know that she was passing *Mujin*'s business secrets to someone in the West?"

Yuriko touched the half dozen thin gold bracelets she wore on one wrist. "The world of business holds little interest for me, so I have to wonder if Hanako would have much interest in it, either. It is difficult to believe that such a lighthearted girl would involve herself in something as mundane as the theft of company secrets. As far as I knew, her only objective was to live her own life, nothing more. Why would she steal *Mujin*'s secrets?"

"Had you paid more attention to your husband's work, you would know the answer to that question without having to be told. And I did not say Hanako stole secrets. I said that she passed them. As for why, the answer is rather obvious. She was asked to do so by Serge Coutain, with whom the three of you are already acquainted, I believe. In the past you have attended his parties and enjoyed his hospitality here in Tokyo, Hong Kong, and Seoul. I'm given to understand that his parties are quite lavish. I should also add that on occasion, the three of you attended those parties without your respective husbands."

"With or without husbands, those parties were related to business," Yuriko said. "I believe you have lectured us on the importance of advancing our husbands' careers. That is what we were doing by attending Mr. Coutain's parties."

Yuka and Oman both covered their mouths with a hand to suppress giggles. If Mrs. Gennai noticed, she said nothing. But she did say, "The danger in attending western social functions without your husband is that you can easily fall victim to those who would exploit your naiveté. I am talking about those who would lure you into betraying your husband and his company."

"With all due respect, let me say that I feel you are making more of this matter than necessary."

"I disagree. Hanako and Serge Coutain became infatuated with one another at one of his parties. Because of this feeling, she agreed to accept certain papers from someone at *Mujin,* someone who could not afford to be seen with Coutain and, at the same time, did not want to put these important papers in the mail."

"The focus today appears to be less on the tea ceremony and more on Hanako, Coutain, and *Mujin*'s business secrets. Speaking for myself, I would like to hear Hanako's side of the story."

"You believe that Coutain is strong enough to protect her, don't you? You feel she is beyond my reach, that I can no longer control her."

Yuriko permitted herself a small smile. "With all due respect, I am surprised you don't know that name of the man who is passing on secrets to Coutain."

"It appears the three of you feel that Hanako's defection indicates a diminishing of my powers. I should warn you: It is a mistake to underestimate me, as you shall soon see. The man who passed on the information to Coutain was Mr. Nikkei."

"One of *Mujin*'s accountants," Yuriko said. "The nice little man who plays classical guitar at company parties."

"Yes. Sad to say, Mr. Nikkei learned that we were on to him and last night he took his own life by hanging himself. He fled to the next world before he could be made to tell me who was behind his treachery. You see, Mr. Nikkei was merely a messenger boy of sorts. He was acting on behalf of a certain Judas, someone who works at *Mujin*. Someone I call *Aikuchi*."

Yuriko gathered her purse and cigarettes. "Your *Aikuchi* and Hanako have something in common. Neither can be dominated now, or coerced or intimidated or pressured, which seems to be the fate of all those who fall into *Mujin*'s web. With all due respect, you will have to excuse me now. I have an appointment with my hairdresser. I took the liberty of making it for this hour because I no longer drink tea. I'm sure you understand."

"Sit down." The Empress's voice was a cold hiss, and it made Yuriko's flesh creep. The younger woman's purse slipped from her hand to the matted floor, but she didn't look at it. Instead her eyes remained glued to the Empress's face.

The older woman said, "I have something I wish the three of you to see."

She clapped her hands twice, a signal. The sliding door was pulled back and two men in dark suits entered. One carried a projector, the other a small, rolled-up film screen and a single can of film. Both walked to the Empress, bowed from the waist, then stood waiting. She nodded, and the two placed the projector, film, and screen on the floor, then cleared the table, handing food and dishes to white-jacketed servants in the hall. Just as quickly, and in silence, the men set the projector on the low cedar wood table, plugged it in, and attached the film to the supply and take-up spindles. The screen was unrolled, then erected at one end of the room. One man closed the paper window, then both stood at attention, eyes on the Empress. She snapped her fan shut. One man stepped to the projector, and the other turned out the light.

A series of unfocused numbers flicked partially onscreen, partially on the wall. The picture, however, was soon focused and centered on the small screen. The film was in color. And it was almost totally without sound. Almost.

The opening shot was of the Arc de Triomphe, indicating that this portion of the film had been taken in Paris. Next came a shot

of the Rue de Rivoli, a charming old street of cafes, tourist and
perfume shops under nineteenth-century arcades. At the end of
the street stood an elegant town house with a cobbled courtyard
and formal French garden. Among the private cars and police
cars jamming the courtyard were a pair of ambulances. Japanese
subtitles explained that the town house was a private hospital for
the wealthy. The subtitles also noted that this was newsreel foot-
age taken by a Paris television station.

Next came a shot of the hospital lobby crowded with television cameramen, reporters, doctors, nurses, and the curious.
Subtitles said that the press wanted information on Serge Coutain's stroke but that security guards were trying to keep the
media from talking to Coutain's family. There was a quick shot of
Coutain himself, one taken through the open doorway of a room
overlooking the courtyard. It showed him glassy-eyed and slack-
jawed and lying in bed with rubber tubes from a life support
machine connected to his nose, arms, and chest. Subtitles said
that he was one of the richest men in France and that he was
suffering from a stroke which had rendered him helpless.

The camera lingered on Coutain for seconds until doctors and
members of Coutain's family filed into the room and a uniformed
security guard violently shoved the cameraman out into the hallway. As the camera focused on the closed door of Coutain's
room, subtitles said that doctors gave no hope of the Frenchman
ever regaining his health. He would be on the life support systems until he died.

An unblinking Yuriko stared at the screen in silent horror,
ignoring the growing ash on the cigarette between her fingers.
The eyes of Yuka and Oman began to tear, while the Empress
fanned herself and stared impassively at the screen, at the next
portion of the film which had been shot by a private cameraman.

It began with a night shot taken from the bow of a yacht
pulling away from a crowded marina of other yachts, sailboats,
and small pleasure craft. A dockside sign, barely visible in the
darkness, read Port-Deauville. On board the moving yacht, the
camera traveled past rowboats and a small helicopter roped to a
mini-landing pad and moved belowdeck, along a narrow, poorly
lit passageway and into a cabin at the far end.

The cabin was bright with light from wall lamps shaped like
sea horses. Two portholes were covered by black curtains, while

much of the pale green walls were covered by white sheets. Except for a bed and an end table, the room was empty of furniture. A nude Japanese woman lay on the bed, hands and feet securely tied to the four corners. She was beautiful and well-formed, and the shape of her eyes had been altered to give her a western "round eyes" look. It was Hanako, and in the silent film her screams went unheard.

Yuriko cried out and attempted to rise from the floor, but one of the men pressed down on her shoulder, keeping her in place. Yuka and Oman huddled together and sobbed aloud.

The camera lingered on Hanako for a few seconds, then swung around to the cabin doorway where a wide-shouldered muscular man stood waiting. His appearance was literally that of a beast, one easily recognized, for this beast appeared in Japanese legends and folklore, in films and books. He was one of the destructive forces Japanese artists used to depict the malignant side of mankind. He was *Oni*. The demon.

The man's head and face were covered by a demon's head, one with horns, bulbous eyes and a wide mouth with fangs. Long gray hair hung from the top of the demon head and down to the man's backside. He wore only a tigerskin loincloth and was barefoot. His bare arms and legs were masses of well-developed muscles. On the fingers of both hands he had attached steel claws.

The demon entered the cabin, his shadow touching the terror-stricken Hanako, and then he was at the foot of the bed, staring down at her, his very ugliness ominous and threatening. He circled the bed, the long and wispy gray hair trailing him like a pale mist. Then he stopped, raised his claw-tipped hands overhead, and looked up at the cabin ceiling, as though invoking gods from a mythic past. He climbed on the bed, straddling Hanako, a knee on either side of her body. He stared down at her with his demon face, watched her squirm beneath him, her head frantically twisting from side to side.

Using the heel of his left hand, he pressed down on her forehead, keeping her head in place against the bare mattress, and as the camera moved closer, the demon pushed a claw-tipped forefinger into Hanako's right eye and gouged it from the socket. Crazed by pain, she twisted her head free from his grip, spraying his bare chest and arms with her blood. And for the first time in the film there was sound, as the half blind Hanako's scream was finally heard, a sudden outcry that was all the more terrifying because of the long silence that had preceded it. The screaming continued as the demon gouged out her remaining eye and used his blooded claws to carve the word *kitsune* into Hanako's chest.

Yuka fainted.

An hysterical Oman threw herself into the arms of a sobbing Yuriko.

And though she slowed her fanning, the Empress never took her eyes from the screen.

The next scene. A crudely scrawled title card read: Bangkok. Then came shots of the city: teak houses, white sandy beaches, a canal lined on either side by wooden houses on stilts, a floating market of *sampans*—narrow boats filled with rice, fruit, liquor, sides of beef, flowers, the boats paddled by men and women with faces hidden by huge straw hats. And suddenly it was night, and the scene was Patpong, Bangkok's notorious red light district. Three square blocks of massage parlors, discotheques, whorehouses, key clubs owned by Golden Triangle druglords, bars owned by expatriate American GIs.

The area was garish with neon. Male Asian and western tourists jammed the sidewalks, overflowing into the streets. Those on scooters, in motor rickshas and minicars slowed down to stare at the dazzling lights, the tinsel streamers that advertised sex shows, the half-clad Thai women in spangled bikinis, who sat on high chairs in front of bars and trawled for customers. One woman with black lipstick and a blond wig left her perch, walked to the camera, and attempted to tongue the lens. Someone shoved her aside.

The screen went dark. Then the camera was inside a shadowy, narrow club with a small stage and a staircase leading to a second floor. The bar, booths, and tables were packed with men; the only women were Thai prostitutes, all of whom wore numbers pinned to their bikini tops.

Men and women watched the stage, where a naked woman danced alone in a bamboo cage. Her face was covered by a silver leather mask shaped like a fox head. Her hair was jet black and appeared to have been recently and crudely cut. Her dance was frenzied, verging out of control, and her small, well-formed body glistened with sweat.

The camera closed in on the woman until the fox mask filled the screen. Without the woman's body to soften it, the mask took on a menacing life of its own, appearing bestial and brutish in the half light. The camera dropped down to the woman's bare chest, where the word *kitsune* had been carved in her flesh in large letters. *Kitsune,* Japanese for fox. The animal that appeared in Japanese mythology and art, where it was known as the trickster, the character who fools others but in the end is fooled himself. Trickster, whose sly pranks often backfired and ended up doing him great harm. The woman was Hanako.

The camera went to her right shoulder, where for a full minute it lingered on a star-shaped birthmark.

Then it pulled back to show a middle-aged, potbellied black man with a round face pitted by ingrown hairs, making his way past the tables and stopping in front of Hanako's cage. He wore a T-shirt from the USS aircraft carrier *Ticonderoga* and had a cigar clenched in his teeth and held an empty beer bottle aloft in one hand. Reaching into the cage, he slammed the floor with the flat of his hand three times, a signal. Hanako stopped dancing. She stood breathing heavily, her breasts rising and falling as she waited.

The black man placed the beer bottle between her feet and again struck the cage floor. Then he took the cigar from his mouth, fingered his crotch, and watched as she slowly squatted, felt for the bottle with her hands, and guided it into her vagina. She pushed herself down further, taking more of the bottle inside. The black man grinned and slowly shook his head. Behind him the male customers applauded wildly.

The screen went dark, followed by a shot of a cramped, untidy room in the sex club. Still nude and wearing the fox mask, Hanako sat perspiring and trembling at a tiny table. Across from her a Thai prostitute with a harelip and steel front teeth dug a blackened tablespoon into a plastic bag of white powder. A label on the bag read: *Golden Tiger Brand*.

The whore added water to the spoon from a battered teakettle, then held the spoon over a candle stub burning in a teacup. When the powder turned to liquid, the prostitute drew it into a hypodermic syringe, left her chair, and walked to Hanako's right side. After examining the masked woman's right arm, the prostitute injected Hanako in the forearm, plunging the needle into a cluster of purple puncture marks. The masked woman immediately stopped shivering. She relaxed and began to breathe deeply. Then her head slowly dropped to her chest and she slumped in her chair.

The screen went black and when the picture returned, Hanako was stomach down on the table in the small room, feet on the floor. The potbellied black man, naked and still smoking his cigar, was behind her. He dipped the fingers of one hand into the melted candle wax, greased his erect penis, and entered her from the rear, leaning forward to grip her hips with thick hands. The elephant hair bracelet he wore on one wrist rubbed Hanako's skin raw. Beads of perspiration dangled from the tip of his flat nose, and as he thrust back and forth, the table inched across the floor. His cigar ashes fell into Hanako's black hair.

When he finished, he dropped a crumpled thousand *baht* note on the table. Hanako, still in a drugged stupor, remained on the table, her face turned away from the camera. The black man began dressing and had put on white boxer shorts and black socks held up by green garters when he stopped to pay attention to something being said to him off camera. He nodded, stepped over to the masked woman, and removed the cigar from his mouth. He grinned, shook his head, and blew on the lit end of the cigar until it glowed bright red. Then he ground it out on Hanako's back.

At the Empress's command, the projector was switched off and the room lights turned on. She ordered the projector and screen removed. The two men obeyed, then positioned themselves in the hallway outside the anteroom, their shadows visible through the rice paper door. Mrs. Gennai fanned herself in silence, noting that all three young women were now weeping. Yuriko seemed to be the most affected by what she had just seen; she covered her face with a handkerchief and rocked back and forth with a grief which appeared to be deeply felt.

But then she had been the closest to Hanako. On occasion the two had been mistaken for sisters, something which had pleased both of them. Unfortunately, they had emerged as the first *Mujin* wives in some time to make a show of their intentionally provocative behavior. Such defiance, the Empress felt, was caused by an inability to remain quiet, a prime failing in today's young people.

She began to speak to the three weeping women, keeping her voice low, saying that for them the film had been a warning. For Hanako, it had been the chronicling of her punishment. Hanako had fled the Empress, accepted a role in the theft of *Mujin*'s business secrets, then felt herself to be safe because she had secured the protection of a rich and powerful man from the West.

Oni, however, had found her, proving that no one was beyond the power of the Empress. Yuriko, Yuka, and Oman had just seen for themselves that Serge Coutain was permanently institutionalized, that he was mindless and immobile and because of *Oni* would be that way for the rest of his days. Both Coutain and Hanako would spend the remainder of their lives paying for their treachery. They had dug a pit for others and fallen into it themselves. Just like the fox.

Mrs. Gennai warned them never to speak of what they had seen here today. Should just one of the three do so, then all would be punished severely. At the same time, they must not forget what they had seen on film. This was proof that the Empress could and would punish any affront or transgression of her law. *Oni* was her retribution. And he was unstoppable.

She said that as Japanese the three wives were all members of a single great tribe, one united by bloodlines and tribal rites that could be traced back to the dawn of history. The tribe was always in danger, from nature, from foreign countries, and therefore there was nothing more important than loyalty from tribal members. Loyalty to the tribe itself, to family, to seniors like Mrs. Gennai, to all that was Japan.

"Fail in your duty to me," she said, "and you fail in your duty to *Mujin*, to your country itself. The future of *Mujin* depends on how each one of you conducts herself. All of you must share in the glory or disgrace earned by every *Mujin* wife."

Defeated, the young women bowed, foreheads touching the mat. *"Hai,"* they said, for now they truly understood her words and the thoughts behind them. Today they had been reminded of their collective responsibility and that there could never be self-gratification at the expense of collective welfare. They had also been reminded that evil did indeed exist in the world, and that the Empress herself was evil. Today they had been forced to yield to a fear of that evil, a fear which would never leave them.

The Empress rose from the floor and said the nail that sticks up gets pounded down. Then she tapped on the door with her folded fan. One of the men in the hallway slid it open, bowed from the waist and stepped aside as she led the three women out of the anteroom and to a room next door. Here the young wives changed into summer kimonos and cleansed their faces with hya-cinth-scented towels. Mrs. Gennai waited until the maid had left, then spoke to them in a gentle manner, a mother correcting chil-dren in need of a mild reprimand.

She suggested that the three not spend so much time together in the future, that instead more time be given to husbands, chil-dren, even to older company wives. Oman was to cease her gam-bling; as a show of good faith, Mrs. Gennai had paid her entire gambling debt, but would keep possession of the young woman's IOUs. Yuka was to give up all thoughts of an affair and instead spend more time with her two children and in supporting *Mujin* charities. Yuriko, of course, was to seriously consider starting a family; the Empress recommended that the decision be made soon.

Above all, the three were to be alert for anything that might link Tetsu Okuhara to the late Mr. Nikkei, for Mrs. Gennai sus-pected Okuhara of being the man who pulled Mr. Nikkei's strings. Mr. Nikkei, sadly, had neither the intelligence nor the courage to mastermind the scheme that had cost him his life. Who better than Okuhara fitted the role of *Aikuchi,* and who stood more to gain than he by the Empress's fall from grace. Attend company social events, Mrs. Gennai told the young wives, and listen carefully. Observe with open eyes, then report back to her twice a week even if there was nothing on Okuhara. She alone would judge the worth of their information. And she would be extremely displeased by any failure to comply with her wishes.

She told them it was now time for the tea ceremony. But first a walk through the garden, among red pines, apricot and green willow trees, wisterias and irises. It was time to enjoy peace, stillness, beauty. A garden was one of life's highest pleasures, a certain cure for anxiety. And remorse. Inside the tea house, she said, they would drink tea from a seventeenth-century bowl as sunlight filtered through the small paper window and bathed them in warm shadows. Each of the three young wives had attended previous tea ceremonies and knew that the conversation must be about the history of the ceremony itself, with great admiration expressed for the historic bowl, tea caddy, whisk, and other implements.

"And what else are we to discuss during the ceremony?" she asked, addressing the question to Yuriko.

Yuriko, red-eyed from weeping, bowed her head. "We must remember to praise you for the beautiful ceremony you planned for us. And we must promise to return here in four days to express our thanks for it."

Yuka and Oman said *hai,* and nodded in agreement.

Mrs. Gennai said, "I am planning another tea ceremony in three weeks."

She waited.

And when all three women said they were looking forward to it and would attend, she pointed to Yuriko, saying that as senior she was *shokyaku,* guest of honor, the one who today would enter the tea room first, crawling inside on her hands and knees. Crawl with the others watching.

The Empress complimented the three on their aesthetic sense and refinement, which brought weak smiles from all except a weeping Yuriko. Mrs. Gennai did not tell them that she had learned to put her trust neither in the glories of dawn, nor in the smiles of those who feared her. It was always a mistake to trust one's enemies.

3

Manhattan, New York

IT WAS NEAR midnight when Edward Penny climbed the staircase to the second floor of Senator Fran Machlis's four-story town house carrying an ECR-1, an Electronic Countermeasures Receiver. Penny was the Senator's chief of security. And the ECR-1 was the most sophisticated device available for detecting hidden wiretaps.

Penny thought it looked like a third world briefcase, one of those portable radio and cassette players popular with black kids. He couldn't afford his own; he'd borrowed this one from an ex-FBI agent now working in the international affairs department of New York's second largest bank. It didn't destroy or deactivate bugs. It found them and let you listen in. With the ECR-1, you bugged the buggers. You learned who was tapping your lines or recording your conversations. It could even pick up microwaves, which was saying something.

Senator Machlis had ordered Penny to learn who was bugging her offices and homes in New York and Washington. Someone was making transcripts of her telephone calls, an act which had left her incensed. Her in-person conversations were also on those transcripts, meaning that a friend or a staff member was wearing a body mike, an act of betrayal she had taken pretty hard. Penny had to do more than just stop the bugging. He had to find out who was behind it and why.

Her East Seventieth Street town house was modeled on a Florence palazzo and stood between a Portuguese synagogue and a Middle Eastern consulate. Directly across the street was a hundred-year-old armory, a mammoth red brick palace with gun bays. With its offices, meeting rooms, and vast drill hall, the armory took up an entire square block. It was an eyesore, a blight and ugly as sin, Fran Machlis told Penny.

Her town house, however, could never be called ugly. Fran Machlis had used money and taste to achieve a successful blend of sumptuousness and simplicity. Bare brick walls, pumpkin pine floors, and understated moldings contrasted with Ming Dynasty armchairs, Baccarat crystal candlesticks, and Jackson Pollack paintings. There were marble baths with sunken tubs, and the master bedroom had a Degas hanging over its fireplace. An office had the latest in computers and telephones. For relaxation and inner peace, there was a stark, unadorned meditation room, whose wrought-iron balcony, unfortunately, overlooked the armory.

Edward Penny liked Fran Machlis; she was candid, kept her word, and never forgot a favor or an insult. She was fiftyish, widowed, bright, and one of twenty or so millionaires in the Senate. Polls ranked her as one of the two most powerful women in Congress, a conclusion she did not deny. Next year she planned to run for a third term and was considered a shoo-in, though like everyone else in politics she had her detractors. There were people in Washington, in the media, in both major parties who wanted her out of Congress. To them she was unmanageable, hard-nosed, someone who didn't play the game as they felt it should be played.

Senator Machlis, however, was a woman who believed in staying the course. "I'm not the type to change, falter, or repent," she told Penny.

And because she had known and trusted him for some time, she told him she did indeed have something to hide, something the wiretappers just might be on to. Something that could blow her career right out of the water. She was having a love affair. It was, she told Penny, the most passionate, demanding, and humiliating of her life. Her lover was a woman named Helen Silks. As for explaining it, the senator couldn't.

"All I know is that I'm caught up in a whirlwind," she said to Penny. "I'm involved in something so intense that to even think about it takes my breath away. If you tell me what I'm doing is wrong and dangerous, hell, I'll be the first to agree with you. But I can't help myself. Somebody once said that love is being stupid together. I think he knew something."

Penny, whose life often depended upon being observant, had a surprise for the senator; he was aware of the affair and had been for some time. He'd seen the looks that passed between the two women, and he'd felt the vibes when he entered a room where they'd been alone. But for what it was worth, he didn't care. It wasn't his business to approve or disapprove, only idiots felt compelled to have an opinion on everything.

He'd been all over the world and had encountered worse things than two women in love with each other. And since they were being frank, Penny said, his mind was still on Central America, on his own problems, his own pain. In any case, he didn't have to tell her what she already knew, that horsing around with Helen Silks was asking for trouble.

The senator said she was aware of this, but could not stop herself. She'd never done anything like this before and wished a hundred times she'd never gotten started. But Helen Silks had a Far Eastern sensuality, something that was overpowering. She was uninhibited and wanton in love. The experience was irresistible.

Fran Machlis showed Penny a photograph of Silks, who was thirtyish, a petite woman with high cheekbones, blond bangs and the frozen smile of self-love. She divided her time between New York and Tokyo, where she taught English; her knowledge of Japanese culture was so thorough that she sometimes worked as a *geisha* without ever giving away her western identity. Lately, however, she had appeared troubled and out of sorts over something she refused to discuss. No matter how hard Fran Machlis tried, she could not get Helen Silks to accept her help with this mysterious problem, whatever it was.

"You think Helen Silks's problems are tied in with your being bugged?" Penny asked the senator.

Fran Machlis covered her eyes with one hand. "Jesus wept. The thought had occurred to me, but I immediately put it out of

my mind. I mean, it's just too painful to think about. Too goddamn painful. Now you know why I've brought this thing to you
in confidence, and no, I haven't mentioned anything to Helen
about the wiretapping. You're the only one I've discussed it with.
The only one I *could* discuss it with."

Fran Machlis had two additional private investigators on her
staff, both of whom reported to Edward Penny. Penny was to
handle the wiretapping problem by himself, at least until he felt
he could trust the other investigators. It went without saying that
the name of Helen Silks was not to come up under any circumstances. Penny had already proven his discretion by handling past
investigations and security jobs for the senator. On a fact-finding
mission to Southeast Asia, he had saved her life. She was now
entrusting him with something even more important. She was
entrusting him with her political life.

Edward Penny was in his mid-thirties, a tall, gaunt man with
sleepy eyes, dark brown hair, and a short beard which hid fairly
recent burn scars. His movements appeared deliberately slow and
drawn out, but they were an athlete's movements, smooth and
with a controlled cadence. Since leaving home at seventeen he
had been a member of the American Special Forces, a bodyguard, a consultant to arms dealers, and a mercenary, and he had
worked for private intelligence agencies. He had also worked as a
martial arts instructor to elite military units in the United States,
Asia, Europe, and Central America.

As for being security chief to a senator, it was something of a
comedown. There was no physical danger, no challenge, no opportunity to use what he knew about combat, and it called for
showing up at too many embassy parties in his tuxedo. He had
taken the position because he had lost much of his self-confi-
dence and couldn't bring himself to do more than the Machlis job
called for. Penny knew what others knew: the Central American
job had all but destroyed him.

It had left him with physical scars—the burn marks on his face,
neck, and shoulders were the most prominent—and emotional
scars as well. All were reminders of the worst failure of his life, a
failure that had left him disillusioned and questioning his combat
skills, the thing he had built his life around. It had also brought him
worldwide publicity. Unwanted publicity. And a heavy burden of
guilt and shame. Until Fran Machlis had talked him into working

for her, he had wondered if he would ever work again.

When he returned from Central America, he had retreated into solitude, the self-assurance, desire, enthusiasm gone. But Fran Machlis was having none of his self-pity, as she put it. She owed him her life and had no qualms about using her considerable powers of persuasion to make him see things her way. The pay would be good, she said, and he would work out of New York and Washington, the only two civilized cities in the country. For a man of his talents, the job wouldn't be demanding, but it would be a job and for his own good, the sooner he returned to work, the better.

He was, she said, the most suitable security chief imaginable, a blend of sophistication and savagery, a well-spoken man who knew a few languages, owned a first-class wardrobe, and was capable of forcible ways when the need arose. He had a number of interesting contacts, which she credited to his acts of skulduggery in dark corners of the world, and he knew how to keep his mouth shut. In these days of terrorism and random violence, a man like Penny was worth his weight in gold.

She went about convincing him in just the right way. She knew he collected first editions, so she sent him a collection of Longfellow's poems and a 1915 edition of Dickens's *A Christmas Carol,* which included beautiful illustrations by Arthur Rackham. She also knew he was partnered in a small business with a former French intelligence agent; the two produced apple cider on Normandy acreage where Penny eventually planned to retire. So Fran Machlis had her friends order cases of apple cider from Penny and George Cancale, a windfall the two men needed badly.

And Penny received telephone calls. They came from people he knew at war colleges, the CIA, foreign embassies, and private security agencies, and they all had the same message: Take the Fran Machlis job because no one else will hire you until you prove you haven't permanently lost your nerve.

Looking for bugs.

On the second floor Penny began his search in the library-dining room, where the senator took most of her meals when she was in New York. She was proud of her cook, and often held business meetings here with her staff, campaign manager, press officer, labor and religious leaders. She had done press interviews in this room and held highly secret meetings with party leaders, the mayor, and financial backers. This was also where she had dined with Helen Silks.

Helen Silks was the reason Penny had decided to handle the New York and Washington debuggings himself and to work at night when the senator's offices and homes were empty or close to it. Should Helen Silks be involved in the bugging, it was a good idea not to broadcast that fact by hiring an outside wireman. Penny hadn't even told the three live-in staff members at the town house why he was in New York. He had told them only when to expect him. He didn't even tell them that he would be returning to Washington tonight without staying over.

He knew what he was looking for: hidden tape recorders, hidden transmitter systems, miniature microphones. He could also be looking for a bug so sophisticated, so advanced that its existence was unknown to everyone in the trade except its inventor. Penny hoped this wasn't the case, that he wasn't after a bug so new that no way yet had been found to counteract it. Any bug, no matter how different or up to the minute, could be defeated eventually; let something new emerge and the antibuggers quickly began scheming to defeat it. The advantage, however, was always with the inventor of a new bug. Until his invention was neutralized, he was free to eavesdrop undisturbed.

Penny turned on the lights in the library-dining room, walked over to a mirrored recess, and placed the ECR-1 on a banquette. The room reminded him of a private club for men in London. Lining the walls were lacquered bookcases filled with leather-bound books. A walnut-veneered table, with early Georgian style chairs, was set with an English silver service featuring two-pronged forks. English snuff boxes of gold, ivory, and tortoise-shell were arranged on a small end table, while another small table held a piece Penny especially liked, an agate dish mounted on a gilded silver statuette of a Greek warrior. It was a seventeenth-century masterwork, the gift of Lord Oliver Coveyduck, one of the senator's oldest friends.

Penny wondered if Coveyduck appeared in the transcripts of Fran Machlis's telephone calls and decided he did, particularly since the Englishman had taken to calling her every week. Coveyduck might find it amusing; until recently he himself had been a politician and was no stranger to backstabbing and dirty tricks. He had just left Parliament to finish a book he had been working on for some time. Penny had met him in Washington, where Coveyduck had been the senator's houseguest while researching at the Library of Congress and collecting documents under the Freedom of Information Act.

Penny found Coveyduck to be charming and interesting, though something of a character. In his mid-sixties, an age when many people were ready for a rocking chair, the Englishman climbed mountains, raced along country roads on a motorbike, and not too long ago he'd made the front pages of British newspapers by using a bow and arrow to attack two men who had been abusing animals. He also stuck to an exclusive diet of peaches and nectarines two days a week, claiming it was the key to health and longevity. He was closed-mouthed about his book, but when he learned that Penny spoke French he said the book was being written because *qui aime bien châtie bien*. He who truly loves will chastise well. Penny had no idea what the hell he meant, and Fran Machlis wasn't much help, either. She'd been sworn to secrecy about the book and would only that it had to do with Coveyduck's wife who'd died in a Japanese prison camp some forty years ago and Penny could read it when the book was published next year. Coveyduck, she said, was obsessive about secrecy.

Near the banquette were Japanese prints of white herons and a pond garden in a Kyoto temple, gifts from Helen Silks. An art deco lamp, something Silks had picked up in France last month, was also in this corner. Next to the lamp was Penny's favorite work in the room, a painting of a nineteenth-century Japanese courtesan done by Aikiko Shaka, a Japanese artist who was one of the most beautiful women Penny had ever seen. They had met in Washington ten days ago when she had begun commuting from her New Jersey studio in preparation for an exhibition of her paintings at a local gallery. The senator had introduced him to Aikiko, who was her houseguest, and the incredible had happened. Penny and she had fallen in love almost immediately. Emotions had been released in him that he had thought were long dead, and he found himself happier than he'd been in a long time.

But his passion for Aikiko was also one of the most terrible things in his life, for he lived in fear of losing her. She was the fire that warmed him; she was the light guiding him back to the land of the living. As for Fran Machlis, nothing was said but Penny had the feeling she didn't approve of the relationship between him and Aikiko. Penny didn't give a shit what she thought. He knew only that he needed Aikiko, needed what she could give him, and he wasn't about to give her up. Aikiko was the reason he planned to return to Washington tonight after debugging the town house and Fran Machlis's Lexington Avenue office.

He switched on the battery-powered ECR-1 and looked at its visual display. Perfect. Then he checked the most important feature, the built-in monitoring capacity which allowed him to bug the buggers, to listen in on whomever might be listening in on the town house. Again, no problem.

It was time to exterminate a few bugs.

He picked up the ECR-1 and carried it to a telephone beside a Queen Anne armchair. The visual display lit up. The monitor began to hum. The ECR-1 wasn't wasting time; it began to hone in on its target, the man at the other end of the tapped telephone. Penny grinned. This was going to be fun. Picking up the receiver, he dialed the time operator. A woman's recorded voice told him it was twelve-oh-three exactly, and she continued to speak, adding seconds as Penny unscrewed the mouthpiece, laid it aside, and looked inside the receiver at the miniature microphone hidden there. This was something new, a bit of metal no larger than a child's fingernail. A nice, compact microphone. Whoever designed it was good. Very good.

Penny didn't want to alert the wireman at the other end, so he left the bug where it was, replaced the mouthpiece, and hung up. He increased the volume on the monitor. Any second now. The wireman who planted the bug was in the neighborhood, listening, recording, and drinking a lot of coffee to keep from falling asleep. He had to be near because this kind of bug sent out radio frequencies to a receiver and tape recorder no more than fifteen hundred feet away. In a few seconds the ECR-1 was going to tell Penny exactly how far away the eavesdropper was.

The visual display now told him there was another bug in the room. He walked over to a wall near the walnut veneer table, took a small pocketknife from a jacket pocket, then unscrewed the metal covering over an electrical outlet. There it was. A bug just like the one inside the telephone. Extra small, extra powerful. Unless you knew what you were looking for, you'd ignore it as being nothing more than a speck of metal. Penny replaced the outlet cover and walked back to the ECR-1. The monitor was humming, indicating that the wireman was practically on top of the town house. Maybe to the left in the synagogue. Maybe to the right in the Middle East consulate—and wouldn't that be something. Penny snapped his fingers. *Of course*. The bastard was across the street in the armory. The most obvious hiding place. And the easiest to get in and out of because of the many entrances and exits. Seconds later, the monitor indicated that Penny was right.

The monitor picked up one voice, then another. A man and a woman. Penny almost laughed out loud. Damn right he knew them. If you knew anything about electronic surveillance, you knew about Aristotle Bellas and his daughter Sophie. Aristotle Bellas was an electronics genius, the best wireman in the business, the man responsible for some of the finest listening devices ever invented. He was a legend among spooks, a man who approached his trade as Rembrandt approached his canvas. Penny had worked with "The Greek," but so had the CIA, FBI, DEA, Pentagon, wise guys, $400-an-hour lawyers, various multinational corporations, Big Labor, Israeli intelligence, beauty pageant promoters, investigative reporters.

Bellas's daughter Sophie was his partner and a good one. She'd inherited much of his talent and under his direction she'd become the best wiretapper around after Bellas himself. She was so good that customers didn't hesitate to hire her when he was unavailable. He insisted that she receive the same high fees as himself and that she be accorded the same professional respect, so it was understandable that Sophie worshiped the ground her father walked on.

Aristotle Bellas's voice on the monitor. A voice raspy from years of Turkish cigarettes and *retsina*. "No more talking, you hear me? Somebody's picking us up over there. Just pack everything and we get to the van. Don't say a word. Not a word."

Sophie must have taken him seriously because from then on Penny heard only dead air. Aristotle Bellas and his little girl were leaving without saying good-bye.

Penny switched off the ECR-1 and patted the machine. Good work, my friend. There were undoubtedly a few bugs in the office. And in the bedrooms, master bedroom in particular. And not your ordinary bugs, but something special invented by the Greek or Sophie. Penny was almost sure the Bellases had invented a new scanner, since he hadn't heard of anything on the market that could pick up the ECR-1. Such a scanner would be worth a small fortune to the Greek, a man always in need of money.

The problem was the Greek's fascination with the stock market. He couldn't keep away from it. He had squandered a fortune on so many can't-miss tips that Penny had told him the only way he'd ever come into money was to screw a woman who was wearing a gold diaphragm. To cover recent losses the Greek was said to be selling surveillance equipment to drug dealers and for five times the money he received from law enforcement agencies. Certain Cubans in Miami and New Jersey and some Dominicans and Colombians in New York had the latest in beepers, scanners, walkie-talkies, and whatever they needed to run counter-surveillance on the police. The bad guys were now tuning into police radios in advance of raids, preventing the loss of millions of dollars in confiscated narcotics, cash, guns. This marketing decision by Aristotle Bellas had not made him popular with cops, but it was easing his problem with his broker.

Penny ran from the library-dining room, down two flights of stairs, and out into the street, slamming the door behind him. The night was warm, quiet, dark and the street was deserted except for a lone cyclist about to turn the corner on Park Avenue. Penny could wrap this thing up tonight. Just grab Aristotle Bellas and force him to come up with two names: his client, plus the name of the staff member involved, the one who'd gotten the Greek inside the town house or planted the bugs for him.

Bellas had mentioned a van. It had to be parked within walking distance of the armory, but in which direction? Penny's adrenaline was starting to flow. Getting pumped up over chasing a middle-aged wiretapper and his daughter. As action went, it wasn't much, but it was something.

Think.

No cars on the armory side of the street. Signs here stated that parking was limited to military vehicles at all times.

On the senator's side of the street, another no-parking zone, this one in front of her town house, the synagogue, and the Middle Eastern consulate. In front of the consulate, a uniformed policeman stood guard twenty-four hours a day, a protection against Jewish militants. No doubt about it, Penny thought. Aristotle and Sophie would avoid this side of the armory to avoid the cop.

Three sides of the armory left. Three blocks of entrances and exits for the dynamic duo of wiretapping to come through. Penny ruled out one side, the block facing Park Avenue. Too much pedestrian and vehicular traffic. Too many chances for Aristotle and Sophie to be seen.

Two blocks of entrances and exits left.

Decisions.

Penny decided. He ran along the block to his right, toward Lexington Avenue and the back of the armory, intending to cover *all* remaining entrances and exits, believing in himself enough to know that he could outrun the Greek and Sophie, which ought to allow him a quick look at the back of the armory *and* the Seventy-first Street side. Hell, neither Aristotle nor his daughter were world-class sprinters and besides, they would be weighed down by suitcases with bugging and taping equipment.

Penny didn't expect any trouble with the Greek; the wireman was a lover, not a fighter, a man with a taste for brown sugar, young, black prostitutes. To get inside the armory, he had probably bribed a guard or used a contact in the mayor's office. It was unlikely that an armory guard would buy into the Greek's trouble, but if that happened Penny was going to take the easy way out. Just open his jacket and flash the twelve-shot Browning Hi-Power he was licensed to carry. Most security guards were unarmed or carried empty guns. The sight of a real gun usually made most people chill out, which Penny was counting on.

He felt it coming back as he ran, the joy of pitting himself against someone else, the satisfaction found in standing his ground against an opponent. The feeling invigorated him as he ran, then sprinted, shortening his stride for speed, arms pumping rhythmically, thinking he ought to go back to a five mile daily run instead of the three he was now doing. He was in shape, maybe not as good as he'd been before Central America, but good enough to get by. He worked out an hour a day—running, weights, judo or karate practice, usually with younger guys who didn't give too much of a fight. Occasionally, he worked out on his own with the *tanto*, the Japanese knife he favored and which he had introduced to a few commandos, mercs, and elite units.

However, there were some things he should be doing, but wasn't. Like spending time on the firing range or polishing his driving, particularly evasive and defensive tactics. Or reviewing his explosives training, with an emphasis on defusing car bombs.

These were things a security chief or bodyguard had to know in order to keep himself and his client alive. But Penny no longer pushed himself as he'd done six months ago. No more balls to the wall training. The urgency just wasn't there anymore.

At the moment, however, his professionalism had taken over; he was definitely excited about getting his hands on the Greek and Sophie. He raced past an elderly doorman standing under the awning of a high rise, past a private school for pubescent rich girls, past a tinted glass and steel art gallery until he reached an almost deserted Lexington Avenue. He stopped, looking north, waiting until a white stretch limousine passed in front of him, then he jogged across the street to the armory and slowed to a walk, keeping close to the begrimed brick wall of the darkened armory and away from the street lights.

A sound ahead of him made Penny freeze. Twenty feet away, in the middle of the block, a metal door opened a crack, sending a thin trace of light into the night. Then the door opened wider, creaking until it swung open completely and slammed into the armory wall. A young man in a U.S. Army uniform, steel helmet, and black combat boots, his back to Penny, stepped outside the armory and held the door in place. The soldier, his rank was sergeant, cast a long shadow in Penny's direction. The armory light was a bright yellow path across the gray pavement and stepping onto that shining path with three suitcases and an attaché case between them were Aristotle and Sophie Bellas. Penny thought they looked like a couple sneaking out of a hotel to avoid paying the bill.

The sergeant lifted a hand to the wiretappers in farewell, pulled on the metal door, and backed into the armory. The door followed him, creaking and scraping across the pavement until it slammed shut with a clang that echoed along the empty street.

Penny rubbed his eyes. No more bright lights. And the Greek was within reach. In the soft street light, the Bellases became silhouettes as they raced north toward Seventy-first Street, the Greek with a suitcase in either hand and Sophie bringing up the rear.

Penny closed in, running on tiptoe, getting a kick out of the misery he knew the Greek was going to feel, because the Greek had his pride and wasn't going to like getting nailed.

Penny increased his speed, his strides taking him past Sophie. Then he grabbed a handful of the Greek's jacket collar from behind and yanked hard. The Greek stopped in place, then went up on his heels, and when Penny pulled back, the wireman fell into his arms. He let the Greek down easy, sitting him on the pavement with his suitcases, then stepped behind Sophie, slipping a hand over her mouth, saying her name a few times, feeling her relax a little. Then he whispered, trying to keep her calm, telling her to put her suitcase and attaché case down and move over to the wall. Keep quiet, he said, or he was going to hurt her father. Sophie, eyes glistening with tears, obeyed.

Penny looked down at Aristotle Bellas, seeing a man in his fifties, burly, wild-eyed and with receding, kinky, gray hair, wearing pink-tinted eyeglasses, pinstriped suit, alligator shoes, and a purple silk shirt open at the neck to reveal white chest hair. Arms resting on one of the suitcases, the startled wireman looked up at Penny, trying to identify him in the street light. Remembering, but not sure. Taking in the weight loss and the beard Penny hadn't worn until recently. At the same time, the wireman was thinking of excuses.

Sophie had eyes only for her father. From the concern on her face, Edward Penny would have thought the Greek had fallen from the top of the World Trade Center and was at death's door. Sophie was in her early thirties, a pudgy woman with permed, reddish hair, a faint moustache, and features almost lost in excess weight. In the poor light Penny thought she was wearing a dark blue jumpsuit until he later saw *Amsterdam Garage* on the breast pocket and realized she was wearing a garage attendant's uniform and with it a pair of scuffed, red cowboy boots and a nondescript, wide leather belt worn by competitive weightlifters. No mistaking Sophie's jewelry, however. It was her trademark and her taste ran strictly to Cartier. She was wearing a few samples tonight: pendant, tank watch, rolling ring. Sophie was what Penny's father would call a distinctive entity.

Penny respected her talents, but he couldn't help feeling sorry for her. He often wondered if she was living a life chosen by someone who was using her, or if she was in the game because she enjoyed it. Someone had to protect her; she was the butt of jokes because of her weight and she was claustrophobic, with a pathological fear of confined spaces. Penny had heard the Albany story, about how she'd freaked out up there when she had to spend a night in jail because she couldn't make bail and how she'd had to go into therapy for a while and how the experience had left her with a fear of being sent to prison. Penny thought her father should have warned her that listening to other people's conversations had its downside.

Outside the armory, Penny asked Sophie which suitcase contained the new scanner and since she was too frightened to lie, she pointed to the one she'd been carrying. Penny picked it up and said, "Sorry about the beard, Greek. It's me, Edward Penny."

He watched Aristotle Bellas nod in agreement, finally recognizing the security chief, but before the wireman could speak, Penny, anxious to spare himself as much bullshit as possible, interrupted. He told the Greek that putting an illegal tap on a United States Senator was a bad career move, and that maybe the three of them ought to go back to the town house and the Greek and Sophie could tell him something good. Like who was paying him to go after Senator Machlis and why.

"Just remember," Penny said, "it's not whether you win or lose, but where you lay the blame."

"You're supposed to be dead," Aristotle Bellas said.

"An exaggeration," Penny said. He touched his beard. "You're tapping Senator Machlis's wires, so I think you knew I was still in the land of the living. Anyway, why don't we talk about you and Sophie and how the two of you have been spending your summer vacation."

Edward Penny and Aristotle Bellas were in the same business, private intelligence, but they weren't friends. Admiring the Greek as a wizard was one thing; trusting him to keep your secrets was another. The two of us are just players, Penny told himself. No more, no less.

The three were in the town house kitchen, a large first floor room of Spanish arches, rust-colored floor tiles, brick walls hung with copper pots, and barred windows overlooking a back garden. Penny didn't bother asking, but the Greek volunteered that the kitchen was clean, that the only bugs in the room had eight legs and wings. Too much noise in here, the Greek said, and besides, people don't discuss important things in the kitchen. Penny said there was nothing like making sure, so he ordered the Greek to sweep the room, anyway . He watched Aristotle Bellas do the job using a hidden wire locator, a hand-held model of his own invention. When the wireman had taken the locator out of a suitcase, Penny had gotten a look at quite a few new toys invented by father and daughter. Meanwhile, the locator turned up nothing.

From this point on, Penny had to proceed with caution. The relationship between Fran Machlis and Helen Silks had to be kept away from the news media, meaning he'd have to arrive at an arrangement with the Greek and his daughter, an arrangement allowing them to walk. After they had talked. Penny could live with that providing he received copies of the tapes, copies he knew the Greek had made before sending the originals on to his clients. Aristotle Bellas had availed himself of other people's mistakes before, especially if the people had been as important as Fran Machlis.

Penny poured coffee into Wedgwood cups for Bellas, Sophie, and himself. He watched Sophie put four lumps of sugar in hers.

He said, "No cops."

"Of course," the Greek said. He smiled, too.

Penny sat down on a butcher block table. "Here's my problem. I can't afford to look bad over this thing because, frankly, there aren't that many jobs around for me at the moment. So I have to produce. There isn't going to be any shoulda-woulda-coulda."

The Greek smiled and said he understood, believe me, he understood.

Penny said he preferred to avoid any publicity, and he got another smile from the Greek. One from Sophie, too. Which could mean they knew about Helen Silks, or they thought Penny had lost his nerve. He wasn't about to let the Greek get away from him, so he said he had to have the Greek's cooperation, and he intended to get it. If he didn't, he was going to turn the Greek's suitcases over to the cops. Either the Greek played ball, or those new toys were going to have a new owner.

The Greek stopped smiling. Penny said, "After the way you've tried to increase your market share among Dominicans and Colombians, the DEA and the FBI would love to get their hands on those suitcases. How much money do you figure to lose?"

Aristotle Bellas looked frightened. "You don't know what you're asking me to do," he said. "You just don't know."

"Names," Penny said.

Sophie looked scared, too. She went to her father, put her arms around him and said, "We've wanted to get out, so let's get out now. Just tell him what he wants to know, then we drop the whole thing. We leave the country, Daddy. We get out for good."

Penny sipped his coffee, thinking, is this thing really that heavy? They look as though they're afraid of being killed. He said to the Greek, "I'm waiting."

"August Carliner," the Greek said. "He's the one who hired me."

Edward Penny put his cup down. "Are you kidding?"

The Greek shook his head and Sophie, arms still around him, said her father was telling the truth. August Carliner, a former secretary of state. Shrewd, charming August Carliner, whom Edward Penny regarded as one of the most untrustworthy men he had ever met in his life. August Carliner. The kind of man you walked away from backwards.

Penny had been asked to work for him on a couple of occasions, but knew too much to even consider saying yes. Carliner would go all out to get you on board and he paid good money, but he tended to lose interest in a hurry and didn't always stand behind those he hired. From the State Department, he had gone into private industry, forming Carliner Associates, a risk consultancy. Risk consultants served multinational corporations by providing written reports, holding seminars, and conducting regular briefings with executives on the advantages and pitfalls of doing business in such troublesome areas as the Middle East, Latin America, and Asia.

Some risk consultants actively engaged in dealing with kidnappings, extortion, and executive protection. Penny had worked with a few firms, teaching martial arts, executive protection, and acting as bodyguard to some of their clients. Teams assembled by risk consultants were usually former U.S. and foreign intelligence agents, and high ranking ex-military and government officials. All were in a position to compile reports based on access to foreign leaders and to sensitive, sometimes secret information acquired in government service.

Ex-CIA directors, FBI executives and White House staffers had formed risk consultancies but August Carliner's was one of the better known and more expensive. A single assessment on an overseas investment by his firm was priced at $150,000. He paid top dollar for staff, but he didn't always back up his people whenever they got into trouble overseas. Edward Penny knew of one Carliner man now doing thirty years in a Turkish prison for bribing a cabinet official. Another was quietly facing trial in Beijing for trying to buy the notes of a secret meeting between the Chinese Communists and the Taiwanese government. Some might say these incidents indicated that August Carliner was the sort of man who left his people twisting slowly, slowly in the wind. Carliner, however, put a different spin on the same events. He included them in reports to his clients as evidence of trouble abroad and how in touch he was with the true picture. There was no more morality or meaning in Carliner's world than he put in it.

When Penny came to work for Fran Machlis, she and August Carliner were in a battle involving his largest client, the *Mujin* group of Japan. She was outspoken in her dislike of Japanese trade practices, which she saw as unethical and below the belt. Japan, she said, was out to win the trade war at any cost and refused to play by the rules. It protected its domestic industries against competition while flooding foreign markets with its exports. And it did this by fair means or foul, she said.

She had learned that *Mujin,* through a front, was attempting to buy a major bank in the Washington area. The bank held records on government and military personnel and would have given *Mujin* invaluable information on people it wanted to influence. Single-handedly, Fran Machlis killed the deal, pointing out that *Mujin* already had influence in Washington with scores of lawyers, registered and unregistered lobbyists, and a few high-powered public relations firms on its payroll. To avoid embarrassing *Mujin* and the Japanese government, the bank story was never made public.

Penny had learned from the senator that *Mujin* was Carliner's largest client, paying one million dollars a year and expenses to assess foreign markets including America. That's why Carliner had gone all out to save the bank deal and in the process had called in quite a few markers, making defeat more than just a casual humiliation.

Edward Penny had asked Fran Machlis if she feared reprisals from August Carliner and she said no, she didn't. She was ready if Carliner wanted to return the favor, but the advantage was hers. She and Carliner were living in Washington, where only two things mattered: power and influence. She had both and Carliner didn't. One could gain them only through politics or government, and August Carliner was no longer an official part of either. He was what Washington called a former person.

Edward Penny, however, had felt he owed the senator a warning about *Mujin*. He told her he understood Asians; he'd fought for and against them, worked for and against them, and he knew that in defeating *Mujin* she had committed a crime against the corporation in its eyes. Like all Asians, the Japanese saw crime and punishment as being inseparable. He warned her to be on guard against *Mujin*.

Edward Penny said to Aristotle Bellas, "Looks like payback time. Carliner and *Mujin* are looking to hurt the senator in next year's election. Is that what you're telling me?"

The Greek snorted through his hooked nose. "That, my friend, is what you're telling *me*. What I'm telling you is that the senator is not the target."

"Great. Her lines are being tapped but she's not the target. You can do better than that, Greek. Try again."

"She's a minor player, nothing more. Carliner's after information. He's interested in what she and a few other people know about Warren Ganis. That's it in a nutshell. It's what these people know about Warren Ganis that counts. Nothing else."

Penny pushed himself away from the butcher block table and gave the Greek a very hard look, a look which made a tense Sophie say that her father was telling the truth. "Can't you see we're both scared?" she asked. That was when Aristotle Bellas patted his daughter's hand, speaking softly to her in Greek. Penny did the only thing he could do: He kept quiet, giving Sophie time to calm down.

He told himself that it wasn't like the Greek to be scared. Aristotle Bellas had been around; he was a survivor who had outlasted friends, enemies, and acquaintances. He wasn't called the Gray Fox for nothing; he was someone more prone to act for himself than for others, and people like that, Penny knew, outlived the rest of God's children. It didn't make sense for Bellas to worry about cops, even if he did give them a hard time now and then. He had worked for them, played cards and gotten drunk with them, and he knew their secrets. So why was he afraid?

Warren Ganis. Penny didn't know the man, but he knew the name. Mr. Ganis was strictly heavy duty. And rich. Serious rich. He owned a New York-based communications empire with interests in magazines, newspapers, cable operations and book publishing, which made him a mover and shaker in the media world. Ganis was an intensely private man who never gave interviews, but he was known to be doing a deal that could be the biggest of his life. He was about to acquire a controlling interest in a rival chain of newspapers, cable stations, and wire services at a cost to him of over $400 million. Added to those he already owned, the additional ninety-four newspapers would give him the largest chain in the country. With this, he would leave the movers and shakers behind and become a full-fledged kingmaker.

It was no secret that Ganis was very pro-Japan, particularly Japanese industry, whose management he held up in his publications as a role model for America. This also made him pro-free trade, strongly on the side of Japanese corporations doing business in the United States, Japan's largest market; therefore, it was no surprise when his views appeared in his publications, which they did with a certain frequency. Despite their differences concerning Japan's trade policies, Fran Machlis and Warren Ganis were friends, though she told Penny that Ganis's intense defense of *Mujin*'s right to buy the Washington bank might have intimidated anyone else but her.

Penny said to Aristotle Bellas, "Who are these other people who are supposed to know something about Warren Ganis?"

He watched the Greek chew a corner of his mouth, thinking the question over. Sophie didn't have to think. She was more frightened than her father. "The sooner we get out of this Carliner thing, the better," she said. "Tell Mr. Penny the truth."

The Greek closed his eyes. Thinking. Then he opened his eyes and stared at the tassels on his alligator shoes. "Coveyduck. Your senator's English friend. He knows. That's what his book's all about, the one the senator is helping him with. Meyer Waxler, he knows, too."

"Waxler. The old newspaper guy who runs the political scandal sheet?"

Bellas nodded. "Ganis ruined him. Made him a poor man and now Meyer's out to get even. He's crazy sometimes, Meyer. Gets this God complex, like he has to save the world. But he's a stand up guy. We're still checking on a couple of other people who might know something about Ganis. Point is, what these people know can bring the big man down. And make trouble for *Mujin* as well, I might add."

Penny's hand went up in a stop signal. "Let's slow it down a minute. How in hell can any of these people hurt Warren Ganis, let alone *Mujin?* Ganis is a heavy hitter. Money, power, the man's got it all. So he's left a few bodies behind him, so what? You don't get to the top of the mountain without punching out a few people. And you know something? I don't even think the public cares anymore. And as far as *Mujin*'s concerned, whatever Coveyduck and anybody else has on them, well it ain't gonna mean diddly squat here or in Japan."

Aristotle Bellas's pride took over. He didn't like having his information doubted. He aimed a forefinger at Penny and spoke from under a curled lip. "Sonny boy, when the Greek tells you something is true, you go out and bet the rent money on it, because you're betting on a sure thing. I'm the man with the golden ears, remember? Knowing things is what I'm good at. I'm the best at what I do, and don't you ever forget it. Suppose, just suppose I told you that a long time ago Mr. Warren Ganis killed some people."

Penny picked up his coffee cup. "Some of the country's best families spilled a little blood on their way up the ladder. Nothing new about that. Go to any country, shake the best family trees, and sure enough, a few assholes are going to drop out. The nicest people don't always get ahead, because the nicest people aren't always willing to do what it takes to get ahead."

A grinning Bellas slapped his palms together, pointed his folded hands at Penny, and leaned forward. "Mr. Edward Penny, sir, you are listening, but you are not hearing me. I did not say that Mr. Warren Ganis killed somebody. I said he killed *people*. In Greek schools people means more than one. I am talking to you about something Mr. Warren Ganis and *Mujin* did together, and they did it forty years ago. It is something that can blow them both right out of the water. Aha, I see by your bearded face that you do not believe me."

Penny said, "A reasonable assumption, considering that you've played fast and loose with the truth on more than one occasion. Face it, Greek, you have the reputation of a man who can be shifty when the need arises, and you could be feeling that need right now. Before we get too sidetracked with Ganis, mind telling me who you've got on the senator's staff?"

The Greek leaned back, fingering his chest hairs. "Why not, my friend. As they said when the first black astronaut landed on the moon, the jig is up." He grinned. "It's a woman, so I guess that makes me an equal opportunity employer. Debbie Previti. You know her, right?"

Edward Penny knew her. And liked her. She was thirtyish, blond, looked good in suedes, and was an administrative assistant to Fran Machlis. His first day on the job had been spent with Debbie showing him around the Washington office, introducing him to many of the fifty-five people who worked for the senator, and filling him in on life in the most political town on earth. The senator was going to be hurt when she learned that Debbie was the traitor in her ranks.

The Greek said, "We only bugged the town houses, this one and the one down in Georgetown. We left the offices alone. We thought if you did a sweep, the office is where you'd look first. Anyway, we weren't interested in politics. Just Warren Ganis. Debbie got us into the town houses when nobody was around, we planted the bugs, one-two-three, and that was it."

"And you body miked Debbie, too, right?"

"She felt funny about that. Didn't want to do it at first. Said her conscience was bothering her, but for what we were paying her, I said to hell with your conscience and wear the damn mike. And speaking of dirty tricks, Mr. Edward Penny, you pulled one on me, didn't you? The senator's not in New York, is she?"

A smile from Penny. And a slow shake of the head. He said, no she wasn't. She was staying overnight in Virginia with friends. Penny had spread the story around the Washington office that the senator had decided to fly to New York for dinner and the ballet with Lord Coveyduck, who was in town for only a day. Penny had preferred to set the trap in New York; with fewer of the senator's people around, there were fewer chances for things to go wrong. He told only the Washington people and, as icing on the cake, he had some of his New York friends telephone the Manhattan town house and leave messages for Coveyduck. This was to keep the wireman interested. In Washington, Debbie Previti had taken the bait. In New York, the Greek had done the same.

Penny said to Aristotle Bellas, "Why now? Why the sudden interest in Warren Ganis after all these years?"

A grim looking Bellas slammed his palms down on his thick

thighs and spoke to his shoes. "Why now? Because, my friend, there is a war going on in Japan, a war to see who controls an empire. To see who controls the *Mujin* group. Yasuda Gennai, the company president, is on his death bed and it's only a matter of time before he climbs those golden stairs. Meanwhile, there's a battle going on to see who steps into his shoes and that, my friend, is where Warren Ganis comes in. Somebody at the company, I don't know who, believes that bringing down Ganis is the way to take over *Mujin*. This somebody could be right."

He looked up at Edward Penny. "So it doesn't make sense, but let me ask you: How far would you go to take over a company that does one hundred billion dollars a year?"

Penny looked into his coffee cup. "You and Sophie aren't just working for August Carliner. You're also spying on him. You're tapping his lines, and I think he found out about it and now you're both scared shitless. When you got cute with Carliner, you got in over your head. You could even lose your head."

His eyes went to Sophie. Her face said Penny was telling the truth. She toyed with a string of pale blue worry beads, eyes on her father. The Greek smiled at Penny. A weak smile. With a nervous tic near the left eye. "Smart, Mr. Penny. Very smart."

Penny said, "That's your style, Greek, playing both ends against the middle when you can get away with it. Make a tape, then sell copies to whoever's interested. Only this time you got caught. The only way you could know about what's going on at *Mujin* and Ganis being involved is to have a tap on Carliner. Which I do not think is cool. My guess is you're running some kind of scam and it's not turning out the way you planned. What did you do, try to make a pile to cover your losses in the market?"

Sophie's worry beads clattered to the tiles. And Aristotle Bellas's large head flopped back on his shoulders. He said, "You know what they say about computers. Shit in equals shit out." He looked at Penny. "That's the way this whole thing's been going, this Ganis business. It started out shitty and it's ending up the same way."

Penny thought, if the Greek had a problem with August Carliner, it was between the two of them. You play, you pay. Penny's job was to take care of Senator Machlis, to keep the lid on her affair with Helen Silks. He wasn't going to mention Helen Silks until after he'd heard the tapes. No sense giving the Greek ideas.

What Penny wanted now were copies of those tapes, copies he knew the Greek had made. Time to play let's make a deal.

He walked over to the Greek's suitcases, picked up two and said, "Let's go." Where, said the Greek. Penny said, follow me. He watched the Greek pick up the remaining suitcase, and the attaché case, then Penny led the way from the kitchen, along a hallway and across a sunken living room, and finally to a marble floored vestibule near the front door of the town house. Penny set his suitcases down.

The Greek raised his eyebrows. "You're letting us go?"

Penny gently pried the attaché case, then the suitcase from the Greek's hands and said, not exactly. The Greek could go. The suitcases and Sophie, however, would remain behind. Penny was proposing a trade: copies of the Fran Machlis tapes in exchange for Sophie, plus the Greek's property, and don't bother denying the existence of any copies. Penny knew better and so did the Greek. The Greek was going to get the tapes and bring them back here. The sooner he left, the sooner he could return. Take it or leave it.

The Greek held out his hand. "My case."

Penny shook his head and said, no tickeee, no laundry. It was a package deal. All or nothing.

The Greek chewed the inside of his mouth and stared at the attaché case for a long time. Then he spoke to his daughter in Greek. At one point he grabbed her by the shoulders, shook her, and yelled in her face to get his words across, bringing her to the verge of tears. All Sophie did was nod her head in agreement and finger her worry beads.

Aristotle Bellas looked at Penny. "I got to drive out to Astoria. Be at least three hours before I get back."

"Good-bye, Greek."

The attaché case.

Edward Penny waited until he was alone before opening it. Getting rid of Sophie had been easy. Nervous and on edge, she'd asked to use the bathroom, so he had taken her to one near the kitchen, then jogged back to the vestibule and opened the attaché case.

Contents.

Snickers bars, unopened box of Tampax, two packs of Turkish cigarettes, miniature screwdriver, wire clippers, bits of paper covered with doodles of electronic devices being developed by the Greek and Sophie. A copy of today's *Wall Street Journal*. A copy of today's stock quotations from *The New York Times*. A copy of last month's *Forbes* magazine. The wireman as captain of industry.

Ignoring these items, Penny removed everything else and hid it in a vestibule closet.

He'd seen it when the Greek had looked at the attaché case, then jumped in his daughter's face in a loud and uncouth manner. What Penny had seen was a frightened man preparing to run a game on him. And all because of the attaché case. Penny's instinct told him so. Instinct and a lifetime of being a professional warrior, of being on guard against treachery and violence in those warriors who would kill him.

Edward Penny had remained this side of the grave by reading people. Reading them before, and not after the fact.

Sophie, somewhat calmer and composed, returned to the living room. Making small talk with her was no easy task, however. She sat in a fringed, upholstered chair near an antique Chinese table, biting her nails and giving monosyllabic answers to Penny's questions. No sense upsetting her, so he began with simple questions and little by little she opened up. Yes, she still went to Atlantic City once a month to see the shows and do a little gambling. She'd seen Diana Ross there twice, but her favorite was Barry Manilow.

The idea for the new scanner was hers, she said. She'd been working on it for over a year and finally got it finished last week. She was saving to buy her own apartment in Manhattan, but prices were high and she didn't know when she'd have enough money for what she wanted. For one thing, she wanted a terrace. Plus a spare room to use as a workshop. Since the spring she had been attending night school twice a week at NYU, taking French and art appreciation.

When they got onto the subject of her father, Sophie's face lit up. He was a genius, the absolute best in his field. Because of him she was making good money, a lot more than she would have made as a dental technician, which is what she had started out to be. Choosing his words carefully, Penny asked her what she and her father were afraid of. He watched her eyes fill with tears. She was quiet for a long time, then said somebody wanted to hurt them. A horrible man. Penny said Carliner and Sophie shook her head. Not him, but someone else. A man who was paid to kill people. A man tied in with Carliner and Warren Ganis.

Penny tried to look indifferent. He nodded, wanting to appear sympathetic without being too curious, and he was about to press her a little, to get a name from her, telling himself to go slow and not blow it, when the telephone rang.

The Greek. He wanted to speak to Sophie. He was in Astoria, but was having trouble finding all the tapes. He needed to talk to Sophie, to learn where she'd put them. Penny passed the receiver to her and watched Sophie speak to her father. In Greek. And tense up once more. Then she handed the receiver to Penny. Her father wanted to speak to him again.

Penny said, "Yeah, Greek."

"I was thinking. We could clean the town house for you tonight, if you like. Run a sweep from top to bottom. Might be better than bringing in somebody else."

From the corner of his eye, Penny watched Sophie edge away from him. He said into the phone, "I'd like that. Don't worry about Washington. I'll take care of that myself."

He looked over his shoulder.

No Sophie.

At the other end of the line, the Greek kept talking. Anything to keep Penny occupied. "Do me a favor," the wireman said. "Tell the senator it was strictly business. Nothing personal. Hell, I'm planning to vote for her next year."

When the Greek began pitching his new ideas, including the new scanner, Penny put the receiver down without hanging up. Then he tiptoed across the living room and looked down into the vestibule in time to see Sophie struggling through the front doorway with a suitcase in either hand. And the attaché case under one arm.

A beige and black van waited at the curb.

Motor running.

No lights.

Back doors open wide.

And who might the driver be? The front of the van was out of sight, but Penny knew who was behind the wheel. Aristotle Bellas. With his cellular car telephone.

Penny stepped away from the stairs and stood with his back to the wall, hearing Sophie enter the town house, grab the last suitcase, and dash out to the van, leaving the town house door open.

He heard the van's doors slam shut and the vehicle pull away. So much for trust in the integrity and character of wiremen. And wire persons.

In the living room he sat down in the upholstered chair, which was still warm from Sophie, and spread the items from the attaché case on the antique Chinese table.

First item.

A copy of the *International Herald Tribune* folded to page three, with a paragraph story circled in red.

Next, a bonanza. The Greek's black book of telephone numbers and addresses, a loss which was going to hurt the wireman. Penny wondered if it were true, that Aristotle Bellas did indeed have the private numbers of all nine Supreme Court justices and at least forty White House personnel.

Then three inexpensive notebooks, cheap ones that couldn't have cost more than ninety cents each.

Putting the notebooks aside, Penny flipped through the black book, looking for the name of a certain Washington call girl. There she was, Andrea Pagan. If you lived in Washington and kept up with gossip, you knew Andrea. She was a current favorite, the lady whom congressmen, retired admirals, high-powered lobbyists, and top civil servants wanted to party with. Andrea the pagan. Nineteen years old, half black-half Filipino and all lust, with a God-given talent for deviant behavior.

Penny wondered what the Greek would say if told that his last sex session with Andrea had tipped Fran Machlis to the wiretaps. On this particular visit, Aristotle Bellas had mistakenly left behind copies of the senator's transcript. The call girl had then shown them to another customer, a representative from North Carolina and a prominent spokesman for the Moral Majority. Fortunately, the representative was a friend of Fran Machlis and also needed her vote on an upcoming tobacco bill. The senator received a warning about the taps and the representative received a very key vote. And though the Greek had retrieved the transcripts, the cat was now out of the bag, thanks to Andrea Pagan.

The *International Herald Tribune* story.

Penny had wanted to discuss this with Sophie, since it was about someone he knew. The story was about Serge Coutain, who had suffered a stroke a few weeks ago and apparently was getting worse. Penny had met him through Georges Cancale, who sometimes bodyguarded Coutain on business trips abroad. Coutain's horse farm was just south of Penny and Cancale's property, and occasionally the French industrialist had invited them to watch the races from his private box in Deauville. That's where Penny had met Hanako, Coutain's beautiful Japanese fiancée.

Hanako of the incredibly beautiful eyes. Georges Cancale's telephone call to Penny about Coutain's stroke had described Hanako as part of *la mystere,* the mystery. On the night Coutain suffered his cerebral hemorrhage, she disappeared and hadn't been seen since. There was nothing to indicate that she had been abducted. She had taken her purse and passport, but left behind expensive clothes, jewelry, and a new BMW, an engagement present from Coutain. *Mystere.*

Who, Penny wondered, was the sick bastard who had destroyed Coutain's prized foal, then left it hanging on the barn door? The answer to that was worth money, since Coutain's family had offered a reward for information leading to the arrest and conviction of the criminal or criminals. Penny and Cancale would both love to solve the crime, not for the reward but for Serge Coutain, whom they liked. Suspicion had fallen on the farm's security guards, as there had been no sign of an intruder and the generator had been destroyed that night, eliminating all alarms. Even Cancale felt it had been an inside job, though try as he may he failed to connect it to Hanako's disappearance in any way. His theory on Hanako? All women are sleight of hand, he said.

Penny decided that Aristotle Bellas knew something about the colt and Hanako. Why else would he be carrying around this particular newspaper story with the word "Bangkok" handwritten beside Hanako's name? The Greek collected information for a living, as a hobby, and because he was obsessed with knowing other people's secrets. Once he collected it, the information was used as currency or a weapon. Penny was going to look up the Greek and lean on him until he explained why he had a copy of this story. And what was meant by the letter *O* drawn beside the story in red and underlined.

The notebooks.

Forget the first one. Penny flipped through it quickly, seeing stock market quotations, related financial jottings, and nothing more. Just something for the Greek to do when the eavesdropping proved slow or boring.

The second notebook.

A bit more interesting. And devoted entirely to Warren Ganis. Pages of dates listing telephone calls between Ganis and August Carliner, proving that the Greek was indeed tapping Carliner's phones. Next to some of the dates was that letter *O* again, always underlined and occasionally followed by an exclamation point. Most of the notebook dealt with a particular time in Ganis's life, the period from 1941 to 1945. Yasuda Gennai's name appeared in this section more than once. Definitely thought provoking.

Third notebook.

First the word *Mujin*, then the names of Yasuda Gennai, Reiko Gennai, Hanzo Gennai, and Tetsu Okuhara. The last two names meant nothing to Penny, but the second name did. She was Yasuda Gennai's wife, the woman known as the Empress and supposedly the power behind the throne at *Mujin*, if you believed all the gossip. A Japanese banker in Hong Kong had told Penny that his country had a saying: Gossip does not endure beyond seventy-five days. The Empress was an exception, the banker said. The gossip about her influence at *Mujin* had gone on for much longer.

Penny was about to turn the page when he saw another name, one hastily scrawled in light pencil almost as an afterthought. Helen Silks. Jesus. The Greek knew. The son of a bitch knew. Penny felt bad for the senator; it was another reason for catching up with the Greek and giving him a hard time until he coughed up the tapes and a few answers besides. Penny had a thought and not a very nice one. He considered the worst possible scenario, which was that Helen Silks had been planted on Fran Machlis by *Mujin*. If that were true . . .

He didn't even want to think about having to tell this to the senator. No wonder Aristotle Bellas wanted his attaché case back. This notebook and the tapes could be enough to knock Fran Machlis out of the next year's senate race.

Next page. Like the man said, anything that begins badly will end worse. This page listed telephone calls between August Carliner and Helen Silks. Between Helen Silks and Warren Ganis. Between Helen Silks and Reiko Gennai, with the notation that these last calls had been made in Japanese. And again the letter *O* beside some of the calls, the letter always circled and underlined. If it was a code of some kind, only the Greek and Sophie knew. Penny couldn't even guess what it meant.

Next page.

A shocker.

Edward Penny's name, along with his Washington, Arizona, and Normandy addresses and telephone numbers. At the bottom of the page Penny's name again, along with the name of Akiko Shaka. Beneath hers was the word *Oni*. Underlined. Not the letter *O* this time, but the full name. A circle had been drawn around all three names, linking them.

Penny leaned back in his chair, eyes closed. He felt suddenly exhausted, and there was a touch of nausea in his stomach, a vile taste creeping toward his throat. He began to shudder as if from cold, and his palms became damp. His heart started to beat faster. Breathing became difficult. He remembered the fire that had burned him in Central America, the torture he had suffered there. He remembered *Oni*, the man responsible for what had happened to him. *Oni*, the man Aristotle Bellas and Sophie now feared. Who had all but destroyed Edward Penny and now threatened him again. *Oni*, who also threatened Akiko.

For a long time, Penny sat slumped in his armchair, staring at the wall with glazed eyes and yielding to the fear of evil.

4

THE BUZZING OF the intercom annoyed Warren Ganis because it interrupted a quiet morning with his Asian art collection. Today was the first opportunity he'd had to examine his newest acquisition, an oil painting of a maharaja and his wife by nineteenth-century Indian artist Ravi Varma. Ganis found Varma sentimental and too influenced by Victorian artists, but nevertheless capable of striking and attractive work. In the past three years Ganis had spent almost twenty-five million dollars on Asian art, most of it smuggled into the country.

He held the Varma in his hands, angling it to catch sunlight coming through a window of his Fifth Avenue apartment, before putting down the painting and picking up the intercom phone. Ioko Waseda was calling. Waseda was his assistant and, among other duties, he dealt with thieves and looters who sold Ganis Far Eastern masterpieces. This morning Waseda was leaving for Thailand to pick up Ceylonese sculptures and Korean scrolls, but minutes ago he had received a long distance call from the man who had stolen these particular *objets*. The thief, an expatriate American GI living in Bangkok, now insisted on more money or the deal was off. Waseda asked, do we pay him or do we back off?

"Pay him, of course," Ganis said. He spoke in Japanese.

Waseda objected strongly. "Pay him? He wants thirty thousand *more* or he says he'll find a new buyer. We had an agreement with this maggot, but now he wants to change the rules at the last minute. I don't like being made a fool of. If it gets around that we can be pressured like this, then—"

"I know, I know. But he has what I want. It's as simple as that."

"The bastard kept saying 'No finance, no romance,' and laughing each time he said it. I would like to pluck out his eyes, put a mask over his stupid face, and set him to dancing in a cage beside our friend Hanako."

Hanako. Warren Ganis knew her. He'd seen her last March at a Tokyo reception for *Mujin* managers, trying to look interested in what was going on and succeeding only in coming across as monumentally bored with it all. He'd thought her to be one of the prettiest company wives at the reception, then decided she was too flighty and giddy for his taste and was probably giving her husband more trouble than he'd bargained for. Waseda, who enjoyed the morbid and macabre, had Polaroids of Hanako wearing a fox mask and dancing naked in a bamboo cage. Warren Ganis had seen the photographs once and that was enough, for the destruction of Hanako had been tantamount to the destruction of a work of art, something too unsettling to contemplate. On the other hand, only a featherbrain like Hanako would have imagined she could defy the Empress and get away with it.

Warren Ganis's three wives, each Japanese, had been chosen for him by Reiko Gennai, who had based her selection on *his* tastes in beauty, intelligence, character. The third and current Mrs. Ganis, while considerably younger than he, met all his requirements with the added plus of being keenly interested in art. Lately she seemed to be a bit distant, somewhat tense, and since she'd been in America less than two years, he had put that down to homesickness for Japan. That was why he accepted her preference for the quiet of their New Jersey estate to the Manhattan apartment. She had never liked New York, calling it filthy and dangerous and filled with people who didn't care about each other or what they did to each other.

He told himself that her present mood was a phase she was going through, that she would never become the problem Hanako had become. Warren Ganis loved his third wife more than he had ever loved the other two, and had no intention of ever allowing the Empress to punish her as she had Hanako. So long as Yasuda Gennai lived, Ganis had a court of last resort and would not hesitate to use it to protect his wife should the need arise.

The Empress had insisted on disposing of his first wife. Ganis had agreed, remembering the first Mrs. Ganis's adulterous liaison with a Japanese U.N. diplomat and her threat to go into an American divorce court and reveal matters best kept secret. No trouble with the second Mrs. Ganis, who'd been a dutiful and obedient spouse until her untimely death from breast cancer. Neither excited him as much as his third wife, his pride and joy. The day she entered his life had been one of the most glorious he could remember. Jealousy being one of the consequences of love, there were times when he could barely tolerate her being out of his sight.

On the intercom phone, Waseda continued railing against the treacherous GI. Perhaps if some harm were to come to the GI's little daughters, Waseda said, it might instruct our thief on the value of keeping his word. The GI and his Thai wife had two daughters, aged nine and twelve, ages especially appealing to the forty-year-old Waseda, who preferred his sex partners no older than twelve. On Bangkok trips, he indulged himself in child prostitutes of both sexes, which Ganis didn't mind since Waseda performed all other tasks efficiently. Waseda, however, felt compelled to relate his sexual experiences to Warren Ganis in boring detail, including the time he had suffocated an eight-year-old boy to death for attempting to steal his watch. Waseda's idea of sexual pleasure invariably included hurting or injuring his young partners.

Ganis said, "I want those Korean scrolls. This is why we will do business with our friend in Bangkok, avaricious though he be. For the moment, art is a seller's market, therefore we need him. It's as simple as that. Just remember: He's one of those people for whom no amount of money is enough, and rest assured, he will eventually hoist himself upon his own petard. That's when we'll make certain he has sufficient cause for regret and sorrow. Pay him what he asks and let that be the end of it."

"Ganis-san, I—"

"Do it, please. Let him continue to think we're fools and that he's putting something over on us. He'll get his due at the allotted time. I'll have the cash drawn from a commercial account. Stop by the Madison Avenue bank on your way to the airport. The money will be waiting for you."

He hung up without waiting for Waseda's reply, one way of insuring obedience, then with a pinky finger traced the emerald and ruby necklace painted around the *Maharani*'s neck. In speaking to the enraged Waseda, Warren Ganis had taken care to appear composed and undisturbed, free from agitation and bother. For once he had curbed his own tendency to outbursts when he didn't get his way, which in this case meant being left alone for thirty minutes each morning. But the interruption, with its haggling over money, had left him feeling irritable. Edgy.

He hated, absolutely hated *anyone* breaking into his morning quiet time, his much needed period of serenity, his time spent alone with his art. But it was self-defeating to get angry with Waseda, who after all was only doing what he had been hired to do. Besides, anger would only have an adverse effect on Warren Ganis's blood pressure, tension headaches, and gastrointestinal disorder, which though slight could get worse if he wasn't careful. Despite having a wife who made him feel young, he was still subject to the gradations of decay. *The passing years steal from us one thing after another.*

In recent months he'd taken to spending time each morning viewing his art collections in New York or at his New Jersey estate. The viewing was then followed by a Japanese massage. Art, he felt, provided the form which life itself seemed to lack. The massage, given by a professionally trained *anma,* Japanese masseur, promoted physiological well-being and general good health. Health, as Ganis's father used to say, was the first wealth.

Warren Ganis's apartment was a triplex in a neighborhood of recycled mansions, deluxe apartment houses, and expensive residential hotels. He'd purchased the flat because he loved art; it faced the Fifth Avenue entrance of the Metropolitan Museum of Art and was in an area containing more museums, archives and cultural exhibitions than any other in the city. The previous owner had been a famed symphony conductor who was said to have entertained his lovers by conducting his own recordings wearing just white gloves and using a jeweled stick.

Warren Ganis had filled most of the forty rooms, which included a private gym, screening room, and sixteen wood burning fireplaces, with Japanese, Chinese, Korean, and Southeast Asian art. At the Met he had underwritten the Stephen and Lucille Ganis Asian Art Room in honor of his dead parents, an excellent tax write-off and excellent public relations as well. He had also loaned works to the museum, made generous yearly donations, and frequently consulted museum curators on works he planned to acquire. Art was his fantasy life, a retreat from the ugliness of the world.

The tension headaches, high blood pressure, and stomach trouble had been building for years, but they had suddenly intensified with the news of Yasuda Gennai's terminal illness. The thought that Yasuda-san was going to die so depressed Warren Ganis that he now found himself constantly frightened. Yasuda-san, his mentor, his dearest friend, the reason behind his becoming a successful publisher. Yasuda-san, who had been his first lover.

And with this blow had come the shocking news that three men were poking about in his past. Oliver Coveyduck and Meyer Waxler were hell-bent on revenge, on inflicting punishment in return for previous injuries. The third man, Aristotle Bellas, was nothing more than a sleazy blackmailer looking to get rich quick, which made him the most despicable of the three.

They intended to do more than expose or discredit him; they planned to destroy him completely, to tear down everything he and the Gennai family had worked for these last forty years. The bastards were sifting the ashes that were his past, prying into events which had happened when he was a boy between the ages of thirteen and seventeen. Coveyduck was doing it because of his wife; Waxler was doing it because Warren Ganis had bankrupted him; Aristotle Bellas was doing it because he saw the chance for easy money. Two of them, Coveyduck and Waxler, were being fed information by someone at *Mujin* whom the Empress called *Aikuchi*, the hidden sword.

Ganis's enemies could not have picked a worse time to attack him, for at the moment he was in the fight of his business life and needed all his energy. In May he had paid eighty million dollars to purchase sixteen percent of Butterfield Publishing, a well known and moderately profitable New England company whose stock was undervalued, making it extremely attractive to anyone looking for a major media buy. He was now attempting to purchase the remaining eighty-four percent for four hundred million, a twenty million dollar increase over what he had offered last week. This had meant raising his price from $370 a share to $410 a share after financial advisers had encouraged Butterfield to hold out for more.

He had never been involved in more delicate negotiations in his life, and they were still going on. Lawyers, bankers, Wall Street analysts, and Butterfield editorial groups were all playing a role, and there were times when Warren Ganis was certain that the quibbling and nitpicking would drive him batty. Like it or not, he had been forced to proceed carefully, to be cautious in speech and action and take his stomach medication as prescribed. Illness was definitely a lesson in humility.

The Empress and her son Hanzo, someone whom Ganis saw as having more ambition than ability, had both given their backing to his plan for purchasing Butterfield. She had even insisted that her cherished son play an active role in the merger, a decision made without consulting Ganis who wasn't too enamored of Hanzo's brainpower. Her insistence on offering Hanzo's services, Ganis knew, meant that, as usual, she was moved by self-interest rather than by selflessness. As she saw it, if *Mujin* was to have a stronger voice in America because of Ganis's expansion, then let some of the glory go to her son for having helped bring it about. She envisioned a successful media merger as a stepping stone for Hanzo in his quest for the presidency of *Mujin*. Reiko Gennai saw her beetle of a son as nothing less than a graceful gazelle.

Yasuda Gennai favored the Butterfield deal, which pleased Warren Ganis no end since it meant other *Mujin* executives would follow their president's lead and give the publisher their support. This also insured the necessary financial help from the Japanese multinational.

He had encountered opposition from just one quarter and that was Tetsu Okuhara, the only major *Mujin* executive to oppose the Butterfield deal. Okuhara argued that the project required too much *Mujin* money to cover costs and that the very size of the deal would attract unwanted publicity to Ganis and his relationship with *Mujin*. Ganis suspected that Okuhara's opposition had more to do with jealousy over Ganis's closeness to Yasuda Gennai than it had to do with a sincere opposition to the Butterfield project. The publisher had to admit that Okuhara was an outstanding executive, certainly head and shoulders above Hanzo, who was too tightly tied to his mother's apron strings. But there was little about Okuhara that was likable. He was overbearing, contemptuous of weaker people, and positively salivating with ambition. It wouldn't surprise Ganis if Okuhara turned out to be the hidden sword, the worm in the apple, so to speak.

When it came to the cost of the Butterfield takeover, Okuhara had a point, unfortunately. In his attempt to gain control of the New England publishing company, Warren Ganis had spent twenty million dollars of *Mujin*'s money and estimated he would need at least ten million more. Should the deal fall through for any reason, all of that money would be lost. For Yasuda Gennai, the Empress, and Hanzo, such a loss would be crushing. In Japan, failure in business was considered a crime and after it one was always alone. Losing thirty million dollars or more would not be tolerated in a Japanese company. Warren Ganis's inability to acquire Butterfield, regardless of why, would mean a shameful death for Yasuda Gennai and the end of Hanzo's dream to succeed his father. It would also strengthen the Empress's enemies at *Mujin*, making her a stranger in her own house and stripping her of power.

Sale of Butterfield required a two-thirds vote of 980,000 shares. The chairman, who was also grandson of the founder, had agreed to vote his 337,000 shares in favor, and Ganis, naturally, would vote his 164,000 shares with him. The swing vote, which Ganis wanted desperately, would be cast by a Wall Street investment firm which managed over two hundred thousand shares for investors. As recently as yesterday Ganis had no idea which way the Wall Street firm would vote, though he'd heard rumors that it intended to support him.

Butterfield was an old, respected, and highly conservative company, the kind which saw publishing as a gentleman's business and traced its history back to the time when men wore spats and women got the vapors. A mere hint of scandal surrounding any deal with Warren Ganis, and both the chairman and the Wall Street investment firm would pull out in record time. Like

Caesar's wife, Warren Ganis must be above suspicion.

He was in his late fifties, a large man with a beefy handsomeness, curly silver hair and movements that were either ponderous or jittery, movements that matched lifelong mood swings ranging from cool-headed to turbulent. He was the chairman of Ganis Communications as well as its majority stockholder, giving him total freedom in running the company which had been founded by his grandfather. He preferred to operate in a hidden and confidential manner, concealing his intentions until the last minute. He rarely acted openly, preferring to achieve his ends without attracting attention. This allowed him to conceal improper and illegal actions toward competitors until it was often too late for anyone to stop him. It was his policy never to be interviewed, to make public statements only through a corporate spokesman, to remain isolated from contact with the general public and from most of the people who worked for him.

Employees and competitors, however, agreed that he had excellent business judgment and that his success was due to an ability to make sound and reasonable decisions quickly and under pressure. As a leader he rarely held out false hopes to those who worked for him. He stood behind any course of action he chose to follow and was willing to pay the price for what he wanted even when it meant sacrificing others. He reserved the power of decision at his company for himself, making sure those who worked for him knew that he was the foremost horse on the team. When asked the secret of leading men, he replied, "You lead them by the nose with money." Warren Ganis, however, knew the true secret: you monopolized all power and destroyed your rivals.

After telephoning his bank to have the money ready for Waseda, he took the elevator to the third floor, to his private gymnasium. Waiting for him at a foam rubber mattress in the center of the floor was his masseur, who was Japanese and blind, a frail, white-haired man with phenomenal skills. In Japan the profession of massaging had once been reserved exclusively for the blind, who were forced to apprentice themselves to a master for long and difficult training. In those days the masseur announced his presence in a neighborhood by playing a flute. Ganis was pleased to see Zasshi, his *anma*, keep to the old ways by kneeling near the mattress and playing a sad, mournful tune on a small wooden flute.

Zasshi was a gift from the Empress. She had put Ganis in touch with the old man, who serviced only Japanese clients. She assured him that Zasshi had been certified by the board of health in the Japanese prefecture where he had once practiced, that he was licensed, well acquainted with the structure of the human body, and even possessed medical knowledge. She praised his skill at *shiatsu,* finger pressure, and at *hari-ryoji,* acupuncture. Ganis knew he had a find in Zasshi when he learned that the *anma* had trained in *Irie, Misono,* and *Sugiyama,* three of the four most famous schools of acupuncture. Zasshi's hands were his instruments, and they were magic. Despite a waiting list, Zasshi had been persuaded by the Empress to accept Warren Ganis not just as a client, but as a preferred client.

After greeting the old man with a bow, Ganis removed his kimono and nude, lay stomach down on the mattress. There was no conversation unless the publisher initiated it, and even then, Zasshi replied in as few words as possible. Useless talk, he told Ganis, wastes much energy. A love of silence only increased Ganis's respect for the old man, whom he saw as a tie to the Japan he had first seen as a boy of twelve and never ceased to love.

Kneeling over the publisher, Zasshi began by rubbing him with scented oil and stroking the spine with his palms. Then, placing his right hand on his left, the old man pressed on the spine for three or four seconds at each hand span, moving from the neck to the buttocks. Occasionally Zasshi stopped to press down extra hard on that portion of the spine which in his words needed to be rectified. The proper alignment of the spine, he said, was of the utmost importance. Ganis didn't question him; the touch of those small hands erased his stiffness, leaving him feeling loose and rested and on the edge of falling asleep.

Then when Zasshi stuck an index finger in Ganis's ear and vibrated it, the last of the tension disappeared and the publisher was ready to take on the world. He had tried doing that himself but never managed the right amount of pressure and speed and in time gave it up for fear of damaging an ear drum.

Next, Zasshi manipulated Ganis's joints, stretching and working out every imaginable kink. The old man had to be doing something right because Ganis's overall health had improved, his blood pressure had dropped, and the stiffness in his joints had eased a great deal. Even his stomach wasn't as tormenting as it used to be, though it did flare up when he worried about the Butterfield deal or his problems with Coveyduck, Waxler, and Bellas.

Hari-ryoji. Acupuncture.

It will make your stomach better, Zasshi said, and he was right. The needles were not only painless, but in Zasshi's hands they drew no blood. Placed properly, he told Ganis, the needles stimulate muscles and nerves and aid the internal organs to function as they should. There were six hundred sixty spots on the body which controlled those muscles and nerves; it was here that the needles were pushed into flesh to stimulate stricken areas. Zasshi's needles were thin, from one to three inches long, and made of gold, silver, and platinum. Neither Ganis nor any other customer was allowed to touch them.

The publisher closed his eyes as Zasshi placed a small, slender tube on his body where the needle was to be thrust. Then, using a thumb, the old man gently pushed a gold needle through the tube and into the oiled flesh. When he had placed nine gold and silver needles in Ganis, the *anma* reached for his velvet-covered tray of platinum needles. These were special, almost a cure unto themselves, Zasshi said. He tapped them into Ganis's flesh with a small silver hammer, no tubes, and when he finished the publisher's back resembled a pin cushion.

Incredibly enough, Ganis felt no pain. He felt rejuvenated. Energetic. Ready to do battle with the world. In his last conversation with the Empress he'd tried to tell her how addicted he'd become to Zasshi's needles, but she'd been in no mood to discuss acupuncture. Her sole concern was that he acquire Butterfield and do it soon. Failure to do so would mean dishonor to Yasuda Gennai, who had been like a father to Warren Ganis. It could also mean the end of her son's career at *Mujin*.

"And you," she said to Ganis, "will no longer have important friends at the company. Tetsu Okuhara will see to that."

"He's already made that clear to me. He says he prefers to see someone else in my place."

"One way or another, Warren-san, it is his intention to withdraw all *Mujin* support from you should he become president.

This will be a severe blow to your business, as I am sure you realize. For your own sake, as well as ours, you must do whatever you can to stop him from succeeding my husband. I beg you, do not fail us, especially since my husband holds you in such high esteem and honor."

Warren Ganis was familiar with the Empress's desire to be first, with her insatiable desire for command, but she was correct in pushing him to do his utmost for Yasuda Gennai. The *Mujin* president had been his rock, his teacher in so many things; it was painful to imagine a universe without the old man's wise and trusted counsel. Ganis couldn't stop him from dying, but bringing the Butterfield deal to a successful conclusion would insure that Yasuda Gennai died peacefully and that his name remain revered.

Yasuda-san had been his first lover. The relationship was the one homosexual experience of Ganis's life, something he had not repeated but which he never regretted. As a boy he had been deeply in love with the older Yasuda, and their relationship was one where sexual love was neither categorized nor seen as shameful. All that mattered, Gennai told Warren Ganis, was that one be capable of giving and receiving love.

For years the publisher had been Yasuda Gennai's instrument in a carefully orchestrated propaganda campaign designed to create a favorable business climate for *Mujin* in America, a campaign that had begun during the waning days of World War II. Ganis, following Gennai's orders, had used his publications and influence to back American politicians, laws, and organizations which favored Japan and its trade policies. Backed by *Mujin* money, he sponsored books, articles, academic study groups, East-West conferences, and foreign affairs associations promoting harmony with Asia. Yasuda Gennai had done the elaborate planning, but Warren Ganis had been the instrument and the deed.

The result was a multibillion-dollar success for *Mujin* in the United States, the world's wealthiest market. With Ganis's help, Yasuda Gennai and *Mujin* had managed to keep Congress at bay for years, stopping lawmakers from passing restrictions inhibiting Japanese trade. *Mujin* funds, laundered through Ganis Communications, found their way into the political campaigns of candidates friendly to Japan. *Mujin* funds also found their way into university think tanks, high-powered publicity firms, press junkets, and expensive trips abroad for congressmen, journalists, and other Americans whom Ganis considered opinion makers.

He knew that many of these tactics were illegal and could not stand the light of day. And while Japan ignored most corporate wrongdoing for nationalistic reasons, Ganis knew that it couldn't ignore the book being written by Lord Coveyduck nor the series of articles by Meyer Waxler on the true relationship between Ganis Communications and Asia's largest multinational corporation. As for the blackmail attempt by Aristotle Bellas, the Empress described it as the beginning of hell on earth and simply not to be excused.

"I hold Carliner responsible," the Empress said. "I've made him aware of my displeasure at hiring such men as Aristotle Bellas. I was led to believe that the matter of tapping a few telephone lines would be a simple one. All we wanted to know was how much information Coveyduck had on *Mujin*. And on you. And we also wanted to establish a connection between Helen Silks and Senator Fran Machlis, which we planned to use in future. But now we seem to have run into a stumbling block, one which could cause problems for me. This is something I cannot and will not tolerate."

Ganis said, "It looks as though Aristotle Bellas came across certain facts and decided to profit by them."

"Those tapes he's holding over your head must not be allowed to remain in his hands. I've ordered Carliner to have his people find them, they're copies, I believe, and destroy them. As for disposing of the men who are your enemies and mine, I've turned that matter over to *Oni*."

Oni. The very word left Warren Ganis petrified. If a name could be said to chill the blood, to make one's hair stand on end, it was the name of this uncommon assassin. Ganis had met him twice, never for long, and only on matters related to the Empress. Merely to be in the company of this blood-soaked psychotic was horrifying. Ganis asked the Empress if there wasn't another way of dealing with the problem rather than use this madman whom no one seemed able to control.

She said, "We are not faced with an imaginary disease; therefore, I do not propose an imaginary cure. I have learned that secrets can be weapons in the wrong hands. I have reached that stage of life where I do not care to have my secrets in the wrong hands. You of all people should understand this. I should add that my husband agrees with me."

Ganis thought, I have only your word for that, madame, since you're not letting me or anyone else speak to your dying husband these days. Which conveniently leaves you free to put words in his mouth, not to mention run *Mujin* as you see fit.

The Empress said that since Carliner wasn't willing to get his hands dirty, *Oni* was the only answer. Hanako had been located in France and *Oni* was being dispatched there to deal with her. Afterwards, *Oni* would stop off in England to deal with Covey-duck before proceeding to America. Ganis was to extend him every cooperation.

"Be glad he's around to prevent you from being victimized by lesser men," she said.

Ganis shuddered, knowing that in truth it was he who had set loose the dog of war called *Oni* forty years ago, knowing that human blood was heavy and the man who had shed it could never run away.

5

Hartford, Connecticut

ON A CHILLY November night in 1941, thirteen-year-old Warren Ganis was running away from home.

He cracked the door to his second floor room, looked along an empty corridor, then stepped outside and softly closed the door behind him. He walked past walls hung with Currier and Ives lithographs, down a narrow staircase, and into a living room whose oak and country furniture of chestnut red and black had been polished to a glossy sheen. He wore a winter coat, woolen cap, high-topped sneakers, and carried a paper bag under one arm.

In the living room he paused to look at his father's Windsor rocking chair with its missing arm. Last week an angry Warren Ganis, who could be violent when upset, had smashed the arm with a poker, then began breaking his mother's collection of Royal Doulton character mugs displayed on an oak low dresser. Before he could attack a forty-six-string pedal harp standing near the fireplace, his father had snatched away the poker and, with his fist, struck Warren Ganis in the face. The blow had loosened two of the boy's teeth.

Ten-forty-five P.M.

A long case clock, its dial painted with a rocking ship against a seascape background, struck the quarter hour. Warren Ganis began to perspire. From his winter clothing. From nerves. He had to hurry. There were things to do before he left the house, before he cut himself off from his family forever.

He took a pen flashlight from his coat pocket, flicked it on, and walked through the quiet house and down into the basement. After turning on the basement light, he walked over to his father's workbench, shoved a hammer into his coat pocket, and left the paper bag among the tools. Then he walked to the furnace, opened its heat-blackened door, and stared in at the glowing coals now beginning to die down. There was a Heinz ketchup cardboard carton to the left of the furnace. Huddled among rags in the box was a small female dog and three newborn puppies. The dog's name was Nyoka, after the heroine in "Perils of Nyoka," Warren's favorite movie serial. She was a tan and white mongrel whom he had raised from a pup, and she had just given birth.

Warren picked her up, brought the dog to his chest, and kissed her cold nose. Then he threw the dog into the furnace and quickly slammed the iron door, covering his ears as the animal yelped and thrashed about in terror and scraped the metal inside of the furnace with its claws. There was a smell, Jiminy Cricket what a smell, like burning rubber and hamburger, and then the yelping and scratching stopped.

Speed it up, bozo, Warren told himself. He opened the furnace door again, didn't look inside, couldn't look inside, then tossed in the three puppies one by one and slammed the door. Now he ran. First across the cement floor to the workbench where he grabbed his paper bag, then out of the basement, leaving by the cellar door and glad, really glad to get outside in the cold, clean air.

He stood in the backyard, breathing deeply to clear the dog smell from his nostrils. His breath was steam in front of his face, and he was this close to vomiting, but nothing came up, just a bitter taste at the back of his throat, and he was glad he didn't have the heaves after all.

He looked at the two-story, white clapboard house in which

he'd been raised, at the top floor where his parents slept in a four-poster bed that had been hand-carved over a hundred years ago by his great-grandfather, a New England whaling captain. No turning back now. Not that he wanted to, because God, did he hate his parents, really hate them for trying to come between him and the best friend he ever had. But no amount of opposition by his parents could keep Warren from the one person he liked, the one person he trusted. Last week when his parents had physically tried to prevent him from leaving the house to meet his friend in Boston, Warren had picked up the poker and gone wild. Just wild. Now he was running away with his friend. They would be together forever, and there was nothing Warren's parents could do about it.

He took the hammer from his pocket and walked across the frozen ground until he reached a weather-beaten doghouse under a maple tree. Laying the hammer down on the ground, he lifted up the doghouse and set it to one side. It appeared that he had uncovered a pile of dried leaves and a metal pie tin half filled with water now starting to freeze. With the claw end of the hammer Warren gently poked the crisp leaves, scattering them to reveal a turtle with head, arms, and legs drawn into its shell. He had named the turtle Joe D., after Joe DiMaggio, who had set a baseball record this year by hitting in fifty-six consecutive games. One end of a long string was tied to the maple tree, the other to a hole drilled in Joe D.'s shell to keep him from wandering off.

Raising the hammer overhead, Warren brought it down on the turtle's shell again and again until the claw end was bloody and the turtle was a broken mass. Finished, Warren remained crouched for almost a full minute, breathing loudly through his open mouth, knowing that *now* he had cut himself off from his parents and his life in Hartford, that he had destroyed all that belonged to him and there was nothing left to connect him to this house and the people in it.

He dropped the bloodstained hammer, picked up the paper bag, and ran from the yard, leaving the wire mesh gate open behind him. He had been told by his friend to bring nothing, no clothes, no money. The trip ahead, he was warned, would be a long one and the less he carried, the better. His needs, all of them, would be taken care of.

The paper bag, however, contained one thing Warren couldn't bear to leave behind. It was a gift from the friend his parents hated. The gift was a cast-iron "Santa Claus" mechanical bank, just six inches high, a toy Warren never tired of playing with. The bank was in the shape of a stubby Santa holding his sack, one arm raised over a chimney which was the actual bank. You slipped a coin into Santa's hand, then watched the hand descend and release the coin into the chimney. A good way for a boy to learn the value of thrift, his mother had said. That was before she learned who had given the bank to her son. After that she had regarded the bank with distaste, and Warren had been forced to hide it in order to prevent her from throwing it away.

No one saw him leave. His parents' house, on the outskirts of Hartford, stood alone in the center of a lot near Nook Farm, the nineteenth-century writers' community which was a tourist attraction because Mark Twain and Harriet Beecher Stowe once had homes there. Warren ran east along a dirt road and toward a car parked a hundred yards away in a clump of basswood trees. The car, motor idling, was a blue Pontiac; its exhaust sent a steady stream of pale fumes into the cold night. A red taillight glowed under a pale quarter moon, and as Warren drew near the back door opened. He reached the Pontiac, leaped on the running board, and threw himself head first into the back seat. Using both hands, he yanked the door closed behind him. His heart was pounding and he was out of breath.

In the back seat with him sat a slim, handsome Japanese wearing a gray homburg and dark Chesterfield coat with an ermine-trimmed collar. One doeskin-gloved hand held a black ivory holder containing a cigarette, while the other rested on the hand-carved monkey head of a walking stick. His small, dark eyes took in everything about Warren's appearance, missing nothing. Instantly the Japanese revealed himself to be a man who reacted immediately and sharply once he reached a decision. Without a word he snatched the paper bag from Warren, rolled down the window, and tossed the bag outside.

Leaning toward Warren, he kissed him and said, "Warren-san, you must learn to obey, to do exactly as I tell you. Follow my instructions to the letter. Always. Do you understand?"

"Yes, Gennai-san, I understand."

Yasuda Gennai, the man in the homburg and Chesterfield,

commanded the driver in Japanese and the Pontiac pulled away from the basswoods, rolling slowly along the dirt road until it reached Farmington Avenue. On the nearly empty street, it picked up speed, passing a tobacco farm, a firearms factory. Once Warren saw a pair of foxes ahead of the car, their eyes emerald green and glowing in the headlights before they sped off into the darkness.

Fifteen minutes later the car reached the center of a deserted Hartford and took Asylum Street into Hartford Plaza, where thousands of lights now glittered for this year's festival of lights. A beautiful sight. Familiar, too. Suddenly Warren wasn't sure he wanted to leave, but then he looked at Yasuda Gennai and felt better. Much better. The car passed through Hartford, turned onto Route 91 and headed north along the banks of the Connecticut River. Warren Ganis was on his way to Japan.

Yasuda Gennai was in his early forties, a slight, handsome man with an abstract charm and a self-mocking smile. The son of a wealthy industrialist, he was a member of Japan's diplomatic corps, attached to the Washington embassy. Warren's father, publisher of a small chain of New England newspapers, had introduced him to Gennai, whom he had been interviewing for a series of articles on Japan's expansion in Asia.

Stephen Ganis was blunt, stiff-necked, and mulish. He never spared the strap when he thought Warren needed it, a habit he'd picked up from his own missionary father. Granddad believed that beating children saved their souls, so he would take the strap to Warren whenever he thought the devil was getting the best of the boy. Just let Warren get caught by his granddad using a swear word or not standing up when his elders came into the room, and out came the strap. Warren's father and mother went along with it, which Warren didn't think was right.

Yasuda Gennai was the kind of father Warren would have preferred. The Japanese was a soft-spoken, brilliant man, who always smelled of fancy shaving lotion, was friendly to Warren, and never raised his voice like Warren's father or his Holy Joe grandfather. It was hard to think that Japan wanted war with America, especially since Yasuda Gennai insisted that his country wanted to be America's friend. This was the idea Gennai wanted to get across in the newspapers, which were an important part of American life.

"Tell your countrymen to lift the embargo against us," Gennai said to Stephen Ganis. "Help us now when we need it most."

"And China?" Stephen Ganis asked.

Warren blushed because Yasuda Gennai was smiling at him, seemingly ignoring Warren's father. But then he saw the Japanese signal a servant to pour tea for Warren's mother Lucille, a chubby, dark-haired woman with a round, graven face, who had remained silent for most of the luncheon, believing that a woman should always defer to her husband. It seemed to Warren that Gennai was looking at him with interest and affection, which was nice, while at the same time being watchful of everything around him. Amazing.

When the white-gloved Japanese servant stepped away from the table to stand behind Lucille Ganis's chair, Yasuda Gennai said, "Japan would appreciate your country's taking no part in events now occurring in its part of the world."

"You mean let you have a free hand with China," Stephen Ganis said.

"Japanese-American relations have been in crisis for many months, and the situation will not be improved by outsiders interfering in Asian affairs. You have the opportunity, Mr. Ganis, to bring our two countries closer together by presenting in your newspapers a more balanced account of Japan's actions. We are fighting for our economic life. Surely, you cannot deny us the right to survive."

Yasuda Gennai said that even now negotiations between America and Japan were being conducted in Washington by the Japanese Ambassador Admiral Nomura. Japan did not want war with America. Stephen Ganis had to get this idea across to the American people.

Warren felt such sympathy for Yasuda Gennai and Japan that he almost apologized for his father's rudeness and bad manners. The Japanese diplomat was charming and certainly trying his best to be fair. Why couldn't Warren's father see that? Why did his father talk as though war with Japan was inevitable? Warren, like many boys his age, often daydreamed that a wonderful stranger would come into his life and take him away from Hartford, away from father and grandfather. With their first meeting he began to imagine Yasuda Gennai as his deliverer.

• • •

Warren had been described by one Hartford teacher as capable of upheaval and uproar when he didn't get his way. Another said he was violent, uncontrolled, and too harsh at games, a boy who made little attempt to get along with other children. Grandfather blamed it on Satan. The old missionary wondered aloud if Warren's disposition wouldn't be improved by a cold bath each morning, followed by castor oil and a solid hour of prayer and hymns.

Warren, however, found that he could get along with Japanese children his own age. He met them at a Washington embassy party to which the Ganises had been invited by Yasuda Gennai. The diplomat wanted newspaper coverage of the party because he said it showed the humanistic values and concerns of the Japanese people. The party was for the twelve-year-old daughter of the military attaché and Warren was the only Western child invited.

A Japanese chauffeur told the children a type of ghost story called *obake*, acting out all parts himself complete with costume changes and sound effects. The story was in Japanese, but the attaché's daughter translated for Warren, who became as frightened and as thrilled by the tale as the Japanese children around him. A boy gave him a wind wheel, a piece of colored paper which had been shaped like a flower and attached to a slim bamboo cane. When Warren blew on it, the flower revolved. Two girls taught him the first stages of *origami*, paper folding. Yasuda Gennai gave him a *shakuhachi*, a bamboo flute.

Warren had entered the party feeling self-conscious and hesitant, intimidated by the cultural and racial differences between himself and the Japanese children. But, encouraged by Yasuda Gennai and the children, he joined in their games and found himself welcomed with a warmth and friendship never shown to him by American children. The Japanese showed him how to play *sugoroku*, a travel game depicting an exciting journey filled with adventures. He played tug of war and *tosen-kyo*, where players tossed an opened fan at a gingko leaf placed in a small box resting on a round weight. To win, one had to knock the box down. And he gazed open-mouthed as a man on stilts, dressed as a samurai warrior, performed superhuman sword tricks within a foot of Warren's face.

He and Yasuda Gennai spent time alone before the party

ended, first looking at the Japanese art decorating some of the
embassy rooms, something in which Warren took an immediate
interest. Then they walked outside on the embassy grounds, talking about themselves and getting to know one another. That was
when the diplomat put an arm around him, saying he was a beautiful boy, with the most appealing blond hair, blue eyes, and fair
skin. Gennai said that regardless of what happened between their
two countries in the days ahead, he sincerely hoped that he and
Warren would always be friends. Looking back, Warren would
always remember that day as the one on which he fell in love
with Yasuda Gennai.

The two frequently spoke on the telephone. To avoid parental
criticism of their friendship, Yasuda Gennai urged Warren to
make his calls from a public booth. Next came secret meetings,
with Warren skipping school and traveling to nearby Boston, returning the same day. At the second of these meetings, Warren
and the diplomat had sex for the first time. For the boy the experience was wonderful—out of this world. To him this meant that
he and Yasuda Gennai were more than just pals. Their relationship, with its secrecy and fear of discovery, was special, something out of the ordinary. Which indicated that Warren himself
was an unusual person, truly one of a kind. Such a person was
not destined to spend his life in a dump like Hartford.

Stephen Ganis learned of these meetings when Warren's
school reported him absent without proper excuse. That same day
a postcard found in his room revealed what Warren had been
doing while avoiding the classroom. The card was from a leading
Boston hotel and had Warren's name written on it in Japanese
characters, a casual token from Yasuda Gennai.

Highly moralistic and piously certain of his own righteous-
ness, Stephen Ganis immediately suspected the worst. The boy
took a severe beating from his father, knowing he was in for
another at the hands of his grandfather and not really caring because Yasuda Gennai was now his entire life. It was when his
father ordered him never to see Gennai again that Warren had
taken a poker to the rocking chair and his mother's character
mugs. Warren was always one to stubbornly adhere to an attitude
or course of action.

November. Yasuda Gennai told Warren he was being recalled

to Japan. All chances for peace with the United States were doomed, and soon Japan would be taking what Gennai referred to as "decisive action." He said this was regrettable and not necessarily in Japan's best interests, for she was about to make an enemy of the strongest industrial power on the face of the globe. Gennai said he could discuss these things with Warren but not with most Japanese, who were quite anxious to go to war with America. Gennai called this a foolish idea, adding that all foolish ideas bring misery.

"From here on," he said to Warren, "one can only forbear the events to come. *Shikata-ga-nai*. There is nothing that can be done."

Warren wept as he'd never wept before and in several telephone calls begged Yasuda Gennai to take him away, too.

December. They arrived in Japan five days before the nation's spectacularly successful attack on Pearl Harbor and, while Yasuda Gennai remained skeptical about the wisdom of such a war, Warren was convinced that people like his father and grandfather could easily be defeated by a superior Japan.

Tokyo

June, 1945

The prison commandant's office.

Seventeen-year-old Warren Ganis took two steps and slapped the English woman's face. Stupid bitch. He should have hit her harder, knocked her out of her chair and made her hear bells. The blow had snapped her head to one side, and he could see the red imprint of his hand on her pale, sweaty skin, but there was no fear in the woman, none at all. There was hatred in her eyes, however. Hatred and contempt for Warren as she held his gaze and refused to look away. Warren struck her again, punching her in the cheekbone and feeling satisfied this time.

She almost fell from the chair, slipping to the floor on one knee and tearing her thin, purple dress along one side, but managing to cling to the back of the chair with both hands. A symbolic act of defiance, this clinging, and both she and Warren knew it.

Angered beyond words at her resistance, he bent down and bit her right hand, digging his teeth into her thumb and knuckle, tasting blood, determined to tear her grip loose if it killed him. Now the bitch fought back, punching him in the face with a small fist, and his rage took over, really took over. He lashed out with his fists, hitting the English woman on the top of the head, the shoulders, the back, never hearing Yasuda Gennai and the other Japanese in the small, bare shack order him to stop, that the English woman was a special prisoner and not to kill her. Warren didn't give a damn. It took the camp commandant and two guards to pull the tall, husky teenager off her and restrain him.

Warren Ganis was indeed in a prisoner of war camp, not as a prisoner, but as a collaborator, fluent in Japanese and proud of his position as interpreter and assistant to Yasuda Gennai, who ran this particular camp. Neither the commandant nor his staff had authority over Warren, which suited him just fine since he considered himself smarter than anyone in the camp, with the exception of Yasuda Gennai, and really didn't feel like accounting to people dumber than he. The commandant himself reported to Yasuda Gennai, who alone had the authority to issue passes necessary for travel in the area and could even order trespassers, civilian or military, shot on sight. In a country with a military government and a repressive secret police, control over a war facility by civilians like Yasuda Gennai was unheard of.

His association with Yasuda Gennai made Warren someone to take seriously around the prison camp, and he enjoyed every minute of his status. He had a pass, as well as a car and driver to take him between the camp and the Tokyo villa he shared with some of the Gennai family. The camp commandant resented having to show respect to a mere boy, a foreign boy at that, but to mistreat Warren was to challenge Yasuda Gennai, and there was no way the commandant could do that and live. When a new prison guard made the mistake of cursing Warren in Japanese, thinking he couldn't understand the language, the boy told Yasuda Gennai and the guard was flogged then left hanging in the sun three days without food and water. Warren found this a fitting punishment, since he regarded himself as inseparable from Yasuda Gennai and therefore entitled to a sense of his own proper dignity. Still he was warned by Yasuda Gennai to avoid an excessively high opinion of himself. Self-interest, Gennai said, prevented a man from seeing the truth.

The prison camp.

It was hidden in the pine and cedar covered mountains northwest of Tokyo, and was so secret that most Japanese were completely unaware of its existence. Nor did it appear on any list of POW camps to be inspected by the International Red Cross. Yasuda Gennai had ordered its construction for reasons known only to himself, his family, government officials, and of course, Warren Ganis. Most of its barracks and supply shacks were hidden inside a long tunnel blasted within a mountain. Guarding the camp were armed troops, killer dogs, an electrified double fence, and a cordon of tanks. The single entrance was protected by four checkpoints, with an additional four checkpoints stretched out along the one road leading to the camp. With artillery pieces and machine guns trained down on the camp from the surrounding mountains, Warren decided that the only place in Japan more secure was the Imperial Palace, home of the emperor and the royal family.

Warren's camp—he thought of it that way—was made special by the inmates. All were *gaijin,* Westerners, captured Americans, English, Europeans, Australians, taken from prison camps in Southeast Asia and the Pacific. Most were civilians and all were elite members of their societies, ninety-seven men and women who had held important positions in politics, journalism, medicine, the arts, diplomatic service, business, the clergy. Warren, perceptive and knowledgeable for his age, and eager to please Yasuda Gennai, had joined him and other Gennais in poring over prisoner records from Japan's conquered territories, selecting from thousands and always, always choosing with great care.

"Choose only the learned and well-schooled," Yasuda Gennai had said. "Choose the most skilled and privileged, the high and mighty, the cream of the crop, the ones who can tell us about America and other Western industrial nations. But let the emphasis be on American business expertise."

The project had been given the code name *kin-boshi,* from sumo wrestling, meaning a grand victory against the grand champion. Because he had been assigned a major role in the project, Warren had been among the first to hear about it at a secret meeting called months ago by Yasuda Gennai and limited to Warren and select Gennais. "Japanese propaganda to the contrary," Yasuda Gennai said, "Japan has lost this war with America and must now prepare for the next one with the Western grand champion, the one to be fought not with bullets, but with minds and wills.

"Our next war with America will be a trade war," he said. "We have only to look at the destruction of our beloved country to see that there can never again be a military solution to our economic dangers. We must come to grips with a changed world, one which threatens to change even faster when war ends, when Western colonies and our conquered territories become sovereign nations, free men in charge of their own resources and manpower, and their own destinies."

With Warren and the others absorbing every word, Gennai said that Japan had always learned from other nations, that its navy had been copied from that of the British, its army from the Germans and its government copied from the French. Since Japan was being crushed by the industrial might of America, did it not make sense to imitate that same industrial might and turn it against America in the trade war which was to come?

"And how do I know of this forthcoming trade war?" he asked. "Because, my brothers, Japan is too small to survive without foreign markets. We cannot survive without being economically aggressive. America is opposing us now for this very reason and will oppose us when this war ends rather than relinquish those markets it controls or covets. America will not share Asia or the Pacific with us, therefore we must fight her for them. But this time we fight America with her own weapons and we join those weapons to the sacred Japanese spirit. I tell you, my brothers, this time we will win. We will defeat the grand champion."

He thrust both arms in the air and shouted, *"Kin-boshi! Kin-boshi! Kin-boshi!"* and Warren was the first to leap to his feet and cheer, with the others quickly joining him, some with tears in their eyes and all aroused to strong emotion, their already intense natures now more inflamed. And in the midst of this special moment, Yasuda Gennai put an arm around Warren, lifted a hand to stay the cheering, the chanting, then said that *kin-boshi* would succeed because Warren-san was an important part of it. Now the Gennai family would see why Warren had been brought to Japan four years ago.

"You will all learn to trust and believe in him as I do," Yasuda

Gennai said. "I give you Warren-san, the heart and soul of *kinboshi*. Warren-san, our spearhead in America."

Warren, fighting back the tears, feeling a pleasurable satisfaction that could never be expressed in words, knowing there would be few moments in his life as proud as this, promised Yasuda-san and the other Gennais that he would do whatever they asked of him and do it gladly.

He was cheered again and again, and never had he felt so loved and so much a part of anything as he did now.

The boy found his mentor to be the most shrewd, yet flexible of the Gennais, bold and patient by turns and at all times aware of what was written in his own soul. Yasuda-san knew when to take risks and when to bide his time, when to take command and when to trust the judgment of a subordinate. Being in his company gave Warren the conviction and will to do anything.

He had been surprised to learn that Yasuda Gennai had been an intelligence agent while serving as a diplomat, but Gennai said this wasn't unusual, that the envoys of most countries doubled as spies. Most fascinating of all to Warren were Yasuda Gennai's ties to the *Mujin* Group, Japan's largest conglomerate, which had been founded by a medieval ancestor. *Mujin*, Warren learned, had first call on the loyalty of all Gennais, who were samurais and traced their line back almost five hundred years.

Yasuda-san had insisted Warren learn the history of the company, which had been founded in the fifteenth century when an ancestor had discovered a small silver mine and called it *Mujin*, eternal, in hopes of being eternally wealthy. Mine profits had been invested in a brewery, then in a dry goods store, and the ancestor had indeed prospered. *Mujin* had been one of the first tax collectors for a *shogun*, using that advantage to become one of the country's first banks. And how had the company survived centuries of civil wars, corrupt emperors, earthquakes, coups, floods, and financial depressions? By planning thirty years ahead.

Mujin employed two million people in businesses such as banking, steel production, mining, real estate, and food processing. The entire conglomerate was controlled by a single holding company; tradition called for that company to be owned by one man, the head of the Gennai family. Along with these riches came the power that went with maintaining close ties to all major political parties and military factions. Thus the man who ran *Mujin* was the uncontested monarch of a feudal kingdom. With his father hospitalized because of serious injuries suffered in an American bombing raid this year, Yasuda Gennai now ruled that kingdom.

Had they been as intelligent or as lucky, two older brothers might have ruled in his stead. But with the war going badly for Japan almost from the beginning, a shock to Warren who had expected an easy Japanese victory, the government had been forced to declare all males between the ages of sixteen and fifty-nine eligible for conscription. Which was how the older brothers found themselves entering military service past the age of fifty, with one eventually dying in the battle for Okinawa and the other dying when his ship was sunk while attempting to run the American naval blockade of Japan. Because his intelligence-gathering skills were essential, Yasuda Gennai remained exempt from the military. Even more essential was his leadership of *Mujin,* which produced needed fighter planes, explosives, firearms, and ship's engines.

Warren needed him, too. Needed him to gain acceptance in this astonishing and exciting country. On arriving in Japan, Warren had been terrified. He felt out of place, unwanted by Yasuda-san's family and he resented being looked upon as some sort of freak due to his white skin. Yasuda-san, however, stood by him, telling the family that Warren was a friend of Japan and would be of great value to the Gennais in the future. Eventually, he came to be accepted, even liked by most of the family.

Kin-boshi

When the first Western prisoners arrived in the special internment camp, Warren immediately went to work as interpreter for Japanese participating in the interrogation. These were Gennai family members and a few government officials who had given official approval to the project. All spoke English, had traveled in the West before the war, and were familiar with America. Warren, with his quick intelligence and youthful energy, was of great assistance. He detected nuances in English that the Japanese sometimes missed, and he was able to point out attempted deceptions, lies, or inaccuracies.

He pursued his assigned task with zeal, feeling flattered at having been asked to participate, always anxious to please the Gennai family and show them that he belonged in their circle. Above all, he enjoyed the power and advantage he held over the prisoners, men and women old enough to have been his parents and teachers back in America. It was a delicious time for the boy who gloried in his authority and willingly worked long hours, interrogating and examining written transcripts of prisoners' answers. In helping to prepare the Japanese for the war that was to come, he came to know his American countrymen as he never imagined possible.

Taking his lead from the Japanese, Warren maintained curiosity about everything from factory production and union wages to the number of streetcar lines in a Texas town and the size of a Chicago airport under construction by the family of a war correspondent captured in Burma. Yasuda Gennai was particularly interested in the racial tensions between American whites and negroes. A festering sore, he called it, one bound to erupt one day with explosive consequences.

Warren learned of the increase in American government agencies formed to fight the war and control inflation with price and wage controls. Government control of unions had eliminated labor strife during the war, but Yasuda Gennai predicted this would set off huge wage demands in peacetime. Let American labor become too expensive, he told Warren, and it will be unable to compete against countries with cheaper labor. Taxes had been raised to fight the war, yet the American government was going into debt borrowing money to handle expenditures taxes couldn't cover.

Warren watched Yasuda Gennai give maps of American cities to the prisoners, then ask for corrections or additions. Gennai also asked about farm fields, factory machines, methods of hauling produce to market, and the role of the press in American life. It was learned that America feared Russia, though the two were allies. Warren himself was surprised to learn how little Americans knew of international affairs. Such ignorance, Yasuda Gennai said to him, must be exploited.

The boy came to admire the Japanese passionate emphasis on

the acquisition of knowledge for its own sake. Different prisoners were asked the same questions and their answers were compared. Sometimes the same prisoner was reexamined a week later, a month later, to confirm whether he or she had been telling the truth. Lying is a prisoner's last weapon against his jailer, Yasuda Gennai told Warren.

Prisoners were given the carrot and stick treatment, privileges granted then withheld when it suited the staff. Some inmates were shown courtesy, while others were handled in a harsh, unbending manner. When a Marine captain, the son of an American congressman, refused to cooperate, Yasuda Gennai ordered guards to pour gasoline on his feet and set fire to them. The Marine was then bayoneted to death, which Warren thought was a fitting punishment for not doing what he was told.

The American representative of an oil company, accused of organizing prisoner resistance within the camp, was forced to run barefoot over broken glass while being struck with thick curtain rods. A pair of Australian diplomats, who'd spent years in America, but whose answers conflicted with one another, were punished by being forced to stand long hours in the sun while holding a heavy log overhead. Warren himself became displeased with an American Air Corps captain and ordered him hung from a tree by his thumbs, feet barely scraping the ground. Nor were women spared. The uncooperative wife of an American automobile manufacturer was force-fed water through a hose until her stomach bulged, then tied with barbed wire. Guards jumped on her stomach and kicked her until she died.

A few prisoners were beheaded, and on one occasion Warren returned to the camp after a few days' absence to find an American priest about to be buried. He had been executed for stealing food to give to the sick; his ears, nose, tongue, and eyes had been cut out. Then there was the college professor from Ohio who was humiliated by simply cutting all the buttons off his clothes, then forcing him to clean the latrines.

On the other hand, Yasuda Gennai had shown kindness to an American woman doctor captured when she had stayed behind with her patients in a Manila hospital. Brutal treatment in a Philippines prison camp had ruined her health, and now she was losing her sight. Gennai ordered Warren to read to her from Jane Austen, her favorite author, and from the Bible. Men and women whose heads had been shaved in other prison camps were allowed to grow hair in this camp. And there were gifts of soap, combs, mirrors, salt. Kindness precedes extraction, Gennai told Warren.

The boy, however, felt little kindness toward one particular prisoner. Her name was Cass Coveyduck and as the wife of a British diplomat once attached to the Tokyo embassy, as well as being the daughter of the president of the British Board of Trade, she was a prized prisoner, one too valuable to kill. She was also an uncooperative one, with a particular contempt for Warren Ganis whom she called a toady and a lickspittle. When the war broke out, she had been in a Tokyo hospital recovering from a miscarriage. At the same time her husband, in Hong Kong on a diplomatic mission, was trapped there by a Japanese siege. Accompanied by a handful of daring souls, including a one-legged Chinese admiral, her husband managed to escape the Crown Colony and make his way to Chungking. War conditions, however, prevented him from reentering Japan, forcing him to return to England without his wife. As for Cass Coveyduck, the International Red Cross had her listed as an inmate in a POW camp near Osaka.

She and Yasuda Gennai's other prisoners received none of their Red Cross packages, which were confiscated by Japanese in all camps. Incoming mail in Gennai's camp was confiscated as well, with an occasional letter given to that prisoner who had proven extraordinarily cooperative. Yasuda Gennai allowed certain prisoners to write home occasionally, but these letters were heavily censored then mailed from other prison camps. He did this in order to receive letters in reply which might contain useful information. Warren, who'd taken an instant dislike to the scornful Mrs. Coveyduck, once burned three of her husband's letters to her while she watched. That was when she spat in his face. If Yasuda-san hadn't stopped him, Warren would have strangled her on the spot. But from then on, she and the boy were enemies.

Minutes after Warren had lost his temper and bitten the Coveyduck woman, he and Yasuda Gennai were outside in the mountain tunnel, strolling toward the tunnel entrance, toward the sunlight. Arm around Warren's shoulders, the Japanese praised him, calling him truly a good lad, extraordinarily bright and industrious and possessed of good instincts in most matters. But there was a volatility to Warren that could be shocking to those who didn't know him.

Speaking calmly, Gennai said that Warren's behavior was both commendable and irrational, that he was intelligent and probing in his questioning of prisoners, but had revealed his hostility to the Coveyduck woman, thereby allowing her to use that rage against him. Yes, Yasuda Gennai was aware that she was a clever woman, one able to walk the line between resistance and cooperation. But Warren was clever, too, and quite capable of dealing with a mere woman if only he controlled himself. Gennai said that Warren had to restrain himself, that all knowledge came from calmness of mind and to achieve this Warren had to relax by maintaining an interest in art, calligraphy, sketching. And though Warren lacked the patience to practice it, meditation was also good for the soul.

They stepped from the tunnel, shaded their eyes against the sudden glare of the sun, and, with Gennai leading the way, walked to a rock garden near a flagpole. The garden had the stark, unadorned beauty which was at the heart of Japanese art. Modeled on the garden at the Ryoanji Temple in Kyoto, it consisted only of fifteen rocks placed on white sand in groups of seven, five, and three. Warren loved it, having learned from Yasuda Gennai that beauty lay in naturalness.

For a few moments the two stared at the garden in silence, closing out the camp around them. When Yasuda Gennai sensed the boy regaining control of himself, he said he was now going to divulge to Warren the most important part of *kin-boshi,* the part which would determine its success or failure and could be executed only by Warren.

Gennai stared at the empty road leading to the camp. "Listen to me carefully, Warren-san. Today is your last day of working with the prisoners. Let me add that it has nothing to do with the English woman. You have something to do for us. It is the next step in *kin-boshi,* and it is also a test of your loyalty."

Warren frowned. "But why must my loyalty be tested, Yasuda-san? Have I not proven myself all these years? I don't understand."

"You have passed all tests, my friend. But you will come to see the need for this final test and I, for one, have no doubt that you will acquit yourself handsomely. Let me say that this test will convince every member of my family, even the most reluctant, that you are, indeed, one of us. The family must be certain of your loyalty. They must know, as I know, that you will serve without question and do whatever is asked of you."

"Ask me anything, Yasuda-san, and it is done. I have no other family but yours. I want no other family but yours."

Both of them saw it at the same time—black smoke rising over Tokyo. The city was under attack by American bombers. A sad Gennai said that war was not an art, that it was the business of fools and brutes, a cruelty that could never be refined. And yet if he wanted *Mujin* to survive, he would have to play this mad game a little longer.

He looked at Warren and said, "You leave Japan in three days. May you stick to your purpose, our purpose, Warren-san, and be a match for heaven."

He took the boy in his arms and held him as he stared at the black smoke rising to the south.

Hartford, Connecticut

July, 1945

It was dark and the rain had slackened when Warren Ganis opened the gate to the wire mesh fence enclosing the backyard. Wire mesh instead of the white picket fence that used to be there. The doghouse was gone, too, and so was the maple tree, now chopped down and reduced to a rotting stump. Warren walked up to the white clapboard house he'd left four years ago and peered through the kitchen window. Almost pitch black inside. And nothing moving around. Good.

He was dressed in black—leather cap, gloves, raincoat, trousers tucked into rubber boots. And a handkerchief tied across his face. In the darkness and rain he was almost invisible. And definitely uncomfortable. The summer rain had brought with it a disagreeable humidity. Under Warren's raincoat his shirt clung to him with a clamminess that made him want to scream. God, he wished this night were over. On the other hand, he was looking forward to it, to the final test. Pass it, and never again could his loyalty be questioned.

Taking a screwdriver from a raincoat pocket, he jabbed at the single window lock until it was loose. Then he pocketed the screwdriver and pushed the bottom window up, tearing the lock free and sending it flying to the kitchen floor. Damn the noise. He climbed inside, scraping his right knee and cursing again, but breathing easier when he saw that he hadn't torn his trousers. "Leave nothing behind," Yasuda-san had said.

Inside, Warren closed the kitchen window, then froze and listened. He heard the refrigerator motor and he heard rain beating gently on the panes behind him. Ahead there was the faint ticking of the long clock coming from the living room. Nothing else. Still, he remained motionless for a long time, holding his breath and listening and feeling the rainwater slide from his cap and down the back of his neck.

Nerves. Maybe that was why he was perspiring so much. He was under orders not to take off any clothes until the job had been completed and he was clear of the house. Yasuda-san's orders. And Warren had learned to obey them without question. His mentor not only gave good advice, but gave one the spirit to act upon it. Warren took out a penlight and ran its beam around the kitchen.

Changes.

New curtains, cupboards, and linoleum in the kitchen. And a bulletin board near the fridge that hadn't been there four years ago. Recipes were pinned to the board, along with a news story written by his father on President Roosevelt's death in April of this year, and a copy of the Sermon on the Mount, no doubt put there by Warren's grandfather. His late grandfather.

A month old copy of the old man's obituary, with an accompanying news story by Warren's father, was also tacked to the bulletin board. The story said that Grandfather Ganis had passed away at home in his sleep, surrounded by loved ones. Warren knew this to be false. But as Yasuda-san had said, referring to Warren's father, a man of good speech can tell a good lie.

Before leaving Japan for America, Warren had been shown a folder containing up-to-date information on the Ganis family. Included in the dossier was the news that Grandfather Ganis had been institutionalized during the last year of his life and had died a raving alcoholic. Gennai said that the old man had probably been unhappy and drank to keep from thinking.

The kitchen smelled of pine disinfectant. Still the compulsive little cleaner, his mother. A woman who couldn't sleep if she knew there was the smallest speck of dust on the floor of her bedroom.

He went looking for the cutlery drawers and found them in the same place, to the left of the kitchen sink, polished metal knobs gleaming, and every implement spotless and resting in the proper compartment. Dear, dear mother. Heart pounding, Warren made his selection. He chose a long-handled bread knife with a nine-inch blade.

Knife in hand, he left the kitchen and walked through the dining room, tracking mud on the newly waxed floor, then entered the living room. He trained the tiny flashlight on his father's Windsor rocking chair. The broken arm had been repaired, while the Royal Doulton character mugs had tripled in number. Warren thought the mugs were ugly, not artistic in any way, and simply an example of money without taste. Frankly, all the art in this room was dismally provincial, indicating that whoever had picked it out lacked the first idea about what was excellent or appropriate. One thing Warren had learned from Yasuda Gennai was taste and a feeling for style.

Behind him the long clock struck four A.M.

He looked at the ceiling, toward the second floor where his parents were sleeping. He'd thought about this moment every day during his lonely three and a half week journey across China and India on his way to Spain. Thought about it during the dangerous Atlantic crossing and all the way down from Canada in that crummy truck, hiding in the back behind cartons of apples and blueberries, getting sick from the smell of rotting fruit and all the while scared to death that the two unwashed and unfriendly men in the front seat were going to murder and rob him. Thought about it when he had to stay hidden in a Massachusetts forest for two days while waiting for the promised rainstorm that would allow him to sneak into his parents' home unobserved.

"Thoughts must result in action," Yasuda Gennai had told him. Warren took several deep breaths, aware of his thumping heart but remembering that Yasuda-san had said he was strong, calling him a lion and a man of mettle.

Following the small flashlight beam, Warren climbed the stairs to the second floor. His parents' bedroom was halfway down the hall on the left. At their door, he paused to listen and heard his father's slight snore and heard the rain start to come down harder. Without turning the flashlight off he slipped it into his raincoat pocket. One more deep breath. Exhale. Then Warren opened the door and stepped into the bedroom.

He walked toward his father's snoring, toward the left side of the bed which was cooled by a small electric fan resting on an end table. He stepped closer to his father, took out the flashlight, and trained it on the bed. Both parents were sleeping on their left side with their backs to him, and were covered by a pink sheet. For a few seconds he held the tiny beam of light on their shoulders and the backs of their heads. Neither parent stirred. Warren made a mental note of their positions, then placed the flashlight on the end table, beam aimed at the bed.

"Kill your father first," Yasuda Gennai had said. "He's strong and the more dangerous of the two. Should he see you attacking your mother, he will become crazed and fight like ten devils to save her life. But if she sees her protector die, she will lose heart and become easier to deal with."

Kin-boshi.

Warren grabbed a handful of his father's graying hair, yanked his head off the pillow, then sliced his throat with the bread knife. Remembering what the prison camp commandant had told him, he tightened his grip on the hair and pulled the head back, enlarging the wound, causing the blood to flow faster. There was a long, loud rasp, the noise of air escaping his father's torn throat, and Warren almost leaped out of his skin.

His mother stirred, her sleep now disturbed by the sound of her husband's dying. As she rolled over on her back to confront him, Warren quickly crawled across his father's bleeding body, straddled his mother, then placed the tip of the bread knife against her throat. With both hands on the handle, he pushed down hard. Her blood spurted up with shocking force, splattering his arms and chest. Some of it got under the handkerchief, wetting his chin and neck. At the same time she kicked the sheets with both her feet and her bowels emptied in a sudden rush. And just as quickly she relaxed and died.

Warren climbed off her, backing away from the bed, the blood, the stink. Then he sat down on the floor and laughed and cried at the same time without knowing why. He felt exhausted, so very, very tired, and was ready to sleep. But he wasn't finished.

He rose from the floor and, following Yasuda Gennai's orders, he ransacked the bedroom, slicing pillows with the bread knife, pulling out bureau drawers and leaving them on the floor, then tearing apart clothes closets and scattering books. Any money and jewelry he found went into his raincoat pocket. The motive must appear to be robbery, Yasuda Gennai had said.

Warren ransacked every room on the second floor, including the one which used to be his. It had been kept exactly as he'd left it, a shrine of sorts, with his baseball bat and glove, a set of electric trains, a chemistry set, and photographs of himself at summer camp, as Miles Standish in a school play, and standing with his mother in front of the Lincoln Memorial in Washington. The room was a sentimental touch which, for a moment, made him feel guilty and terribly alone. But everything in this house belonged to another world and time. Even God couldn't undo the past. One could never go back.

When he finished in the house, Warren left by the kitchen door and stood outside in the yard, face turned up into the warm rain. He stared into a starless sky and thought, it's the same sky that covers Japan, and I wish I were there with Yasuda-san to tell him what I've just done and to see the look of pride on his face. Warren now felt more energetic than he had in a long time. Very lively. Full of vim and vinegar.

He walked across the yard, the mud sucking at his boots, and when he was outside on the road he ran as he'd done four years ago, running toward a car parked in a clump of basswood trees, a car that was the first step on a return journey to Japan.

Tokyo

August 30, 1945

Tense and perspiring under a noon sun, Warren Ganis followed Yasuda Gennai, his wife Reiko, and a Shinto priest into the prison commandant's shack. The small room was packed with prison staff, and smelled of cigarettes, sweat, vinegared rice, and fear. When Yasuda Gennai and Reiko had seated themselves in two empty chairs placed in the center of the room, Gennai snapped his fingers and ordered an officer to stand and give his chair to Warren. As the chair was placed to Yasuda's left, Warren bowed his head in gratitude, knowing this was not only a kindness to him but an expression of contempt for the military in general because it was they who had brought this terrible defeat upon Japan.

Two weeks ago the country had surrendered to the Americans. The official signing of the surrender, however, was scheduled for eight A.M., the morning of September 2 on board the American battleship *Missouri* in Tokyo Bay. Sometime today the Eleventh Airborne Division of the American Army was due to land at Atsugi Airfield. Also today the Fourth Marine Regiment would be landing at the naval base in Yokosuka. The American occupation was only hours away.

Warren was making his second visit to the prison camp since returning from America, and again the Gennais and others had given him a hero's welcome. He'd seen the American press cuttings which, as Yasuda Gennai had predicted, attributed the murders of Mr. and Mrs. Stephen Ganis to person or persons unknown. The motive, it seemed, was robbery. This bloody episode, the press said, was the final chapter in a tragedy which had begun four years ago with the mysterious disappearance of young Warren Ganis, Stephen and Lucille's only child. And to this day no one knew whether the boy was a runaway or a kidnap victim.

Yasuda Gennai said the way was now clear for Warren to return to America, assume control of his father's newspapers, and be the spearhead for *Mujin*'s forthcoming war with America. *Kin-boshi*. This time, Yasuda Gennai said, Japan would fight a wiser war than the one it had just lost.

Warren had listened to him tell the family of a final meeting with the emperor a few days ago, one which included both civilian and military leaders. The civilians wanted peace while the military, to no one's surprise, insisted on fighting. The military had no desire to surrender, Yasuda said, even in the face of continuing defeats—the Russian slaughter of seven hundred thousand Japanese troops in Manchuria, and the horror of the new American weapon, the atom bomb, which had devastated Hiroshima and Nagasaki. Even the unflappable Yasuda Gennai had been left shaken by the atom bomb. Warren found it too terrible for belief. His mind refused to accept such information.

Yasuda Gennai said that in the end the emperor, unshaven, thin from a loss of weight, and with gray in his hair and moustache, was told that he alone could decide whether to continue fighting or surrender. This time neither generals nor political extremists would be allowed to pressure or intimidate him.

"The unendurable must be endured," the emperor said. "The war must end."

In the prison commandant's office, Yasuda Gennai said that Warren would soon be returning to America to continue his work for Japan and *Mujin*. However, there was one loose end to be disposed of. The prisoners. They had to die, for all could identify Warren as a traitor, a collaborator with the enemy.

There was a long silence, then the commandant said, "I speak with respect, Gennai-san, but I must question this order. Our emperor has told us that the war has ended, that no more shots are to be fired. To kill the prisoners is to disobey him, a serious matter for myself and others in this room. How can we go against he who is the representative of God on this earth?"

Yasuda Gennai thought for a few seconds, smoothing the crease in his right trouser leg, letting the silence build, then, "This camp could not have come into existence without the emperor's support. He knows how important our work is to Japan's survival. He knows that if *Mujin* has no future, then neither does Japan. In years to come, our sacred nation can only be as strong as the *zaibatsu*. They alone can deliver that wealth which our armies have failed to provide. Japan now faces the combined hostile powers of America, Russia, China and Great Britain. Let us ask ourselves, will they be as generous in victory?"

He rose from his chair and addressed the room. *"Will they be generous in victory?* I think not, my friends. These are the same people whose war propaganda has labeled us a twisted, dwarf race, a nation of half-humans who revel in torture and bloodshed. Therefore, is it not best that we depend upon ourselves and not those who have contempt for us? Let us remember our purpose in starting this camp, which was to become as industrially productive as our enemy in America. This cannot be achieved unless Warren-san can return safely to the United States and live there without fear of retribution from his countrymen. If we agree on this, then we have no choice but to dispose of the prisoners. It is their lives against the lives of Warren-san and our nation."

The commandant looked down at the floor and spoke without lifting his eyes. "I am at your disposal, Gennai-san."

Yasuda Gennai placed a hand on the commandant's shoulder, then motioned to the Shinto priest, a white-haired, toothless old man in a tattered and frayed saffron-colored robe. The priest shuffled to Gennai's side, then waved his *gohei,* sacred wand with strips of white paper, to his right and left, cleansing all in the room of sins and impurities.

Warren, head bowed, eyes closed, kept a hand inside his jacket and on the *Nambu* 8mm pistol given him by Yasuda Gennai as a birthday gift. With his thumb he stroked his initials which were engraved in gold on the walnut grip, feeling keyed up, afraid of the future and, above all, feeling angry at the so-called Allies for having destroyed Japan and his life here.

When the priest finished chanting, Yasuda Gennai issued his orders. Members of his family were to take part in the elimination of the prisoners, for it was only right that the burden of killing be shared by all. Machine guns had already been set up at the south end of the camp. Warren, Reiko, and several guards were to go to the women's barracks and escort those prisoners to the killing ground. The executions were to take place immediately.

In the women's barracks, Warren leaned inside the lower bunk bed where a thin, feverish Cass Coveyduck lay looking up at him. Her skin was blotched and blistered, and she was too ill to walk, but she was still able to show her disregard for him. Sunshine coming through a window behind Warren threw his shadow across her body, hiding her face but not her voice. It came out of the darkness, a needle piercing him, and he knew he would always be uneasy if she lived.

"We've won and you've lost," she said in a hoarse voice. "You have lost, you frightened little man. Your day of reckoning has arrived at last, and I hope to be there when they hang you." She began coughing up blood.

Warren thought, She knows my secret. She knows I am afraid and have spent my life trying to prove I'm not. She was stronger than he, and in her place he would have broken long ago. He sensed how ugly he must look in her eyes, all because of his fear.

He shot her in the head three times. And for reasons he was never sure of, he felt sadder at killing her than he had at killing his parents. He stared down at her corpse, oblivious to Reiko Gennai and the guards who herded the screaming, weeping women out of the barracks at gunpoint.

Two days later, American occupation troops found the secret prison camp and Warren Ganis, sole survivor among eighty-eight men and women, all Westerners and primarily Americans. There was no one else in the camp to talk to because staff and guards had fled, taking with them those records which they hadn't burned.

Warren said he'd managed to stay alive by pretending to be hit by gunfire, then falling into a shallow grave with prisoners who hadn't been as fortunate. He'd been terrified the entire time, and still didn't know how he'd managed to stay alive. As far as he knew, the prisoners had been executed to prevent them from testifying at possible war crimes trials. As for the all-white inmate population, Warren said the camp was meant to be a bargaining chip, with ranking Westerners to be exchanged for ranking Japanese POWs. Somehow the idea never worked out, and the Western prisoners became expendable. Warren had survived only through luck.

He admitted to being a runaway some four years ago. He'd stowed away on board a Japanese freighter leaving New York and ended up in Japan, where he'd spent the entire war as a prisoner. A childish thing to do, but he had certainly paid for it many times over. He had nothing else to say.

The soldiers who found him thought it sad that after having lived through this ordeal he now had no family to return to in America. The ill-fated youngster would have to start his new life alone.

6

England

August, 1985

LORD OLIVER COVEYDUCK stood beside his cat in the kitchen of the converted fifteenth-century barn that was Coveyduck's home. They were a matched pair: round-faced and gray, with chunky bodies and hair jutting from their ears. At sixty-eight and still charged with restlessness, the big-nosed, baggy-eyed Coveyduck was the younger of the two. The cat, called Edwin Drood, was twelve—old age in animal years.

Coveyduck had learned that being elderly did not stop Mr. Drood from being the most arrogant little bugger in England. Early on in their relationship he had attempted to teach the cat subservience. Teach it obedience with a bit of cringing thrown in for good measure. Bloody waste of time that was. Cats, damn them, were freeborn and ungrateful to boot. Coveyduck had failed to subjugate the beast, failed because he and Mr. Drood were too much alike. Both possessed an independence of spirit which people found fascinating. Both were by nature solitary

animals. And both were hunters, relying chiefly on ʂ̶
catch their prey.

Tonight Coveyduck was preparing Mr. E. Drood's Frida͇ ͏n-
ner: half-cooked chicken livers chopped into small pieces, then
mixed with raw egg yolks, a tablespoon of lager, and a bit of
lemon barley. Revolting, to say the least. Mr. Drood, on the other
hand, saw it as epicurean, more succulent even than a dormouse
or a budgerigar, creatures he had previously victimized for his
own gratification.

While readying this concoction, Coveyduck wore rubber
gloves, regretting only that he didn't wear a face mask as well.
The smell gave new meaning to the word putrid. Mr. Drood's
taste in food confirmed Coveyduck's suspicions that cats were
indeed an example of sophistication minus civilization. Still, why
indulge the beast who, after all, was in the winter of his life and
not getting any younger.

After scraping Edwin Drood's dinner from a wooden mixing
bowl and into a nineteenth-century butter dish with fan handles,
Coveyduck removed the rubber gloves and placed the dish on a
pine duck board which he used as a tray. Then he washed his
hands and prepared his own meal: sliced peaches, Norwegian
bread, marmalade, cheddar cheese, and a small pot of Twinings
Earl Grey tea. He placed his food on the tray, picked the tray up,
and walked toward a raised platform at the south end of the barn,
his writing and library area. Mr. Drood led the way.

On the platform, Coveyduck placed the tray in the middle of a
large, Victorian mahogany desk. After pushing aside a pair of
Baccarat paperweights, he slid a thesaurus in their place and set
Edwin Drood's dish on top of it. He popped a bit of cheese into
his own mouth, then reached down for the cat and deposited him
in front of the eagerly awaited and repulsive looking meal. *Bon
appetit,* Droodie me lad.

Coveyduck sat down in a Renaissance throne chair that ended
in massive ball and claw feet and reached for a lined yellow pad
on which he had been writing in long hand until twenty minutes
ago. He stopped chewing and read, feeling the same cold satisfaction he always did each time he worked on the book that was
going to expose Warren Ganis as the killer of Coveyduck's wife
some forty years ago. The book, to be called *The Grand Victory,*
was almost finished. God willing, he'd have it done and in the

hands of his publisher by fall and then poor Cass could rest easier in her grave.

She was buried seventy-five yards away from Coveyduck's bedroom window, at the base of a huge beech tree, the gravesite covered with bluebells and marsh marigolds. Buried in her wedding dress, with the prayer book she'd been carrying the day they married. And with a copy of Browning's poems, for she had dearly loved them. *"Ah, but a man's reach should exceed his grasp or what's a heaven for?"*

Coveyduck's home sat alone at the base of a ridge which was covered with beechwood trees and surrounded by dense, green-gladed places full of paths he never tired of exploring. It was located a half-mile outside of Amersham, an old town of gabled and timbered inns, Georgian houses, and thatched cottages with cobbled courtyards. He lived by himself, save for Edwin Drood, and had decorated the barn according to his own eclectic tastes, combining Renaissance bronzes and George III mahogany bookcases with art deco mirrors and a fourteen-key barrel playing organ. The outside remained as it had for centuries, a rust-colored tile roof and walls of rough stone covered by clinging vines, peonies, and hydrangeas.

At his desk Coveyduck bit into marmalade-covered bread, then picked up a damask napkin. Edwin Drood had stopped eating to stare at an open window. An owl hooted. A nightingale sang in a nearby cypress. Coveyduck used the napkin to wipe bits of liver from Edwin Drood's whiskers and said, "Droodie me lad, you may be long in the tooth, but you're still keen of ear. Would you please finish eating your abominable compound before it destroys me sense of smell?"

He watched the cat drop its head and resume eating from the butter dish which had cost Coveyduck seven hundred pounds at an antique stall in London's Portobello Road. His reputation as an eccentric had apparently preceded him, for when he'd told the dealer that a cat would be taking its meals from the dish, the dealer simply said, "That's nice, your Lordship," and wrapped it without a further word. What else could you say to a man who had once purchased a Swiss banker's private collection of Hitler memorabilia for over one hundred thousand pounds, then publicly burned every item? A man who, as a staunch anti-vivisectionist, had been arrested for leading an attack on an animal research center with a bow and arrow; who, as a member of Parliament, was feared for his stinging putdowns and high-pitched laughter.

Oliver Ronald Coveyduck was an energetic intellectual who appeared to have everything. The son of a prosperous Lloyds of London underwriter and self-made millionaire, he had attended Harrow, been president of the Oxford Union, won a first in philosophy and Asian history, then came top in civil service exams. But even Whitehall couldn't stop him from being a cutup and an oddball with the thick skin of a rhinoceros. At parties he leaped into swimming pools in full evening dress, at work he showed up in bright yellow double-breasted waistcoat. He took a leave of absence from the civil service to work as a farm laborer for the experience and caused an outcry by suggesting that Mrs. Wallis Simpson, the American divorcée who had married the Duke of Windsor, be paid ten million pounds to leave him.

But he was a Japanese-speaking expert on the Far East, and his papers analyzing the growth of Japan's empire during the thirties were brilliant. He boldly described her territorial ambitions in the Pacific, a truth some at Whitehall didn't want to hear since England had allied itself with Japan, a means of protecting its own Asian colonies from Russia. Coveyduck said this was shortsighted and stupid, that the Japanese dragon was every bit as greedy as the Russian bear. After feasting on its neighbors' lands, Japan wouldn't stop to pick its teeth before swallowing Britain's colonies.

In 1941 Coveyduck was offered a post in the Tokyo embassy, a chance to evaluate Japan's territorial ambitions firsthand. But he was in love and hesitated to leave England. Cassandra Sarah Loelia Beatty was her name. Lovely. Intelligent. And he was irresistibly drawn to her because Cass was as courageous in private as she was in front of all the world. Super sense of humor, Cass had. Her family motto was *Courage Above Cowardice*. Cass's version: *Courage Above Guiness*, employing the names of two leading British beers.

She showed promise as a writer, collected ostrich-feathered hats, had been a 1939 deb, and loved gossip, especially tidbits about the royal family and cafe society. Coveyduck called her a walking bush telegraph. Cass, who loved cats and the film *Gone With the Wind* and Coveyduck reading to her from Robert

Browning, and who had walked out on a "good match" with the
son of a duke—after she'd bought her wedding dress—to marry
Coveyduck. Cass, who never saw him as being eccentric, who
saw him only as a man who wouldn't yield to anyone else's
control, a man who wouldn't queue up behind someone or something else. "That is why I love you," she said.

And because he loved her with a biblical bone-of-my-bones,
flesh-of-my-flesh intensity, because he knew she was the best
thing for him in this life, because she was the partner of his soul,
he never forgave himself for not getting her out of Japan. *If only
they'd been more careful and she hadn't gotten pregnant and had
the miscarriage and had to be left in hospital. If only...*

Guilt-ridden, he avoided self-destruction only by throwing
himself into his work at the War Office in London. When Japan
surrendered, he pulled strings to be assigned to the War Crimes
Tribunal in Tokyo as an investigator. There were trials on Bor-
neo, the Philippines, Singapore, and Hong Kong, but the Tokyo
trial was the one which interested Coveyduck and a new friend,
Alain Coutain, a French war crimes investigator. A former Japanese POW in Indochina, Coutain had lost a hand to torture by the
Kempetai, Japan's military police, and also contracted the
chronic hepatitis that would eventually kill him. Living well is
not the best revenge, he told Coveyduck. Revenge is the best
revenge.

Working together, they searched the world for witnesses and
key documents. They also collected affidavits and located sus-
pects. Each man was dedicated to getting the indictments that
would lead to swift prosecutions and dispositions of trials. They
even managed to get the goods on conglomerates like the *Mujin*
Group. Had these companies dead to rights, with proof positive
that *Mujin* and others had supported the military government and
gotten rich doing it, feathering their nests from defense industries
and new colonies. Any schoolboy could see that without the conglomerates the military machine would have come to a swift halt.

So when the order came down from the Allies to break up the
conglomerates and sell their shares, Coveyduck and Alain
Coutain were ecstatic, figuring this marked the end of *Mujin* and
the other *zaibatsu*. No such luck. *Mujin* did not lose a paper clip,
and you could bloody well thank the Americans for that.

By 1946 America and Russia were at each other's throats.

And in Asia the Communists were seeking control of China, the Philippines, and Malaya. America now had an overwhelming fear of the Red Menace and decided it needed a strong Pacific ally to stand beside it in the holy war against Godless Marxism. Therefore the *zaibatsu* could not be broken up, the U.S. said. Nor would they have to pay reparations. All was forgiven. Why? Because the *zaibatsu* were needed in the "Cold War." Japan would now receive American trade credits and all the help it needed to find markets to replace those it had lost in Asia and the Pacific. An angry Coveyduck could only wonder how America, a critic of Japan's economic expansion not too long ago, could suddenly switch and support this same economic aggressiveness now. Mystifying, to say the least.

The Tokyo trial results left him even more enraged. Brimming with hypocritical piety, the Americans had insisted on what they called "international legality," resulting in a three-year-long trial and a sentence of hanging for only seven Jap leaders. *Seven*. And guess who decided to spare Emperor Hirohito, a decision so moronic that Coveyduck almost wept when he heard it and apologized out loud to his dead wife. General Douglas MacArthur, America's own, and a man Coveyduck saw as a pompous ass with an itch for the praise of fools—Browning's phrase—had insisted that the emperor not be placed on trial.

Why? Because to destroy Hirohito, MacArthur said, was to destroy the Japanese nation. Coveyduck said to Coutain, "Silly me. All this time I was under the impression that the point of going to war *was* to destroy the fucking Japanese nation. I say we hang this slant-eyed little bastard and be done with it, for as sure as the sun rises in the east, he knew what was going on and bloody well played his part in it. Believe you me, there are no virgins in whorehouses."

However, it was the emperor who indirectly pointed the finger at the murderer of Coveyduck's wife.

On a gray winter afternoon a thin, nervous Japanese in a dark, threadbare suit appeared at Coveyduck and Coutain's Tokyo office, saying that his conscience would not leave him in peace, that he must cleanse his soul. He had defied the emperor's orders to lay down his arms, and in doing so he had violated his own honor. He said that it was a soldier's duty to kill during war, but to slaughter helpless prisoners after the emperor had ordered all soldiers to cease fighting was breaking God's law, for the emperor was God's representative on earth.

The man wanted to erase this stain from his honor, then with his wife and two children leave Japan for life in another country. His name, he said, was Captain Oshima, and he had been the commandant of the prison camp in which Mrs. Coveyduck and the others had been murdered. He would now reveal the true story of Warren Ganis's "miraculous survival."

But first he told Coveyduck things which could have been known only by someone who'd been in the prison camp with Cass. Oshima said that Warren Ganis had burned Coveyduck's letters to his wife, but not before translating them for the Gennai family, who ran the camp and the camp staff. In one letter Coveyduck had written about a wonderful evening they'd had at a French embassy banquet where Winston Churchill had been a guest. He'd also written about seeing Fred Astaire at the Derby and attending a performance of "The Importance of Being Earnest" at the Globe Theatre.

A stunned Coveyduck took a few minutes to compose himself. When Oshima continued, Coveyduck wept as the Japanese named Warren Ganis and the *Mujin* people Yasuda and Reiko Gennai as murderers. Then Oshima detailed the conspiracy designed to enrich the *Mujin* Group in the future, and said that he would never repeat these accusations in open court because he feared for his life. And he wanted money and help in emigrating to another Asian country, where he planned to change his name and pray that the Gennai family never found him.

Coveyduck begged the Executive Committee of the Allied Powers to approve a closed hearing for Captain Oshima, to give him the status of protected witness. The committee's decision: a split one. Some favored Coveyduck's request, while others insisted that Oshima testify openly so that *Mujin* would be publicly identified with the massacre. As for Warren Ganis, the committee refused to believe he'd had a hand in the killings. Too preposterous to even consider, they said. The boy had been a prisoner, nothing more. American youngsters didn't go around committing such heinous crimes. It went against the laws of God and man.

Coveyduck chose to ignore such asinine reasoning and instead accepted Oshima's version of Warren Ganis. The American youth appeared to have had heaven's help in staying alive. Few in the war had found fortune so favorable. Fate had dealt him the best of hands, while Cass had come up a loser. The more Coveyduck thought about it, the more it seemed to him that Warren Ganis owed his survival to more than just good luck.

The committee, however, did not share his suspicions. It declared the matter closed, saying that Warren Ganis was now in America where he'd become a figure of great public sympathy, understandable when one thought of all the youngster had been through. And nothing could be more farfetched than Oshima's claim that Warren Ganis had left Japan, killed his parents, then returned to Japan and waited for the Allies to discover him. And all as part of some future scheme to enrich *Mujin*. Pure eyewash.

The matter of an American youngster being charged as a war criminal was too incredible to consider, the committee said. The American government was not going to create a public relations disaster for itself merely because Coveyduck asked it to. Americans loved heroes and, by God, there was no bigger hero in the country at the moment than young Mr. Ganis. No one, not Coveyduck or Oshima, was going to take this moment away from the American people.

All the committee could do was meet privately with Oshima and see if his testimony warranted proceeding further. But before Coveyduck could contact him, the former camp commandant, along with his wife and children, was killed when his car burned in a collision with a gasoline truck outside of Tokyo. Both Coveyduck and Coutain called it murder, noting that Oshima had not owned a car and was too damn poor to buy one. Oshima, Coveyduck told the committee, could barely scrape up enough rice to feed his family each day.

By now, Coveyduck was a man possessed. It was his constant badgering which forced the Executive Committee of the Allied Powers to bring Yasuda and Reiko Gennai in for questioning. And while he insisted they had been behind the prison camp killings, he was speaking as a man who *felt* they were guilty, *knew* they were guilty, but couldn't prove it.

And without Oshima, he never would. The committee dismissed the Gennais for lack of corroborating evidence and ordered Coveyduck not to pursue the matter any further. But as the Gennais left the hearing room, Coveyduck blocked their way and said, "Be warned, both of you. I shan't let go of this thing until

I've laid Cass's murder at your doorstep. And you can tell your young Mr. Ganis to keep looking over his shoulder, for it's I who'll be stepping on his shadow for years to come. Now go to hell, both of you."

He spat in Yasuda Gennai's face and would have struck him if Coutain and a white-helmeted American Military Police hadn't held him back. A week-long binge of drink, self-pity, and tears followed. Coutain helped him to live through it, listening while Coveyduck explained that the loss of someone you love was worse than any death, and he would die a thousand times in order to hold Cass in his arms once more. Her loss, he said, had killed something in him forever. He could no longer love, but he could hate. He looked at the files on *Mujin* and the Gennai family which were scattered around his office and said, "I can hate."

He left military service in 1949, knowing he could never return to the restrictions encountered in the civil service, knowing that England had changed as much as he had. The upper classes, damn their eyes, were carrying on as though the war had never occurred. But for most people, the postwar years were the most austere in the country's history, with tighter rationing than had been known during the war.

True, there were splendid balls at Windsor, Sutton Place and in assorted stately homes, but the winds of change were blowing hard. The government was preparing anti-upper-class legislation, something bound to tighten every aristocratic asshole in the British Isles. Privilege of any kind was about to be flushed down the toilet, and the era of the common man was upon the land. A different England, a better England was a possibility.

Anxious to bring this about, Coveyduck ran for Parliament. To his surprise, he won. But after years of battling Conservatives, Labour, senile Lords, imbecilic Socialists and assorted fanatics, he resigned. There was a limit to how long a man could watch politicians swallow their own lies.

By now he was rich enough to do as he pleased. His mother had died during the Blitz, while his father had died in a hunting accident in Yorkshire, leaving him a wealthy man. He sold the Surrey properties and the Mayfair home in London, then moved north to Amersham where Cass was buried. He was sixty, with no intention of retiring, and with no end of things to keep him busy. He lectured at Oxford on Asian studies, wrote about Japan and China for *The New Statesman* and *Times Literary Supplement*, and served as a BBC radio commentator.

Above all, he remained a *Mujin* watcher, filling file cabinets with information on the company, its personnel, its policies, its successes and failures. Some of this information formed the basis of a book on Japan's "economic miracle," and linked Warren Ganis to that, though there was no mention of the prison camp massacre or the death of Ganis's parents. No mention because there had been no proof.

Until recently, when Coveyduck had received a sudden flow of damaging information on *Mujin*, the Gennai family, and Ganis. Someone wanted to be top dog at *Mujin* badly enough to air the company's dirty linen in public and to link America's most important media czar to a long-forgotten mass murder. Someone who had used Serge Coutain, Alain's son, and a Japanese woman named Hanako Watanabe as conduits to Coveyduck.

Both Serge Coutain and Hanako had told Coveyduck they were getting their information from Mr. Nikkei, a *Mujin* accountant who was not the true source, just a middleman. The true source was unknown to them. There was no reason to doubt their word; Coveyduck had known Serge since birth and found him to be a good chap, perhaps a little too fond of the ladies, but a good chap. Hanako was a beauty, more interested in burning the candle at both ends than in any form of intrigue. Yes, they were telling the truth. Coveyduck believed that his unknown benefactor at *Mujin*, someone in a position to know the company's darkest secrets, preferred a buffer between himself and Coveyduck. And with good reason. Coveyduck knew enough about *Mujin* to confidently predict that sooner or later he'd uncover the identity of the person who called himself—or herself—*Aikuchi*, hidden sword. Meanwhile, let the dirt pile up and let the files in the barn grow fatter and let Coveyduck, after forty long years, get his own back.

He owed it to Cass and to Alain, who hadn't lived long enough to see *Mujin* brought down. *Aikuchi* obviously knew about Alain's relationship with Coveyduck, otherwise, why use Serge as a messenger boy?

Coveyduck's concern about *Mujin* was shared by one American, Senator Fran Machlis from New York, an occasionally strident lady but one not entirely devoid of charm, manners, and intelligence. Her involvement with a Congressional Asian Affairs Committee had led her to see something rather sinister in Japan's worldwide business success. She was one of the first in her country to question Japan's trade policies in America.

A few years ago Coveyduck had written to congratulate her on leading a fight in Congress to penalize *Mujin*'s electronics division for dumping television sets in America, for selling them at less than fair value, an underhanded way to take over the market. *Mujin*, she said, was determined to force American television manufacturers out of business by offering their own sets at prices so low they couldn't be resisted. Then when it had the market to itself, prices would be raised to ensure a profit.

Coveyduck had written her of his own interest in *Mujin*, noting that she was correct in her analysis of the conglomerate's intentions. But he predicted that the American Congress would take no action. "It is difficult, if not impossible," he said, "for a legislative body to arrive at a consensus on any subject." Politics was the business of ignoring facts. Politics was the fool's hope.

But wasn't Coveyduck a fool for wanting to avenge Cass, for keeping that particular wound open and bleeding, preventing it from ever healing? He didn't think so. He owed Cass for the love she'd given him, for having joined her life to his, if only for a moment. Finishing *The Grand Victory* and destroying Warren Ganis would be Coveyduck's answer to God when asked what kind of life he'd led.

Coveyduck fed bits of cheddar to a purring Edwin Drood, who'd finished his chopped liver and had now taken up residence on Coveyduck's lap. *Damn*. Coveyduck had forgotten about today's mail now sitting on his desk and staring him in the face. Frightfully busy working on the book, he'd also received a telephone call from his editor in London who'd said that the publisher's lawyers wanted a look at what he'd written and would be ever so grateful if they could view the manuscript. Could Coveyduck put it in the post straightaway? Coveyduck could not.

Bloody lawyers. Retards whose opinions are worthless unless you're paying for them. Liars with a permit to practice. Coveyduck said that no editor, no publisher, and no lawyer was going to view so much as a single comma until the entire book was finished. This especially applied to the unnecessary evil called lawyers.

He picked up the pile of envelopes, saw one from his publisher and, remembering the conversation with his twit of an editor, threw the envelope over his shoulder unopened. Rest of the mail: notices from a book club, his accountant, a London cinema club he'd dropped out of years ago. And a plain white envelope addressed to him, postmarked Zurich, dated two days ago, no return address. Could it be that the gnomes of Switzerland were informing him that a distant relation had died and left him untold millions? Curiosity being the lust of the mind, he picked up a letter opener and slit the envelope.

He removed a single sheet of paper from the envelope, unfolded it, and let his eyes drop down to the bottom, to the signature. *Aikuchi.* Just the one word, typed like the rest of the words on the page. *Aikuchi.* The so far unimpeachable source of *Mujin*'s dirty doings and Warren Ganis's murderous past. Heart beating faster, Coveyduck slipped on his bifocals, sat Edwin Drood down on the desk in front of the peaches and cream, and began reading.

Dear Mr. Lord Coveyduck:

As you are aware of, I cannot reveal my identity to you, but I am the person who is advancing you information which until recently you have been getting through Mr. Serge Coutain and Hanako Watanabe. My proof of who I am is that I am aware of the book you write about the Mujin *Group and Warren Ganis and why you write because it involves the murder of your wife by Warren Ganis. I also know that the last information you receive from Serge Coutain was the details of Captain Masataka Oshima's murder during July, 1947.*

With the murder of Serge Coutain and the kidnapping of Hanako Watanabe, I am forced to contact you directly at great risk to myself please to understand. I am mailing this letter from Zurich to keep myself secret and no personal information about me can come from this letter. I am taking care to see this does not occur.

Coveyduck thought: Wrong, mate, I do know something about you. You're a Jap, you're with the *Mujin* executives now in Zurich finalizing a deal to take over the city's oldest department store, and you're desperate to bring down your own. I know there's a lot of hate in you, my friend. Oh, I know something about you. I do, indeed.

I have some truths for you, Mr. Lord Coveyduck. I say Serge Coutain is murdered and he was, even though he still lives, for he is brain dead because of poison and will never enjoy life again. Viktor Poltava has done this, the assassin known as Oni. *Poltava has also kidnapped Hanako Watanabe, Coutain's fiancée, and she can be found in Bangkok bar called Stack's on Patpong Road and this place is owned by a former American Navy Chief Petty Officer Tyrone Brice. Reiko Gennai ordered this to be done. She knew about Mr. Coutain and Miss Watanabe, and she also knows about your book. Reiko Gennai wants to protect her position at* Mujin *and protect Warren Ganis.*

Miss Watanabe has very sad fate. She must work as a prostitute because she has been made into a heroin addict. Reiko Gennai does this to Mujin *wives who displease her, and she has them taken to brothels in Thailand, Hong Kong, Taiwan, and the Philippines, and all the times these women are made to take heroin and be whores. You must have someone visit Stack's bar and see Watanabe woman there. She is wearing silver fox mask.*

Please know that soon I give you physical evidence that Warren Ganis murdered your wife. This evidence will be final and you will need nothing else to use against him for your revenge. May I say that this evidence is important for it will be the final piece in the puzzle and by then the game will be over and I will have done what I set out to do. Reiko Gennai and Warren Ganis will be no more with this evidence. I also take opportunity to warn you that Poltava seeks to destroy you and others in the west so you must have caution.

Aikuchi.

Letter in one hand, Coveyduck chewed on a stem of his bifocals and leaned back in the throne chair thinking, now here's something unexpected, a bit of news to jar the brain cells and upset the emotions and what, pray tell, can we do about it. He felt upset, disturbed. And curious about the physical evidence to come. He was also a bit frightened about the possibility of a visit from Viktor Poltava.

Did he believe the contents of this letter? Instinct told him to believe every word. An inner voice, in fact, screamed at him to believe every word. Reiko Gennai had killed before. No reason why she shouldn't kill now, especially with a kingdom at stake. Yes, *Aikuchi* was telling the truth. His mention of Oshima's murder was proof enough, and the existence of Viktor Poltava was an incontestable fact. *Oni.* The most wanted international thug since Carlos the Jackal, and more mentally unbalanced to boot. How could one sleep soundly after hearing that he was heading in your direction?

Oni. An animal in human skin. One who had come by his name honestly enough, with some of the most cold-blooded and marble-hearted behavior within human memory. Coveyduck had heard rumors linking him to *Mujin,* but this letter was the closest he'd come to having those rumors confirmed. As for Reiko Gennai, the Empress, she was no rumor. In the tradition of Japan's shadow rulers, she was the true master of the kingdom called *Mujin,* one who had destroyed rivals, spent and made fortunes, and degraded and demoralized men and women around her all in the name of power. A woman like that wouldn't hesitate to forge an alliance with *Oni.*

Coveyduck tossed his bifocals on the desk. Bloody shame about Serge. Coveyduck had known the lad since he'd been a toddler. Guested at his homes in Paris and Deauville, and enjoyed his company immensely, which is more than one could say about the majority of Frenchmen, who were disagreeable and contemptible, a people who did everything and knew nothing.

Hanako. Disgusting what the Empress had done to her. Coveyduck would have the British Embassy in Bangkok look into the matter of Hanako's abduction. Might also be a good idea to contact MI5 in the morning and ring London's Metropolitan Police as well, both of whom were more equipped to deal with *Oni* than the local Amersham constabulary. Police the world over would love to get their hands on Mr. Poltava.

First thing in the morning, he'd ring MI5 and the Met lads. Let them tell Coveyduck what to do regarding the hellish Mr. Poltava.

Edwin Drood suddenly lifted his head out of the peaches and

cream, stared at the opened window, then arched his back, tail erect and stiff as a broom handle. He spat in the direction of the window. Bloody insane. What in God's name had gotten into the animal? Coveyduck watched Droodie's ears flatten against his skull. He'd never seen the cat so defensive, so threatened.

Something flew through the window, a dark object that landed just feet away from the desk. It was small, dust-covered, the size of a book. A *book*. Coveyduck left his throne chair, stepped down from the platform, and picked it up. Mother of God! It was the prayer book that had been buried with Cass. Some fiend, some ghoulish bastard, had desecrated Cass's grave. Dug up her coffin and . . .

Coveyduck was boiling. Furious. The desecration of his wife's grave was a foul deed, utterly foul, and left him feeling a remorseless fury. Such a heinous crime would not go unpunished. He himself would punish the criminal, a promise he was making this instant before God and all that was holy. To hell with being civilized, with acting his age, with turning the other cheek. He was ragingly violent and didn't care who knew it. He was also over-excited. Out of breath. He had to inhale several times before finding his voice. Then, he shouted, "Bastard! Stinking bloody bastard, whoever you are!" at the open window.

Near the window someone laughed.

Coveyduck blinked away tears. Then he looked around for his whalebone cane, the walking stick that was strong enough to split a man's skull, which is exactly what he planned to do with it.

More breaking glass. This time from the back of the barn, near his carved oak tester bed. Coveyduck saw another small dark object being tossed through the broken window to land on top of the handmade bed quilt. Prayer book clutched to his chest, he hurried to the bed.

The object on the bed was the now-crumbling copy of Browning's poems which he'd placed in Cass's coffin.

He sat down on the bed and wept, making no attempt to hold back his grief, his sadness. A nightmare. That's what it was, a bloody nightmare, and he wished with all his heart that he could wake up. But damn it, he was angry beyond belief, so he rose, ready to go outside and deal with the animal who had done this unspeakable thing.

He heard glass breaking in the kitchen. He ran there, books in his hands, and saw the oddest thing. Quite unbelievable, really. The ghoul—what else could you call the person responsible for this—had knocked all the glass from one pane and was now pushing a filthy, discolored sheet through the empty space. Grotesque. Inexplicably grotesque.

The sheet toppled a potted geranium from the windowsill, sending it crashing into the sink, smashing dirty plates and cups, and then the sheet was through the pane and filling the sink, hiding the geranium, dishes, and faucets. Coveyduck couldn't make sense out of what he was seeing, but seconds later he *knew* and when he knew, when he understood that he wasn't looking at a sheet, but at Cass's mildewed, rotting wedding dress, he dropped to his knees in despair.

Coveyduck reached out to touch the dress, and the barn was plunged into darkness. The front door was kicked open, flying into a wall to shatter an art deco mirror. The noise scared Coveyduck out of his wits, causing him to fall back against the sink, crying out, "Who's there? I say who's there?"

No answer. And no one came through the door.

He blinked tears from his eyes, the anger still with him, but also with him was an increasing uneasiness, a growing dread over what was happening.

"Who's there?"

Silence.

The doorway still remained empty. Coveyduck looked out and saw only a moonlit road and a clump of cypress trees he'd planted his first summer in the barn.

Then he heard someone speak. A male voice near the doorway. English speaking, but with a foreign accent. A hoarse voice. Coming from deep in the chest. Chilling.

"You ran away and left her, old man. You failed your wife when she needed you most. That makes your life a lie, doesn't it? Would you like me to tell you how the prison guards treated her? How they enjoyed her in ways you never did?"

Coveyduck got to his feet and took one step toward the voice. He had the wedding dress in his hands, and his anger was stronger than ever. He needed a weapon. Anything. A kitchen knife. A poker from the fireplace.

The voice. "She's not in her coffin anymore, old man. You might say I have arranged for you to see your precious wife again. She's out here waiting for you. Lying on the ground, staring up at the stars. But I tell you something, old man: You better get out here soon before the dogs and rats have at her. The worms have already done their part, I can assure you. You know those books I just sent you by air mail. Ha-ha-ha. Air mail. Don't you think that's funny? Maybe you sell those books and buy yourself some peaches. I understand you're quite fond of peaches, old man."

Coveyduck had had enough of this monster. It was time to deal with him man to man, even if Coveyduck must do it with his bare hands. People like this didn't deserve to live. Not after what he had just done to Cass.

Coveyduck saw it through the doorway: Twin points of light coming along the twisted road leading to the barn. A car. And as it drew closer, he saw the blue light flashing on top and almost screamed for joy. *The police*. Praise God. Praise, praise God. He shouted, "The police are here and we have you now, you fucking bastard! We'll get you, and when we do, I'll personally beat you to within an inch of your miserable life! You have my word on that!"

Coveyduck's eyes were getting used to the darkness, and there was a bit of moonlight coming through the windows and doorway. He looked around the barn, saw the outline of the fireplace and, with Cass's wedding dress still clutched in his hands, stumbled toward the fireplace, toward a poker. Annihilate the man outside. That's what Coveyduck was going to do and no one, not the police, not Jesus, Son of God, was going to stop him.

Viktor Poltava was surprised by the appearance of the British police car, and his surprise led to anger. Anger, however, could be a problem. It would assume control of his mind, causing him to lose mental sharpness, his prudence, the ability to separate sheep from goats, as his Russian father might say. No, he would not permit himself to become angry at this unexpected and unwelcomed turn of events. He would adjust—and adjust quickly.

Poltava's plan had been to unbalance Coveyduck's mind by desecrating his wife's grave. If that didn't drive the old man to suicide, then Poltava had planned to kill him and make it appear as though Coveyduck had taken his own life. Poltava also planned to steal the Englishman's book on *Mujin* and Warren

Ganis, along with other relevant papers. This material would then be turned over to Ganis, who was to evaluate it before passing it on to Mrs. Gennai. Simple. A matter of hours. Two days at the most, if Poltava was skillful enough and he was. He most certainly was.

But now he watched the small police car navigate the curves on the dirt road and told himself, this was no coincidence. Coveyduck couldn't have phoned them, because Poltava had cut the electrical and telephone lines. Was this visit by the police a casual one? Or had he made a mistake somewhere along the line and not realized it? Fate was capricious. Anything was possible.

Survival meant being vigilantly attentive. Alert to danger. There was always the possibility that the appearance by the police *was* a coincidence, that he had nothing to worry about, that no one was on to him. But he would have to change tactics.

The warrior must avoid what is strong and strike at what is weak, said Sun Tzu.

As Poltava watched, the headlights drew closer, their beams creeping along the road, their glare illuminating a mailbox, a sagging wooden fence covered in orange monkey blossoms, a small abandoned windmill.

Strike at what is weak.

The black-clad Poltava crawled into the darkened barn on his hands and knees, stopping to the right of the entrance and away from the open doorway, his keen night vision allowing him to avoid pieces of broken mirror. He could see the old man clearly, see his tear-stained, red face, see the poker in one hand, see the other hand shade his eyes to better view his salvation, the police car.

Poltava slammed the door shut, plunging the barn back into darkness, making Coveyduck stiffen with surprise. *Hai, surprise.*

"Who's there? Someone's in here with me. I know it. Show yourself, why don't you?"

Poltava thought, old man, when you see me, it will be too late. Fucking old fool with the poker resting on your shoulder like some sort of rifle. Ready to fight for your wife's honor, as though it were a sacred cause. Do you expect her to thank you? Fucking old fool.

Coveyduck said, "It's you, you rotten bastard, the one who violated Cass's grave. I can smell the stink of you. Well, we have

you now, we do. Police outside, me inside, and you with nowhere to run. You're trapped, and you know it."

Poltava rose from his crouch, slowly, carefully, not moving
his feet because he didn't want to step on the glass around him.
Not yet. He deliberately kept his breathing shallow. Silent.
Didn't want to give himself away. Out of the corner of his eye he
saw light. A faint ray from the police car as it neared the barn,
the light brushing the window before moving on. Seconds later,
the light entered the barn from beneath the door. It wasn't much,
but Poltava knew it was enough to give the old man courage.

Poltava himself was beyond courage. He was self-controlled,
unruffled, his mind a waveless ocean. Only the extraordinary
brightness of his eyes indicated his murderous nature.

Distance between him and the Englishman: a little under six
feet. The Englishman's night vision: none. Too dark for old, untrained eyes to see much. But the old man could cry out—and
would, unless silenced.

Poltava pulled at his belt buckle and, when the small knife
was in his hand, he tossed it to Coveyduck's right, hearing a soft,
off-key note as the knife landed inside a harpsichord, on the
strings. When the Englishman turned toward the sound, poker
raised high overhead, Poltava charged. Two steps and he was
directly behind Coveyduck.

Crouching, Poltava punched the Englishman in the kidney
with a right uppercut, breaking his balance to the rear. Coveyduck dropped the poker, then began flailing the air to keep his
balance. Poltava kicked him in the back of the right knee, driving
the Englishman to the floor on both knees. Coveyduck started to
cry out as Poltava's left arm went around his neck, cutting off all
sound. Then, with Coveyduck's larynx trapped in the crook of his
left elbow, Poltava placed his right hand at the base of his skull
and stepped back with his right foot, breaking the Englishman's
neck. He continued to squeeze for several seconds, making sure
Coveyduck was dead. When he heard the police car stop in front
of the barn, he released his grip on the dead man, letting him fall
to the floor. Then he jogged to the harpsichord, retrieved his
knife, and reattached it to his belt.

A knock at the front door. He froze, listening as a voice iden-
tifying itself as Inspector Barbon said he was here to speak to his
lordship on a most urgent matter. Poltava thought of escaping,

then decided no, he must do what he came here to do, what the Empress had paid him to do. He had to get the manuscript and some of Coveyduck's papers.

He tiptoed to the entrance, to a window to the right of the door, avoiding broken glass and ignoring a fat gray cat which sat and stared at the dead Coveyduck. Crouching at the window, Poltava cautiously peeked outside. Two policemen. One in civilian clothes, tweed hat, lighting a cigarette. The other in uniform, looking around, bored to tears. Just two. And he would have to kill them both if he wanted to search the barn.

He watched the one in civilian clothes, the inspector, knock on the door again, impatient this time. The inspector whispered his complaints to the uniformed constable, complaints at being dragged from bed at an ungodly hour because of a telephone call from the high and mighty London Metropolitan Police. The inspector said it was probably a false alarm anyway, that his lordship was undoubtedly asleep in his pink pajamas, curled up with his teddy bear and at peace with the world. Bloody Americans, the inspector said. They've got their knickers in a twist over this *Oni* character, and now the entire population of Amersham is forced to go meandering about in the dark.

Surprise.

Poltava's heart jumped. Something *had* gone wrong. They knew he was here and this was terribly upsetting. Who had tipped off the police? Who had brought him as close to being captured as he'd come in quite a while? It was enough to turn his world upside down. *Unless* . . . unless he remained calm. He *had* to remain calm if he intended to survive this night.

Suddenly he smiled. He was elated. Because if the police were sure of his whereabouts, they would have come after him in larger numbers. Much larger numbers. He was absolutely certain of it. He was *Oni*, the most dangerous man alive, a force beyond control.

He thought, if they knew I was here, the tactics would have been different. Experience had made him familiar with the world's police, secret police, and elite forces such as Britain's SAS, Royal Marine Commandos, and the Parachute Regiment. That same experience said that the British would surely have come after him with the Blue Berets from the D11 Squad, the firearms instructors who were elite rifle marksmen.

Still, Poltava would have to kill the two at the front of the barn, for when they discovered Coveyduck's body, they would raise the alarm, confirming his presence in England.

He began jogging toward the rear of the barn, toward the window over the big bed. His escape route.

At the door Inspector Barbon said, "We've come this far, we might as well finish the job."

"Go in, you mean," said the uniformed constable.

"Very astute, Sergeant. I can see that you have a brilliant future ahead of you. Your grasp of the obvious is nothing less than astounding."

"Thank you, sir."

"I'm glad you've grasped the big picture, Sergeant. You see, unless we enter the premises, it will not be possible to gather his lordship and bring him into town and into protective custody, as requested by the esteemed Metropolitan Police of London. You, being a reasonable man, might have your doubts as to the value of night labor, but ours is not to reason why."

Under his breath the Inspector said, "Wakee, wakee, hands off snakee, your lordship."

A final knock, then the door creaked as it was slowly pushed open. Inspector Barbon said, "What's all this broken glass about, and where's the flippin' light switch? Lord Coveyduck? Your lordship? Sorry to wake you."

Poltava smiled. And leaped on the bed, scrambled across it on his hands and knees, and lifted up the window as quietly as possible. He was out of the barn in seconds, blending with the darkness and disappearing as though he had never existed.

Inspector Herbert Barbon, a small, forty-six-year-old Welshman with a permanent frown, stepped from Lord Coveyduck's barn with a flashlight in his hand and followed the beam toward the police car, shaking his head and not at all pleased at the way events were unfolding. For starters, his lordship had climbed the golden staircase. The late Lord Coveyduck was lying dead on the floor of his own domicile, apparently dead of a broken neck. Whether accidental or otherwise, leave that to the forensic boys.

A quick examination of the premises revealed broken windows, a pudgy, gray cat who didn't have much to say for itself, and, not far from the deceased—explain this if you will—a filthy wedding dress and a poker. A bit of a muddle, if you asked Herbert J. Barbon. No telephone or electricity, either. At the moment, Police Constable Jonathan Spenser was checking the outside of the barn for damaged power lines or broken cables. And for a possible intruder, a yobbo who might have broken the windows. His lordship could have broken them himself, a possibility since he was known to be a bit balmy.

Meanwhile there was the corpse to contend with. Not just any corpse, mind you, but one of England's more prominent citizens, a former MP and right wealthy gent to boot. This would bring the powers that be and the press to Amersham in large numbers, thereby complicating Herbert J. Barbon's life. Damn little chance of him and the wife getting away tomorrow evening for a long-planned anniversary dinner and show in London. They had tickets to see Tommy Steele in "Singing In The Rain" and the missus was quite looking forward to it.

But come tomorrow he would be swamped with visitors and paper work, all of it to do with the late Oliver Lord Coveyduck. Barbon himself was sure to be questioned, something he could well do without since he was a most private man and not at ease talking to strangers. From this moment on he was going to be up to his ass in aggravation and all because his lordship had answered the final summons. Bye, bye, Tommy Steele.

At his car Barbon opened the door, slid behind the wheel, and turned on the light. He put his flashlight on the dashboard, then picked up the radio mike. Might as well get started. The Chief Constable first. Wake him up and bring him into the picture even though he wasn't going to be happy at having his beauty sleep disturbed, but to hell with him. Barbon thought, our peerless leader will be more cheesed off if the Metropolitan Police down in London get the news of Coveyduck's death before he does.

And where the hell was PC Spenser? He'd been gone a full five minutes, maybe longer, and Barbon hadn't heard a peep out of him. All Spenser had been asked to do was look around back, which didn't appear to be too demanding a task. Maybe the sod had snuck off and was home watching "Dynasty" or some other American trash he found so fascinating on the telly.

Barbon took a notebook from inside his jacket, flipped it open, and angled it to see better in the car light. If he had to get the chief out of bed, it might be a good idea to pass on a few names, such as the people Barbon had spoken to from the Metropolitan Police and the man from the American Embassy in London who'd telephoned the Met and gotten this whole business started. The chief might want to familiarize himself with these names before the big boys and the press showed up tomorrow.

Barbon had the microphone to his mouth when he saw Spenser, flashlight aimed at the ground, walk toward him out of the darkness. Made out his flat cap and the bright buttons on his uniform jacket and Barbon was about to ask him if he'd seen anything and what had taken him so long, when Spenser was at the car, shining his flashlight in Barbon's face, making him duck his head and turn away, getting him highly annoyed and he ordered Spenser to get that damn light out of his eyes and stop fiddle-arsing around and that's when Poltava, wearing Spenser's cap and jacket, leaned in the car and cut Barbon's throat.

When he had wiped his knife clean on the dead Inspector's chest, Poltava reattached it to his belt, then picked up Barbon's notebook, leaning into the car to read it. He saw the names Senator Fran Machlis and Edward Penny and smiled. He whispered the name Edward Penny several times before putting the notebook in his pocket and walking toward the barn. His eyes were extraordinarily bright.

7

VIKTOR POLTAVA WAS born in Japan in 1955, the bastard son of a Russian journalist and a Tokyo waitress. The elder Poltava was a sadistic alcoholic who abused mother and son, beating them with his fists and a nail-studded paddle. He also burned the boy with lit cigarettes. Eventually the beatings cost the mother her hearing and the ability to speak. Her dumbness then so incensed the Russian that he strangled her to death with a dish towel and was sentenced to life imprisonment without possibility of parole. When an escape attempt failed, he committed suicide by eating peaches laced with DDT.

Viktor was raised by his Japanese grandmother who found the boy to be exceptionally intelligent. He was capable of reading and writing from the age of four. However, he was far from normal. Scarred by his father's cruelty and his mother's violent death, he grew up starved of parental affection. In time he came to love his grandmother deeply, save with this one exception he cut himself off from all emotion but contempt and hatred. He lived with constant nightmares and fantasies about death. He enjoyed torturing animals and was to suffer a lifelong fear of sex.

Viktor and his grandmother shared a small wooden house

among a cluster of old homes at the bottom of a hill leading to *Yushima* shrine in northern Tokyo. The god of this shrine was the patron of scholars. During the examination months of winter and early spring, Viktor would stare from his bedroom window at the hordes of students climbing the hill to pray for higher grades and admission to the country's top universities. The attempt to pass university entrance examinations often led to mental and physical breakdowns. Some students committed suicide. In Viktor's opinion such people were fools. They had good heads but they lacked brains.

At school Viktor himself was an impossible pupil, showing a violent temper and little respect for authority. Teachers disciplined him for unacceptable and uncivilized behavior, warning him that in Japan individual desires and whims had to be suppressed for the good of all. Japanese society called for cooperation and self-restraint. Success or failure in school determined the sort of life one could expect as an adult. One's future depended entirely on scholastic achievement.

Viktor found this advice confusing. On one hand he was told to make himself indistinguishable from the Japanese. Yet the Japanese themselves discouraged him from doing so. Those teachers who cautioned him to show restraint would join students in ridiculing him for being a *gaijin,* a foreigner. While he'd had a Japanese mother, his father had been Russian, meaning Viktor was not fully Japanese. Therefore he was *gaijin.* An outsider.

Schoolmates saw his white skin and blue eyes as freakish. Japanese children called him *bastard,* a word that made Viktor feel physically disfigured. They taunted him for having no parents to dress him in fine clothes and take him to Shinto shrines for festivals.

The cruelest blow of all was being reminded that he lacked a mother to devote all her time and energy to him, as Japanese mothers traditionally did with their children. All he had was his old grandmother, and she was the laughingstock of the neighborhood. Her mind was in ruins. She had been mentally unbalanced for years.

Her name was Yosano Akashi and she was a slender woman with a high forehead, deep voice, and strangely dilated eyes. Her white hair hung to the back of her knees, and many saw her as hovering on the edge of madness. Viktor, however, found his only peace in her presence. When he was overexcited, she alone was able to calm him, using a combination of caresses, words, and her breath blown gently on his face and neck. When he suffered from depression, she had him sit at her feet while she stroked his hair and soothed him with tales of supernatural visions and Asian myths.

Yosano Akashi had devoted her life to the occult and because of it she had been branded a witch and sorceress. Others used the less complimentary names of hag, ogress, gorgon.

As a young girl she had been a *miko,* a shrine maiden consecrated to the gods. She had worn a white kimono and red shirt and performed sacred Shinto dances. She had assisted priests in ancient Shinto rituals and sold charms and oracles to shrine visitors. The Japanese had always used youngsters as temple attendants, believing that children represented purity of soul and possessed an untainted mind.

But as Yosano Akashi grew into a woman she underwent a severe change. She became extremely vain and was disrespectful to shrine authorities. She was no longer content to be a servant. She demanded to be served, to be held in the highest esteem as if she, too, were a deity. "I will no longer drop to my knees and mumble before old men," she said. "Let them worship me."

Her parents, both strongly religious, were shamed by her mental disorder. They begged priests to free her from the evil spirits now in possession of her soul, to save her before she destroyed herself. But before priests could perform the exorcism that might save her, it was learned that Yosano had seduced a young priest. This was a major scandal, one which threatened the sanctity of the shrine and the reputation of the priest's family.

The young priest confessed his guilt, promising to erase the shame he had brought upon the shrine and his family, which he did by setting fire to himself in a public park and burning to death. Yosano Akashi, now pregnant with Viktor's mother, was driven from the shrine—*Yushima* shrine—forbidden ever to enter its grounds again. Her parents refused her any help and publicly announced they no longer had a daughter.

To support herself and her illegitimate child, Yosano Akashi became a medium *miko,* an occupation which the government considered illegal. Medium *mikos,* it said, were charlatans. Spiritual fakes who cheated the ignorant and desperate. Priests shunned them, denying medium *mikos* even the smallest role in religious celebrations or festivals. Frauds like these, they said, had no place among genuine devotees.

But medium *mikos* were eagerly sought after by believers in black magic, omens, and witchcraft, by the uneducated and the superstitious. Yosano Akashi was called upon to treat the sick by driving out the devil with her prayers, to go into a trance and talk with the dead, to cure the most serious illness with a touch. Many would not begin a journey, change jobs or marry without first consulting her.

Viktor grew up watching his grandmother move back and forth between the realms of the living and the dead. Inevitably his mind became quite influenced by the supernatural. But as she told him, this was not unusual in Japan, where every aspect of life was touched by the supernatural, the other worldly, the mystical.

When he first came to his grandmother, he had been covered in burns, welts, and bruises received at the hands of his father. His grandmother had cured these wounds by means Viktor had considered supernatural.

She had healed his cigarette burns by using a poultice of egg white and soy sauce. To eliminate his intestinal parasites, she'd had him chew handfuls of raw brown rice. A constantly upset stomach had disappeared when he'd swallowed cups of charred, powdered bamboo and water. And his body became more resistant to disease when he followed his grandmother's orders and ate garlic, ginseng, and pickled red plums. This was the healing side of what she called *yagen*, pharmacy. But *yagen* had its destructive side, particularly in the making of poisons.

Poisons were made from male rats, green tea, blowfish, green plums, copper rust, wolfbane, arsenic, and animal and human excrement. Some were designed to paralyze, while others killed immediately or created the appearance of a lingering illness followed by natural death. As usual with things he found interesting, Viktor gave the study of pharmacy his undivided attention, particularly the business of poisons.

Viktor's grandmother had an intense sympathy for him. "The opinions of those who criticize us do not matter," she said, "for we are unique, you and I. In you I have found another self like my own." She understood Viktor, she said, for she knew what the world was trying to do. It was trying to crush him as it had tried to crush her. "Your pain is in my heart," she said, moving Viktor to tears for one of the few times in his life. She questioned none of his cruelties and she tolerated them all. Viktor became extremely devoted to her. She was the one person to whom he would have given his soul.

She was his protector. But in time, he became hers.

It began when, in a final attempt to fit in with his Japanese classmates, he changed his name to Fumio Akashi, combining his mother's surname with the first name of a distant Japanese uncle. The gesture evoked contemptuous laughter and insults at school, turning Viktor into an isolated and sullen youngster. He was now more determined than ever to retaliate against a world that had struck first.

Blow for blow. Measure for measure.

What better way to get back at his tormentors than by breaking their necks as he did with birds and stray dogs? This led him to study karate, which he combined with weight training to give him added strength. Karate engrossed him from the beginning, capturing his undivided attention as school never had, challenging him in ways he hadn't thought possible. In time, revenging himself upon his classmates became secondary; his goal was now to obtain the ultimate performance from his body, to never accept mediocrity from himself, to pursue karate to an infinitely extended dimension. He would submerge himself in this fighting form as his grandmother had done with the supernatural, and his mastery of it would set him apart from everyone around him. From this point on Viktor had little interest in anything else.

He approached karate with his intelligence, physical strength and emotional intensity, all of which were considerable. Against older, more experienced fighters he learned that strength was not enough. Power had to be used correctly, which meant using it in conjunction with speed and timing. The strong but slow use of power in weight lifting was not as effective in karate as power delivered with great speed. He learned to concentrate his power when striking or kicking, then quickly release it for the next action.

His efforts to gain a thorough insight into this fighting art were extraordinary. He spoke with various instructors, seeking them out along with their top students. He fought in numerous tournaments, attended exhibitions, collected books and articles on karate, and kept his own series of notebooks on combat. By the time he was fifteen, Viktor was the talk of Tokyo's martial arts circles. Not all of the talk, however, was good.

He had no trouble defeating boys his own age, either in or out of the *dojo*. His karate ability, coupled with his strength and savagery, allowed him to intimidate his schoolmates at will, even to extort money from them when it suited him. No *dojo* allowed him to spar with anyone his age. Wherever he trained he was asked to practice with seniors, some of whom were twice his age and had years of tournament experience. A half dozen clubs banned him from training under any circumstances because he had injured students and showed little remorse. All opponents found him difficult, for he looked upon even the most casual encounter as one he had to win.

No one questioned his ability as a fighter. A few even predicted that he would become the youngest all-Japan karate champion on record, one of the country's most prestigious sports achievements. Others, however, were disturbed by his lack of sportsmanship and humility. He was too headstrong, they said. Too inflexible and intent on victory at all costs. Viktor Poltava, they said, loved the excitement and cruelty of combat.

Unbending. Merciless. Viktor himself would have been the first to admit these words applied to him, not that he cared what others thought. The older he grew the more determined he was to follow his own will in all things and be subject to no man. He was, however, determined to find a club that would allow him to use his full abilities, energies, and resources without placing any restrictions in his way.

He found the *dojo* he was seeking in Tokyo's *Ikebukuro* section, a run-down area of cheap wooden and bamboo houses, sleazy hostess bars, all-night movie theaters and *pachinko* parlors, where players endlessly flipped ball-bearings into metal cups marked "win" or "lose." The karate club itself was little better than a hole in the wall, a long smelly room with concrete walls, filthy windows, torn mats, and a cracked, leaky ceiling. It smelled of sweat and dampness and food odors from a nearby *soba-ya* noodle shop.

The fighters in this *Ikebukuro* club were strong, unyielding, and as hard as nails. They were ranked among Tokyo's best. And toughest. In or out of the *dojo,* few abided by any rules. Nor did they accept victory or defeat graciously. Practice was a vigorous, no-holds-barred affair, and injuries were frequent. This was an outlaw club, one not connected with any organized system of karate. The rule here was survival of the fittest. Those who couldn't defend themselves would not be defended.

The *dojo* will have an aura, his grandmother said, a spiritual current which ebbs and flows, and Viktor should be aware of those times when the current was strongest, for this would aid him in his fighting. She had come to realize that fighting was his life, that it lived inside him.

Viktor said that through karate he had found his identity. Fighting exalted him. As a fighter the responsibility for his fate was on his own shoulders. One had to know how to fight, he told her, for in this world right and wrong did not matter. What mattered was being strong. In the *dojo* he felt alive every second. He had a fever for combat. His grandmother nodded. She understood.

Which was why she insisted that he train among the dead for three nights. "Enter the cemetery at midnight and remain until dawn," she said. "Practice alone and make certain no one sees you. Select a site near the tomb or mausoleum of one who had recently died, for they are still close to the land of the living. You will be able to feel their aura."

Viktor had never feared death. To him it had always been a friend, a means to end the pain and confusion of life. He had always imagined it to be a beautiful adventure. Thanks to his grandmother, Viktor had grown up quite comfortable with the spirit world and had always found the emphasis on death more stimulating than everyday life. Everyday life was boring. Dry as dust. Death lived in his thoughts more often than the past or the future.

He had always been a dreamer, his only refuge after being knocked about by his prick of a father. He had started to dream of a world undefiled by life's misery and suffering. Such a world was death, and he had seen it as bright, with an immense and endless promise. To a frightened little boy with a scrotum covered in cigarette burns, death was freedom. Viktor had always envied the dead.

Viktor's grandmother had selected Yanaka Cemetery for his training because members of her family were buried here. He was to carry the small brocade bag that was his talisman and wear a silken headband his grandmother had made especially for this training. It was blood red and marked with the Japanese characters for *Oni*. Demon.

Talisman. And the mark of the demon. His defenses against the evil of the spirit world.

Demons. Viktor was drawn to them. Supernatural creatures who moved between *Naka-tsu-kuni*, the world of the living, and *Yomi-no-kuni*, the world of the dead. His grandmother spoke of them frequently, saying they were everywhere. 'Above ground and with the living. In the air and under the sun. Everywhere. Viktor, of course, believed her. He believed her so much that he sometimes left food by his bedside at night in case a demon came visiting.

Demons were destructive. They were feared, though not by Viktor who had something in common with them. They were angry and so was he, so why shouldn't he be drawn to them? He especially liked a demon's looks. It was ugly, with long white hair, a square-shaped face, two sharp horns pointing straight up, and a wide mouth with bared teeth and fangs. Its only clothing was a tiger loincloth, and its toes and fingers were claws. And its voice was that of the thunder and wind gods. The louder a demon wailed, the angrier the storm. A demon had only to pull a dark cloud from its bag to release a heavy downpour or typhoon.

Seeing his love of demons, Viktor's grandmother bought him a demon mask, a rubber one complete with horns, bulbous eyes, and a wide mouth with plastic fangs. It had long gray hair attached to the top, and when he wore the mask, the hair went across the top of his head and hung below his shoulders. To complete the appearance of a mythical *Oni*, Viktor purchased a tiger loincloth. Sometimes, alone in his room, he practiced karate wearing the loincloth and mask. Practiced with a wild joy brought on by the sight of the muscular half-naked demon staring back at him from the mirror.

Demons, however, could sometimes be protectors. Viktor's

grandmother told him of the ancient priest Gazan Ryogen, a pious soul who built a temple for his followers and who loved them all so much that after his death he had returned as a demon to protect the temple. Yosano Akashi's small home was her temple, and it was now under Viktor's protection. At sixteen, powerfully built and with outstanding fighting skills, he was a formidable foe. Now he eagerly looked forward to handling unruly complications encountered by his grandmother.

Drunks no longer hurled bottles through the windows and cursed her for being a witch. They'd stopped when Viktor took on two of them in a fight, breaking one man's collarbone and sending the other to the hospital with a concussion and torn neck ligaments. He also dealt with those who used her services and refused to pay. A woman who owed Yosano Akashi money and had ignored the debt found the inside of her new car crawling with poisonous centipedes, and Viktor standing nearby, calmly watching her scream. She paid.

His grandmother no longer had to fear the mentally disturbed who sought her help, then sometimes lost control and threatened her life. A factory worker, whom Viktor immediately recognized as being a dangerous crackpot, came to the house and requested that Yosano Akashi speak to his dead wife. But the stars were not right. Nor did the old woman feel the cooperation of the spirit.

When she told this to the man, he attempted to strangle her. Viktor went berserk. He broke both of the man's arms and was systematically breaking all of his fingers when the factory worker's screams drew police. Only his grandmother's insistence that he had acted to save her life, kept Viktor from prison.

This incident and the neighborhood's fear created Viktor the demon.

Fourth night of the fourth month.

Because legend said that demons swooped down from their stone houses in the northeast, Viktor entered Yanaka Cemetery from that direction. He carried his rolled *gi* under one arm and wore the headband made for him by his grandmother. His talisman, the brocade bag, hung from the belt of his trousers. His energy was high. Yosano Akashi had insisted that he eat a protein-rich meal of tofu, salted plums, dried trout, and genmai juice

made from unpolished rice. He felt strong enough to enter the
tiger's den and walk out with the tiger's cub.

In the cemetery he crouched beside a moss-covered tombstone
and shivered in the April chill. Seconds later he stared up at the
sky. When a full moon slipped behind black clouds, he rose and
began walking south. He moved from shadow to shadow, from
trees to giant mausoleums. And he ignored the whispers of warning sounded by the wind as it blew through pine and cypress
trees. Even a far-off car horn sounded menacing. A tenacious
Viktor, however, held steadily and firmly to his purpose.

Viktor walked a quarter of a mile before locating the grave he
sought. It lay at the end of a path leading to a grove of cherry
trees. He knew it was a fresh grave because yesterday he had
watched the ashes of a Buddhist nun being buried here by long-
faced relatives dressed in black and Buddhist priests wearing yellow robes.

Tonight, as he approached the grave, he was a bit nervous. It
wasn't fear; he would never allow himself to be frightened. But
there were butterflies in his stomach, and he could feel himself
becoming tense. He would warm up before getting started. A
very good warm up. *How would the dead receive him?*

He walked to within inches of the nun's grave and stopped.
Her tombstone was a *stupa*, pagoda-shaped, and in five parts to
represent sky, wind, fire, water and earth. He touched the stone,
closed his eyes, and felt the night grow suddenly colder. When an
owl hooted in a cherry tree, Viktor opened his eyes. The graveyard appeared darker, more foreboding. No matter. He wasn't
turning back. He undressed and hung his clothes on the nun's
tombstone. Seconds later he was in his *gi*.

He stared at the tombstone. Twice he cleared his dry throat. A
vein throbbed on his forehead. No, he wasn't going to turn and
run. This was where he wanted to be, standing on the edge of the
unknown and feeling free. *Feeling the dead looking on and ready
to help him.*

The moon disappeared once more, easing behind black
clouds, and the graveyard was almost totally dark. The wind
blew stronger, and the trees seemed to whisper *Oni*. An emotion-
ally aroused Viktor smiled. His mind understood what had to be
done.

Warm-up. He began by stretching his neck, then his arms—

forward, back, and to the side. He paid careful attention to his spine, ankle joints, and knee joints. Other exercises stretched his hamstrings and remaining leg tendons. A perspiring Viktor finished his twenty-minute warm-up with high kicks to the front, back, and sides.

Training. His punches had never felt so strong. He punched with the power of his hips as he had been taught to, but soon, as though by miracle, he was able to transmit that power to his chest, shoulders, arms, and fists, tensing his body precisely at the moment of impact against an imaginary opponent. All of his muscles were working together in a harmony he had never been able to achieve until this instant.

Kicking techniques were equally as powerful. His upper body remained balanced at all times, his supporting foot anchored strongly on the ground, and his hips pushed forward during each kick, making the attack devastating. None of his kicks had ever been this smooth or this destructive before. Viktor was elated.

He no longer felt the cold or heard the wind. He moved in a dazed state, functioning between sleep and waking. He dropped to his knees in exhaustion at one point, then pushed to his feet and continued in a stupor, stumbling through the movements as the hours went on, but refusing to stop as he summoned from within himself an energy that defied normal physical laws. Tonight he was removing forever any limits that could restrict him as a fighter. He had to continue until dawn; he must not show weakness before the underworld spirits he had challenged.

Only when the tip of the sun pushed itself above the horizon did a painfully fatigued Viktor sink to the ground. He clung to the nun's tombstone with both arms to keep from falling face down. The past five hours had left him drained. Totally depleted. His *gi* was soaked with his perspiration; his hair lay wet and flat against his skull. He breathed through his open mouth and his lungs burned with each breath. He wanted to sleep, to lay down on the cool, cool ground and close his eyes.

His eyes began to close and his hands slid down the tombstone. But he shook his head to clear it and, with his last ounce of strength, he pulled himself to his knees. His body was betraying him; he would have to force his body to obey his mind. He reached into his pants pocket and pulled out a pocketknife. Then he collapsed back into a sitting position, feeling sleep rush to overtake him, but he opened the knife, filled his lungs with air, then pushed the tip of the blade into his right thigh, tensing when the pain raced through his body, pushing the blade a bit deeper.

The pain awakened him. He kept the blade in his flesh while he breathed deeply and stared at the sun, gaining strength from its warmth and light, feeling his breathing become more stable, less rapid. Two minutes later, he pulled the knife from his thigh, stood up and removed his *gi*. He wrapped the headband around the wound, which wasn't serious, then dressed and walked slowly from the nun's grave, heading toward the northeast where demons come from.

Ikebukuro Dojo.

The chief instructor was a fiftyish, balding Korean named Cho Park Yi, a muscular, heavy-jowled man with small, empty eyes and a rasping hiss of a voice. He was a fanatical supporter of right wing political causes, mistrustful of strangers and new ideas, and ran his *dojo* with an iron fist. He bodyguarded Japanese industrialists, popular entertainers, and visiting Korean CIA officials. He also did strongman work for the *yakuza*, Japan's Mafia. To him, karate was neither an exercise nor a sport to be practiced under controlled conditions. It was the science of destruction, to be taught with a cruel discipline.

Park Yi's ruthlessness in a fight was legendary. He was a vengeful adversary, one who never forgot a wrong done to him no matter how small. He was called "The Pig Man" because, in an attempt to persuade a wealthy client to hire him as a bodyguard, Yi had driven a hand into the chest of a live pig, pulled out the heart, and eaten it. He was a rabid baseball fan, and from April to October could often be found at *Korakuen* Stadium in a seat behind third base. Other addictions were TV game shows, his favorite aired weekly at six A.M., and Coca Cola. A Coke machine in his *dojo* office was solely for his private use. New students had the responsibility of seeing that the machine was never empty.

Park Yi's training emphasized endurance and power. Punching, striking, blocking, and kicking techniques were repeated endlessly until both offensive and defensive movements became instinctive. Yi demanded maximum speed at all times and did not hesitate to hit those who didn't move fast enough to suit him.

Each session was filled with a variety of techniques, and students were expected to remember them all correctly. "The body offers many weapons," he said. "Hands, feet, elbows, and knees are the most frequently used, and should be selected according to the situation. Above all else," Yi told his students, "a fighter must develop confidence. One who believes in himself can lead the world."

Viktor trained hard, absorbing Yi's teachings while expanding on what he already knew. He increased his flexibility, improved his breath control and concentration. Because of tougher competition, he was forced to learn how to correctly predict his opponent's movements and instinctively counter them, performing both parts of this process as a single act. He sharpened his throwing techniques and continued his weight training, adding to his strength.

From his first practice session, Viktor stood out. He demonstrated a superior hand speed and power which even the most experienced students had trouble containing. He received his share of bruises and sprains: his grandmother often washed bloodstains, his and other students', from his *gi*. Viktor, however, refused to complain about anything. He found this sort of training gratifying. The most grueling sessions would often leave him in high spirits. And he always gave as good as he got.

He had been at Yi's *dojo* almost two months before encountering serious trouble with any of the students. Until then he had kept to himself, training hard and making a point of being polite to Yi and all senior students since he felt at home among these outcasts and looked forward to remaining with them for a while. Yi himself rarely praised his students, but he did afford Viktor a special distinction. The teenager became one of a handful never struck or cursed. This was a rare privilege earned by following Yi's instructions to the letter and making a minimum of mistakes.

Viktor's trouble came from a twenty-four-year-old, thickset ex-biker named Chiba, whose closed-cropped hair, mangled left ear and three steel front teeth gave him a formidable appearance. Chiba was taller than Viktor, outweighed him by fifty pounds and was strong enough to poke a hole in an apple with one finger. He'd recently been accepted into a *yakuza* mob and hadn't appeared at the *dojo* since Viktor had begun training. On his first evening of practice, he'd been confronted with Viktor's reputation as a fighter, by Park Yi's unspoken appreciation of Viktor's ability, by seniors who confessed to him privately that they were a bit afraid of the new boy. *Seniors afraid of a new boy?* Chiba thought this was crap. He was Yi's toughest fighter and he wasn't afraid of anyone, let alone a newcomer. Someone had to put Mr. Viktor in his place. Chiba nominated himself for the job.

Before joining Park Yi's club, Viktor had taken his grandmother's advice and gone there as a spectator. Which was when he'd seen Chiba and made a mental note of him as a potential enemy. Chiba was a bully who used his strength against new or weaker students. His technique was good but nothing special; it was all power, with no finesse, no fakes and little strategy. His style was to attack the body, destroying his opponents with blows and kicks to the stomach, chest, ribs. He called it "tearing down a man's house." He would take punches to get to his opponent, barrelling in like a speeding train out of control. A very predictable fighter.

When Chiba returned to the dojo as a full-fledged *yakuza*, he returned as a conquering hero, a poor boy who'd made good. He wore his *yakuza* lapel pin, a flat top haircut and he was dressed in a pinstripe suit with a black shirt and white tie, which Japanese gangsters borrowed from Hollywood gangster movies. Viktor watched Yi's students fawn over Chiba and enviously admire his chunky gold watch, flashy gold cufflinks and pointy toe black and white shoes. It was all too showy for Viktor's taste.

Chiba basked in the attention. He bragged about his steady pay, the *yakuza* big shots he hung around with, the whores who were his for the asking, the important businessmen he had done "special" favors for. In the changing room his bare chest was a source of admiration; Chiba was undergoing ritual *yakuza* tattooing, another reason to toot his own horn. His chest, back, arms and legs contained unfinished but beautiful designs of flowers, tigers and religious symbols, a painful process done over a period of months with bamboo needles that pricked holes in the skin so that dyes could be inserted to form the stunning patterns. These elaborate tattoos set a *yakuza* apart from ordinary men. They indicated that he was someone special. Viktor saw it as boasting, which as any fool knew was not courage.

On this particular night, Viktor had deliberately avoided

Chiba, choosing instead to practice with other students. The decision to stay away from Chiba was strictly a strategic one. Viktor had watched Chiba and other seniors whispering to each other, then seen Chiba look at him with contempt. Sooner or later Chiba would seek him out and test him. So why spar with a bully boy and give away fighting secrets? A clever hawk conceals its claws.

It happened after practice, in the changing room called "The Zoo" because of its barred windows, foul odors, loud talk and occasional fights. Viktor had towelled himself dry, dressed and was tying his shoes when the room went quiet. He hesitated a second or two, but didn't look up. Someone dropped keys on the cement floor. Not far away, one student farted. Chiba said, "Hey, you. Russian bastard. I'm talking to you." Viktor finished tying his shoes, then folded his *gi,* tucked the damp towel inside and wrapped his black belt tightly around the *gi.* Only then did he stand up and face Chiba.

"The next time I call," Chiba said, "you better show some respect. You look at me, you understand? And do it right away." The brawny *yakuza,* barechested and barefoot and wearing white boxer shorts, strolled toward Viktor. Chiba's sweat-soaked, soiled *gi* hung from one arm. Six feet away he stopped and hurled the *gi* at the teenager. Viktor caught it, then held the jacket in one hand and trousers in the other and stared at them as though seeing a *gi* for the first time.

"Listen carefully, Russian bastard," Chiba said. "I want my *gi* cleaned and pressed and waiting for me here in the *dojo* when I show up tomorrow night. 7:30 promptly. And if you're even one minute late, I'm going to drag you by your balls over to the toilet and shove your Russian head into the bowl." He pointed to the stinking, sluggish toilet near the far wall.

Some students laughed. Others were too frightened to say anything. One or two left, knowing there was going to be trouble. Why witness something like this when you didn't have to? And there were some who knew a fight was on the way, and didn't want to miss it. Even those who disliked Chiba knew he would win. He was a son of a bitch. That's why he was *yakuza.*

Park Yi rarely interfered with any happenings in "The Zoo." Here seniors were allowed to rule as they saw fit, so long as no one was killed and the *dojo* was not damaged. Until now no one had attempted to give Viktor a hard time in or out of "The Zoo." The most experienced senior now knew the Russian-Japanese teenager was a handful. Chiba hadn't seen Viktor before tonight and in any case the young *yakuza* was too full of himself to walk softly around anyone else, especially a foreigner with blue eyes. If others lacked the nerve to take him on, Chiba didn't. The Russian bastard in the demon headband was going to be brought to heel. Right here and now.

Chiba said, "Half Russian, half Japanese, and all nothing." He jerked his head towards the toilet. "It might do you some good to have your big head shoved into the bowl tonight. Maybe when you eat some Japanese shit, you'll learn to respect us seniors."

Viktor smiled at Chiba and thought, if one is going to pull out the eyes of the stallion one must act boldly. The way he handled Chiba from this moment on would determine whether or not he could continue practicing at this *dojo*. Chiba the body puncher. A dangerous fighter and capable of inspiring mindless fear in just about anybody.

But as his grandmother often reminded him, Viktor wasn't just anybody. She had always known he was special, surpassing what was common or unusual. He was intelligent, she said, but possessed something even more valuable and that was the ability to concentrate all of his mental powers on a single object. This would enable him to accomplish anything he desired.

And there was his talent for combat, which set him apart from everyone else. And he was entirely without fear. In any fight, he was indifferent to his own fate. Why waste time and energy on such idle thoughts as injury or defeat? In combat he stuck to his purpose which was to destroy his opponent. He didn't fear death, so why fear Chiba or anyone else for that matter. And pain had always been the seed-bed of Viktor's pleasure.

Bright-eyed and still smiling, he held up Chiba's *gi,* then crouched and laid the jacket on the cement floor. Next he put the pants inside, folded the jacket over them and rolled it into a compact bundle. The prescribed way to carry one's *gi* to and from practice. Viktor turned his smile to Chiba who nodded in approval. The new boy was shaping up. All it took was a firm hand.

Viktor, rolled *gi* under one arm, rose and walked toward the far wall. His smile appeared to be turned inward, as though pursuing a very private and exquisite pleasure. His sneakered feet made no sound as he stepped across the concrete floor. All eyes were on him. No one spoke. At the far wall, he turned to face Chiba and dropped the rolled *gi* into the toilet bowl.

Now he stared at the brawny *yakuza* with eyes that were blue ice. The smile was gone.

At first a stunned Chiba was rooted to the spot. He stared at the new boy, not believing what he'd just seen. If the room had been hit by an earthquake, the shock could not have been greater. This Russian bastard had challenged him. Worse, he had shamed Chiba in front of others. A white-hot hatred took over the young *yakuza*. He shuddered with loathing and the tattoos on his muscular body quivered with a life of their own. There was only one way to save face now: beat this Russian fool so severely that he would bear Chiba's mark forever. *Destroy his house*. Taste his blood.

Viktor saw it all in Chiba's face. The determination to regain lost honor. The belief in his own size and physical strength. The teenager also saw Chiba's passion destroy his judgment. Viktor sensed the room withdraw from him, leaving him alone to face Chiba's fury. But he felt an excitement rising within his mind and body. *Viktor wanted this fight*.

He concentrated on the breathing, bringing it under control, slowing his heartbeat. He did not feel vulnerable. Nor did he have the slightest concern for himself.

Chiba, blood boiling, ran at him, bare feet slapping the concrete floor, so anxious to get his hands on the new boy that he shoved students out of the way and kicked a stool aside, sending it bouncing off someone's arm. Viktor, seemingly doomed, stood his ground. Only when Chiba was a step away did he go into action.

He quickly yanked Chiba's *gi* from the toilet and whipped it across the *yakuza*'s face, stopping him dead in his tracks, arms high in self-protection and because Chiba's arms blocked his vision he never saw Viktor strike.

Viktor leaped forward, grabbed Chiba around the waist and drove his right knee into Chiba's left thigh, crippling the leg, sending the *yakuza* staggering sideways, face contorted with pain, and when Chiba bent down to clutch the damaged leg with both hands, Viktor stepped left and double punched him in the rib cage, using both hands and hitting with full power, deliberately striking in the same spot to intensify the pain, hearing Chiba scream, and when Chiba spun around to face him, Viktor broke his nose with a quick left hook. Chiba, face covered in blood, now thought only of saving himself and limped backwards, defeated and destroyed, but Viktor, showing no mercy, leaped forward and drove his right knee into Chiba's stomach, lifting him in the air, sending him flying into a group of watching students. Chiba and the students all hit the floor, arms and legs flailing, the students crawling away from the pileup to leave a glassy-eyed Chiba lying on his back, mouth open. Blood from his crushed nose began staining his teeth and darkening the concrete floor beneath his head.

A smiling Viktor walked across the silent room to stand before a cracked, dirty mirror where he combed his hair as if nothing had happened. Then he picked up his rolled *gi* and walked toward the exit without looking back. No one attempted to stop him from leaving. They watched him disappear up the narrow staircase leading to the practice area and for a few seconds they listened, no one moving or speaking until they heard the faint sound of the *dojo*'s front door close behind him.

As Viktor's grandmother grew older, she often sat at a back window of their home and stared up the hill at *Yushima* shrine, once her spiritual home. Occasionally she would turn from the shrine to silently read from a small, worn book. When Viktor learned the contents of the book, he began to worry. It was a book of prayers for the dead, which could only mean that Yosana Akashi now sensed the approach of her own death. The worn garment that was her aged body was about to be cast off by her eternal soul.

An uneasy Viktor dreaded losing her. The thought of it preyed on his mind and left him depressed. For a time he even had trouble sleeping. No one, but no one could take her place. When he asked her why she spent so much time looking at the shrine, she said she wanted to visit it at least once more before dying.

"No, I do not expect to die soon," she said, attempting to calm him. "But it is inevitable that I die sooner than we both would prefer, my little demon. So I wish to go to the shrine and beg the gods' forgiveness before it is too late."

Viktor accepted many of her ideas about gods, especially anything she said about the supernatural. But for the most part, his thoughts tended to center and concentrate on himself. Still, he gave some thought to his grandmother at this time and came to see that she was afraid to die, that she wanted to prepare herself for this final journey to the unknown with a farewell visit to *Yushima* shrine.

As her protector, it was Viktor's duty to take matters into his own hands, which he did. On a wet June day he told his grandmother that they were going to visit the shrine. Immediately. She would have her chance to talk to the gods in their home. Viktor would give her the opportunity to make her final peace.

A teary Yosano Akashi thanked him, but said she did not have the courage to violate the ban by walking on *Yushima*'s sacred ground. "You won't be violating the ban," Viktor said. "I'm going to carry you up the hill on my back and you'll remain on my back while we're there. Your feet won't touch the ground. If the gods wish to be angry with someone, let them be angry with me."

She looked at the floor. "I'm afraid."

"I'm not," he said. "Leave this matter to me."

He placed an old straw hat on her head, pulling it down to hide her face. Then he draped a raincoat around her shoulders, taking care to hide her long white hair. "Climb on my back," he said, "and hold tight."

She didn't move. Then she began to tremble and Viktor had to support her to keep her from falling. Now it was he who soothed her with words of encouragement, holding her in his arms and whispering softly that she must go, that she had a right to go. He would answer to the gods for taking her to the shrine.

He smiled, turned his back to her, and crouched down. She hesitated, then stepped forward, put her arms around his neck, and leaned against him. Viktor straightened up, clasped her legs, and walked from the house.

It was late evening when they began their ascent up the hill. Viktor had carefully selected the time for their visit to the shrine. June was the season of the *baiu,* the plum rain welcomed by the rice farmers. It wasn't raining this evening, but there was a misty drizzle which most people, city dwellers in particular, hated because it dampened their clothing for days. The drizzle and the late hour meant fewer worshipers at the shrine, lessening the chances of Viktor's grandmother being recognized.

He climbed the hill with ease, carrying his grandmother effortlessly and feeling her grow tense as they neared the shrine. At the top, they paused in a cool evening mist now beginning to envelop the shrine and its sacred pine and cypress trees. Viktor's grandmother breathed rapidly; she needed to catch her breath. He sensed her edginess and spoke softly to her, saying there was nothing to fear or to be concerned about. "Today *I* am your talisman," he said.

"I am a burden to you," she said. "Put me down. If it is the will of the gods that I be struck dead, then I am prepared to die."

Viktor chuckled. He wasn't weary in the least, and told her so. She was as light as a feather, and he could have carted her several miles if he had to. "I'm as sturdy as an ox," he said.

For a few minutes the two stared at the shrine and its almost empty grounds. They saw several unpainted wooden buildings, none over two stories tall and all made of Japanese cypress. Since this was a Shinto shrine, all of the buildings were fairly new. Shinto was a religion of renewal, and every twenty years all of its buildings were demolished and reconstructed in exactly the same form.

Viktor walked through the *torii,* the wooden arch that represented the gateway cutting off the everyday world from the spirit world. He headed first toward the *mizuya* or water place several feet away. This was a roofed stone basin where worshipers purified themselves before entering the shrine. Here Viktor crouched to allow his grandmother to pick up a long-handled wood dipper and fill it with water. After pouring a bit over the fingers of both hands and rinsing her mouth, she lay the dipper on the basin's edge. Viktor had no intention of purifying himself. His interest in the spirit world was rooted in dark things, things more base and ominous.

But coming to the shrine had made him aware of how frail his grandmother had become. Her body was bent with age, she was almost seventy and her hands were gnarled and heavily veined. She was having difficulty with her vision and a persistent soreness in one hip caused her to limp noticeably. There was no denying that she was near the end, that her work was almost done. Viktor found this a very disturbing idea. He could not bear to lose the one person who had strengthened and protected him when he'd needed it most.

The mist grew thicker, an impenetrable whiteness that almost blotted out the sacred trees. Viktor felt the drizzle begin to find its way through his clothing; it was only a matter of time until he was soaked to the skin, something he'd rather avoid. He preferred to be indoors, but then his grandmother said she wanted to see everything. Would Viktor mind strolling the grounds for a few minutes? Of course not. He would gladly take her wherever she wanted to go.

They left the watering place just as a mother and two small daughters in identical yellow kimonos approached to purify themselves. Following his grandmother's directions, Viktor walked out past a waist high stone lantern, then stopped to allow her to touch the *shimenawa,* a thick rope tied between pine trees to indicate a purified area. From there she pointed toward the *honden,* the main building, and asked to be taken there. This is where she had performed her duties as a young attendant, she told Viktor. She touched one of the two stone lions guarding the building's entrance, then lapsed into silence. A full minute passed before Viktor realized that she had been weeping.

Finally she asked him for a few coins to put into the collection box; she'd left the house without money and had nothing to offer the gods. Viktor took money from his pocket and watched his grandmother take it with a trembling hand. She dropped the coins in the box, clapped her hands three times to alert the gods to her presence, then bowed her head and prayed. Viktor wondered if the gods were ready to change their laws on behalf of one old woman.

Their time at the shrine was brief. Less than an hour after arriving, they were approached by a novice priest, a small, chinless man with a flat nose, who quietly told them that the sacred grounds were closing for the day. By now Yosano Akashi was quite ready to leave. Her first visit to the shrine in almost fifty years had been a most satisfying one, she told Viktor. Her one uncomfortable moment had occurred when an old priest had come toward them, tottering on his stick, eyes down on the ground, mind lost in things not of this world. A frightened Yosano Akashi had whispered, "I know this one. He will surely

recognize me. What should I do?" She tightened her grip around
Viktor's neck.

Viktor said, "Don't worry. There's no reason to be frightened." No one would recognize her in the raincoat and hat. It was
quite possible that the old priest was half-blind, even senile, and
if he wasn't, his thoughts were obviously somewhere else. But
Viktor did change directions, turning his back to the old priest
and heading toward a building whose walls were covered in
wooden tablets bearing prayers, not only from students, but from
men and women seeking divine help in everything from finding a
mate to recovering a lost dog. The old priest never looked at the
couple.

At the *torii,* Viktor stopped and turned around to allow his
grandmother a final look at the shrine. Two novice priests, white
robes darkened by the rain, stood near the arch and bade farewell
to the handful of departing worshipers. Like all who were leaving, Viktor and Yosano Akashi received the priests' blessing, a
gesture he saw as serving no purpose. Unlike other visitors, the
teenager and the old woman also received a gift. The youngest of
the two priests gave Yosano Akashi the bamboo and oil paper
umbrella he'd been using to protect himself against the rain. He
also praised Viktor for doing a good turn by carrying a worshiper
on his back. Such kindness would always insure that the gods
grant solace and comfort to his soul.

On the return journey down the hill she was beside herself
with excitement. The visit to the shrine had revived her; she was
more lively and energetic than she'd been in some time. She
talked over the sound of rain drumming on the paper umbrella,
cheerfully recounting the visit to Viktor as though he hadn't been
there with her. He played along, allowing himself to be caught up
in her joy and listening attentively, adding a word here and there,
but letting her tell the tale in her own fashion. She thanked him
again and again for having made this glorious day possible. The
gods had blessed her with a most thoughtful grandson, one who
had gladdened her heart every day since he had come to live with
her. Should she die on this day of days she would be eternally in
Viktor's debt.

But it was he who owed her, he insisted, and she was going to
live a long time. "You'll see *Yushima* shrine torn down twenty
years from now and rebuilt," he said. "I myself will carry you up

the hill to see the new one. *Hai,* I will take you up the hill anytime you wish to go. We will make many trips there, you and I. You will see, Grandmother. You will."

A cheerful Viktor began to slowly jog down the hill, bringing whoops of delight from his grandmother. Halfway down he stopped in the rain and spun around in a circle, gently bouncing her on his back, making her shriek with the joy of a child. In her joy, she threw the umbrella in the air, and raindrops beaded on her face.

The following evening, Viktor finished karate practice and hurried to the changing room, anxious to get dressed and be out before the room became crowded. He hated masses of people. They made him feel trapped, and their noise prevented him from losing himself in thought. Yesterday's visit to *Yushima* shrine, with its open spaces and smell of cypress trees, had been surprisingly relaxing. He'd been able to move about without bumping into anyone. He'd also been removed from the gibber-jabber now surging around him. The *dojo* changing room, with its chattering and constant horseplay, was a loony bin.

Viktor wondered if anybody in the changing room knew the meaning of the word silence. Everyone was running off at the mouth, attacking Viktor's ears with rubbish about American Westerns, rock music, and their scruffy little sex lives. Two seniors, both of them bikers, practically stood on his toes while discussing the student riots now breaking out on University campuses across Japan. Bikers, Viktor had learned, were die-hard conservatives, and this pair was no exception.

Both were slow to accept the unfamiliar and quick to register their hatreds. Even if this were the 1970s, a time of worldwide turmoil and unrest, they made it known that they stood opposed to any changes in Japan's traditional values. Students who felt differently were little more than troublemakers and could expect to get hurt. Viktor found the bikers, Yutaka and Kimura, to be know-nothings, the sort of mutton-heads who were clever only to themselves.

"It's all the fault of the Communists," Yutaka said. He was in his early twenties, a small balding man with a high, nasal voice that Viktor found unbearable. He was also a vicious little bastard when aroused. When Park Yi wasn't around, Yutaka was one of the seniors who ran things. And bullied anyone who let him get away with it.

"Left-wing students and their professors," Yutaka said. "You can blame it all on them and your damned Marxist agitators. Trade unionists, left-wing journalists, women's groups. Your free thinkers, and I say they can all go to hell."

An excited Yutaka stood on tiptoe, naked and sweating, forefinger held high as he sprayed Viktor with saliva and insisted the only way to handle the bloody Commies was to knock some sense into their heads. Give the bastards the once-over.

"That's our job," said Kimura. He was nineteen, a chubby, dull-witted loner who could neither read nor write. He was the product of a rape, born to a deranged mother who had been sexually assaulted by an attendant in a mental hospital. Now he stared at the swollen knuckle on one hand, then smiled idiotically at Viktor in an attempt to bring him into the conversation. "We bash in their faces and loosen their teeth," he said. "That's how we earn our money. We lay into those college boys with all we've got. I think you should join us. You would have fun. We enjoy ourselves, don't we, Yutaka?"

Yutaka, Kimura, and others at the *dojo*, Viktor included, had all been given the chance by Park Yi to make a bit of money from the riots. All they had to do was infiltrate the demonstrators at Tokyo University and beat up the riot leaders. Give those intellectual smart asses the trashing they had coming. Have fun and get paid for it.

Viktor had refused. Not because he favored the rioting students or believed in any rules of good behavior. He refused because he preferred to seek his own profit in his own good time. And because he, like everyone else in the club, knew that Park Yi was being paid a pretty penny to sic his bully boys on the students. You didn't have to be a college professor to figure out that the Korean was keeping the lion's share of the money for himself and throwing crumbs to anyone dumb enough to work for him. Yi's greed operated at all times and upon all persons. Well, it wasn't going to operate on Viktor.

Viktor crouched down to tie his shoes, wishing that he could shove something in Yutaka's mouth to squelch that detestable voice.

"It's all a matter of morale," Yutaka said. "Those Commie

students, damn them, are upsetting everyone at a time when Japan needs workers willing to do what they are told and do it cheerfully."

Viktor thought, this fool is not only talking himself blue in the face, but he's robbing me of my peace of mind.

Shoes tied, Viktor began folding his *gi*, deliberately keeping his back to Yutaka. The balding little man was not discouraged, however. He simply stepped in front of Viktor, continuing to babble on, continuing to mistake dullness for seriousness. "The riots have shamed Japan," he said. "It is wrong that the government's time has to be taken up with this student nonsense." He slammed a fist into his palm, saying that the only solution was to put the students out of business. Then he held his wrist near Viktor's face, showing off a brown leather bracelet studded with red and green, oval-shaped rhinestones. Something new he'd bought for himself with the money he'd earned from beating up students. What did Viktor think of it?

Viktor thought the bracelet was rubbish, second-rate trash, but he said nothing. He simply finished folding his *gi* then stood up to find Yutaka and Kimura blocking his way, preventing him from moving forward. The bikers were beginning to get on his nerves. Something of his hard feelings toward the pair must have shown on his face because the oafish, hare-brained Kimura nervously said, "You can't go just yet, Viktor."

"I can't. And why not?"

"Because . . . because we're supposed to talk to you."

A suddenly angry Yutaka glared at Kimura as though wanting to tear out his heart. Viktor watched a hint of some understanding worm its way into Kimura's thick skull, for the chubby biker's face reddened and he looked down at the floor, avoiding Yutaka's heated gaze. They want me to join them in beating up the students, Viktor thought. Park Yi's idea, no doubt. Get the Russian bastard to change his mind.

Like it or not, the Russian bastard was now the best fighter in the *dojo,* and anyone who disagreed would be wise to keep his opinion to himself. Of course, Park Yi wanted Viktor to join the campus punch-up tomorrow. In combat Viktor was a whirlwind, and the businessmen would definitely be getting their money's worth. And Park Yi, of course, would look good in the eyes of his rich friends. It was just like the bullheaded Korean to insist on having his way.

"Tell Park Yi the answer is still no," Viktor said. "I fight for myself and no one else. And I don't like anyone putting pressure on me, understand?"

Yutaka looked relieved. He smiled quickly while smoothing sparse, wet hair forward on his head. "Whatever you say, Viktor. We're not here to argue with you, Kimura and me. You really are a good fighter and with you beside us, well, those students wouldn't stand a chance. But we understand how you feel. You are your own man, and we respect you for that."

"We respect you, Viktor," Kimura said. His voice was barely audible and he continued to stare at the ground, as though waiting to be punished by Yutaka.

Viktor thought, it's not respect you two feel. You fear me and, like all inferior people, you will always fear something.

He was about to order them to stand aside when Yutaka said, "By the way, your old friend Chiba will be with us tomorrow when we go after the students at Tokyo University."

A sly wink from Yutaka.

An imbecilic grin from Kimura.

Two insufferable fools, thought Viktor. Each one born an ass and destined to die that way. Chiba hadn't set foot in the *dojo* in a week, not since the run-in with Viktor. No great loss, to hear some students tell it. These were the ones who made a point of letting Viktor know that Chiba had been a swine, a swaggering boor who'd finally received the knocking about he so richly deserved.

The single negative reaction had come from Park Yi, no great surprise to Viktor since Chiba had been one of the Korean's favorites. Together they attended baseball games, sumo wrestling matches, and motor bike races. Both drank excessively, were drawn to prostitutes, and enjoyed long evenings in *karaoke* bars, where patrons sang live to prerecorded music.

It was Park Yi who had recommended Chiba to one of Tokyo's major *yakuza* groups. Viktor's defeat of Chiba, therefore, had proved embarrassing to the Korean, especially since Chiba hadn't struck a single blow in his own defense. For Park Yi this meant a loss of face with mob bosses, now said to be reluctant to accept his recommendations of new members. This stain on Yi's honor was blamed squarely on Viktor, the Russian bastard. And the Korean, as Viktor had come to learn, was not the type to forgive or forget.

He was now cool and distant toward the teenager. Even the offer to join the student bashers had come through Yutaka. When Yi did speak to Viktor, it was to harshly correct so-called mistakes in training. Viktor wasn't cowered by these criticisms. The Korean was simply getting hot-headed over what had happened to one of his toadying bootlickers. It was enough to make Viktor wonder if Yi's feelings for Chiba didn't go beyond those of brotherly love.

Tonight Viktor had come to the *dojo* to confront Yi, to stand his ground and go head to head with the arrogant blowhard. However, the Korean wasn't there, leaving Viktor to work out his frustrations on other *karateka*. This he did with a fury that left a few of them shaken up. Yutaka, the squeaky voiced windbag, had been in charge. He had opened the training hall, collected dues, and conducted the class in his usual self-important manner. When Viktor asked him about Yi, the balding little biker said the Korean was off doing a special job for a very important businessman. Then Yutaka, usually quite talkative, suddenly went silent and looked away. Viktor understood. If there was going to be trouble between Yi and the Russian bastard, Yutaka knew which side his bread was buttered on. He was squarely in the camp of Park Yi, his lord and master, his connection to a lucrative job in the Tokyo underworld.

Viktor didn't give a damn if Yutaka and all of Japan snubbed him from now until judgment day. He was used to getting the cold shoulder and being treated like a leper. That's why he'd learned never to rely on others or circumstances. Others were unreliable, circumstances uncertain. He preferred to be in charge of his own actions. He never wanted to be subject to the whims and caprices of others.

He left the *dojo* annoyed at Yutaka and Kimura for having delayed him long enough to miss the 9:15 tram from *Ikebukuro* station. Trams were scarce this time of night; the next one wouldn't be along for another hour. Yutaka and Kimura had invited him to join them at a bar near the *dojo*, an invitation Viktor had gladly declined. He had nothing in common with those lamebrains, since he never touched alcohol, tobacco, or women, and had no intention of ever doing so.

It was almost eleven o'clock when Viktor stepped from a quiet alley lined with wood and paper houses, then walked the last few yards to his home. Under a new moon, he placed his shoes on the doorsill, pushed aside the *amado*, an outside sliding door of thin boards, and stepped into a darkened front room. A *hibachi* in one corner offered the only light, its burning charcoal casting a pale red glow over a portion of the *tatami* covered floor. Mustn't wake Grandmother, thought Viktor.

He supposed that his grandmother had probably grown tired of waiting for him and was now asleep in the back room, a picture of a *baku* under her pillow. Bearlike, with shiny fur and a small, pointed head, the *baku* was a mythical animal who ate unpleasant dreams, guaranteeing one a peaceful sleep. Grandmother Akashi said the *baku* always ate her nightmares, and she refused to go to sleep without a picture of one beneath her head.

He looked down at the hibachi, expecting to see his supper being warmed, eagerly anticipating a promised meal of broiled eel and steaming hot rice. Instead he saw a battered black teakettle, the only kettle they owned. Strange. It wasn't like Grandmother to go to bed without first making sure he had enough to eat. She pampered Viktor, bestowing on him the attention and indulgence due a favored child. *Why hadn't she left food out for him?*

On the floor near the kettle were cups, saucers, hand towels, and an unopened packet of green tea leaves, all neatly arranged and apparently untouched. Viktor's grandmother always prepared tea for anyone dropping by to consult her. This evening she'd been expecting Mr. Taira, a minor official employed by a large Tokyo bank. An old customer, Taira had sent her a note impressed with his *mitome*, family seal, saying he had to see her at once on a matter of some urgency. The note contained nothing about his problem. He did, however, insist on seeing Grandmother Akashi tonight.

Viktor hadn't bothered hanging around. He'd met Mr. Taira on several occasions and found him to be a sad-looking little man who seemed to be waiting for the tears to flow. Absolutely no danger to anyone. The bank official was middle-aged and small, with a shiny forehead, eyebrows joined at the top of his nose, and a fondness for black-and-white polka-dot ties. He was also very respectful of Grandmother Akashi, usually bringing her generous gifts of food and cash. In the past he'd consulted her on building a new home and on selecting a surgeon for his wife's mastectomy. He'd also taken her advice and cancelled his daughter's wedding to a man later arrested for theft and arson. Mr. Taira's loyalty to Grandmother Akashi was strong and unwavering.

Kettle, teacups, hand towels. Exactly where his grandmother had placed them hours ago.

Was something wrong?

Perhaps Mr. Taira hadn't kept his appointment. If so, then Viktor's food should have been warming on the *hibachi*. Or had Grandmother suddenly been taken ill? A bit concerned about her, Viktor switched on a bamboo floor lamp and called her name. He blinked, adjusting his eyes to the pleasant diffused light coming from behind a gray lampshade hand-painted with silver cranes in flight. He was about to call her again when he looked at the *tokonoma*. Always orderly and precise, Yosano Akashi kept a vase of arranged flowers and a hanging picture scroll in the alcove. Both were now on the floor, the scroll ripped to shreds, the water from the flower vase darkening the *tatami*.

And the footprints. They led from the alcove to the back rooms. Some lout had worn shoes into the house, a disgusting thing to do. Shoes touched the earth and were made unclean, and unclean things didn't belong in the home. Viktor's eyes hardened and a vein throbbed in his temple. He clenched both fists until the knuckles whitened. None of this would have happened had he been here. If he'd skipped practice and stayed home, he'd have taken care of the intruder. Viktor would have gone berserk, make no mistake about it, and whoever had walked on the mat with shoes and torn apart the *tokonoma* would have wished they've never been born.

If he had been here.

An unthinkable idea started to worm its way into his brain, an idea so dreadful it left him cold. Moving as though in a horrible, hopeless dream, he dropped his *gi* and ran toward the back of the small house. Stepping into a narrow, darkened corridor, he slid open the second door on his left. His grandmother's room. He moaned, a low, inarticulate sound of fear and grief at the sight of two bodies lying on the floor in moonlight coming through torn rice paper covering a small window.

Sobbing and breathing convulsively, Viktor stepped over the bloodied and battered form of Mr. Taira, then knelt down beside his grandmother. Whimpering in a low whining voice, he gently drew her dead body to him. He kissed the white hair now matted with blood, kissed the small, wizened face that had been beaten almost beyond recognition. Rocking back and forth, he repeated her name.

He had never hated being alive so much as he did at this moment. The silence around him, he knew, was to be a silence within him forever. Sorrow would never leave him; he would never be happy again. Grief now possessed him with a terrible power. It robbed him of everything—strength, intelligence, and above all, the wish to live. He was a frightened child once more, and he cursed himself for not having loved his grandmother more.

"Come back to me," he pleaded. "Please, please come back." He listened for her voice, expecting to hear it and knowing he wouldn't. He glanced at Taira's corpse, neat in a black suit and polka dot tie, not really seeing it. In the same way his eyes passed over the room and saw that *oshiire,* closets, had been torn open, and bedding and clothing tossed around. A sliding door which served as a divider between her room and Viktor's was partially pulled back, and he could see that his room had also been torn apart in a frenzied search. His books and notes on combat and torture had been scattered everywhere.

He continued kneeling on the floor, clinging to his grandmother and rocking back and forth and making a soft mournful sound deep in his throat. Bright eyes shimmering behind tears, he sorrowed alone in the darkness.

Giggling and a bit unsteady on his feet, Yutaka arrived alone at Park Yi's *dojo* shortly before midnight. The little biker was drunk and didn't give a damn who knew it. Inside the *dojo,* Yutaka slammed the door behind him. Switched on the light. Frowned as he tried to remember why he'd come here.

The note from Park Yi.

It had been delivered to Yutaka at a bar just up the street, a stool bar—no hostesses, no telephone, no television. Just a bar, several stools, and lots of cheap liquor. The messenger who'd delivered the note: a blind beggar. A stoop-shouldered old man with ulcerated sores on both ankles and missing most of his teeth.

An emergency, Park Yi had written. Police know we're coming after the students tomorrow. We must change plans. Come to the *dojo* at once. Will explain the new plan.

So the police had put their foot down. Yutaka wasn't surprised. The police didn't like the students, but they also didn't like Yi's boys joining the riots. Perhaps the police had warned Yi off.

Yutaka pushed himself away from the front door and staggered toward Yi's office. Had to get to the Korean's private toilet before the Korean showed his face, which could be any moment now. Yi didn't want anyone in his office when he wasn't there. Didn't want anyone poking around his private papers or walking off with something.

Yutaka made it to the small toilet and did his best to pee accurately. Mustn't let his golden shower touch the floor. And he prayed to the gods that he wouldn't get sick and heave all over the place.

He finished, flushed the toilet, then stepped to the basin. He looked in the mirror. Bloodshot eyes. Hair disappearing too fast. Face as gray as a snake's belly. He cupped his hands, filled them with cold water, and bathed his face, thinking he was damned clever to have tricked Mr. Viktor Poltava, the Russian bastard. Kept him here in the *dojo* just like Park Yi ordered. Delayed him long enough to miss his train. "Do whatever you have to," Yi had said, "but make sure he doesn't catch that train." Yutaka had done it, no thanks to Kimura the dimwit, who almost gave the game away. Damn fool. Poltava wasn't stupid; for one heart-stopping second Yutaka thought the Russian had caught on.

"Taira has to be neutralized," Yi had said. "He knows too much. He could send an important man to prison. And if Taira's talked to the old woman, to his *miko*, then she knows too much. She has to be neutralized, as well." Yi hadn't said anything about being afraid of Viktor Poltava. All he'd said was, things would go better if the Russian weren't at the house. "See that he's kept away."

Yutaka finished bathing his face, then dried it with his shirttail, vigorously rubbing his temples to get the blood circulating. Had to be alert when Yi arrived. But he still felt light-headed.

Dizzy. Who cares, he thought. Let Yi tell me the new plan, then I'll return to the bar and my buddies and I'll drink until I'm booze blind and cross-eyed and seeing two moons and they have to put me to bed with a shovel. He giggled and looked into the mirror. And saw Viktor Poltava.

Yutaka blinked. Shook his head. Had to drive *that* reflection from his mind.

But Viktor Poltava, the blue-eyed Russian bastard, refused to disappear. He continued to stare back at him. Yutaka's throat went dry. He had a strong feeling of dread, something he was powerless to avoid. He forced himself to smile. And began to feel sick to his stomach.

He started to turn, mouth opened to speak. Viktor kicked him in the base of the spine, sending the little biker crashing into the basin, pain tearing at every nerve in his back and brain. The collision with the basin made him vomit, and he doubled over, head down in the bowl. Viktor punched him in the kidneys, once, twice.

Yutaka's head snapped up, and he sprayed the mirror with half-digested food. Showing no emotion or feeling, Viktor kicked him in the back of the right knee, dropping Yutaka to the floor in a sitting position. Before Yutaka could cry out, Viktor knelt behind him, slipped his right arm around the biker's neck, and pulled back hard, forearm cutting into his throat.

Yutaka gagged. His face turned red. His eyes grew glassy. Then Viktor eased the pressure. Just a bit. Yutaka's breathing was raspy.

Viktor said, "I know why you and Kimura kept me from leaving the *dojo*. Now tell me who ordered you to do it. And why."

Park Yi was furious. He slid from his Nissan, slammed the car door behind him, and quickly walked the few steps to his *dojo*. That drunken little shit Yutaka. He'd telephoned Yi saying the *dojo* was on fire. Pulled him out of a sound sleep, screaming in his ear to come quick. "You have to save what you can." Well, Yi was here and the *dojo* was not on fire. No smoke, no flames, no fucking fire. When he got his hands on Yutaka, the bastard was going to wish he'd never been born.

He'd probably been out drinking with his mates. Gotten as drunk as a lord. Then somebody had bet him that he didn't have the balls to call Yi and get him down to the *dojo.* Yi was going to break every bone in his body. After tonight, the biker would choose victims of his pranks a lot more carefully.

Yi should have known nothing was wrong when he turned onto the street and saw the beat cop strolling back to the *koban,* the small police post found in every neighborhood. The entire street was as quiet as a graveyard. By the time Yi drove up to the *dojo,* he was beside himself with anger.

The *dojo.*

Front door open. Corridor light on, which was a waste of Yi's money. Something else for Yutaka to answer for. At least Yutaka and his stupid friend Kimura had managed to keep Poltava away long enough for Yi and Chiba to dispose of Taira and the old woman. The witch, Chiba called her. He'd hated her on sight, blaming the old woman for the beating he'd suffered at her grandson's hands. A beating that had humiliated him in the eyes of the *yakuza.*

It was the *yakuza* who'd asked Yi to kill Taira and Poltava's grandmother. "We're simply messengers on this one," the mob bosses had said. "We're speaking to you on behalf of Mr. Andōs, whom you have previously done some work for." The mob bosses then went on to remind Yi how important Andōs-san was, that he was a banking official who knew how to take care of his friends, meaning he laundered money for certain businessmen, politicians, and, of course, the *yakuza.*

It was now time for Andōs's friends to take care of him, and this could be done by killing Mr. Taira, the little man who wore polka-dot bow ties. As long as Mr. Taira lived, Andōs stood a very good chance of going to prison, a fate to be avoided at all costs.

Why did Andōs-san fear this shy, inoffensive man?

Both worked at the same bank, where Andōs was Taira's superior. Unfortunately, Taira had discovered, quite by accident, that his superior was an embezzler. Andōs was using the stolen funds to purchase money orders, cashier's checks, and treasurer's checks, always in modest amounts to avoid arousing suspicion. Checks and money orders were then deposited in dummy accounts in Hong Kong, Seoul, and Singapore. These accounts were then used to buy bearer bonds and securities in Europe. The money was now untraceable.

The hard-working, modest Mr. Taira did not wish to bring dishonor upon the bank he'd served so loyally for so many years. To find a solution to this difficult problem, he'd sought out Poltava's grandmother. It was no secret that he'd relied upon the *miko* in the past and considered her to be divine.

Yi knew how valuable Andōs was to the *yakuza*. No one could move money around the world easier than a banker, and the underworld had plenty of money to move. Yi himself had acted as a *yakuza* courier on occasion, carrying cash to Hawaii, Hong Kong, and once he'd gone as far as San Francisco. As for Andōs, Yi had bodyguarded him when the banker received kidnapping threats from the Japanese Red Army. Yi suspected the threats had nothing to do with the JRA, that they'd come from small-time hoods out to get rich in a hurry. Yi had kept the banker alive and made a pretty penny doing it, even though Andōs tried to hide the fact that he disliked Koreans. Goddamn Japanese. Quick to let you know how much they thought of themselves and how little they thought of everyone else.

Yi didn't mind doing the *yakuza*'s dirty work. The pay was good, and it gave him a chance to get in with the mob, to call on them should he need a favor. The granting of such favors eased the dark journey of life. As for Chiba, the *yakuza* had ordered him to work with Yi on this Taira business and use this chance to redeem himself. And let nothing go wrong.

"We have promised Mr. Andōs secrecy," the *yakuza* said to Yi. "Taira is to carry his knowledge of Andōs's affairs to his grave. And the old woman is to carry to her grave anything Taira may have told her. Search her home for notes she may have made of conversations with Taira. Collect every scrap of evidence that might betray Andōs. Leave nothing behind. One disgrace leads to another."

Mr. Andōs had made arrangements to be on holiday in Macau when the killings took place. As far as he was concerned, his burden had been shifted to someone else and he was free to pursue his life as he saw fit. All the advantages of this world were his; he lived in that particular class called privilege. He viewed himself as a peacock in a world of sparrows. And in his view, sparrows such as Taira and Poltava's grandmother were subject to consumption.

• • •

The *dojo*. Yi walked along the corridor to his office, calling Yutaka's name and cursing him for not answering. Couldn't wait to get his hands on that bloody drunkard. He'd have Yutaka's balls for cuff links.

Ahead Yi noticed that the door to his office was open. The office was dark, but there was a light coming from a small toilet set in the wall behind his desk. The toilet door was slightly ajar. Perhaps Yutaka was inside, kneeling over the procelain throne, flinging his dinner in every fucking direction. Yi was about to do a little flinging of his own.

He ran to the office and to the toilet, yanked open the door and found Yutaka nailed to the inside of the door, hands and wrists fastened to the wood. His ears and tongue had been removed and also nailed to the door. There were deep gouges in his face, across his forehead, eyes, and down his cheek and neck. It was as though he'd been clawed by an animal. Or a demon.

Park Yi's blood turned cold. He considered himself to be a hard man, able to face any situation in life no matter how frightening. But nothing had prepared him for this. Absolutely nothing. He began to shiver as though standing naked in deep snow.

He could not tear his eyes from the horror that was Yutaka. And he never saw a dark figure step into the doorway of the toilet and stand watching him. Suddenly Yi flinched. He'd just become aware of the shadow now covering Yutaka's corpse. The dark figure. Yi turned toward it. Too late. The figure kicked him in the balls.

Eyes bulging. Yi dropped to his knees in pain. He sucked in air through his open mouth, instinctively fighting against passing out. Seconds later, he collapsed on his back. He fought for breath, tried to rise, tried to focus his gaze. And found himself unable to move. Found himself looking up at a *demon*.

Yi shook his head to clear it. But the demon remained in place. A muscular, stocky figure wearing only a demon mask and tiger-skin loincloth. Barefoot. With claws.

Lifting his right leg, the demon brought his heel down on Yi's nose, crushing it. Yi rolled away and, calling on all his strength and training, got to his knees. But the kick to his balls had severely weakened him and, before he could stand, the demon kicked him in the head, sending Yi flying backwards. Almost unconscious, the Korean rolled over on his stomach, again trying to stand, tasting his own blood and knowing his jaw was broken. But the demon was on him, a knee pressing down hard between Yi's shoulder blades and keeping him in place. Yi's arms were then yanked behind him and his thumbs quickly wired together.

With one foot, the demon flipped Yi over on his back and knelt beside him. A dazed Yi truly believed he had been attacked by a real demon because no man could kick that hard. The pain in his balls was unbearable. Nor would his head stop throbbing. And the wire around his thumbs had sliced into the flesh, cutting off circulation in his hands and lower arms. And he feared the demon's claws. No they weren't claws. They were *kitchen forks bent in half*. Kitchen forks with bloodied prongs.

Seating himself on Yi's chest, the demon pressed a hand down on the Korean's mouth. Then he pushed the prongs of one fork against Yi's temple and slowly raked the fork across his forehead, gouging the head to the bone. A wide-eyed Yi attempted to buck the demon off and failed.

Jamming the same fork into the flesh near Yi's eye socket, the demon slowly pulled it down to the jawbone. Again Yi attempted to throw off the demon. Again he failed.

The demon took his hand from Yi's mouth and quickly raked the bloodied fork across his lips, then once more covered the Korean's mouth. And still the demon refused to speak.

Now the demon touched the bloodied fork to Yi's right eye, but did not press down.

The hand came away from Yi's mouth and the demon said, "Where is Chiba?"

A terrified Yi shook his head violently. "I do not know. I—"

The hand was pushed down over his mouth and the bloodied fork pushed into his eye the barest fraction of an inch. Yi thrashed about like a wild man. The demon remained in place on his chest.

Again the hand came away from Yi's mouth and again the demon asked where Chiba was.

Yi spoke quickly. "Whore. He is with a whore, but I do not know which one. He has so many since he became *yakuza*. I swear this is true. Swear it is true. Tomorrow. You can find him tomorrow at Tokyo University. That's when he, we are supposed to attack the students."

The demon remained silent. Then he covered Yi's mouth and,

with a fork, clawed at the Korean's ear until he'd torn off the lobe. Next, he clawed at a corner of Yi's mouth until he drew blood, then hooked the fork into one of Yi's nostrils.

Yi kicked, whimpered, pleaded with his eyes. Blood ran down his face and onto the demon's hand. Keeping the fork hooked in Yi's nostrils, the demon said, "Tell me about the man who ordered you to kill my grandmother."

Tokyo University. The student rally began in front of the Yasuda lecture hall around noon. This was the university's main building, the gift of a wealthy businessman, and the building occupied by rioting students four years ago in 1968. At that time it had taken almost nine-thousand riot police with helicopters, tear gas and the assistance of fire fighters to drive them out. The students fought back with clubs, bricks, and burning beams. Although they were defeated, the building was no longer usable. Now it was an empty shell, an ugly reminder of the bitter resistance to the university's ties to the business world.

Today over three-thousand students had gathered to hear a group of militants lead a protest against a major car manufacturer, whose industrial robots had accidentally killed two female factory workers. The militants claimed robots were literally removing human labor from the face of the earth. We're speaking for those Japanese workers who fear for their jobs, said the militants. Those workers were becoming alarmed over the increased use of robots, who were quick, undemanding, precise, and performing at a much lower cost than humans. Businessmen and politicians, however, were highly in favor of robots, seeing them as another chapter in Japan's economic success story, the greatest such story in the world's history.

Privately, certain businessmen said that anyone denouncing the miraculous industrial tool that was the robot should be considered a traitor. And traitors should be punished. Punished severely. They should be forced to wear the yoke of their wrongdoing.

It was warfare. And the students were prepared.

They protected themselves with cyclists' helmets and shields. And they fought with staves and bottles, bricks and chains, hands and feet. They fought club-swinging police whose faces were hidden behind acrylic helmets. And they fought the *wolf dogs*, Yi's boys, who yielded lead pipes.

Noise from the campus riot was loud and prolonged, an ear-splitting din of incoherent curses, roars of defiance, screams of pain. It was a crashing wave of sound that seemed capable of toppling buildings. It was the cry of those who had grown savage, who had chosen violence for their rhetoric, who had abandoned reason.

Chiba fought with a temporary madness. He stayed close to Kanda, the emperor's former bodyguard, a wiry, long-headed man with a scarred nose. Together they led a handful of *wolf dogs* toward the student leaders. They hacked their way through student spectators until they reached the platform. Four policemen stood between them and the top of the platform. Chiba and the others ruthlessly cut them down. It was Chiba who led the way up the small staircase to the student leaders.

Top of the staircase. Chiba stopped to catch his breath. One arm was bleeding, his shirt was torn, and there was a slight pain in one shoulder where he'd taken some sort of blow. But all of it, the pain, the blood, the noise, left him with an unspeakable satisfaction. He wondered if there were not some sort of pleasure in being mad.

He looked across the platform. Five people down. Two were crying out; the others were unconscious and bleeding. Two of those were policemen. Chiba counted six students still able to fight, one masked by a motorcycle helmet. Leaders or bodyguards, it didn't matter. The *wolf dogs* would lay waste to them all.

He watched Kanda and the moronic Kimura go after the student who wore the motorcycle helmet and whose weapon was a *nunchaku*, a pair of foot long pieces of wood connected at one end by a four-inch chain. But to Chiba's horror the masked student disposed of both fighters with frightening ease.

Dropping to one knee the student whipped an end of the *nunchaku* between Kimura's legs, striking him in the balls. As Kimura dropping shrieking to the platform, Kanda stepped past him and attacked. He was a trained professional, good enough to have served the emperor and more than good enough to deal with the bookworm in front of him. Kanda was no Kimura.

Kanda leaped to his right, a fake. Just as quickly he leaped left and backhanded the pipe at the student's rib cage, fully expecting the blow to land and break a few bones and make the bookworm wet his pants. It was a good tactic. Kanda had used it successfully more than once.

The masked student ignored the fake and when Kanda leaped to his left, the student dropped stomach down on the platform. The blow passed over his body, missing him completely. Still prone, he swung the *nunchaku*, wrapping the free end around Kanda's ankle. Yanking hard, he pulled the leg out from under the ex-bodyguard, sending him flying, arms and legs flailing in the air.

Leaping to his feet, both sticks of the *nunchaku* in one hand, the student clubbed the fallen Kanda in the head. When a wobbly-legged Kimura attempted to stand, the student whacked him in the face with the *nunchaku*. Kimura dropped like a stone.

Poltava. The name sprang into Chiba's mind, rooting him to the spot. His mind was so jarred that for a few seconds he forgot where he was. *The masked student was Viktor Poltava*. Chiba was at once amazed, horrified, and elated to see the Russian bastard in front of him. From this point on, nothing else existed for Chiba; he was now consumed by a single thought: to kill Poltava or die.

As Viktor prepared to turn, he was struck from behind and there was a terrible pain in his right side. The blow knocked him to the platform; the *nunchaku* went flying. Instinctively he rolled away from danger, head bouncing awkwardly across the wooden slats, and came up standing. He looked around for weapons and saw none. But he saw the wild-eyed Chiba rushing toward him, shrieking to give himself courage and to frighten Viktor.

Viktor yanked off his crash helmet and threw it in Chiba's face, striking him in the forehead, forcing him to stretch both arms out sideways to maintain his balance. For a few seconds he was defenseless, out of control, and in that time Viktor killed him.

He punched Chiba in the balls, then snatched the iron pipe from his hand and clubbed him in the head, knocking him to the platform. Chiba lay at Viktor's feet, bleeding, moaning and making no resistance as Viktor squatted, lifted the *wolf dog* up, and cradled him in his arms. A second later, Viktor dropped to the platform on one knee, bringing Chiba's body down on the upraised knee and breaking his spine.

Someone hit Viktor from behind, the blows landing on his shoulders, back, head, and on his broken ribs. He spun around, arms high for self-protection, saw two policemen, each with a long staff, and he charged them both, enraged beyond words that they had stopped him from fully destroying Chiba. Was Chiba dead? It didn't matter. Viktor's rage was not depleted. He had not concluded his business with this villain who had murdered his grandmother. Anyone attempting to stop him from having his revenge risked a sharp reprisal.

He took a few more blows from the policemen, not caring about the pain because he wanted to punish them for coming between him and Chiba. Viktor and the two policemen were wrestling now; and at close range, the long staves were useless. Viktor kneed one cop in the groin, causing him to drop his staff. Then he drove his heel into the second cop's instep, wrested his staff away, and turned it against the two of them, swinging wildly, striking the cops on the helmet, the back, the legs, and knocking them down.

Viktor opened his eyes; he was on his knees, propped up by the staff. He'd almost passed out. Bleeding and in great pain, he tried to stand up. He failed the first time. He tried again.

A girl was running toward Viktor. Two students were close on her heels. When they reached Viktor, he forced himself to his feet and backed away. He felt so weak. He wanted to flee, to get away, to be with his grandmother who'd know how to cure him.

He'd done what he'd come here for. Chiba lay a few feet away. *Hai*, he was dead. That would have to be enough.

Viktor felt hands lifting him to his feet. He'd passed out totally this time. And he didn't remember speaking but he must have said something because the girl replied, "No, that is out of the question. You cannot go home. You will have to come with us. We will hide you."

One of the male students said that Viktor had just killed three policemen and would have to get out of Japan. *Three*. Viktor didn't remember killing three. But he looked across the platform and there they were. Three uniformed bodies lying near Chiba.

Viktor's head was in agony and it was an effort for him to breathe. Getting to his feet was impossible.

A student said, "You are one of us, brother. And we will repay you for what you have done here today. We are the *Rengo Sekigan* and we forget neither our friends nor our enemies."

Viktor pulled away from them and crawled toward the staircase. But the pain in his head exploded into a blinding light, and he fell face down on the platform, into a darkness that immediately became a greater darkness.

The Japanese Police launched an intense manhunt for Viktor Poltava.

Members of the Prefectural Police, Regional Police bureaus, the National Police Agency, and the country's four intelligence agencies received copies made from a photograph of Viktor found in his grandmother's home. Facts regarding his life history, education, martial arts training, along with fingerprints, dental records, blood type, and personal habits were fed into computers and stored in data banks. This information was then sent to Israel's Mossad, as well as to intelligence services in Europe, the United States, and Latin America. The KGB obtained a copy of Viktor's file from East German intelligence, which had gotten it through the efforts of an attractive secretary-spy planted in the *Bundesmt fur Verfassungsschutz*, West Germany's counterespionage service. Like western intelligence, the KGB was always interested in terrorists. Poltava's file listed him, erroneously, as a member of the *Rengo Sekigan*, the Japanese Red Army, among the most feared of all terrorist groups.

Charged with five murders, he was now one of the most wanted men in the far east. And he was half Russian. Yes, the KGB definitely wanted to know more about him.

After examining his file, the KGB ordered an investigation into Viktor Poltava's life and times. It was to be headed by Colonel Melor Feltsman, who was in his early fifties. A small, strong, bearded man, Feltsman was restless and lived on his nerves and made a point of walking upright in order to appear taller than he really was. In the grim, gray seven-story building that was KGB headquarters in Moscow, Feltsman saw the Poltava family enter his life for the second time.

Poltava was a familiar name to Feltsman; he'd used the father and other journalists in disinformation campaigns, getting them to plant false information, rumors, and altered facts in Asian newspapers. The father had also worked as a KGB courier. Feltsman had dropped him after catching the elder Poltava padding his expenses once too often. And there'd also been the matter of his drinking. Add that to a foul temper and you had someone who drew too much attention to himself. Feltsman had been happy to see the last of *Guzzle Guts*, the KGB's nickname for Poltava. No one in Moscow had been surprised to see him end up in prison.

As for the son, Feltsman's Japanese contacts reported a story that clashed with the one being circulated by Japanese police officials. Eyewitnesses confirmed the gruesome but interesting fact that Viktor Poltava had indeed killed five men during a student demonstration at Tokyo University. Three of the dead had been policemen. But contrary to official reports, the remaining two had not been students in pursuit of academic excellence. They'd been hooligans, thugs hired by a right-wing millionaire to silence student protests against capitalism, the lifeblood of Japan.

Another error or downright lie: Viktor Poltava was not a member of the *Rengo Sekigan*, the Japanese Red Army. *DGI*, Cuba's secret service, confirmed this. Nor was he a member of Italy's Red Brigades, Germany's Baader-Meinhoff gang, the PLO or IRA. He was not involved in any of the European, South American, or Palestinian urban terrorist organizations. *DGI* trained members of these groups in guerrilla camps partially paid for by the KGB.

Feltsman was certain that the Japanese Red Army would attempt to recruit young Poltava. The Russian-Japanese youngster seemed to be the sort of suicidal fanatic the organization preferred. Japanese terrorists did their recruiting among the most extreme left-wing students and had simply crossed paths with Poltava on that fateful day, a fact police had twisted to suit themselves.

Feltsman also learned the following: Young Poltava's grandmother, of whom he appeared to be quite fond, had been murdered just hours before he'd gone on his killing spree. A Tokyo banking official had been slain with her. And then there were the murders of Poltava's karate instructor and a fellow karate student. Were these four killings somehow connected with one another? Feltsman, no believer in coincidence, was willing to bet two quarts of vodka that they were. A coincidence was a coincidence only to the ignorant.

He asked himself these questions: why the press silence over the deaths of Viktor Poltava's grandmother and the bank official Mr. Taira? Why, also, had there been no mention of the murder of the two karate men? And why falsely claim that Poltava was a member of the Japanese Red Army?

With the Japanese nothing was ever the way it seemed. Feltsman found them to be nothing more than economic animals and among the most illogical and inconsistent people on the face of the earth. A people with a talent for survival. Experts at being deliberately unclear or misleading.

Sensing hidden truths waiting to be uncovered, Feltsman applied himself more diligently to the matter of Viktor Poltava. He sifted through information from telephone calls, moles, informants, ciphered messages, bulging folders. He worked in his office and from the back seat of his chauffeured black Volga. On weekends he worked at his *dacha*, his comfortable country home in Peredelkino, a pleasant little village fifteen miles outside of Moscow. Here he chain-smoked Russian-made Marlboros, sipped vodka flavored with pepper leaves, and made notes in a small neat script. Whenever he grew restless or encountered an obstacle, he stopped and lifted weights until he was exhausted and could think better.

But in time his instincts were confirmed. The Japs, no surprise, were lying. Whether you called it disinformation or dirty tricks, it came down to a highly calculated deceit aimed at blackening the name of young Poltava. The purpose? To protect a Tokyo banker named Andōs, a man of more than relative rank in his native land. And rank had its privileges.

Andōs, Feltsman learned, was also an embezzler; to hide his crimes he'd ordered the murders of Poltava's grandmother and a co-worker named Taira. The business of removing these two from this world had been entrusted to a Korean named Park Yi, whose ties to the Korean CIA and certain Japanese fascists had earned him a page or two in KGB files. A karate instructor and gangster-for-hire, Yi was not the brightest of men. He was called level-headed only because he drooled from both sides of his mouth.

The story concocted by Japanese police had Yi and an accomplice murdering and robbing Poltava's granny and Mr. Taira, then having a falling out over the spoils. The accomplice, Fujio

Chiba, then eliminated Yi and another man who'd played a minor part in the crime. In turn, the disgruntled Chiba had himself been erased by a vengeful Viktor Poltava. Case closed. Leaving Andōs, the instigator of this unrighteousness, free to continue his role in Japan's irresistible economic expansion.

As for young Poltava, he was a convenient scapegoat. The warrant for his arrest charged him with the murder of Chiba and a man named Kimura, a pair of hooligans whom Japanese police insisted on listing as Tokyo University "students." With the exception of Poltava, no one else had been accused of a criminal act. Japanese capitalists, Feltsman observed, were held to be above all wrongdoing. When a rich man shits in his pants, the world calls it honey.

While stalking Fujio Chiba, Poltava had also found time to dispatch three policemen, a feat so prodigious as to inspire wonder. It would appear he had all the makings of a top-drawer assassin. Feltsman took special note of this fact; the KGB would always have the need or occasion to employ individuals possessing this sort of flair.

As for Poltava's whereabouts, he was in Iraq at a guerrilla training camp operated by the PFLP with KGB assistance. The PFLP (Popular Front for the Liberation of Palestine) trained, equipped, and financed the Japanese Red Army, which had smuggled Poltava out of Japan aboard a North Korean freighter. At present he was recuperating from his wounds and apparently grateful to the JRA for helping him avoid the police. Initial reports also said he was being indoctrinated in the Marxist-Lenin system of thought and had shown some interest in it.

Subsequent reports to Feltsman said Poltava had become thoroughly convinced that the class struggle was absolutely necessary to lead society from bourgeois democracy under capitalism to a socialist society under Communism. Simply put, Poltava wanted to kill not only Mr. Andōs but all the Andōses of this world. Grandmother's murder was going to be avenged.

KGB instructors in the Iraqui camp were enthusiastic in their praise of the young man. He was that rarity, a born assassin; one didn't run across his kind of talent that often. He was violent, remorseless when it came to seeking retribution, and had more than a modicum of intelligence. Handled correctly, he could be a valuable asset to the KGB.

Feltsman was surprised to learn that Poltava read constantly, particularly history, Marxist philosophy and books on the martial arts. He was obsessed by Sun Tzu's *The Art of War,* a work much admired by Feltsman who read it twice a year. Tzu's little book was 2500 years old, a very rational approach to the conduct and planning of military operations and still required reading among Russian officers. If Viktor Poltava was attracted to Sun Tzu, he was certainly no numbskull, something which could not be said of his late, unlamented father.

The thought of the elder Poltava undergoing the guerrilla training his son was now taking made Melor Feltsman chuckle. *Guzzle Guts* wouldn't have lasted two minutes; the son, however, took to it like a duck to water. Working alongside revolutionaries from a dozen countries, Viktor received six months of very rigorous terrorist training. And enjoyed every minute of it.

He ran six miles each morning before breakfast. Then came a minimum of four hours of physical training, which included hand-to-hand combat with North Korean instructors. From personal experience, Feltsman knew these instructors were neither gentle nor tender-hearted. They prided themselves on sending camp recruits to the field hospital. Viktor, however, proved to be a rude awakening for a pair of them; he sent one to the hospital with a fractured skull and gave the other a permanent case of kidney damage. He also showed a talent for weapons, excelling with pistols, automatic weapons, and grenades, though showing a preference for a small-bladed knife. Poltava, it would seem, had found his calling in life. He had found the ideal which justified his cruelty.

KGB officers at the Iraqui camp took a shine to him. He was flattered, showered with praise and given a few gifts. Very few, since the KGB was notoriously tight with money. He was fed the party line and appeared to have swallowed it hook, line, and sinker. Why all this attention for a pockmarked boy still wet behind the ears? Because the time to befriend a talented junior was *before* he became a star on the international terrorist scene.

The KGB flew him to Moscow for a brief course of study at Patrice Lumumba People's Friendship University. They attempted to keep Viktor away from GRU, military intelligence and the KGB's arch rival, but failed to do so. GRU pulled strings with the party and was allowed a brief opportunity to chat up the youngster. They, too, laid on the flattery by inviting him to a hand-to-hand combat session with *Spetsnaz*, their elite commando unit.

No one told him the invitation was really a test to see if this stocky man-child was as good as the reputation that had preceded him. *Spetsnaz*, Russia's toughest troops, had its own reputation to uphold; those men scheduled to practice with Viktor were in no mood to be defeated by a mongrel boy. Viktor, on the other hand, was in no mood to be tricked. He knocked two commandos unconscious and broke the shoulder of a third before the test was called off. The KGB was quite pleased.

Feltsman met him, finding Viktor to be an interesting if somewhat intimidating young man. Quick thinking and with an agile mind. Outsized energy, but the sort who played his cards close to the vest. More than a bit inflexible in his opinions, as well. Apparently without vices, a trait Feltsman found peculiar in a supposedly virile young man. Viktor had no interest in girls, little boys, alcohol, or drugs. Very self-contained, our little half-caste.

Feltsman and he lifted weights, dined together, spent a few hours on the firing range, and had long discussions about Sun Tzu's *The Art of War*. Feltsman found the Chinese philosopher's writing to be an enlightened and perceptive approach to the tactics of war. Viktor, one could say, was more pragmatic; he saw the book as a helpful guide to being ruthless. As Feltsman told his superior, it would not be going out on a limb to say that Viktor's aim in life was to destroy or oppress as many people as possible.

The KGB was certain that Viktor's Moscow trip was the first step in molding him to their will. He was an outsider, neither Russian nor Japanese, and they were offering him a chance to belong, to be accepted, to be *nash*, one of ours. Why shouldn't he accept such an honor? There was even talk of making Colonel Feltsman his control; he'd used the father, so why not do the same with the son?

Feltsman, however, declined the opportunity, pleading a heavy workload. In truth, Feltsman wanted as little to do with Viktor Poltava as possible. The half-caste was a madman, crippled in mind and possessed of a dead soul. Anyone who thought young Viktor was going to be easily manipulated was feebleminded. Better to walk a highwire in windstorm than spend time nursing the demon, as he was called. Young Viktor was trouble, the kind that could destroy a man's career if he wasn't careful.

Feltsman did his duty and mentioned this to his superiors, the *Icons* as they were known because of their arrogance, and he did so, knowing in advance what their reaction would be. They didn't disappoint him. They ignored Feltsman as he knew they would. All had been seduced by the thought of directing the destiny of the next truly accomplished assassin. Poltava was going to go great things; KGB careers were riding on this assumption. The *Icons* were bound for glory and intended to get there on Poltava's back. Was Feltsman blind? Didn't he see the possibilities?

What Feltsman saw were vain old men, short-sighted imbeciles who wouldn't recognize a sociopath if he pissed in their soup. Young Viktor was a ticking bomb, a conniving young man maniacally bent on self-justification and having absolute control of his life. "You cannot ignore his sadism," Feltsman said. "And what about the rumors that he carries around his grandmother's hair, along with her heart, which he has encased in gold?"

The *Icons* didn't want to hear any of this. Feltsman, they said, was no longer responsive to new ideas, new methods, new people. Perhaps it would be better if someone else took over the young man's life. Let someone nearer Viktor's age be his control.

Tell the truth and run, went the Yugoslavian proverb. Feltsman could do no more. Continued opposition to young Poltava was dangerous. It meant openly criticizing the *Icons,* and only a fool would do that. The *Icons* dealt with open criticism by calling it treason, punishable by death or imprisonment in a labor camp.

He had Mischa, his driver, take him to *Leninskiye Gory,* Lenin Hills, from where you could view all of Moscow. During the ninety-minute drive, Feltsman sat in the back of his Volga and drank from a quart of Vodka, thinking about the silly business of getting smacked about by the *Icons*. The more he thought about it, the wider his smile grew.

By the time he reached Lenin Hills, the smile was glued to his face. He knew the *Icons* had outsmarted themselves regarding Viktor Poltava and in the end it wouldn't be Feltsman who would be smacked around. He was going to survive because he was no longer involved with the demon.

• • •

Viktor's first action with the Japanese Red Army took place in Israel. He hadn't forgotten Mr. Andōs; revenge, however, would have to wait. The PFLP and Iraquis had to be paid for the training, weapons, and sanctuary given Viktor and the JRA. Paid, not in cash, but in armed propaganda. The Arabs wanted a violent incident to make their presence known to the world and call attention to their cause, the destruction of Israel.

Viktor and three JRA comrades were given a few weeks of special training at a PFLP guerrilla camp in Lebanon, then supplied with false passports and flown to Athens. From here they entered Israel as tourists, lost among thousands arriving on a cool March morning for the splendid rituals of Holy Week and Easter. They rode a chartered bus from the airport to the narrow cobblestone alleys of West Jerusalem, checking into a small hotel not far from *Via Dolorosa*, Way of Sorrows, the road Jesus was said to have walked carrying his cross from Praetorium to Calvary.

At the hotel they were met by Palestinians from Jordan and Lebanon, who gave them semi-automatic pistols and grenades. They also received further details on the target and on the escape route to Syria.

In the afternoon Viktor and his JRA comrades left the hotel, each carrying a camera case as they walked beneath ancient archways and past bazaars and old churches until they reached the *Via Dolorosa*. Here they pushed their way into a crowd of Franciscan fathers leading pilgrims in retracing Christ's steps along the dark, narrow street. On Al-Wad Road, the terrorists turned left and walked toward a group of French tourists boarding a chartered bus. When they were almost on the tourists, the terrorists opened their camera cases, removed pistols, and fired from point blank range. The attack was a Palestinian response to France for selling fighter planes to Israel.

As panic-stricken spectators tried to escape, Viktor and the others emptied their pistols into the screaming French. While two comrades reloaded, Viktor and a baby-faced terrorist named Osami tossed grenades through shattered bus windows. Then all of the JRA terrorists ran along Al-Wad Road, toward a side street yards away where four men on motorbikes waited to speed them out of the city.

With the approach of the fleeing terrorists, the motorbikes turned over with a single roar. And then the roar was swallowed up in the sound of exploding grenades. Neither Viktor nor his three comrades turned around.

Slamming a full clip into his pistol, Viktor led the run for the motorbikes. But the crack of gunfire forced him to look over his shoulder and he saw Osami writhing on the ground, bleeding from both legs. Their leader Itoh, a thin, bespectacled leftist, lay sprawled across an overturned chair in front of a sidewalk cafe, his pistol dangling from lifeless fingers. The third comrade Nagano, the handsome son of a Kyoto judge, had stopped, wasting valuable seconds to stare at his fallen brothers. Then he decided to shoot at two khaki-clad policemen now crouched behind an overturned table near Itoh's body. Tearing his gaze from the dead Japanese, Nagano raised his pistol and was shot in the head and chest.

The weak defend, the strong attack, Sun Tzu had written.

Viktor stepped toward two Bedouin women in caftans who cowered near a boutique, motioning with his pistol for them to stand. When the weeping women refused, he kicked them into position between him and the policemen. Along the street, traffic had come to a halt; on the sidewalk, people lay face down or crouched in doorways. Viktor, an arm around the throat of one woman, his shield, pushed his pistol into the second woman's side. All three backed away from the police, who could do nothing.

Viktor thought about stepping into the street, using donkeys, small cars and bicycles as cover, but decided the police would do the same, so he kept to the sidewalk, pulling the women with him and keeping his pistol at the ready, not caring about the women who shrieked in Arabic and wept. When the two cops left the shelter of the overturned table and started toward him, Viktor tightened his grip on one woman and shot the second in the head.

The cops froze. As Viktor knew they would.

He backed toward the side street and the roaring motorbikes, dragging his last hostage with him, the pistol jammed against her neck as he watched drivers abandon their vehicles in the rush to get out of his way. For the first time in his life he was experiencing the power that came from the barrel of a gun. Such power, he decided, was the only pleasure. And the only good.

•   •   •

Viktor's debut as a terrorist won high marks from all revolutionary groups involved in the people's war and from the KGB, as
well. JRA leaders immediately ordered him to participate in several international operations in Europe and Asia. It would be
years before he returned to Japan.

During that time he and JRA members teamed with PFLP to
hijack and blow up Japan Air Lines planes in Manila and Kara-
chi. In Manila, television news cameras filmed Viktor shooting
the plane's pilot in the neck, then tossing his corpse onto the
runway. In the takeover of Japan's embassy in Kuwait, Viktor
strangled the wife of the Sri Lankan ambassador; to save the lives
of others in the embassy, Kuwaiti authorities met the JRA's demands for money and a plane to Damascus.

In West Germany, Viktor and the JRA worked with the
Baader-Meinhoff gang in placing pipe bombs at the American
Army's 5 Corps headquarters in Frankfurt, killing three officers
and wounding twenty-five enlisted men and civilians. This oper-
ation was in retaliation for the American bombing of North Viet-
nam. If European comrades hated American imperialism, the
Japanese hated it even more. The North Vietnamese were their
Asian brothers, and the JRA not only wanted America out of
Vietnam, but wanted American support bases out of Japan as
well.

In Rome Viktor and the JRA teamed with the Red Brigades in
an attempt to kidnap a Japanese businessman and hold him for
ransom. They rammed his car, but when the businessman tried to
flee Viktor was forced to shoot him. Other kidnappings of Japanese and European businessmen and diplomats were more successful, earning the JRA and fellow revolutionaries millions of
dollars in ransom. Marxism was Viktor's religion, his reason for
joining the JRA. His commitment to the People's War on capitalism was total.

After each operation he found sanctuary in Palestinian training
camps in Libya, Lebanon, Syria, Iraq, and North and South
Yemen. He used this time to recover from wounds and familiarize
himself with new weapons while memorizing new codes and im-
proving his language skills. He met revolutionaries from around
the world and instructed them and Palestinians in hand-to-hand
combat. Alone in his tent, he studied Sun Tzu. And spent long
hours thinking of his dead grandmother. In his mind he punished

Andōs hourly. These were private moments when he asked to be left alone. Private moments when no one saw him weep.

To those JRA comrades training with Palestinians in the Middle East, he was a hero. To comrades in Japan, he was mythic. All took pride in his victories against the pig police and capitalistic oppressors in different nations. Every revolutionary held Viktor the demon in high regard, giving each Japanese terrorist a sense of worth. His glory was their glory.

From one training camp to another, all hailed his devotion to the cause of socialism. His devotion to his grandmother earned high praise as well. In time she became a socialist heroine in her own right, an honor based on her having been a victim of capitalism. JRA comrades kept Viktor up on Andōs the banker. Whenever Viktor decided to suppress—kill—Andōs, Palestinian and European revolutionaries stood ready to help. Viktor had only to ask.

He smiled and quietly thanked those who had offered their help in this matter which was so important to him. Life was fortified by friendships, and it was gratifying to see his comrades declare their love. But behind Viktor's mask of a face lay a silent truth: He had become too feared to be ignored.

Kamakura, Japan

June, 1975

Yuneo Andōs's breathing was shallow, more forced than it had been just minutes ago. Asthma. Not fatal but it could be disruptive.

In his garden he removed a small inhaler from his kimono and placed the nozzle in his mouth. Two puffs and the wheezing stopped. He continued pruning a tiny red maple tree, one of several bonsai on wooden shelves attached to the bamboo fence enclosing the small garden. The tree, Andōs's favorite, was in a silver tray, its roots clinging to a thin layer of damp earth. It had been in his family for over six-hundred years.

Bonsai, miniature trees, were dwarfed by pruning, wiring, or limiting their space. The desired shape could never be achieved through the efforts of one man, no matter how long he lived or how expert his touch. Andōs's ancestors had patiently and gently shaped the red maple over many lifetimes. When he died, one of his two sons, probably the eldest, would pick up where he left off. A bonsai was beauty and a reminder of the uncertainty of life. It was also a living connection with the past, something revered by all Japanese.

Pruning the red maple was a way for Andōs to take his mind off Mifune, his beloved miniature collie. The dog had disappeared three days ago. Police couldn't find a trace of him, which left Andōs depressed because he was quite attached to the animal. Mifune, bless his soul, was a good fellow. Loyal, affectionate, and always grateful for any kindness, no matter how small. Andōs blamed his wife for the dog's disappearance, cursing her every day the dog was missing. She bore this abuse as she did all of his tyranny, with patience, forbearance, and a quiet dignity. After so many years with him, she had come to realize that in their relationship he knew no rules except his own selfishness.

It was almost sunset when he finished wiring two branches on the red maple. The next thirty minutes were spent pruning his fruiting bonsai—crabapple, persimmon, and chestnut trees—and then it was time to light the pair of stone lanterns at the garden entrance. On this last day of August it was time to rest, to enjoy the peace of this beautiful town and smell the sea which was only a twenty-minute walk away.

Hai, he was fatigued, which his wife said made him cranky and hard to live with. He ignored her comments, since women never reasoned and were ignorant of most things in life. But he had to admit that gardening could leave him with a shortness of breath. And doctors had warned him that even the mildest exercise might trigger an asthma attack or muscle spasm that could trap stale air in his lungs and keep out fresh air.

Andōs, however, was like most Japanese; he was hopelessly addicted to gardening, holding it to be one of life's indispensable pleasures. The sliding door between his garden and house was kept permanently open, allowing the empty doorway to frame the garden as though it were a lovely landscape painting. He prided himself on being Japanese, for they were a fortunate race, one deserving of beauty.

Andōs's worst asthma attacks were those he suffered in Tokyo, where he lived most of the year. In the summer he fled fifty kilometers south to Kamakura, a green valley surrounded by rolling hills and sandy beaches. This was old Japan, with dozens of temples, shrines, and back lanes lined with exquisite Japanese homes surrounded by bamboo fences. That was even a little old, slow-moving local train straight out of the past, with three green wooden cars that bounced along narrow tracks and was a delight to ride.

The only drawback to Kamakura were the densely packed beaches in summer, along with trainloads of visitors who came each weekend to visit the *Daibutsu*, the giant bronze Buddha that was over eleven meters tall and twenty-nine meters wide. The inside was hollow, with a staircase leading to the shoulder level. Because he found it difficult to breathe in crowds, Andōs hadn't visited the *Daibutsu* in years and probably would never go again.

At his age, a walk on the beach was as much as he could hope for. He had retired from banking, leaving him and his wife free to spend as much time in Kamakura as they wanted to. Their sons were grown, living away from home with families of their own. As for money, his savings, investments, pension, and what he'd stole from the bank was more than enough to afford him the modest luxuries he had come to depend on. All in all, he'd gotten what he wanted from life and had outlived his mistakes. But then he had been the architect of his own good fortune, which had almost been swept away by a meddlesome little man named Taira and an old woman whose name Andōs couldn't even remember. It was preordained from eternity that those two die and allow him to live out his last days in peace.

Andōs sat in a beach chair and sipped green tea as he stared at the flickering flame in one of the lanterns near the garden entrance. He felt content, at peace. He had conquered unhappiness and could live out the rest of his days within sight of the sea. He was seriously thinking of selling his Tokyo home and moving here to Kamakura permanently. Since he wasn't working, why did he need a Tokyo home at all?

He had money, property, and a wife he no longer had to beat because she now had the good sense to obey him instantly and without question. His sons respected him, and he didn't miss the hurly-burly of Tokyo and banking as much as he thought he might. The only reason for possibly visiting Tokyo would be to pay a visit to an old mistress with whom he'd spent many happy hours. At the moment, however, there was nothing more he could ask of life. Except, perhaps, to get Mifune back. Tomorrow morning Andōs was going to telephone the police and demand they find him. He missed that little rascal. An evening walk along the beach just wasn't the same without him.

Andōs felt a tug on his sleeves and opened his eyes. He'd dozed off. The flickering yellow flame in the stone lantern, the smell of sea air, the garden. All of it had relaxed him and he'd fallen asleep with a half-filled teacup still on his lap. Now he looked up to see his wife, her head bowed, apologizing for disturbing him but the police had come. They stood behind her. Two young men in gray jackets and trousers, with white shirts and black ties. Very smart looking.

Andōs dismissed his wife with a wave, ignoring her as she backed away with her head down. Nothing here for her. Police talk was man's business. A woman couldn't possibly understand it. Both officers bowed their heads in respect. In return, Andōs gave them only a slight nod. He was impatient. Let them get on with their business.

Good news. Mifune had been found. The little collie was outside in the police car. He was a bit frightened and he'd lost weight. Otherwise, he was doing just fine.

A delighted Andōs pushed himself out of the beach chair and shook hands with both officers. He would show his appreciation in the proper manner, he said, but right now he wanted to see his dear Mifune. He was sure the officers understood. They did.

Andōs led the way from the garden to the house, removing straw sandals before stepping into the living room and hurrying to the front door where he put on a pair of clogs and walked outside. He ignored the police; they didn't need his help to retrieve their shoes from a shelf at the entrance of his home. All he could think about was his beloved Mifune.

His heart pounding, Andōs walked toward the white police car. One hand was in the pocket of his kimono and on the inhaler. The excitement of seeing Mifune again could trigger an asthma attack.

A third policeman waited at the car. He was stocky, muscular, and wore his cap pulled low on his forehead. His eyes were hidden by dark glasses. Seeing Andōs, he opened the back door of the car and waited.

At the car, Andōs rudely pushed past the stocky cop and looked inside at the back seat. Expecting to see Mifune, he started to call the dog's name, then stopped because the back seat was empty. *Empty*.

An angry Andōs looked over his shoulder, ready to demand some answers of the stocky cop. In that instant the cop stepped closer and injected him in the thigh with a hypodermic needle. Andōs pushed at the cop with both hands. A waste of time.

He lost consciousness just as the other two officers entered the car.

From atop a steep green hill, Viktor stared down at Kamakura's main street, a tree-lined avenue leading from the statue of the Great Buddha to the sea. It was almost dark; except for a handful of strolling lovers and the odd beachcomber, the beaches were empty. Lights were being turned on, and Viktor could hear the faint sounds of temple bells calling monks to evening prayers.

He stood in the shadow of a cedar tree, half hidden in darkness with only his bare legs visible. His two JRA comrades were also concealed; they sat in the front seat of the squad car parked just off a narrow dirt road. Thirty yards of tangled underbrush and trees separated them from Viktor.

There had been a bit of sunlight when Viktor, carrying Yuneo Andōs over one shoulder, had led the way through the undergrowth to a clump of cedar trees overlooking the sea. Then he had ordered his comrades to return to the car and wait for him. He would handle the rest alone. No one had to be warned about spying on him. He was Viktor the demon, as skilled at inflicting punishment as a surgeon with a scalpel.

In the growing darkness he stared down at the lights of Kamakura, remembering his grandmother had come here often as a little girl. Her parents had loved the sea air and also wanted to see the Great Buddha. Once they had taken her to the *Zeni-Arai Benten* shrine, where she'd followed the custom of washing her money in its sacred waters. All she'd had were a few coins, she'd told Viktor, but she'd washed them anyway because the ritual was supposed to make her money double in value. Had her money doubled? Viktor had asked. No, she said. She'd lost it all the same day. The two of them had laughed over that.

He moved away from the cedar trees and walked a few feet to the grave he'd dug yesterday. A coffin, uncovered, rested beside the grave. Inside the coffin, an unmoving Andōs. Arms folded across his chest. Eyes closed. Flies buzzing around his open mouth. Viktor squatted beside the coffin and stared at Andōs. And waited.

Andōs stirred.

The injection was wearing off.

Good. Because Viktor wanted him to know. All of this would be wasted if he didn't know.

Andōs opened his eyes. And saw a demon. Long white hair, demon face, tigerskin loincloth. Andōs blinked, becoming more awake and frightened out of his wits. For a few seconds he was petrified; he couldn't move. Couldn't breathe. Then he began to shake with fear; he wept, he whimpered. A sudden, sharp pain in his lungs only added to his terror. An asthma attack was about to start.

He attempted to sit up, but the demon placed a hand on his chest and roughly shoved him back into the coffin. Pinned him there. And with the other hand he picked up something from the ground and dropped it on Andōs's face. The former banker gagged, convulsing as he struggled for air because the smell of the damp, furry thing was repulsive and vile beyond words. Absolutely detestable.

He immediately felt nauseous, sick to his stomach at the feel and odor of the thing. But when he attempted to push the stinking, loathsome thing away from him and felt the fur, the small snout, and tiny paws, he realized what it was and he screamed, squirming around in the coffin as he shoved the body of his dead collie down around his feet. He managed to raise himself to a sitting position, coughing loudly, great racking coughs that painfully stabbed his lungs and filled his eyes with tears. He jammed a hand in his kimono pocket, desperate to find his inhaler and cortisone pills. They were gone.

He panicked, succumbing to an overpowering fear, wanting air, wanting to flee. And then the demon again shoved him back into the coffin, pulled the coffin lid from atop a nearby pile of earth, and fitted it to the top of the coffin. Andōs kicked and scratched the lid, screaming for his life, pleading for his inhaler, breaking his nails against the lid and feeling an unspeakable horror as the knowledge of what was about to happen became a grim reality.

The demon's strength was immense. Overwhelming. He kept

the lid in place and secured all the locks, doing everything as he'd planned. When all the locks had been tightened, the demon spoke to Andōs. "She was the only person who ever loved me," the demon said. "You should not have killed her."

Viktor pushed the coffin into the grave then picked up a shovel and filled the grave with earth. When he'd finished, he covered the site with cut branches and twigs. For a few minutes he hunkered down beside the grave and stared at it in silence, and soon he began to weep, silently at first, then he moaned aloud. His hands caressed a small, hard object that glittered as it caught the moonlight. It was the size of a human heart and was covered in gold. Viktor squeezed it and sobbed.

The sounds of his grief were heartrendering; they echoed in the dark wood and floated toward the sea. Then, suddenly, he became silent. But he remained crouched over Andōs's grave for more than an hour, never moving, never speaking.

Then he stood up, removed the demon costume, and put it, along with the gold-encrusted heart, into a rucksack. Minutes later he had changed into the policeman's uniform and was staring up at the moon, his eyes glistening with tears. It was the last time Viktor would ever weep.

8

Tokyo

1982

BECAUSE SHE LOVED her only son with a terrible and generous passion, Reiko Gennai chose Viktor Poltava to avenge his kidnapping.

Before contacting him, she paid a ransom of four million American dollars to the kidnappers, a Hong Kong gang called the Big Circle. Then she waited until her son Hanzo had sufficiently recovered from a three-week ordeal of captivity that had begun during a business trip to Hong Kong. She took him in her arms and vowed to punish those who had put the two of them through such agony. It was important that he show himself to be stronger than those who had injured him. He was her son. He must never be struck without striking back.

But her son opposed hiring Viktor Poltava. "He is too much his own man. These days he is accountable to no one," Hanzo said. "He is on a course marked out for himself, and we have absolutely no way of controlling him. I find the man too uncommitted and therefore too dangerous."

Viktor Poltava was no longer a terrorist. He was now a professional killer, an Asian "Carlos the Jackal," for hire to Taiwanese generals, Thai businessmen, Singapore bankers, South Korean industrialists, Golden Triangle druglords. His service with the Japanese Red Army and other urban guerrilla groups was behind him. These days he murdered for money and had been known to charge as much as a million American dollars for a single killing.

Reiko Gennai said, "Poltava is not the danger. The danger lies in allowing yourself to be dishonored and to do nothing about it. I have chosen you to succeed your father as head of *Mujin*. He is old and grows weaker every day. He cannot live much longer. You will take his place because I wish it to be so. But if you are to sit in his chair, you must make yourself feared and respected, particularly by those who might think to harm you. Remember the story of young Julius Caesar."

Hanzo nodded. It was one of his mother's favorites, and she never tired of telling it.

"When Caesar was a boy, he was kidnapped by pirates and held for ransom," said Reiko Gennai. "His kidnappers found him amusing and quite the delightful little fellow. No one took him seriously when he promised that he would one day hunt them down and hang every man. But when the ransom was paid and he was free, that is precisely what he did."

She smiled, taking her son's face in her hands. "So it shall be with you. I intend to see that this kidnapping business becomes a glorious incident for you, my son. In its own way, it will help gain the *Mujin* presidency for you. The incident and your reaction to it will never be publicized. But people shall know of it. Oh, they shall, my darling. And in future, anyone who even dreams of showing you disrespect will be forced to think twice. Leave Mr. Poltava to me, my son."

"I think you are playing with fire," Hanzo said. "No one controls Poltava. No one."

"I can. I can control any man. Have I not done so?"

"He is different, this one. It is my feeling that any relationship with him will cost us dearly in the long run. I do not like the idea of him getting too close to us."

"Dear Hanzo, did I ever tell you that every individual or situation has a particular tone, a certain essence? To achieve control, it is necessary to seize and manipulate this essence. Take our Mr. Poltava. He is obsessed with violence."

"I would say so, yes."

"And he has great pride."

"And he works for money," Hanzo said.

She nodded. "Exactly. So we have three links in the chain. Violence. Pride. Money. The correct reading of any of these links will help you to understand the entire chain. Oh, I understand him well enough, my son. And more importantly, I do not fear him. My sole concern is that men fear you. And they will not do so if you refuse to avenge your kidnapping."

Hanzo stroked his withered left arm. "No one knows of the kidnapping. You kept the news away from the press. We need not be embarrassed—"

She touched his lips with the tip of her folded fan, silencing him. "My beloved son, your kidnapping is also an insult to *Mujin* itself. To me. And no one insults me. No one. Now leave Poltava to me. I know quite a bit about our little demon."

Reiko Gennai's knowledge of Viktor Poltava lay in a single copy of a long, detailed report hidden in a safe whose existence was known only to her. It was in the basement of her Tokyo villa and had been installed by a Frenchman imported from Nice. He had done the job while her husband was out of the country on a business trip, working eighteen hours nonstop. During that time all servants had been ordered out of the villa. And the Frenchman had been paid in cash.

Two weeks after returning to Nice, the Frenchman was found dead in the back room of his locksmith's shop, the apparent victim of a drug overdose. The secret of the safe now belonged exclusively to the Empress.

As for the report, Poltava's sadism leaped from its pages. He was truly a demon. He appeared to relish the role of a strongman, going after defectors and informants with unbridled enthusiasm, and disposing of them in rather horrid ways.

He was no less a psychopath today than he'd been a few years ago. The demon had changed in only one respect—he was no longer a political innocent anxious to destroy the rich. Ideologies and creeds now impressed him as nonsense. The Empress didn't find this too surprising. Personality disorders aside, Poltava was quite intelligent.

In his mind the revolution had failed to achieve any political aims or attract popular support—the dream of all terrorists. Furthermore, no revolution could succeed so long as its goal was to join capitalism rather than confront it. The PLO had become a financial giant with assets worth billions of dollars. What was once a commando unit was now a government with an army, air force, and tax collectors.

The Empress agreed with Poltava. He'd done enough for his Bolshevik chums; it was time to look out for number one. You had to admire a man inclined to mold his life into some form of his own choosing. Such men, she told Hanzo, were rare. Very rare.

But in his new life the demon could not afford to let his guard down, for he'd accumulated more than a few enemies. Israel, West Germany, Italy, England, and America, not to mention Japan, all had reasons to see him dead. And there were his former comrades, some of whom considered him a traitor for having left the movement. Even the Russians had become disenchanted with Poltava. After all, he'd murdered a KGB officer, an action not designed to warm Soviet hearts.

The Empress found this incident fascinating, for it showed how effective Poltava could be when facing seemingly insurmountable odds. The KGB was known for exacting revenge on traitors, defectors, enemy moles, and especially anyone who terminated its agents. In Poltava's case, however, it had done nothing. And wasn't about to do anything.

After eliminating one of its officers, the demon knew the KGB would seek retribution. So he had sent a letter to KGB Moscow headquarters at Dzershinsky Square. Should they attempt to kill him, he wrote, he would start killing the children of KGB officers stationed at Russian embassies around the world. He would strike anywhere: Beijing, Cairo, Rio de Janeiro, it didn't matter. True, the KGB might catch him eventually, though there was no guarantee of that. Meanwhile, any number of Russian children would die very painful deaths.

After careful deliberation the Russians did the only sensible thing. They took the demon at his word and let it be known that the business of the KGB officer would be overlooked. Hanzo said this was proof of Poltava's insanity. Mother, however, had the last word. It was her right to return evil for evil. She would not rest until Hanzo's kidnappers had been dealt with.

"You cannot rule a kingdom and be innocent," she said. "You survive only by being as harsh as necessary, by acting in spite of the pain it may cause you or someone else. You must hear and be deaf. You must see and be blind. Confide in no one, trust no one, depend on no one. Be easy to serve and difficult to please. But unless you enforce your will, you cannot hope to command. Poltava will let the world know that your will is strong, that you are fit to join me in ruling *Mujin*."

To locate the demon, Reiko Gennai contacted Nuan Chakri, a captain in Thailand's para-military police force. For years he had been in the pay of Chinese generals who grew opium along the Burma-Thailand border. He was also paid to look the other way by airlines who flew the opium and other contraband out of Bangkok. The Empress paid him to keep her informed on everything from the state of the King's health to the problems of the country's rubber crop.

And it was Chakri who helped her to discipline troublesome *Mujin* wives. To control company executives, Reiko Gennai selected their wives; at the same time, she ordered the women to spy on their husbands and report to her. Those who refused or who betrayed her in any way were taken to Thailand where Chakri injected them with heroin until they became addicts. To feed drug habits, these wives were then forced to work as prostitutes in brothels and massage parlors Chakri owned in Bangkok's Patpong Road.

At the Empress's command, Chakri appeared in Tokyo for a talk concerning Viktor Poltava. Chakri had connections among Asian opium dealers, gun runners, Hong Kong investment brokers, and Macau gamblers, people who had used the demon to relieve select individuals of their lives. She knew Chakri, a small, dark, bowlegged man, could find Viktor Poltava. And she ordered him to do it.

"I assume you do not want me to mention your name to him."

She nodded.

Chakri slowly shook his head. "It won't work. I will do as you say, you know that. But Poltava—well, let me say he is the one who likes to call the tune. No matter how hard I try to keep your name out of this thing, he will learn the truth. He will learn it is you and not me who wants these Chinese people dead. Perhaps it has something to do with his being part demon."

"All seeing, all knowing," Hanzo said. "Can he levitate as well? And he is no demon. He is a man. Flesh and blood like the rest of us."

The Empress said, "Leave Poltava to me. You find him, then tell him who it is that must be killed. Pay his price without arguing. If and when he becomes curious about me and my son, then I shall take action. I do not believe in poisoning my life with anxiety. To give in to fear is to become powerless. Fear comes from uncertainty, and I am never uncertain. I see no problem with Poltava."

Yes, Poltava was shrewd, she thought. He was a creature who trusted his own instincts in everything. But neither he nor anyone else was strong enough to force her to become consumed with thoughts of her own safety. She feared no one. She'd handled difficult men before. Clever men. Rich men. Powerful men. None had gotten the best of her. And neither would Viktor Poltava.

Two weeks after the Chakri meeting, Hanzo came to his mother with a problem. He was being followed by a man on a motorbike. No, Hanzo couldn't see the man's face; it was hidden behind a crash helmet and visor. The whole business left him feeling uncomfortable, especially since he still had nightmares about his recent kidnapping. And even when he didn't see the man on the motorbike, Hanzo still felt he was being watched. When he left his home. The office. The golf course. It was a feeling he remembered from being kidnapped, when his captors watched his every move. When his life was controlled by them to the extent that he had to ask permission to pee.

The Empress was sympathetic. Poor Hanzo. She understood. Of course the Hong Kong experience had been terrible. And he was working long hours and he was upset over his wife's third miscarriage. She would never again conceive, physicians said. This was a tough blow to Hanzo, who wanted so much to be a father. Naturally, he would have to divorce his wife and marry someone who could give him sons. "Leave that to me," the Empress said. "I will find the appropriate wife."

As for being followed, who did Hanzo think might do such a thing?

"Viktor Poltava," he said.

His mother studied his face. Her eyes narrowed as she concentrated on his every word.

Hanzo said, "Poltava is a great one for strategy, is he not? He devours Sun Tzu, who is the master of strategy. He always works from a plan, is this not so?"

She nodded. "Go on."

Hanzo massaged his withered arm. "I think he wants to know our strengths and weaknesses. His strategy for dealing with the Gennais begins with knowing all there is to know about us. I am positive he is the man on the motorbike. Somehow he has learned that Chakri works for us. I know this is so. I know it."

"According to you, then, the demon knows our identities."

"*Hai.*"

She smiled. And said nothing for a long time. "I am not surprised."

"You expected this?"

She nodded.

A clearly frightened Hanzo said, "What do we do now?"

"Nothing. The mistake is clearly his."

"I don't understand."

"He has made his first mistake in dealing with me. Assuming he is the man you claim is following you, then I can only say he has revealed more about himself than he should have."

"What has he revealed?" Hanzo asked.

"He has shown me that he can be counted on to react, especially given the proper stimulus. Most men react; they do not reason. Nor is it always wise to rush to get ahead of others, my dear one. It would be just like Poltava to rush to learn all there is to know about people who have hired him. He is a creature of habit, after all. But he makes himself visible when he comes this close to us. A risky tactic, yes? And have you noticed something else about our demon?"

A fascinated Hanzo shook his head.

"He is a man addicted to preparation," the Empress said. "He will not move without carefully laying the groundwork in advance. Our little demon absolutely depends on preparation." Smiling, she leaned forward and whispered, "I wonder how well he would fare were he forced into action without any time to prepare. Think of that, my son. Think of that."

Using a handkerchief, Hanzo dabbed at his perspiring forehead. "How do we handle him now that he is in Japan?"

"We do nothing."

"Nothing?"

"Any action on our part would only alert Poltava and, once alert, he changes course. He shifts tactics. No, let us keep his feet on what has become a very predictable path."

"I'm not sure—"

"I am. Let us accept the fact that Poltava is watching us. Why? To confirm that we are who we say we are. He still has enemies, remember? So let him satisfy himself that he is not walking into a trap. We are in no danger from him. None at all. If you saw him then obviously he was not being overly cautious. No, he doesn't see the Gennais as a threat."

"I hope you're right," Hanzo said.

"I *am* right, my son. We will not let Mr. Poltava know we're on to his little game. No warning. We give him no warning. Should it ever become necessary to oppose him for any reason, I would like to think he remains predictable in certain areas. Let him live by his plans and strategy. Experience will teach him that he is not master of this world. He will come to learn that life always modifies one's schemes. It is important to know how to wait. Mr. Poltava will come to see this. If he lives, that is."

Two weeks later, Reiko Gennai handed her son a copy of an English language newspaper printed in Hong Kong. It was one day old and she had encircled a small personal ad on the front page in green ink. The ad read: *Package two days late. Send receipt to Bank of Geneva, c/o Mr. Longman.*

A coded message from Chakri, the Empress said to Hanzo. Poltava had agreed to work for them. Price: Two million dollars. Payable in advance to the Bank of Geneva, the account of Mr. Longman.

"So the punishment has begun," Hanzo said. He looked uneasy.

She shook her head. "No. Justice has begun." She looked pleased.

• • •

Eighteen days after the money was wired to Geneva, an unmarked envelope was hand-delivered to the Empress at her Tokyo home. Inside were press cuttings from two English language newspapers printed in Hong Kong. The cuttings were almost a week old and told of the deaths of three leaders of the Big Circle Gang. One had been poisoned to death in his favorite restaurant. Another had been found in the trunk of his car, his throat cut and eyes gouged out. The third had been thrown from the twentieth-floor apartment of a mistress who had been strangled to death. Police suspected a gang war or an attempt by young Turks to push out the older mob leaders and take over.

"How many more of these Chinese gangsters will he kill?" Hanzo asked.

"Does it matter?"

"You seem satisfied with what he's done."

"Very."

"And father? You have told him, haven't you?"

"Of course." She put down one of the cuttings and picked up another.

"What did he say?"

"He said what he usually says. He told me to do what I think best. Which is exactly what I have done."

"Everything near a rotting fish stinks. Poltava is that rotting fish."

She pushed aside the cuttings. "He takes orders from me and that is all he does. The axe strikes the chisel, the chisel strikes the wood. I am the axe, he is the chisel."

Hanzo fingered the cuttings. "Will you use him again when this business with the Chinese ends?"

She closed her eyes briefly, then opened them and looked at him. "The future is uncertain. Who is to say what my needs will be in a month, six months, a year? I am sure of this: I will do anything to protect *Mujin*."

"Would you yoke yourself to a demon, my mother?"

How far would Reiko Gennai go to maintain her position at *Mujin?* The question had been answered during the final hours of World War II when she plotted with young Warren Ganis to murder his parents, when she took part in the slaughter of western prisoners in the secret prison camp. When over the years she blackmailed, manipulated, threatened, and killed anyone who threatened her husband's position at *Mujin*, thereby threatening her as well.

Poltava? He was only the means to an end. He was hired to cool the dishes so that she might eat the food. Looking ahead, she saw a battle emerging over who would succeed her aging husband Yasuda, a man whose body and mind were losing their vigor every day. The only person she could trust to follow him as leader, and whom she could control totally, was Hanzo. Unfortunately, Yasuda had doubts about Hanzo's leadership ability and was leaning toward his own godson as successor. Hanzo was too soft and boneless to suit his father, who'd been quite ruthless in his day.

At the moment the fight for the presidency was not so acute. But if Yasuda's health took a sudden turn for the worse, the vultures would be out in force, picking his bones clean and staking their own claim at the presidency. Nor would they be too kind to Reiko Gennai, who had used her power harshly, a power that would disappear with her husband's retirement or death. Hanzo had to succeed his father, or she would be destroyed by her enemies.

Would she yoke herself to a demon? She'd already done so, and the demon's name was power.

She was a captive of her ambition and had come to learn that it was the enemy of peace. It was too late, however, for her to be free of that ambition or to question her methods of fulfilling it. She could only deal with the challenges to her hunger.

The greatest challenge of her life would be to win the *Mujin* presidency for Hanzo. No previous task would be as critical. Or carry so severe a penalty for failure. She would need every weapon at her command to beat back those who would trample her husband's grave in the rush to make an end of her. In Poltava she had the means to deal with the most intense hostility.

Mujin was worth embracing a demon.

9

England

August, 1985

ON A RAINY, almost chilly afternoon, Viktor Poltava walked along the dark hallway of a seedy, tumbledown hotel in Soho, London's largest foreign quarter. One hand gripped the handle of a small battered suitcase; the other held a shopping bag from a Japanese restaurant on nearby Gerrard Street. The shopping bag contained his marketing, including copies of eight London newspapers. The suitcase held his night fighting clothes—black trousers, shirt, hooded mask, high-top sneakers. Plus his demon costume, grandmother's heart, and an extra belt knife. And it held the manuscript and private papers of Oliver Coveyduck, the Englishman he'd killed last night.

Had Poltava left the suitcase in his room, it might have disappeared during his absence. The hotel guests were a sleazy lot—prostitutes, old-age pensioners, Bengali students, Maltese pimps, Chinese living ten to a room. The sort who made a habit of finding things before you lost them.

Soho. Narrow, dowdy streets crammed with striptease clubs,

porn book shops, inexpensive Chinese and Italian restaurants,
wine shops, and the city's liveliest open air fruit and vegetable
market. Poltava had chosen to stay here because the London safe
houses controlled by the Palestinians and his former European
comrades were off limits to him. It was unlikely he'd be welcome
in these places or even recognized.

He was now thirty, older than most revolutionaries who were
usually thumb-sucking babies more interested in seeing their
names in the paper than in leading a normal life. And there was
the operation on his face, which he'd had done in Damascus
several weeks ago. It had changed his looks. Not radically, but
enough. The dyed hair, slight weight loss and brown contact
lenses also added to his new appearance.

Soho. Thousands of Asians living here were the perfect cover
for the Eurasian looking Poltava. And the hotels, bless them,
asked no questions of their guests. On checking in this morning
he'd shown a Portuguese passport, one of four he carried. No
problem. The desk clerk, an obese, balding Cypriot, barely
glanced at it.

As for Soho itself, Poltava found the emphasis on lurid pleasures disgusting. And if the smells coming from the cheap take-
away restaurants was anything to go by, the food was inedible.
On his first trip to London nine years ago, Poltava had made the
mistake of trying a Scotch Egg, a hard-boiled egg encased in
sausage meat, rolled in breadcrumbs, deep fried, and eaten cold.
Absolutely foul. He'd eaten half of it, gotten sick, and vomited.
A French comrade had been on target when he said, wherever an
Englishman sets foot, cooking dies.

In front of his hotel room Poltava put down the suitcase and
shopping bag, then crouched in front of the door. He touched the
lock with a forefinger, looking for the hair he'd placed over the
keyhole. Still there. He reached down near the base of the door
and pulled out the small piece of folded newspaper he'd shoved
between the door and floor. Then he stood up and ran his fingers
between the top of the door and the doorjamb. He smiled. The
two folded bits of newspaper were exactly where he'd left them.
He'd had no visitors.

He entered the small, almost bare room, closed the door behind him, and looked around. Listened. Cash deliberately left on

a night table appeared untouched. Twelve British pounds, six American dollars. Not much, but enough to tempt an intruder. A cheap sports jacket and a pair of trousers were visible in the closet where he'd left them. A pair of black shoes was still under the bed. Nothing in the room was missing. Poltava had not become the victim of atrocious deeds.

He was hungry. First he made himself comfortable by stripping down to his white boxer shorts, carefully hanging his shirt and trousers in the closet and placing his running shoes under the bed. Then he sat on the edge of the bed and wolfed down a carton of fried soybeans mixed with vegetables and seaweed he'd purchased from the Japanese restaurant.

He ate a second carton of soybean curd, not as fast this time, and followed that with fish broth, wheat flour dumplings, and a carton of rice cooked with small pieces of chicken. For sweets he ate three buns stuffed with sweet bean paste and a half dozen thin pancakes stuffed with sweet red-bean paste. He washed it all down with green tea mixed with roasted popped rice which gave the tea a smoky flavor. It was his first proper meal in days. During that time he'd lived on dried survival foods, which while nutritious, didn't have the savor of real food. Poltava found little in life more pleasant than eating.

He leaned back against the pillows, sipped tea, and read the London newspapers. Only three mentioned Lord Coveyduck's death. The stories were small, but these were the early editions, and the information had probably come in too late to get a big play. Lord Coveyduck committed suicide, two papers said. Coveyduck's home destroyed by a fire of suspicious origin, said a third. This one also said that Coveyduck himself had been found dead in the ruins of his once-magnificent home. No mention of murder or suicide here.

Poltava grunted in satisfaction. It would appear he'd covered his tracks well. He'd hoped to delay a murder verdict on Coveyduck until he'd left England. Delay it so that police wouldn't be on guard and make it difficult for him to get out of the country. Apparently he'd done just that. He'd broken Coveyduck's neck, then knotted two sheets together and hung Coveyduck from a beam in the converted barn that had been his home. Then Poltava had set fire to the barn. And left an illusion in place of reality.

As for the two English policemen he'd been forced to kill,

Poltava had put their bodies in the squad car and driven it a mile
or so from Coveyduck's home. He'd parked the car on a deserted
dirt road in the shadow of a giant elm tree, then cut the sleeve
from one policeman's jacket and stuffed it into the gas tank. A
touch of a lit match to the sleeve and it became a fuse. He'd then
started running and didn't look back when the car exploded. Another mystery for the British police to ponder.

He wasn't foolish enough to think he could put anything over
on the authorities for long. But he could confuse them. Slow
down their investigation. Misdirect their efforts and buy time.
Time to get out of England before authorities knew they were
looking for *Oni* and mounted an all out search. Eventually they'd
learn that Coveyduck and the two cops had been murdered. But
by then Poltava would be in America, disposing of the three
people who posed a problem for the Empress.

He skimmed over Coveyduck's papers. Quickly at first, then
slowly. Letters, notes, memorandums. All dealing with the Englishman's book on *Mujin* and Warren Ganis. Poltava had expected this material to be dull. It wasn't. On the contrary, he
found it quite interesting. Wonderfully malicious.

The Gennai family and Warren Ganis had cause to worry. War
criminals, Coveyduck called them. Murderers who'd killed his
wife and over ninety other westerners held captive in a secret
World War II prison camp. Greedy businessmen who'd bribed
and corrupted any number of people in an elaborate plot for economic supremacy, a plot that had begun forty years ago when
Yasuda Gennai, *Mujin*'s president, lured a twelve-year-old Warren Ganis to Japan.

Poltava's own investigation of the Gennai family had not been
nearly as detailed as the information that had somehow ended up
in Coveyduck's hands. The assassin's curiosity was definitely
aroused. Setting aside the notes and letters, he picked up Coveyduck's manuscript and began to read. Well, what have we here.

After a while he sat up in bed, still continuing to read, still
engrossed in what he was reading. He smiled. No wonder the
Empress insisted that the Englishman's papers and manuscript not
be mailed to her, but instead be hand-delivered to Warren Ganis
in New York. He was to turn everything over to her son Hanzo,
scheduled to visit America on business. Coveyduck's book and
notes were nothing less than explosive. At the very least the book

would cost the Gennais and Warren Ganis millions of dollars. At worst, it could send some of them to prison.

It pleased Poltava to learn that Warren Ganis had dirtied his lily-white hands in the prison camp massacre. This captain of industry had a filthy side to his nature. Poltava found him to be a pompous ass, conceited and puffed up with self-love. Too aware of his position; he needed to be reminded that his position had been handed him on a plate by the Gennai family and he held it at their pleasure. Wealth and influence aside, Mr. Ganis was little more than _Mujin_'s pet monkey.

Give him his due; the monkey had served his Japanese masters well over the years, using his newspapers, magazines, and television stations to spread the gospel according to _Mujin_ throughout America. Coveyduck had come within a hair of exposing this cozy relationship. A sleeping misfortune had almost been awakened.

Poltava's introduction to the Empress had convinced him it would be wise to learn everything possible about her and _Mujin_. She was a clever woman, and clever people preyed on others. As for _Mujin_, it existed by exploiting others and plundering the universe. What Poltava had first uncovered about her and the company had led him to view both as indestructible. Coveyduck's book, however, was changing his mind.

The Englishman had put it all down in black and white. The Empress's role in the forced drug addiction and sexual enslavement of those _Mujin_ wives who displeased her. Warren Ganis's role in the disappearance and murder of his second wife. And there were "accidental" deaths that Coveyduck claimed were actually murder. The Thai journalist who'd tried a bit of blackmail regarding the heroin-addicted _Mujin_ wives on Patpong Road. The Taiwanese banker who'd mismanaged a secret _Mujin_ account. A New York police detective who'd gotten too curious about the disappearance of Ganis's second wife. Poltava smiled. He had arranged these "accidents" at the request of the Empress.

He had nothing to fear from the book's publication; his reputation had already been established. Poltava had been known for his works long before Coveyduck ever decided to put pen to paper. Others, however, stood to suffer incurable wounds if this book ever saw the light of day. Farewell to Warren Ganis's dream of purchasing the Butterfield newspaper chain. Farewell to Reiko

Gennai's rule at *Mujin* and to her dream of having her son succeed his father as company president. Farewell to thirty million
dollars of *Mujin*'s money, the cost of trying to acquire the Butterfield properties. There was going to be more than enough misfortune to share.

Unless . . .

Enter Viktor Poltava. He'd already disposed of Lord Coveyduck. That left the Jew, Meyer Waxler. And the Greek wiretapper, Aristotle Bellas, along with his fat daughter Sophie. Three
men and a nervous woman who'd been harmless until they'd
come across information that could crush Reiko Gennai. And
ruin the American press lord who hopped to her command.
Blame this on someone who called himself *Aikuchi*, Hidden
Sword.

Laying the manuscript aside, Poltava swung his feet to the
floor and stared across the room at nothing in particular. At first
he listened to the rain, then he began drumming on his thighs
with his fingers. Thinking. He knew a bit about informants,
about individuals like Hidden Sword. The people's war had its
share of those bastards who could hurt you when they started
talking to police.

He hated these turncoats who couldn't be true to anything.
Why did they do it? For revenge. Or to cut a deal with police and
save themselves. Some did it for a feeling of power. Others did it
for money. Almost all of them were bloody madmen who were
better off dead. Poltava had willingly killed his share.

Why did Hidden Sword want to destroy the Empress and
Mujin? Why the obsession to bring down Warren Ganis? Poltava
shook his head. Not for money. Definitely not for money. The
Empress was a tough customer. You opposed her only if you
were committed to total, all out war. Poltava has seen such commitment in revolutionary comrades, and they had not been the
type to do anything for money. They acted as they did because
they were fanatics, uncompromising true believers who were
more dangerous than starving tigers. This sort was never moti-
vated by money. Only a Johnny-come-lately to the movement
went to sleep counting dollar signs, and in the end he or she made
a poor revolutionary.

Was Hidden Sword under police pressure? Poltava thought
not. Were that the case, all information would have been going to

police instead of to an American journalist and an English eccentric. Since Coveyduck—and Poltava—were convinced that Hidden Sword was Japanese, any official pressure for information would logically come from Japanese police. But it was unlikely that the Japanese government would allow *Mujin* to be investigated for any reason. Japanese corporations had the protection of the country's leaders. The government also ignored any and all war crimes, an infuriating attitude to those Asian countries who'd suffered under the Japanese military machine.

Was Hidden Sword interested in power? Possibly. It was no secret that Yasuda Gennai, *Mujin*'s president, was dying. Suppose a company executive had decided to challenge the Empress and make a run for the top spot. Such a man would have to be unique, smart as well as courageous, resourceful, and with access to all company secrets. Such a man was Tetsu Okuhara, Yasuda Gennai's godson. Okuhara had once been the Empress's lover, the affair ending on a bitter note. Did Coveyduck and Hidden Sword know this? Poltava did.

If Okuhara was Hidden Sword, why should he damage the company he wanted to control? Because that's exactly what Hidden Sword was doing. Exposing Warren Ganis meant the end of *Mujin*'s powerful press arm. It meant investigations by the American Congress, FBI, the CIA. It meant the American press would be sniffing around Ganis like hyenas around the carcass of a dead lion. Did Okuhara really want this? Poltava had to wonder if Hidden Sword's motive really was power. The assassin shook his head. His instinct said the motive wasn't power.

In truth, anyone at *Mujin* could be the traitor: a security guard the Empress had abused once too often; an ordinary clerk with access to computers and data banks and with a desire to hurt someone; a trusted servant who wanted to see the mighty brought to their knees; a *Mujin* executive who was fed up with bowing down to the Empress; someone related to a *Mujin* wife who'd been sent to Bangkok's Patpong Road.

Revenge. Steepling his fingers under his nose, Poltava gently rocked back and forth on the edge of the bed. Revenge. The most likely reason of all. Why? Because the Empress was the sort of woman who inspired inexhaustible hatred. How many people had been frustrated at their inability to defeat her? Hatred was the only pleasure left to the frustrated; it had more power than love.

With love, you surrendered. With hatred you carried on for a long, long time. Hatred was the coward's revenge.

Poltava rose from the bed, scratched his stomach, and walked to the closet. He took his suitcase from a bare shelf, opened it, and removed the hair he'd cut from Hanako, the Japanese woman he'd kidnapped and punished aboard the Empress's yacht. Returning to the bed, he sat down on the edge and spread the hair across his thighs. It was dark, beautiful, and smelled of her perfume. It also smelled of her woman-scent. The feel of the hair against his bare skin raised goose bumps along his legs.

He began to braid the hair. His plan was to make a rope, one he could depend on and trust his life to. Like the ancient *ninja*, he preferred a rope made from a woman's hair because it was strong and resilient, less likely to fray and was amazingly light. As he worked he thought about Hidden Sword. The Empress would give anything to know his name. Millions, perhaps. An idea concerning the informant's identity tried to worm its way into Poltava's mind, but he was having trouble concentrating. The sensuous feel of the hair made him think of the woman and the first time he'd seen her. A lovely creature with hair almost to her waist, she'd been lying in bed beside the Frenchman. Lying as still as a corpse, her breathing very, very shallow. She seemed to be dead, Poltava remembered himself thinking, and with that thought he'd become sexually aroused. Now, in his Soho room, he stopped braiding and began to stroke the hair. The feeling of sexual arousal had returned.

Placing the hair on top of Coveyduck's manuscript, he stood up. There was a pleasurable tension in his groin. He removed his shorts. Nude, he picked up several newspapers and the shopping bag and walked to the closet. He spread newspaper on the worn carpet in front of a cracked, full-length mirror on the inside of the closet door. Then he stood on the newspaper, stared at his reflection in the mirror, and sucked his thumb, feeling very, very young once more. The shopping bag stood next to his left leg.

After a few seconds, Poltava looked down at his penis. It was permanently shriveled. Very small. And wrinkled. It stood out in bizarre contrast to the rest of his powerfully muscled body. And it was dotted with scar tissue.

Outside in the hallway, a man and woman walked past his door, the two speaking in Chinese. Poltava recognized the dialect. Cantonese. Spoken quickly and in singsong fashion and damned impossible to learn. He'd heard it often enough in Hong Kong, where he lived several months a year and which he preferred to North Africa and the Middle East, his other hiding places. He owned a fair amount of property in Hong Kong—a go-cart track, a downtown high-rise, a restaurant boat in Quarry Bay. *Keep thy shop and thy shop will keep thee.* It was a saying he'd picked up from his Hong Kong investment broker, a tall, bald Englishman named Pigott-Speakes who knew him as Anton Damrak, a Dutch-Indonesian business consultant. Mr. Damrak's work with various Asian companies kept him out of Hong Kong for months at a time, and for a modest fee Pigott-Speakes gladly kept an eye on his assets.

In the hallway, the Chinese woman laughed and suddenly Poltava, eyes still on his penis, remembered the Russian.

It had been more than three years ago. The meeting between Poltava and the Russian took place outdoors during a snowfall in Frankfurt, West Germany. As planned they met at noon in the Palm Garden, the botanical gardens whose fifty-five acres of gardens, meadows, ponds, trees and footpaths offered a welcome sanctuary from the bustling city. This particular rendezvous was a *treff,* a meeting between an agent and his control in a neutral country.

The Russian had insisted they get together. He was a KGB major from Paris, a handsome, husky forty-year-old named Khosta, and his intention was to talk Poltava out of leaving the terrorist movement.

"You have a duty to socialism," Khosta said. "We will pay you extra money, if that is what you wish. But you cannot leave. We demand that you stay. You are our eyes and ears among the Palestinians. Plus there are a few special jobs we would like you to do for us."

"Fuck you and your special jobs," Poltava said. And meant it. Special jobs meant suppressing someone for the Russians. Doing their killing for them. No, thank you.

Poltava ran the Palestinian supply network out of Paris and only occasionally reported to Khosta, his KGB control. Eventually he told the Russian to go to hell, to leave him alone. Poltava had his hands full working with the Palestinians and their European comrades; there was no time to be the KGB's errand boy.

Whatever understanding he and the KGB had was now off. He didn't want to hear from them again.

Over lunch—Khosta insisted each man pay for himself—the Russian came on strong. Poltava could not leave the movement. He could not go out on his own. A lot of people wouldn't like it. If Poltava knew what was good for him, he would reconsider his decision. From where Khosta sat, Poltava's future looked ominous.

The Russian was a heavy drinker. He washed down thick frankfurters, cabbage and pizza with dark beer, wine, and vodka. Poltava stuck to mineral water and tea, and for that Khosta taunted him, calling him a nun, a schoolboy, a prissy old maid. The insults went unanswered; Poltava never argued with anyone. He either ignored rude remarks or dealt with them in a violent fashion.

After lunch, they walked through the huge gardens. Khosta led him along various footpaths, talking a mile a minute and dominating the conversation, turning red in the face under his fur hat as he waved his arms and did his best to convince Poltava to change his mind. The terrorist, growing angrier by the minute, stuck to his guns. He was leaving and that was that.

Then Khosta turned nasty, accusing Poltava of cowardice, saying he'd lost his nerve. He was chicken-hearted. A weakling who'd grown afraid of his own shadow. "I've got to pee," Khosta said. "You're damned lucky I don't do it on you." After looking around to make sure they were alone, he stepped off the path into knee-high snow, almost stumbling because he'd had too much to drink, but somehow plowing his way to a stubby, snow-covered blue spruce. He unzipped his fly and began to urinate. The trouble, he said, was that Poltava didn't have enough Russian blood in him.

Poltava, seething at the Russian's insults, followed him to the blue spruce. He'd had enough of Khosta's shit. It was time to warn him that he was dangerously close to crossing the line. Viktor was hard to provoke. But once provoked, he was not easy to pacify.

He'd also followed Khosta to the blue spruce because he, too, had to pee. His mind was on his rage and for a few seconds he forgot that he'd always hidden his penis, never let a soul see it because he'd been taunted about it by schoolmates and *karateka* in various *dojos,* no one knowing that his father had tortured him and destroyed his penis when he was very young.

Khosta saw Viktor's penis and whooped. Shrieked. Pointed to it and laughed at the top of his voice, getting red-faced and almost choking, but finally pushing out the words, still pointing and calling it the little finger, a midget's whore-pipe, two-inch knocker, and little Nippy. The Russian threw back his head when he laughed, opening his mouth and showing silver fillings and a very pink tongue.

Khosta's cackle and cruel shouts echoed across the empty, snow-covered grounds, touching hidden and painful cords in Poltava's memory, causing pieces of his past to flash into life with a terrible precision and an absolutely enraged Viktor had had enough. He yelled at Khosta to shut up, but the Russian said I'm drunk and I don't care, do you understand? I don't care. Shut up, Viktor said.

Khosta shouted, fuck you, you no-dick bastard, and Poltava rushed him, ramming his shoulder into the KGB major's chest, knocking him onto his back in the snow, leaping on top of him and then Poltava cupped Khosta's head in both hands and snapped his neck.

In his Soho room, a naked Poltava stood on newspapers spread in front of the closet mirror and stared at his shriveled penis. He fingered it, stroked it with the ball of his thumb, and once he looked over his shoulder at the woman's hair on his bed. Then he reached down into the shopping bag, removed a two-pound bag of white flour, and pulled off the top. After staring at the flour, he raised the bag high and poured the flour over himself, sending it cascading down his head and face, onto his shoulders, chest, buttocks. When the sack was empty, he dropped it into the shopping bag, took out a second container of flour, and also poured that over himself.

An eerie white figure stared back at him from the mirror.

White. The color of death. And death was the port where he one day hoped to find refuge. Death, his friend and comforter. Death was not a punishment but a gift. A gift to his sexual hunger, for it was only the thought of death that allowed him to feel any sensuous excitement.

He felt his penis harden, and he began to breathe deeply. He reached down into the shopping bag, took out a cheap disposable lighter, feeling an irresistible pull toward the sexual pleasure that was to be his, and then he thumbed the lighter's wheel, once, twice. When he saw the flame, he smiled and lowered his hand, slowly, slowly, prolonging the pleasure, remembering that it had begun with his father and how in the end Poltava had come to love it. Now, naked and alone in front of the mirror, he touched the flame to his penis, stiffening at the pain-pleasure, moving the flame along his penis, searing the flesh. Gratification was near and he dropped to his knees, penis totally erect now. And then the warm juice rushed from his loins and he fell to his side on the flour-covered newspaper, body jerking as he ejaculated and stiffened in brief seconds of unbelievable ecstasy. He collapsed. Spent. Drained.

He lay on the newspaper, relaxed and pleasantly tired, his eyes seeking and finding Hanako's hair. He smiled. Hidden Sword had brought him and the lady of the long, beautiful hair together.

Hidden Sword.

Poltava froze, eyes narrowed and almost closed. Thinking. Piecing together in his shrewd mind what he knew about *Mujin* and its executives. What he knew about Warren Ganis and the Gennai family.

He sat up quickly. His eyes were extraordinarily bright.

He knew the name of *Mujin*'s Judas.

He knew the identity of Hidden Sword.

10

TIRED AND DEPRESSED, Edward Penny drove a rented Chrysler past the Capitol Building shortly before eleven A.M. He glanced at a sign on the grounds saying there would be a free concert here tonight by the Marine Corps band. Nice, if you like military music. His eyes went back to the rearview mirror. He was still being followed. Three black men and a black woman in a gray Pontiac 2000 with Virginia plates.

They'd been on him since he'd left Senator Fran Machlis's Georgetown town house an hour ago. Stayed with him while he made telephone calls from a public booth and picked up his breakfast, such as it was, from a downtown luncheonette. Maybe they were Jehovah's Witnesses looking to preach the word. Or maybe they were trapped in their car and needed help to get out. Penny read them as dope heads looking for a quick score.

He was tired because he'd had only four hours sleep. And he was depressed because he'd just learned that Aikiko Shaka, the twenty-eight-year-old Japanese artist he'd met ten days ago, was

206

married. Beautiful Aikiko with the full mouth and lustrous blue-black hair, the woman who had caused him to forget all else and simply love her, was married. She hadn't told him; he had stumbled across that little piece of news himself. Confronted with the truth, she had broken down and cried, admitting it was true, admitting she should have told him about it before now. Penny agreed. Why hadn't she? Because she was afraid he might be intimidated by her husband, a very powerful, very possessive man and one who would do anything to hold on to her.

An angry Penny said he knew who her husband was, thanks to Fran Machlis. But he would have preferred hearing from Aikiko herself. He felt he had been used so that Aikiko could escape from herself for a few hours. He didn't say he was hurt. He didn't have to because it was in his face, in his voice. He asked had she begun their affair out of pity and she said no, that she had loved him from the first because he was gracious and beautiful and strong. Penny said thanks for the compliment, but at the moment he didn't feel very gracious.

He turned his back on her tears, leaving before she could say more, and going to his own room where he had lain awake until dawn, thinking how quickly he had become dependent on her. Ten days. And in that short time he had withheld nothing from her. His heart, his secrets, his dreams. He had withheld nothing. With her he had come alive again. Without her he felt empty.

Edward Penny braked the Chrysler for a red light, thinking that at another time he'd have gone after the four in the Pontiac without waiting for them to come to him. Taken them out before they knew what hit them. But at the moment he had a few other things on his mind. Like Aristotle Bellas and any tapes he might have linking the senator to Helen Silks. And Viktor Poltava. And Aikiko. Forget about bothering with a car full of dope heads. Let them make the first move.

Penny was on his way to meet Meyer Waxler and wasn't too thrilled about that, either. Waxler, supposedly on Viktor Poltava's hit list, was a cranky old bastard, a man with his ass on his shoulders most of the time. He hadn't wanted to see Penny and had agreed to do it only as a favor to Fran Machlis. Which didn't stop Mr. Waxler from giving Penny a hint of things to come. Over the phone he'd said, "You want something, otherwise I wouldn't be having the pleasure of your company. Well, from me to you, Edward Penny, don't count on getting it. I agreed to see you and that is all I agreed to. Remember that." End of conversation.

Penny, of course, did want something. He wanted to know what Waxler had on *Mujin* that Fran Machlis might use to hit back when *Mujin* tried to blackmail her over the affair with Helen Silks. The trick was to get it without mentioning Helen Silks. He'd told Fran Machlis, "Now's the time to call in any markers you've got with Waxler. But let me handle him. You just set up a meeting between us." Fran had said, "Be careful he doesn't handle you. Meyer Waxler will cloud up and rain on you in a second."

Penny turned right on East Capitol Street and drove past the Library of Congress and the Folger Shakespeare Library. He was in the Capitol Hill area, not the Capitol Hill of congressmen, judges, and lobbyists, but a residential neighborhood of the same name. Fifteen blocks of tree-lined streets and marvelous old Victorian, Federal style and bay-fronted frame Edwardian homes. Penny had a room in Fran Machlis's Georgetown home, but Capitol Hill is where he'd live if he were considering a permanent home in Washington. The area had a turn-of-the-century look which he liked. The houses had personality. They were likable.

Edward Penny slowed down the Chrysler, coming to a stop in front of a gray Edwardian home with a pillared porch and hanging ferns in all of its ground floor windows. Without taking his eyes from the rearview mirror, he reached for a paper bag on the seat beside him and placed it on his lap. He removed a sandwich, western omelette on whole wheat toast, peeled off the tin foil, and began to eat. He was sipping light coffee when the Pontiac drew abreast of him, bringing with it the sweet sound of a Whitney Houston tape. Then her voice faded as the Pontiac passed him, continuing straight and in the direction of Lincoln Park only blocks away. Just before reaching the park, the Pontiac made a right and disappeared. Paranoia time, courtesy of Viktor Poltava. Depression courtesy of Aikiko Shaka.

Penny finished eating, wiped his mouth and fingers with a napkin, then felt the urge for a cigarette and remembered he hadn't had one since Central America. Five months without the weed. Not bad. He rubbed the back of his neck, then lightly pounded it with a fist to get his circulation going and increase his energy. Time to check in.

He took an attaché case from the seat, opened it, then removed the cellular phone and dialed the Georgetown house. A maid answered and he sent her after Bob Hutchings, one of two other security men working for the senator. Hutchings, a bulky fifty-five-year-old ex-Secret Service agent finishing his first year in Alcoholics Anonymous, had been left in charge of carrying out the changes Penny felt were needed to make the town house less vulnerable. With Viktor Poltava in the picture, the senator needed all the protection she could get.

Hutchings came to the phone and said no problem, that the changes were proceeding as scheduled, and that he hadn't heard from the senator who was at the Senate Office Building. This was no surprise to Penny since she was a member of three committees and nine subcommittees and could be scheduled for half a dozen hearings any morning. Hutchings asked Penny if he knew why the senator was in such a shitty mood. Word had it that she was mad enough to spit tacks. She had given one staff member her walking papers today. Did Penny know anything about this?

Penny said he'd look into it later, then told Hutchings to make sure that Bud Rogue, the lanky young black who was the other security man, knew he was to stay close to the senator until Penny relieved him. Penny had already contacted a local agency run by people he knew and arranged for additional guards. The senator would have round-the-clock protection at her house, and no guard would work more than a single eight-hour shift without a break. Before hanging up he reminded Hutchings there was to be no discussion of Viktor Poltava with anyone except the security guards, and if the press should start nosing around, Hutchings and the guards were to dummy up. The word for the day was no comment.

He didn't tell Hutchings that what happened between Penny and Viktor Poltava in Central America five months ago was one thing, and what was between Poltava, *Mujin,* and the senator was something different. But if the press got wind of any of this, it might result in some very lurid stories.

Following last night's run-in with Aristotle Bellas in New York, Penny had telephoned Fran Machlis at her friends' home in Virginia. Surprise. She wasn't there. Apparently she couldn't stand hiding out and instead preferred to catch up on some work, so she had returned to her Georgetown town house. Penny wasn't going to call her there, not until he'd done a sweep on the phones. He hopped the first shuttle to Washington and used the ECR-1 on the ground floor of the town house, turning up three bugs, genuine Sophie specials. The other floors could wait until he'd had some sleep, but there wouldn't be any sleep until he'd woken up the senator and given her the bad news. The kind of news that couldn't wait until tomorrow.

Debbie Previti, Helen Silks, Warren Ganis, August Carliner. And *Oni*. Penny spared Fran Machlis nothing. He couldn't afford to. Not if he wanted to save her political career and perhaps her life as well. There was only one conclusion to be drawn from the Greek's record of Helen Silks's telephone calls to Reiko Gennai, August Carliner, and Warren Ganis: Someone had put together a neat little plot to finish Senator Fran Machlis's career in public office, and Helen Silks was in it up to her eyebrows. Penny had no idea why *Mujin* wanted to protect Warren Ganis's past from exposure, but if Viktor Poltava was in the picture, then they were talking heavy secret. Very, very heavy.

Fran Machlis said she didn't give a shit about Warren Ganis or how many times Aristotle Bellas had marked *O* for Oni in his notebooks. Nor did she care if August Carliner lived or died. And while Debbie Previti's betrayal was a bitter pill to swallow, she'd managed to live with it somehow. What she did care about was Helen and this is where Penny saw her fall apart, grieving and shedding tears as though someone in her family had just died. Penny felt sorry for her, but there was nothing he could do but watch.

She had once told him about her husband, Calvin, a hard-nosed businessman who was devoted to free enterprise because he claimed it gave him an unimpeded right to get rich at anyone's expense. From him she had learned enough to survive in politics. She had even learned enough to double the value of the stock he'd left her in a successful paper box company, which was now worth almost 150 million dollars. But Calvin Machlis hadn't warned his wife that sometimes love is nothing more than being stupid together. Fran Machlis would be stupid if she didn't act on what Penny had just told her about Helen Silks.

Then it was the senator's turn to drop a bombshell, and drop one she did. Red-faced and weeping, she said, "You really should have been told this earlier. But with Warren somehow involved in all this, I think it's time you knew."

"Knew what?"

"Aikiko. She's married to Warren."

All Penny could do was shake his head and say no. No. *No*.

Fran said, "The timing's shitty, I know, but you have to be told. I had no idea this thing, this relationship between you two would develop so fast. My God, one minute I'm introducing the two of you and the next minute you're both staring into each other's eyes like Bogie and Bacall."

"Now I know why you didn't approve of me and her together."

"I didn't approve of your getting hurt, that's what I didn't approve of. Lord knows I'm in no position to lecture you or anyone else on moral behavior. But I knew how it would end, because Warren's not the type to give up easily, and if she was thinking of leaving him, well, all I can say to her is good luck."

"Warren Ganis's wife. Damn." Penny wanted a cigarette in the worst way.

"She's much younger than he, something like half his age. And she uses her maiden name on her work, so not that many people know she's married to him. Also, Warren's something of a freak for privacy, so who knows what his personal life is really like. I mean, even I don't know that much about the man."

"And she never said a word. Not a word."

"I should have said something sooner. I really should have."

For Penny, the first few seconds of pain on hearing that Aikiko Shaka was Ganis's wife were as long as their ten days together. He turned from the senator and looked at the staircase leading to the next floor where Aikiko was sleeping in a guest room, waiting for him to wake her and tell her that he loved her. It had been too good to be true. He'd been afraid something like this might happen, that he might lose her. Ten days together and all he had to show for it was a new scar, one that wouldn't show, but Christ, did it hurt. He had been broken when he'd come to her, and she had helped him to mend. Now he was broken again.

"Are you going to talk to her tonight?" Fran asked.

He nodded, eyes still on the staircase. "After you and I finish going over a few things. I still have a job to do, remember?" *God isn't dead. He just won't come to the phone.* Penny tore his gaze away from the staircase and focused on the senator.

"Helen's due in America in three days," Fran said. "She's coming in from Tokyo to attend a language teachers' conference in New York. She's supposed to stay with me. What do I tell her?"

"Tell her you're busy. You're a senator, and senators are always busy. Emergency vote in Congress. An unscheduled meeting with your constituents. Lunch with Ron and Nancy. We'll think of something."

"Edward, I've got to see her at least one more time. I want to hear from her why she did this to me."

"She did it for the money. Which isn't to say she doesn't feel something for you. Just remember, she's connected with *Mujin*, and they've got a reason to come after you. I'd prefer you not see her at all, but if you insist, let me pick the time and place. I don't want you alone with her. Not anymore. You've got too much to lose, understand what I'm saying?"

"Yes."

"I don't know how tight she is with Viktor Poltava, and that scares me. The guy's got a peculiar mind. Totally unpredictable. You can't really plan with him. And he'll do whatever's necessary to get the job done. The more I think about it, the more I'm convinced he put Serge Coutain in a coma and kidnapped Hanako. The Greek seems to feel the same way. The thing with the dead colt is a Poltava touch. Nothing's sacred with that guy. I should know."

Fran Machlis covered her face with her hands. "Why did she do this to me? Why in hell did she do this to me?"

"She's done it. That's what we have to deal with right now. There's a chance Aristotle Bellas has contacted August Carliner and told him I've got the notebooks and address book. If that's true, Helen Silks will be warned, so maybe you won't hear from her again."

Fran Machlis shook her head. "Carliner and Poltava."

Penny shrugged. "No different from ex-CIA guys selling weapons to Colonel Khadafy, knowing full well those same weapons could be used to shoot up American tourists at airports. Or your upstanding American businessman who breaks the law by selling the latest technology to the Russians or anyone else who'll pay. They do it for the money, and because they're hooked on the intrigue. Most of all, they do it for the money."

"Can she really ruin me? I mean, what can we do about—" Fran didn't finish the sentence.

"One thing's for sure," Penny said. "We do it *before* she makes her move, not after. The only answer that comes to mind is to fight fire with fire. Get some dirt on *Mujin* and do a deal. Use it to make them back off."

"Oh, God, do you think it'll work?"

"What choice do we have? We know Coveyduck's digging into *Mujin* and Warren Ganis. And so's Meyer Waxler. I vote we try and cut a deal with Waxler. He's closer."

"Oliver's a friend, and he might help, though Lord knows I don't want to tell him why I need his help. Meyer's a different story. Very much his own man, to put it mildly. But he does owe me a few favors. I've opened doors for him from time to time, confirmed some of his red-hot tips, and even put a little money into that scandal sheet he calls a newspaper."

Penny said, "That ought to be enough to get me through the front door. After that I plan to make him an offer he can't refuse."

"Such as?"

"A trade. What he's got in exchange for what I know. Maybe I should say what I *think* I know. Such as the truth behind Serge Coutain's illness and the disappearance of his fiancée. Such as, 'Excuse me, Mr. Waxler, but are you aware that you're on Viktor Poltava's hit list, the same Mr. Poltava who is the world's most wanted terrorist?' If I don't get his attention with that last one, something's wrong. Plus Mr. Waxler will always have the knowledge he's helped a United States senator, which I'm sure he'll capitalize on in the future."

Fran Machlis used a tissue to dry her eyes. "Meyer's turned into a terribly bitter human being. Then again, he has the right to, considering what Warren did to him."

According to the senator, Warren Ganis had reduced Meyer Waxler's life to almost nothing. Years ago Waxler and his partner Ryan Land owned nine small weekly and daily newspapers in Virginia, Maryland, and Washington. Waxler, the journalist, handled the editorial side. Management and finances were left to

Land, a back-slapping, good old boy with a degree in business administration from Harvard and an eye toward becoming a press magnate. The two prospered, but not enough for Land, who believed that money was God in action.

It was Land who pushed for expansion into outdoor advertising companies, into radio and television stations. Unfortunately, he pushed too hard and too fast. Banks refused further loans, forcing Land to find other sources of financing, most of which came from front companies controlled by Warren Ganis. Waxler, who learned of this too late, turned on his partner. How could Land have been so stupid as to get involved with Warren Ganis, a man with a reputation for swallowing competing newspapers? Ganis was a greedy son of a bitch; he and the devil drank through the same straw.

Ganis ran true to form. It was his habit to wait until a city grew big enough to make it worth his while to move in with his own papers, and that's what he did to Waxler and Ryan Land, taking away their advertisers and readers with his larger circulation. He also called in their loans and when the two couldn't pay, they lost everything. A crushed Ryan Land blew his own brains out with a shotgun. Feeling responsible for his partner's death, Waxler became an alcoholic.

Fran Machlis said, "Meyer's wife Benita got him started again. She helped him kick the booze, and when she came into a small inheritance, she used it to back a small weekly and get him into journalism again. Sad thing is, she had a stroke not long ago. But Meyer refuses to put her in a nursing home. Keeps her with him. Pays for her care by taking speaking engagements when he can get them, or by giving journalism seminars to graduate schools, high schools, any place that will have him. He's devoted to Benita. She's probably the one thing in this world he cares about."

Penny said, "I can see where he might want to cut the heart out of Warren Ganis."

"You might say they don't see eye to eye."

"I'd like you to do something. Do it now. Telephone Coveyduck and warn him about Poltava. Do it through the London embassy and have them contact the Metropolitan Police. Not Scotland Yard, but the Metropolitan. Scotland Yard's only the Detective Division attached to the Metropolitan. I'll give you a name. Make sure this guy knows I'm involved, that I'm working for you. Tell the embassy that the Metropolitan is to place Coveyduck under guard as soon as possible. Got that? As soon as possible."

Penny said the business with Serge Coutain and Hanako meant that Poltava was in Europe, close enough to reach out for Coveyduck. Penny would warn Waxler in the morning and maybe do a sweep on Waxler's place to impress him. As for Debbie Previti, the senator knew what to do.

Fran Machlis said she sure as hell did. She wanted to bury Debbie face down so that if she woke up, she'd start digging the wrong way. The senator was beginning to suspect that there was no point in life. No point at all. She said, "One of my daughters, the youngest one, told me long ago that it's a good thing love is blind, otherwise you'd see too much. They're both married, my kids. Happy as clams, or so it would appear."

Penny said he was going upstairs to talk to Aikiko. He didn't know what good it would do, but it was best to get it over with. This particular confrontation had been postponed long enough. Talking to her or not talking to her, either choice was bound to keep him awake for most of the night.

The senator said, "She's afraid of her husband. Please don't forget that. Try not to be too hard on her. I thought you two were good for each other, which is why I didn't want to interfere despite my misgivings. But now I suppose we're in the same boat, you and I. And the boat appears to be past the point of leaking. It seems to be in a right old state of collapse."

When she tried to hold back the tears and failed, Penny took her in his arms.

In the morning he walked past Aikiko's room, hearing her end of a telephone conversation with someone who Penny guessed was her husband. No reason for her to hide her ties to Warren Ganis now. The cat was out of the bag. Penny didn't stop to talk to her; they'd done their talking last night, and there was nothing else to say. Downstairs he joined the senator in the dining room for coffee and told her that his mind was on *Oni*, on the possibility that the terrorist might already have her in his crosshairs. Security at the house had to be tightened immediately. Fran Machlis didn't feel like talking about it. She didn't feel like talking about anything. Helen Silks, it seemed, was still very much with her.

Penny, she said, could do whatever he liked regarding security. When he told her about proposed changes, she listened only halfheartedly. She okayed the installation of outside lighting, sixty watt bulbs near the doors and along the path leading to a garden. She approved the installation of warning stickers on windows and doors, and the severe trimming of hedges and shrubbery that hid windows and doors. On the question of leaving keys under the mat for maids, staff, or whoever, she agreed it had to stop.

She said yes to putting dead bolt locks on front and back entry doors, vent locks on ground-floor windows. She already had an alarm system; it rang at the security company which had installed it, and the company then contacted the police. Too slow a response time, Penny said. Get an on-site bell alarm to go with the silent alarm that was in place and add a backup battery in case of power failure. Approved.

But when he recommended she get rid of the hollow door in the back and replace it with a metal door, she refused, claiming metal was ugly and clashed with the overall architectural design. Nor did she want her lawn dug up and rose bushes installed so that their thorns could slow down intruders. She had spent a fortune on the lawn and preferred it the way it was, thank you. And Penny could not remove the biggest danger of all, a wide column arbor which shaded rooms facing the garden and eliminated the need for drapes. Unfortunately, it also made it easy for an intruder to approach the house by day or night almost unseen.

They argued over this, but Fran Machlis dug in her heels and that was that. On a related subject they agreed for the time being not to call in the police or FBI, since this would only lead to unwanted press coverage and highly damaging publicity about Helen Silks. Besides, Penny could offer no hard evidence that Viktor Poltava was actually on his way to America. He had only the Greek's notebooks to offer in support of his suspicions. As for the arbor, Penny could wire the French doors opening into it from the house, but that was as far as he could go. Fran Machlis wasn't going to turn her house upside down merely on the possibility that some psycho *might* pay her a visit one fine day. She excused herself to talk to Debbie Previti, who was waiting for her in the music room.

Penny drove away from the Georgetown house without eating breakfast, his way of avoiding Aikiko, then stopped off at a downtown bank for some rolls of quarters. Time to make a few calls and do it from a public booth because he wanted privacy. The senator's phones were now clean, but Penny didn't want to risk being overheard, not even accidentally. Not when he was talking about *Oni*.

The first call was to Georges Cancale in Deauville. Speaking in French, Penny told his partner that Viktor Poltava was probably responsible for Serge Coutain's stroke, Hanako's disappearance, and the destruction of the valuable colt. All Penny had to go on were the notebooks belonging to Aristotle Bellas, but the events which had occurred in Deauville very much resembled *Oni*'s handiwork. He asked Cancale to poke around the Coutain farm. Start with the barn where the colt was killed. Cancale knew *Oni*'s way of working. Cancale would know what he was looking for when he found it. Don't contact the French police yet, but check in with Penny if anything turned up. Cancale said the reward for the colt's killer had doubled; a pair of French racing associations had matched the money put up by Coutain's family. The reward didn't matter, Penny said. This was something they owed Serge.

The next call was to Bangkok, to Nick Maximillian, who had worked with him as bodyguard, merc, security expert, and who, outside of Georges Cancale, was his closest friend. Nickie Max was a former SEAL who'd done two tours in Nam, a free spirit who preferred life in Southeast Asia to being a Wisconsin dairy farmer. Nickie Max, who believed that conning people was an art form, who believed that if you had an angle, you could survive anywhere in the world, and who five months ago in Central America had put his ass on the line to save Edward Penny's life.

Penny told him about Serge Coutain and Hanako, that she might be in Bangkok and to ask around. Get back to him if there was any news, but be careful. This was *Oni*'s handiwork. Nickie Max said, "We owe that fucker, and if I ever see him, I'll grease him on the spot. A full clip in the head and a grenade up his ass to make sure."

"Stay awake," Penny said. "You know how *Oni* plays the game. Don't let him con you, too." Nick Max said no problem and could Penny send him a carton of Chunky bars because those suckers were just about impossible to get in Asia, and could he also send him some video cassettes of the last two Linda Blair prison pictures. He had this thing for Linda Blair and owned cassettes of most of her flicks. Send him the last two which were "Savage Island" and "Chained Heat."

Penny asked about his family and Nickie Max said his Thai wife was fine, his two daughters were fine and had Penny heard the joke about the bum who finds this lamp, rubs it and turns out it's a magic lamp. Genii comes out, Nickie Max said, and grants the bum three wishes. So the bum wishes for a million bucks and boom, just like that he's got the million piled in front of him. Bum asks for a Rolls Royce and wham, the Rolls is right there, chauffeur sitting behind the wheel. Bum says, I want a dick that touches the ground. Wham, the genii cuts off his legs.

Penny agreed to send off a care package. "Get back to me. And whatever you do, don't play *Oni* cheap. I'm telling you," he said to Nickie, "do not play this man cheap."

In the Chrysler, Penny stared at Meyer Waxler's house and wished he didn't have to leave the air-conditioned car. Washington could be hot in August, and today was no exception. The temperature had already hit eighty, with matching humidity, and it wasn't noon. Nor was he keen on talking to Waxler, but it had to be done. He wondered what Waxler would do if somehow he learned about the affair between Helen Silks and Fran Machlis.

He thought about telephoning Fran Machlis at the Senate Office Building, then decided not to, that she couldn't talk about Helen Silks. He thought about Aristotle Bellas and Sophie. On the run and scared shitless, and who could blame them. What was it the Greek had said? *Something Warren Ganis and Mujin did together forty years ago. Something that can blow them both right out of the water. . . .*

The Greek had also said, *Somebody at Mujin believes that bringing down Ganis is the only way to take over the company. This somebody could be right.* Maybe if Penny knew what this big secret was, he wouldn't have to bother with Meyer Waxler. On the other hand, if he knew, he might have to bother with Viktor Poltava. He shivered. And not from the air conditioning.

He left the Chrysler carrying the cellular phone and the ECR-1. The Greek's notebooks and address book were in the phone's attaché case. At the front door, Penny rang the bell, looked up and down the quiet street, and waited. And waited. Waxler took his time answering and when he did open the door, he eyed Penny as he would a serial killer. Meyer Franklin Waxler. A short, chubby, stone-faced Polish-Jew in his late sixties, with the last remaining strands of red hair pulled sideways across a shiny pink scalp. Penny remembered what he'd heard about the man. Abrasive intelligence. Continual skepticism. Perenially looking down on those above him. This was going to be a fun meeting.

"Penny?" A grunt from Waxler, who had a cigar stub in one corner of a wide mouth.

"Yes." Penny put down the ECR-1 and extended his hand. It was ignored.

Waxler shut the door behind Penny then walked ahead, bending from the waist like a fighter coming off his stool at the sound of the bell, dressed in a terry-cloth robe and carpet slippers with crushed backs, leading the way along a dark, narrow hallway whose walls were hung with front pages of newspapers turned brown by the time. Penny glanced at a few. *The Lindbergh Kidnapping. Wall Street Crash of '29. Capone Jailed on Tax Rap. A-Bomb Dropped on Japan. Kennedy Assassinated in Dallas. Nixon Resigns.* Big, big stories. Events forming the substance of history.

Just before reaching a staircase leading to the second floor Waxler turned right, stepping into a large, high-ceilinged living room which he'd turned into a work area. Still ignoring Penny, the old newsman crossed the room to sit down at a nineteenth-century walnut cylinder top desk, where he picked up the receiver of a ringing telephone. Penny decided to find a chair, no easy task. The room was a mess. Colorful, but a mess. Chairs and tables were piled with books, newspapers, file folders, typed pages, press releases. The phone rang without a break, the lights on its four call buttons blinking continually. Oddly enough, Penny found the room appealing, seeing it as a small town newspaper office at the turn of the century. From all appearances, Meyer Waxler had completed the circle, ending up where he'd started, a newsman going one-on-one with the world in a search for the truth.

A bay window facing the street framed a tufted sofa covered with books, while a walk-in fireplace was home to a copying machine. A brass carriage clock stood on the cherrywood mantel of the fireplace and much of the wall space was lined with book-cases. There was a faded, lime-green Moroccan carpet edged in floral motifs on the floor, and a pair of faded leather armchairs near the cylinder desk. Most eye-catching of all was a display hanging over several metal file cabinets at the far end of the room. Spellbinding. Morbid, but spellbinding.

Waxler had collected newspaper pages and photographs deal-ing with Lincoln's assassination and the conspiracy surrounding it. Also impressive was a collection of journalism awards proudly displayed on top of the file cabinets; all of the awards had Meyer Waxler's name on them, and two were Pulitzer Prizes.

Penny turned to see Waxler hard at work, typing with two fingers on an old-fashioned manual and acting as though he were alone in the room. To Waxler's left, a small black-and-white tele-vision set was turned to *Lifestyles of the Rich and Famous,* and Penny could hear Robin Leach saying he hoped life brought each viewer champagne wishes and caviar dreams. Since Waxler never looked at the set, Penny guessed it was for company.

He crossed the room and stopped at a folding chair near the sofa in front of the bay window, just feet away from Waxler's desk. He put down the ECR-1 and attaché case, removed a pile of foreign newspapers from the chair and placed them on the floor, then sat facing Waxler. It was cool in the big room, which was fortunate since Waxler obviously didn't believe in air condition-ing. The closest thing was a small fan with blue plastic blades, which Waxler had cooling his feet.

Since the newsman continued to type, Penny took a Carlos Fuentes novel from books piled on the sofa and began thumbing through it.

Without looking at Penny or ceasing to type or taking the cigar from his mouth, Waxler said, "We have a scholar in our midst. Will wonders never cease."

Penny closed the book and put it back on the pile. "His short stories are better than his later novels."

Waxler stopped typing. He removed his cigar from his mouth, dropped his chin to his chest, and stared at Penny through black horn-rimmed glasses. "Are they, now? Let me get this straight. We are talking about the stories of Carlos Fuentes and not *Soldier of Fortune* magazine."

"They're in a collection, *Burnt Water,* published in 1981. I came across a first edition a few months ago."

Waxler grinned and ignored his ringing phone.

"Well, I have to say I am surprised. I expected someone less refined, someone more basic, for want of a better word. Offhand, I'd say you're the type to move his lips when he reads. I take it you're familiar with the works of Garcia Marquez?"

"Before or after he won the Nobel Prize?"

Waxler chuckled. "And I thought today was going to be just another dull day in our nation's capital. How does a man in your line of work get to be so literate, outside of a brain transplant?"

"I read. Travel a great deal in my line of work, as you put it. I was an Army brat, moving from base to base, country to country. That was education in itself. I also collect first editions."

"Well now, since you're neither a common leg-breaker nor a bloodthirsty retard, exactly what is your title these days?"

"Head of security for Senator Machlis. By the way, times have changed, Mr. Waxler."

"Meyer. And I'll take the liberty of calling you Edward. Fran says you dislike Ed or Eddie."

"That's right."

"Well, now, Edward Penny, how have times changed?"

Penny said that muscle wasn't enough in a security man or bodyguard anymore, that when a client was spending a half million dollars a year on protection for himself and his family, he expected intelligence as well as a talent for blending into the client's circle.

Then Penny had a question: Explain the Lincoln death display at the other end of the room.

Waxler pointed to it with his cigar stub and said it represented wishful thinking, the dream story he would have given anything to cover because it had it all. Every goddamn thing a reporter could ask for. History, conspiracy, government cover-up, the death of an important man, a lunatic of an assassin who just happened to be an actor. It even had a beautiful woman, the dark-haired Mary Surratt. Waxler had written the story in his head a hundred times and never gotten bored with it.

He picked up the telephone receiver and had it to his ear when Penny rose from the folding chair and told him to hang up. Waxler, hand over the mouth of the receiver, said, "We should get something straight, Edward Penny, and that is nobody tells me what to do."

Penny switched on the ECR-1, held it near the phone and, when the indicator lit up, he said, "Your phone's bugged."

Waxler slammed down the receiver. His face was red. His eyes were hard slits. "Who?" he asked.

Penny put down the ECR-1, picked up the receiver, and unscrewed the mouthpiece. When he'd picked up the bug, he gave it to Waxler. "Shouldn't be hard to figure that out."

"Damn it, I said *who?*"

"Before we go any further, it might be a good idea if I did a quick sweep of the room, see what I come up with."

"We trade. Tell me what you want from me, but you give me the name of the bastard who's tapping my phone."

"After I do a sweep. Tell your answering service to pick up all calls."

Waxler made the call and Penny made the sweep, turning up a bug hidden in a drape and one planted under the sofa.

"Room's clean," he said to Waxler. "It's okay to talk now. But before we start, there's something else I think you should know. Viktor Poltava's been hired to kill you."

Penny watched Waxler shift the cigar stub from one corner of his mouth to another, then bite down hard. Waxler looked up at the ceiling, scratched his throat, then removed the cigar and looked at Penny. When he spoke he was more subdued. "He's the one they call *Oni*. The demon."

Penny nodded.

"The one you got mixed up with in Central America, the one who almost punched your ticket."

"That's him. The person who hired him to kill you also paid to have your phone tapped."

Waxler leaned forward in his swivel chair, blocking out a television rerun of *Family Feud*. "You can prove this?"

"I can prove some of it, enough of it, let's say. Let me start by giving you a name. You tell me if this is the kind of person who would hire Viktor Poltava. Reiko Gennai."

Meyer Waxler slumped back in his chair, then began to swivel first right, then left, moving slowly to the applause of the studio audience on *Family Feud*. He stared at the ceiling, both hands gripping the arms of the chair. Ashes from the cigar in his fingers fell onto the carpet. "The Empress," he said softly. "The Empress. That is one tough lady. So tough she stands up to shit. Yes, sir, she would definitely put a price on my head. On anyone's head. Viktor Poltava—Russian father, Japanese mother. Ran with the Japanese Red Army, Italian Red Brigade, the Baader-Meinhoff gang. Worked for Russian military intelligence and any Asian druglord who could afford his fee. He's got some kind of pedigree, our Mr. Poltava. Except that his roof ain't nailed on too tight."

He stopped swiveling and faced Penny. "I understand Mr. Poltava isn't in it for the ideology anymore. These days he does it for the money."

"Strictly for the bucks. And he gets paid in advance."

"Who's crazy enough to stiff the son of a bitch? By the way, who tipped you to all this, or is that classified?"

"It's not classified. Aristotle Bellas. He's the wireman. I caught him at it, him and his daughter Sophie."

"Ah, yes, the talented Sophie. She's no Brooke Shields, but what the hell, I hear the gal's got smarts."

"I also have some notes Bellas made concerning this particular job and they all have to do with Warren Ganis, *Mujin,* and Viktor Poltava."

"Now there's something I wouldn't mind having a peek at. Any idea why Bellas was tapping the senator's lines, or do you want to play that one close to the vest?"

Penny thought, he doesn't know about Helen Silks. It's in his voice, his eyes, the way he's paying attention to everything I say. He doesn't know. Penny said, "Remember the run-in she had with *Mujin* over the attempted bank takeover?"

"Yeah, I remember. You're saying *Mujin*'s tampering with an American election, a serious charge. Don't get me wrong. They're perfectly capable of doing it. I just want to make sure."

"I'm not saying anything for publication, and I'd appreciate it if you held back on this one or at least check with the senator before you print anything. I don't want her being pressed too closely on this thing by the FBI or the police. Even when you're clean, the presence of the FBI in a senator's life might bring on the wrong kind of press coverage. People read senator and FBI and come up with something like ABSCAM."

Waxler said maybe he owed Fran Machlis and Penny something for the tip about Viktor Poltava and the tapped phone, though it was possible that Penny himself had put on the tap and had warned him just to keep Waxler off-balance. Penny said if he'd put on the tap, he'd have sat around listening to Waxler's calls until he heard what he wanted to hear. And he wouldn't have had to talk to Waxler at all.

Waxler said, good point. So what did Penny want to hear?

"I'll be up-front about it," Penny said.

"Please do."

"We'd like some dirt on *Mujin* so that the senator can protect herself. It's that simple."

"My dear Edward Penny, in a town of a pointy-headed congressmen, thieving bureaucrats who'd steal food from your mouth while you yawn, and lawyers slick enough to hold their own in a pond full of eels, nothing is ever that simple."

"You're working on an exposé of Warren Ganis, which means you're bound to come across a few uncomplimentary facts about *Mujin*. The senator knows this. So does Coveyduck. Bellas knows it, too."

Waxler chuckled. "Maybe I should start pulling the shade down when I change my clothes. All of a sudden everybody knows my life story."

"Coveyduck's working on a book that's supposed to be damaging to Ganis and *Mujin*. Bellas says you and Coveyduck are getting information from someone inside the company. Someone with a big hate for Reiko Gennai."

Waxler took his cigar stub from his mouth and stared at it. "Half the world must hate that woman. My guess is Tetsu Okuhara is the 'Deep Throat' on this thing. Or 'Deep Sushi,' if you will."

"I'm not familiar with the name."

"He's the godson of Yasuda Gennai, Reiko's husband and the president of *Mujin*. Tetsu wants to be the next president, but Gennai's son is in the way. Yasuda's dying, no great loss to the world, since the man's mean as a snake. He is one grand rascal, our Mr. Gennai, and he's created Warren Ganis in his very own image. Which is another story entirely. Just out of curiosity, do you know if August Carliner's involved in this?"

"Up to his eyeballs. He hired Bellas to tap you and the senator."

"That's what Carliner's paid to do, to handle *Mujin*'s dirty work in America, and he's paid plenty. Do you know what *Aikuchi* means?"

Penny said it meant hidden sword, a weapon usually carried by Japanese gangsters. The sword was small enough to be worn under a jacket or tucked in the small of the back, and you usually didn't see it until it was too late, until it was in a thug's hand and he was using it.

Waxler thumbed a disposable lighter into flame and lit his cold cigar. "My informant is calling him or herself *Aikuchi*. Now pay attention because here comes the good stuff, stuff Fran Machlis might find of interest—and you never heard it from me."

"Understood."

"Right. Now according to Hidden Sword, or Mr. Sword if you prefer, Carliner's due to get a big boost in his fee from *Mujin* this year and next. A very big boost. But Carliner himself won't see a penny of the increase. Not one red cent. The increase is scheduled to find its way into the campaign of Fran Machlis's opponent, whoever he turns out to be."

Penny said, "Carliner's washing money for *Mujin?*"

"Shit, he's done it before. For that matter, so has Warren Ganis. No, my friend, what I'm talking about here is illegal campaign contributions and election tampering, both of which are definitely against the law, both of which are right up Fran Machlis's alley."

"I understand."

"You might also tell her that August Carliner has had his dirty fingers in two other elections, a senatorial election in Florida and a congressional election in Vermont, and both times on *Mujin's* behalf. *Mujin* only wants people in Congress who see things its way."

Waxler said, "Let's talk bribery and labor unions. August Carliner and Warren Ganis both paid bribes on *Mujin's* behalf to certain top American labor union officials. Why? So that these officials would fight a trade boycott of *Mujin* proposed by their own union brothers." Waxler also had the names of senior White House officials and a dozen congressmen who had accepted secret all-expense-paid trips to Japan, courtesy of *Mujin*, trips which included cash gifts and female companionship. Trips arranged by Warren Ganis or August Carliner.

Waxler had zeroed in on Warren Ganis in particular, learning among other things that *Mujin* money was behind his publication empire. Ganis was no more than a front, the advance man for the biggest Japanese conglomerate operating in America. At the moment, *Mujin* was pouring money into Ganis's takeover bid of the Butterfield Publishing Company, a deal so important that if it didn't go through Ganis would lose the *Mujin* backing he'd enjoyed for many years. This was the gospel according to *Aikuchi,* Mr. Sword, and Waxler saw no reason to doubt it.

"It's goddamn ironic when you think about it," Waxler said. "You got this big multinational, *Mujin,* and who's calling the shots? Who's telling everybody at the company what to do? A woman. Reiko Gennai's the chief honcho, and she's been cracking the whip for years. She must be one very sharp lady and nobody to fuck with. Did you know that she chooses the wives of all top company executives?"

Penny said, no, he didn't.

"Old Japanese custom dating back to the *shogun* days," Waxler said. "It's always been part of a woman's success kit."

"What has?" Penny asked.

"The altar of love, my friend. The fly trap, pleasure garden, the harbor of hope, nature's tufted treasure. Also known as nookie, among other things."

"And centrally located, if nothing else."

Waxler chuckled and ground out his cigar stub in a clam shell that served as an ashtray.

"*Mujin*'s used that same system for years," he said, "but then *Mujin*'s a sovereign state and a law unto itself. The president's wife has always chosen the wives of top executives, and anyone who doesn't like it can clear out his desk and move on. That is, if he can get another job in a country where you're expected to spend your life with one company. They're big on loyalty, the Japanese. And at *Mujin* loyalty means letting Reiko Gennai tell you who to marry."

Penny said, "Say a wife becomes a problem. What happens then?"

"That wife turns up in a whorehouse in Hong Kong, Manila, Bangkok, or Taiwan, and not by choice, my friend. There's a big sex industry in Asia, aimed mostly at western tourists."

"I know."

"What you don't know is that the Empress, nasty little bitch that she is, has uncooperative or difficult wives turned into junkies. Doesn't take long. Not with number four heroin. Then when the wife's hooked, she has to whore to feed her habit. A real fucking sweetheart, the Empress."

Penny said he knew of one *Mujin* wife who had run afoul of Reiko Gennai, and he told Meyer Waxler about Hanako Watanabe and Serge Coutain. And about Viktor Poltava's role in their fate.

Waxler shivered. "Creepy. Sounds like something the Empress might do. Damn. I can't contact *Aikuchi*. Son of a bitch always contacts me. By mail. I'd love to ask him about Hanako and Coutain. That's a story in itself, especially if you're right about Poltava. It all comes back to Ganis. He's the centerpiece, the man Reiko Gennai wants to shelter from the storm. What the hell can he be hiding?"

Penny said, "Bellas says it happened forty years ago and could still make big trouble for both Ganis and *Mujin,* which seems hard to believe. But I have to believe the Greek because Poltava's in the picture, and he doesn't play unless the stakes are high. He's not the kind of guy you bring in just because your neighbor won't return your garden hose. Bellas said the trouble had to do with killing people. I suppose if I'd leaned on him a bit harder I might have gotten more out of him. Both he and Sophie are terrified, and I think it's Poltava they're scared of. Like you said, it all comes back to Ganis."

Waxler said, "Can't wait to hear from Mr. Sword again. So far, he's only given me bits and pieces at a time. It's as though he finds it inconvenient to sit down and write long letters. Like maybe someone's looking over his shoulder."

"Could be a clue to his identity," Penny said.

"Never thought of that. You might have something there, my friend. You just might have something. In any case, I wish Mr. Sword would get a move on. The sooner I nail Warren Ganis to the cross, the better."

He tapped his nose with a forefinger. "Got a theory, and it says Ganis's secret has something to do with a prison camp massacre that happened just outside of Tokyo. I've used the Freedom of Information Act to get my hands on documents dealing with those years Ganis spent in the camp when he was a kid. I also managed to get documents from the Army Archives in St. Louis. Didn't turn up anything indicating Ganis hadn't been kosher during that time, but the records did say some questions had been raised."

"What kind of questions?" asked Penny.

"Questions about him being the only survivor. Coveyduck, for one, pursued that line of thought. Ran into a stone wall. Got nowhere. I tried talking to him about it a couple of times, but he was very tight-lipped on the subject, to put it mildly. Goddamn British are big on maintaining secrecy even when it's not necessary."

"Coveyduck was digging into Ganis forty years ago?"

"He had the right. His wife died in that massacre, along with some ninety other people. All of them died just hours before the U.S. occupation forces reached them. All, that is, except Warren Ganis. A lucky, lucky man, it would appear."

Waxler shook his head. "Our Mr. Ganis returns to America a shining hero, and everybody shakes his hand and tells him what a spunky little lad he was during his time of trial. They were even going to make a movie out of his experiences, about him running away from home and spending four years in a Japanese prison camp, but nothing came of it. For one thing, Ganis himself was never too keen on the idea."

"Aristotle Bellas tells me the problem has to do with killing people," Penny said, "so what else could it be but this massacre you're talking about."

"I don't know. Remember, you've got four years of Ganis's life unaccounted for, so it could be anything."

"Except that Coveyduck's involved and, like you say, he lost his wife in that massacre. Maybe that's why he's on Ganis's case."

Waxler, corners of his wide mouth turned down, shrugged. "Could be. Anything's possible. That might explain why Mr. Hidden Sword is dealing with Coveyduck and me as separate entities, why he's made no move to get Warren Ganis. Edward Penny, I think you just might have come up with something. Let's hope Mr. Hidden Sword sees fit to enlighten me on this point in the not-too-distant future. I also imagine he could tell me a thing or two about Serge Coutain and Hanako."

Penny said a friend in Bangkok was trying to track down Hanako. If and when they found her, would Waxler be interested in the story? Waxler said does a bear shit in the woods? Damn right he wanted the story and would go front page with it, photographs, interview, bold-faced headlines, the works. Penny promised to pass on anything he turned up, but insisted that Fran Machlis not be hurt in any way. "She ain't the target," Waxler said. "Warren Ganis is, and in this case we're talking about a man who ain't worth dried spit."

The doorbell rang. "The nurse," Waxler said. "Jamaican woman who helps me with my wife. Can only afford her part time, but she's worth every cent. Bossy as hell, but she does her job." Penny said he'd heard about Mrs. Waxler's illness and was sorry.

Waxler rose from the swivel chair and looked around for his slippers. "Benita. She's my sun and moon, that woman. Wasn't for her, I wouldn't be on this earth today. Went through a bad time there at one point, but she pulled me through. Told me to go after Ganis, to get even with the son of a bitch, and I tell you, my friend, that's precisely what I intend to do. I want to preach at that man's funeral. I truly do."

The doorbell rang again. Waxler said, "Working on this story about a congressman who likes his whiskey the way he likes his women—twelve years old. Erna, the nurse, tipped me to this one. Her cousin works for the congressman as a maid."

He shuffled across the rug, bent forward, heels dragging, pulling a cigar from a pocket of his robe and dropping the cellophane wrapper behind him. Penny watched him disappear into the hallway, then left his chair and walked to the bay window. He stared out at the quiet street in front of the house, thinking it wasn't easy to grow old and that Waxler deserved a pat on the back for finding new ways to use what he already knew. Nobody lives forever, but Waxler had apparently decided to live as if he expected to. Hell, why not?

He watched a glass-topped tourist bus roll by, and in the house he heard Waxler and a black woman talking. The woman kept saying, "I need help. I'm sick real bad and can't make it to the hospital." She was excited, close to hysterical, and her voice was high, the words coming on top of one another. Penny thought, Waxler's not going to get much out of the Jamaican today. Sounds as if she's lucky to have gotten this far. Really, really sick, the woman was saying.

Penny had his own problems and Viktor Poltava was at the top of the list, meaning it was time for Penny to get his act together. For one thing, he had to give more thought to Fran Machlis, to the possibility that she just might become a target of Poltava, a changeable, resourceful, unpredictable prick. Penny was familiar with her medical history and could be of help in case she was a hostage, but it would also be a good idea to make sure the other security guards had the same information. He intended to ask around and see if any agency had anything new on *Oni*. Get an update on the man who was a state-of-the-art assassin. And it was definitely time to get back on the firing range and bear down in the *dojo*, to stop dragging his ass during training.

After hearing that Viktor Poltava was a player, Penny had changed the bullets in his Browning Hi-Power to jacketed hollow points for stronger stopping power. He'd also changed holsters; the Browning was now in a Horseshoe leather, the gun hanging butt down for quick access. He'd added a backup, a Smith and Wesson Model 60 silver-plated, two-inch barrel, and he wore it in a nylon belt holster.

For the first time since Central America, he was carrying the *tanto*, wearing it in a sheath strapped to the inside of his left forearm. His was a *kozuka*, a small backup knife favored by samurai for a thousand years. The three-inch blade had been handcrafted, hammer on anvil forging and was a mixture of high carbon steel and wrought iron, the mixture heated and hammered then folded back again to yield over five hundred tightly packed layers of steel. The handle was finished black ebony wood. There was no guard between blade and handle, allowing for easy concealment and a comfortable grip. The small knife could also be easily manipulated and because he could grip it tightly, it was difficult for anyone to pull it out of his hand in a fight. The blade was sharp enough to slice metal from an automobile.

Through the bay window Penny watched two middle-aged, male joggers approach from his left, the pair carrying on a conversation as they headed toward Lincoln Park, and his mind was on *Oni*, on how to keep the senator and Helen Silks apart, on what he and Aikiko were going to say to each other when they met again. He really wasn't concentrating on the street in front of Waxler's house. His eyes saw the street, but he hadn't connected his mind to his eyes and so he missed something important, something almost directly in front of him. He half-heard a low rumble of voices at the front door and thought maybe he ought to go help Waxler and the nurse. Only then did Penny's eyes pick up the gray Pontiac 2000 parked across the street, and by then it was too late.

In the room behind him a young male voice said, "Yo, fool. You at the window. Want to put your hands on your head and turn around real slow? No sense y'all gettin' excited in this heat, now ain't that right?"

Penny closed his eyes. Shit. He opened them and put his hands on his head. If brains were dynamite, he wouldn't have enough to blow his nose. Too smart, too late. The story of his life. He turned around. Real slow.

Four black teenagers. The same four who followed him from Georgetown in the gray Pontiac. Three boys and one very pregnant girl, with two of the boys on either side of a badly shaken Meyer Waxler. One shoved Waxler forward and to the floor, put a sneakered foot on his head and kept it there, then grinned and extended his right arm, aiming a .22 at Penny's head, saying in a soft voice, "Bet you thought we was the Young Republicans, now ain't that right."

He was the leader, a man-child who Penny could see was trying his damnedest to grow a moustache. Sixteen at the most, slim and light-skinned, with close-cropped red hair parted on the side, a whispy goatee under a full lower lip, and dressed in a pink track suit, low-cut white Filas sneakers, gold chains, and mirrored sunglasses. Track Suit's male friends were bigger, more intimidating. One was at least six feet and hard-muscled, with large hands and widely spaced teeth in a coal-black, square face. He wore a black leather vest over a bare, hairless chest, a do-rag tied over his hair, and carried a Luger. The third male was built like a fire hydrant, short and wide, with a drooping moustache and a knife scar in the middle of one eyebrow. He wore a red leather beret, wraparound dark glasses, and a *Los Angeles Lakers* sweat shirt with the sleeves cut off, showing muscular arms. He carried no weapon that Penny could see.

The pregnant girl, who'd tricked Waxler into opening the front door, appeared to be the youngest. Penny figured her for fifteen at the most. Round face, eyes dark with blue eye shadow, corn-rowed braids hanging down her forehead. Stuffed into black spandex pants and her belly high under a man's denim shirt with the sleeves rolled up. Sharpened screwdriver in one hand, pointed at Meyer Waxler. Penny and the Waxlers were now in what could be called a serious and compromising situation.

Track Suit looked around. "My, my," he said. "This room so big it be Monday at one end and Friday at the other." He looked at Penny, gun hand now at his right side to show he was cool, that he had his shit together and was on top of the situation. Grinning, he took his foot from Waxler's head and walked toward Penny, diddy-bop stride all the way, a half-limp, half-bounce with the left shoulder held higher than the right, going for the attitude and intimidation that kiddie killers flaunted on their turf, except that Penny was too pissed off at himself to be intimidated. And he had played this game with harder, more seasoned players who knew that attitude was a waste of time, men who killed without posing. Still, he reminded himself that the kids in this room would kill, probably had, and he mustn't forget it.

Track Suit stopped near Meyer Waxler's desk and said to Penny, "Y'all mind coming over here? Sun from that window get in my eyes. Now, before we take care of business, brother man, I be checkin' you out for weapons. Emmett."

The bare-chested black in the do-rag and vest jogged across the room, positioned himself to Penny's left, and motioned with his Luger for Penny to stand between him and Track Suit. When Penny was in position, Track Suit shifted a toothpick from the corner of his mouth to the center, stepped forward, and politely unbuttoned Penny's jacket. His eyebrows went up. "Well, fuck me. Nice. Real nice. You carryin' around two. Man, you know how long I been wantin' to cop a Browning? You don't mind if I borrow it?"

Penny said, "No, help yourself."

Track Suit turned toward the door and yelled, "Yo Marvell!" and underhanded his .22 to the black in the red beret who, with the pregnant girl, stood guard over Meyer Waxler. Track Suit looked at Penny. "See, I always take care of my people." He pulled Penny's guns from the holsters. He shoved the Smith and Wesson in a pants pocket and held the Browning in his hand, smiling at it. "You got anything else I might be interested in?" he said.

Penny slowly took his hands from his head and held his jacket

open so that Track Suit could see. "No. Check it out, if you
want."

Track Suit fingered the toothpick between his lips, smiled,
then patted him down. Rib cage, small of the back, pockets. And
he ran his hand up and down Penny's legs and inseam. He never
went near his arms. But he did remove Penny's wallet.

Eyes on the wallet, he said, "How much we got?"

Penny removed a handkerchief and dabbed at his forehead. "A
couple hundred. Some credit cards."

Track Suit put the wallet in his pants pocket. "You got sweat
on your top lip, dude. You know that?"

"It's hot in here. No air conditioning."

"You ain't scared, right?" Track Suit cocked his head to one
side, eyes invisible behind the mirrored sunglasses, enjoying his
power. Cat and mouse time.

Penny *was* scared. Scared enough to be pumped up. Edgy.
Ready to make his move when he had to. The adrenaline was
flowing, forcing him to think and ask himself why had these four
followed him into the house. There had to be easier targets
around. So why go out of their way to take him off?

Scared? Hell, he was a pro, had been one for years, and it was
time to start acting like one again. Still, why antagonize these
dick heads? So he said he was scared, that he had seen better
days and Track Suit snickered, pointing his toothpick at Penny,
saying, "I bet you have, my man. I bet you have."

Then he said, "We come for them papers, them notebooks.
You want to tell me where they at?"

Bingo.

Almost without thinking, Penny said, "What papers are you
talking about?"

Track Suit fingered his crotch. "Let me tell you how it is,
brother man. See, I be puttin' your brains all over this rug you
start messin' with me. We been told 'bout them papers, and I
seen you leave that woman's crib this morning carrying a briefcase which got all kinds of shit in it. Like maybe that's what I'm
looking for, that case over there on the floor. While we at it, we
pick up a few other things, too."

He looked at Do-Rag, then jerked his head toward the back of
the room. "You and Marvell go do it."

Marvell was the other male, and Penny watched him and Do-

Rag smile at the fun they were going to have, then he saw the two race from the room. He heard them rush up the stairs, whooping like kids at summer camp and saw Waxler hook his glasses over his ears and try to push himself from the floor and get shoved back by the pregnant girl who held the screwdriver near his face. "I put yo' eye out you start acting funny," she said.

Waxler pleaded, "My wife's up there. Let me go to her. She's sick."

Track Suit's eyes were on Penny, but his words were for Waxler. "Chill out, young blood. Brothers ain't going to fuck the bitch, leastwise I don't think so. But you can never tell about these things. See, they do what I tell them, and if I say do something bad, they do that. Maybe I tell them to put the hurt on your wife. How you like that?"

Track Suit waited for Penny's reaction and when he received none he leaned toward him and said, "My crew is what you call collectors. They collect money, jewels, stereos, shit like that. Okay with you, brother man?"

"Help yourself," Penny said, knowing the robbery was a cover-up. Jesus, he really should have picked up on that Pontiac out front before he did.

He decided to go for it now, before the other two came back. He had a chance against a boy and a pregnant girl, against only one gun. Against three guns he was going to get fucked. There was a chance that whoever had hired these four had told them to kill Penny and the Waxlers.

Track Suit said, "I hear you used to be bad. Like nobody used to mess with you. They say you ain't so bad now, that you sort of retired 'cause you too scared. Why you carry all them guns if you scared?"

"Habit, I guess," Penny said. He looked at the entrance to the living room, then at Track Suit. "You're right about the stuff you want being in that case on the floor."

Track Suit, still eyeing Penny, chewed his toothpick and said absentmindedly, "Oh yeah, the notebooks. Must be some heavy shit, right?"

"Right." Penny played with the handkerchief in his hands and wondered who'd sent Track Suit and his crew after him. He said, "We made copies of everything. They're on the big desk behind you." Penny saw Waxler look at him and he held his breath. But Waxler said nothing.

Track Suit said, "Why you be tellin' me 'bout the copies? Nobody said nothing 'bout no copies."

"Look, I just don't want people coming after me anymore, that's all. I'd rather clear this thing up now, understand?"

"I can dig it. You really scared now, ain't that right? You figure we hear 'bout them copies and we come back for your ass."

"Like I said, I just don't want anyone coming after me." Penny wiped perspiration from the back of his neck. He avoided eye contact with the teenager.

Track Suit used his authority to pass judgment. "Shit, man, you nothing but a punk, you know that? A faggot. Guys like you get fucked up the ass and they enjoy it, now ain't that right?"

Penny's hands were now at his waist and hidden by the handkerchief. He smiled, indicating his agreement with Track Suit's assessment of his character. Beneath the handkerchief he unfastened the sheath inside his left sleeve and slowly drew out the *tanto*. "Look," he said, "just take the case and the copies and leave me alone. I'm only a messenger boy on this thing. My job was to bring the stuff to the old guy over there and he was to run it in his newspaper. I'll get the copies for you, then you people can be on your way, okay?"

Track Suit shook his head sadly. "Man, you are something, you know that? You suppose to be so bad and now you peein' in your pants. Next thing, you be cryin' for yo' momma. Why don't you get me them copies before I put another hole in your dumb ass."

Penny tightened his grip on the *tanto* and continued smiling, showing that he wanted nothing more than to be a nice guy and survive. "I'm not looking for trouble," he said. He took a step toward Track Suit and the desk, hesitated, then took another. Steady smiling. Positioning Track Suit with his smile. Coming on like a man scared shitless.

He attacked with his third step.

He threw the handkerchief in Track Suit's face and, when the boy ducked, Penny stepped in. The Browning came up, but Penny's left hand pushed it down and to the side, knowing the thumb safety was still on. With the *tanto* he sliced Track Suit's wrist and bicep, cutting through cloth, muscle, tendons, and cutting deep, using the ancient knife correctly by pulling it toward himself with each stroke. A screaming Track Suit dropped the Browning and tried to pull away, but Penny tightened his grip on the boy's wrist, yanked him forward, and kneed him in the balls. Then he raised his knife hand straight overhead and quickly brought the *tanto* down handle first, hammering Track Suit in the temple and dropping him unconscious to the floor.

The girl was hysterical. "Marvell! Emmett! Come quick! He kill William! He kill William!"

Penny dropped the bloodied *tanto* into a jacket pocket, then shoved the .38 back into his belt holster. And when he picked up the Browning, he automatically thumbed off the safety. William wasn't dead, he was just cold-cocked. On the other hand, if the bleeding wasn't stopped, William was going to be history. Not that Penny cared. You play, you pay.

"I kill him! I mean it!" The girl was crouched behind Waxler, who sat on the floor, the point of the screwdriver pressed against the side of his neck. "You come near me, he dead. Marvell, Emmett! He got his guns back, you hear me? He got his guns, that white man. Y'all do somethin' quick."

Penny ran across the room to the entrance and flattened himself against the wall to the left, both hands gripping the butt of the Browning, ignoring the girl only because the two boys on the second floor were a bigger problem. Those fuckers had guns. Back to the wall, Penny slid down to the floor, then inched forward, through the entrance and out to the staircase. It was empty. But near the top of the staircase and out of sight, a male voice said, "We hear you, girl! We be making our move! Know we do that for sure."

Penny looked at the girl. Defiant, scared, and with one arm around Waxler's throat. She was an amateur, which meant she might do anything. Waxler was having difficulty breathing due to her grip, but she didn't seem to care. A goddamn hard case, she was. And pregnant to boot.

She aimed her chin at Penny. "We know about you," she said. "You ain't gon' shoot me. You ain't gon' kill no girl. You just ain't gon' do it."

Her worlds caused Penny to feel a chill between his shoulder blades and coming on top of learning that Aikiko was married, he suddenly had the impression that his life was FUBAR, as they used to say in Nam. Fucked Up Beyond All Recognition. First Track Suit and now the girl. Both had told him he didn't have the nerve to fight, that he had lost his balls somewhere along the way, and he wondered who kept them informed about his life and times. People were out to make trouble for him, after having first been told that he was a weak sister, that at this point in time he couldn't hit the ground if he fell. The idea didn't win acceptance with him at all.

From the stairs, one of the boys yelled, "Hey, white man, check this out. Show your face and see what we got."

Penny lay stomach down on the floor, and with the closing theme of *Family Feud* coming from the television set behind him, crawled to the room entrance and peeked out the hall.

They were all at the top of the stairs, in plain view, the three of them. Do-Rag, Red Beret, and Meyer Waxler's sick wife. She was between the two blacks, a small, frail, white-haired woman in a pink night dress, her eyes all whites in her fear. Do-Rag's Luger was pressed against the side of her neck. He grinned, showing widely spaced teeth. "She dead if you don't put down that gun, you know what I'm saying? I take the bitch off in two seconds. Don't mean shit to me, Jim. She just another honky broad. It's up to you. Just put down your gun and everything be cool."

Penny watched them ease down the stairs, the three close together, Waxler's wife whimpering and calling for her husband in a small voice, and Red Beret behind her, grim and unsmiling, his .22 held shoulder high and pointed at the ceiling.

Penny blinked away the perspiration that had fallen into his eyes and he felt the beginning of stomach cramps, the kind he'd had for weeks after being tortured in Central America. It was Central America all over again, right here in D.C., and he had to make a choice that could mean a woman's life, the kind of choice he had made five months ago and prayed he would never have to make again.

He backed into the living room, away from the stairs and

Meyer Waxler's wife, and sat on the floor. Sick to his stomach.
Staring at the ceiling and remembering.

Remembering Central America.

And *Oni*.

11

La Merced, San Augustín

December, 1984

EDWARD PENNY WENT where the work was. Overseas work meant getting certain answers up front. Before the boat sailed, not after. Questions: Was payment to be made in American dollars or local currency? What about insurance coverage? Housing? What kind of security clearances were needed? What type of weapons were available and what problems, if any, would an American military adviser run into with local police and military?

For answers to other questions, Penny reached out to contacts in the CIA, State Department, and Pentagon. That was when he learned that if he was going to work in San Augustín, he should beware of Colonel Efrain Asbun, head of the secret police. Asbun didn't like gringos. He especially didn't like gringos who were coming into his country to do a job he felt should have gone to him.

Fabio Ochoa said to Penny, "Asbun doesn't want you in my country." Fabio was the son of San Augustín president Nelson Ochoa, and he'd given Penny a six-month, six-figure contract to train the presidential bodyguard and a new anti-terrorist unit. "Asbun is going to be polite about it," Fabio said, "but to him you're just another foreign mercenary, somebody hired to kill as many people as possible. People who have never done anything to you."

Penny insisted that the job called for training people, not killing them. Fabio said, "You have to understand that Asbun is a man of great pride. He is jealous of you because he knows you are a war hero, a karate expert, a good knife fighter. So he feels threatened. He sees himself as the best unarmed combat fighter in San Augustín. He flies his own private plane to Taiwan to compete in *kung fu* championships every year, and the man places in the top five all the time. He's the war expert in my country. Even the generals ask his advice.

"Now you are the man the generals are talking about," Fabio told Penny. "The gringo with the big pair of balls. The soldier who has fought in a hundred countries and has many medals. Asbun? What has he done? He has shot a few peasants and cut off the ears of some students and that is all."

Penny said, "I think he's done a little more than that."

Fabio said, "I am glad we have you to push the colonel's face in the mud for us. That man, he loves power like you and I love women. Who can be comfortable around somebody like that, right?"

What Penny should have said was, "Forget it. You want to keep Asbun off-balance, you and your father, you find another boy because I need political intrigue like I need cancer." But he needed money for a retarded daughter living in Oregon with a divorced second wife. And he needed money for back taxes he and Georges Cancale owed on their cider business in France. Money was the price of life.

Meanwhile, he planned to fulfill the contract and let Fabio handle any problems that might come up with Asbun. Penny had no interest in politics; it was full of fools and compromises and, like Churchill said, it was something that could kill you many times. His friend Nickie Max said to him, "Let's just do the fucking job, then hop the first fucking plane out of this fucking Mickey Mouse country. Know why pigeons fly upside down in San Augustín?" Nickie Max asked. "Because there ain't nothing here worth shittin' on."

Nick Maximillian. Thirtyish, pudgy, and balding, with a drooping Fu Manchu moustache and a short ponytail held in place by a thick rubber band. A man with his own ideas on Colonel Asbun. "The guy's jealous of you," he said to Penny. "We been here a month and he hasn't set foot in one of your karate classes and he's supposed to be a hotshot *kung fu* man, right?"

Nickie Max said, "Let me tell you something. The man won't work out with you because he doesn't want to look bad and that's all there is to it. He's probably seen you work out, I mean he's done it on the sly and he knows you can wax his ass and he don't want that happening in front of his own people and that's why the dude ain't ever going to be your friend."

That was Nickie Max. Doing it straight from the heart and getting down to basics the first time out. They'd met in Nam, where Nickie, a SEAL, and Penny, Special Forces, had been involved in ICEX, Intelligence and Exploitation, a program designed to kill or capture Viet Cong leaders, uncover hidden arms caches, and scout for American and South Vietnamese units operating in the Delta.

Talk about being happy in your work. Nickie Max got a charge out of being in Nam, him and his "Hush Puppy," a silenced Smith & Wesson Mark .22 pistol he used for assassinations, kidnappings, and reconnaissance missions. Nickie Boom-Boom they called him, because he got off on working with explosives. Shot in both legs, he was once trapped in a VC weapons factory, and Penny had gone in alone to get him. He'd killed three Cong, but Nickie Max had insisted on finishing the job, planting C-4 explosives to take out the factory, with Penny dragging him around. Only after the charges were in place did they leave, Nickie Max, tourniquets on both legs, slung across Penny's shoulders and stoned on morphine, singing the theme song from *The Flintstones* as the two hauled ass out of the factory with the timer set for two minutes. *The Flintstones*. Yabba-dabba-doo. You had to love Nickie Max.

Why were they friends? Because both had proved themselves in time of need, and there was no more needy time than combat. Because despite differences—Penny read constantly, Nickie Max never opened a book—there was between them the good understanding, something that was there on first meeting or not at all.

This allowed them to expect a great deal from each other while never asking for it. And they were friends because each voluntarily ignored the faults of the other. "You're my unresolved side," Penny told Nickie Max. "You're the last of the free spirits. You're exempt from existing rules, and I love you for it. Envy you for it, too." Nickie Max said, "You read books, dress nice, have dignity and decorum. You're what I want to be when I grow up."

They shared a small, walled villa in La Merced, San Augustín's capital, living on a tree-lined street of old adobe houses built around flowered patios and cool fountains. Fabio Ochoa owned the villa; he and his father owned a lot of things in San Augustín, starting with a quarter of La Merced's choicest real estate. The villa loaned to Penny and Nickie Max came with servants, two cars, color television, and a supply of porn cassettes, a couple of which featured Fabio in action.

Alicia Colón was one of the maids. She was a thin, dark, twenty-year-old with a gently nervous face and a five-year-old son Tómas, who was illegitimate, blind in one eye, and suffered from cystic fibrosis. Nickie Max took one look at the kid and said, "Talk about getting fucked from day one." Penny said nothing. But he thought of Deidre, his daughter, and how he still couldn't accept the way she was. He didn't discuss anything with Nickie Max, but he did something about the boy. Clothes, food, toys. Maybe he gave the kid too much, but what the hell.

Taught Tómas a little English, too. Made him laugh and showed him how to throw a curve ball, Dwight Gooden style, and Alicia, watching, cried. After a while, Penny began to look forward to being with Tómas. Call it a change of pace. A temporary halt to hostilities. A few minutes when he didn't have to be on guard.

And that was what Nickie Max objected to. "So I'm fucking paranoid, so what?" he said to Penny. "But in our line of work, my man, I do not think it is cool to become attached to the people we meet."

Penny said, "He's only a kid, and he hasn't got long to live, not with his lungs."

Nickie Max said, "You're a pro. The best. My hero. Do I have to tell you to keep a cool head, to stay alert at all times? What

I'm saying is, okay, feel sorry for the kid. I feel sorry for him, but stay loose, know what I mean? You don't want to get too close to anybody in a place like this, 'cause those kind of feelings they slow you down and the next thing you know, you're history."

Thinking of Deidre, Penny said, "Lighten up. I know what I'm doing. Tómas, he can die in a month, maybe days. It's a gesture, that's all it is. A gesture."

Nickie Max said, "How do you know the kid ain't working for Asbun? For sure Alicia and a few other people in our happy home are telling Asbun what we eat for breakfast and how many times a day we pee. Asbun. Fuck that man where he breathes. Better yet, I'd rather throw the meat to Fabio's sister. Jesus, what I wouldn't give to jump that broad."

He saw the look on Penny's face and up went Nickie Max's hands, a gesture of surrender, followed by a quick smile, nicotine-stained teeth on view, not to mention receding gums that were becoming a problem. "Only kidding," he said. "Just funning, Edward, my man."

Penny said that if Nickie wanted to continue pursuing the great art of living, he'd better be kidding, because there was nothing or nobody in San Augustín more off-limits than Fleur Ochoa. Long-legged Fleur with her green eyes, twenty-two-year-old ass, auburn hair, and a luscious mouth full of promise. A bit of a flirt and a spoiled little bitch and the apple of Daddy's eye.

Penny and Nickie Max, with a couple of locals, had bodyguarded her on a shopping trip to Mexico City where she'd spent $150,000 in two days, not counting hotel and travel expenses. *El presidente* indulged her every whim, giving his little darling the best of everything from Swiss finishing schools to a yearly salary that equalled the gross national product of an emerging nation.

Penny said to Nickie, "Let me run this down for you one last time: It's not a good idea to covet the daughter of a man who is president because he eliminated his chief rival by having his heart pulled out from the back."

Nickie Max said, "Shit, I only want to show her my tattoo." At which point he dropped his pants, his drawers and, grinning, pointed to his tattoo. His pride and joy. Right there on the tip of his cock. A bird's claws pulling at his foreskin.

Penny said, "That's real classy, Nickie." And then the two of them howled.

Penny loved Nickie, but he had to keep an eye on the round little man because Nickie Boom-Boom wasn't above running a little hustle here and there or going off and doing something so crazy you couldn't find the words to say how crazy it was.

Good old Nickie, who when told that his San Augustín security clearance would require samples of his urine, stool, and semen, asked if he couldn't hand over a pair of his drawers instead. Good old Nickie, who said it wouldn't surprise him if one fine day Penny and Colonel Asbun didn't tear up a few corn rows, Wisconsin farm boy talk for have a knock-down, drag-out fight. "Forget hiding behind Fabio," he told Penny. "It's you and Asbun, and either you clean his plow or he cleans yours. That's how it's going to be, homeboy."

Asbun. When they met at the colonel's home for an interview regarding a security clearance, Penny thought, we've got a fashion plate here. The man's straight out of *GQ* by way of *Saturday Night Fever*. Asbun was in his late thirties, a slender man with graying hair and extraordinary good looks saved from being too feminine by a waxed moustache and slightly crossed eyes. He rarely wore a uniform, Penny learned. The colonel believed in style, on duty and off. He was partial to tailored navy blue blazers, beige silk shirts, and blue suede boots. And he wore a Vacheron Constantine watch made with emerald-cut diamonds. He was intelligent, polite and spoke excellent English. On meeting Penny one of his first questions was, "Is cocksucker one word or two?"

Asbun's home, with its pre-Colombian art collection, waterfall in the living room, and dinner parties serenaded by two marimba bands, was one of the loveliest in La Merced. Forget living like the poorer citizens in some raggedy-assed hillside shack made of tin, cardboard, and old drums. The colonel lived in a suburban villa on a beachfront road lined with colonial mansions and new luxury apartment buildings. And, as if all this wasn't enough, he had a new wife, an eighteen-year-old beauty queen who had been third runner-up in the last "Miss World" pageant. Penny thought, if the man's living by choice, he has yet to make a wrong choice.

Asbun played polo and tennis, and held black belts in *ju-jitsu* and *kung fu*. Edward Penny attended a couple of his dinner parties and came away impressed with his knowledge of military history, weapons, and tactics. For the son of a postal clerk, Asbun had come a long way. The trouble was that he wouldn't let anyone forget it. He was quick to demand all the power and consideration he rightfully believed was his, no surprise in a country where *machismo* was a way of life.

He could be human when the mood struck him. A number of poor children received medical treatment at his expense, and he was leading a drive to restore the country's oldest bullring, personally guaranteeing the cost of preserving its sixteenth-century facade. This was the benevolent Asbun, the man capable of giving aid and showing mercy.

And there was the Asbun that Edward Penny had been warned about. This Asbun was a drug trafficker, one of the more violent ones peddling the white powder his countrymen called *Gift of the Sun God*. A month before Penny arrived in San Augustín, Asbun was said to have dealt with a competitor by tying him hand and foot, then dropping him 30,000 feet from a plane into an extinct volcano.

This Asbun was the founder of a death squad called *Los Cuchillos Blancos,* the White Knives. Some of their victims were found with throats cut and tongues pulled through the slit to rest on the breastbone in what was called the San Augustín necktie. A bunch of loonies, a CIA contact told Penny.

Asbun himself was big on torture by fire. Something about flame on skin seemed to fascinate him. He got his kicks, the CIA guy said, by turning prisoners into crispy critters, doing it in a hidden courtyard behind the wine cellar of his home. The local nickname for Asbun was Colonel Kentucky.

Penny's interview with Asbun for a security clearance revealed that the colonel knew a lot about him. Almost too much. For example, he knew that by the time Penny was seventeen he'd spent more than half his life abroad, following his father, an Army master sergeant, from base to base. Picking up a couple of languages as easily as he picked up unarmed combat from the Military Police. Asbun asked where had he learned knife fighting, and Penny said in the Philippines, where his father had been assigned to a naval base. Penny and Asbun agreed that the Filipinos were the best knife fighters in the world, bar none, and that the Japanese knife, the *tanto,* with its superb cutting edge, was growing in popularity among commando units.

Suddenly Asbun got personal. He said, "Your father did not die well. Does this disturb you in any way?"

Penny said nothing, his way of controlling his anger. He simply shook his head and let that be his answer. He let the silence hang, not caring if Asbun thought this was an attitude because if the colonel was out to trash Master Sergeant Devon Roy Penny, he could fucking well do it without Edward Penny's help. Edward Penny never knew his natural father. The Sarge and his wife Rita had adopted him at the age of six months, given him a good home, and treated him right. He owed them something for that. One thing he owed them was not to discuss their deaths in front of strangers.

He'd loved them both, Sarge with his high-pitched laughter and childlike fascination with magic tricks, and Rita, a round-faced woman with a sad smile, who'd wanted to be a tap dancer but ended up teaching grade school. She'd passed on to her adopted son her love of literature.

But everything had ended badly one night in Fort Bliss, Texas, when Sarge came home and found nothing to drink in the house. Sarge had loved his liquor, loved it more than a little bit, and when he finally recognized that he had a booze problem, he devised what he thought was a foolproof way of handling it. One month on the booze, one month off. Nothing to it.

And for a time the system worked, until the night he'd come home during an off month with a craving for alcohol, a craving he had to satisfy. So he went down to the basement and swallowed paint thinner, getting smashed out of his skull, then staggering to the hall closet where he kept his .45. Going to have him some fun.

There he was, Sarge, lying on the floor roaring drunk, three sheets to the wind, feeling no pain, shooting at fucking mosquitoes and accidentally blowing Rita's brains through the top of her skull. A civil court gave him twenty years for involuntary manslaughter, but Sarge had been punished before he'd set foot in court. He'd killed the woman he loved. And the paint thinner had left him permanently blind. Ten days after arriving in prison, he was dead, not of a heart attack as the coroner's report stated, but, as Edward Penny knew, of a broken heart over what he'd done to Rita.

And none of it was any of Asbun's fucking business. None of it.

What else did the colonel know? He knew that Edward Penny was a gifted athlete—a high school forward good enough to win offers of basketball scholarships to six colleges; a promising amateur golfer who attracted the attention of the PGA; the co-record holder of the fastest half mile in Arizona high school history; a black belt in *Tae Kwon Do* at the age of sixteen. The record showed that Edward Penny had the talent, pride, and confidence of a superior athlete.

But after the deaths of Sarge and Rita, the only family Penny felt drawn to was the Army; he enlisted in the 82nd Airborne Division on his eighteenth birthday. He'd always enjoyed military life with its camaraderie and travel; and above all he'd grown up impressed by the best qualities of military professionalism. He'd seen in the American professional soldier a tradition of excellence that had saved the world in two wars. It was a way of life, Sarge said, that belonged to the last of the romantics, to knight errants and pursuers of ideals, to men who could be violent and often extravagant, while being idealists and impassioned true believers.

Asbun was a nosy bastard; it was his business to poke and pry and shine his light into dark corners. But there were some things he'd never know because to know them, you had to live them. He'd never know Penny's feeling when he made his first parachute jump, leaping into a cold silence broken only by the sound of the wind. Then came the long, heart-stopping seconds before his main chute opened and Jesus, he was floating gently to earth, happier than he'd ever been in his life, weeping and calling to Sarge and Rita because he wanted to share this moment with them, and then the ground was rushing up toward him much too quickly, and he barely had time to put his feet together and hit and roll.

One jump and he had a confidence that had never wavered. One jump and he'd become aware of his powers and abilities.

Committed to being totally involved with military life, he cared for nothing else. So he listened when a warrant officer who'd been a longtime friend of the family said that if Penny was serious about being a lifetaker and a heartbreaker, check out Special Forces. Cream of the crop, said the warrant officer. Elite troops. Unconventional as hell. The training's realistic, the standards are high, and most guys can't cut it.

Sounds good to me, Penny said, filling out the application form the next day. Shit, he was young. He had the itch for honor and glory. Did he know what he was letting himself in for? Fuck no. He was in a state of mind that knew only hope and brighter tomorrows. So he joined. And worked his ass off from day one.

Seventeen-hour days that began with a six-mile march while carrying a forty-five pound pack. Parachute training tougher than anything he'd undergone in the 82nd. Unarmed combat. Learning the ins and outs of over eighty modern small arms. Dropped into some very rough territory with only a knife to keep him alive and living off the land while being hunted by trained aggressors. Learning languages, communications, engineering, intelligence gathering. Working with explosives, booby traps, and unconventional weapons like a crossbow and a garrote.

Penny worked his balls off. He completed the course. Seventy-five percent of the men who started with him didn't.

Elite units. An idea whose time had come. New fighters with new tactics, the only way to meet the combination of terrorism and new technology. State-of-the-art warriors to handle warfare that had become too sensitive and too complex to be turned over to troops who did the old things in the old way. In Special Forces you had to be ready to do what you'd never done before. And do it perfectly. Or get yourself and a few other people killed.

Penny watched Asbun lift a page in the file folder and study the page beneath it. "Winner of the Silver Star, it says here," Asbun said. "A Bronze Star, as well. Important decorations in your country. You appear to be a man born for the military life. Ah, but your record as a husband is not so good."

Penny shook a Winston from a pack, lit it, and blew smoke at the ceiling. "Some things work out, some things don't. The army's hard on a marriage."

"Two times married, two times divorced. One child. A daughter."

"That is correct, yes." Using a thumb and forefinger, Penny

squeezed the bridge of his nose. Waiting for Asbun to get to the
part that hurt. "Your daughter is retarded and living with her
mother who is now remarried and, it says here, living in Oregon."

"Yes."

"You send money to help with the child's care."

"Yes."

Asbun smiled. "That is very good. I also believe in helping
unfortunate children. The Bible says they are a heritage of the
Lord."

"The poor man's riches."

A grinning Asbun shook his head. "You might get an argu-
ment on that, my friend." He tapped the open file folder with a
forefinger. "Everything here says you were quite the soldier. Very
uncompromising in your determination to distinguish yourself in
the military. And yet you left the army you loved so much."

"I suppose you could say I reached the point of no return."

"A man like you, a highly qualified professional soldier, a
hero, he leaves the regular army to become a mercenary. Pardon
my saying so, but isn't that a step down?"

"Nothing lasts forever. Let's say it was time for a change."

"Here today, gone later today. David Lee Roth said that. My
wife likes David Lee Roth."

"Really."

"I think she has every Van Halen record he ever made. My-
self, I prefer black musicians. George Benson, Oscar Peterson,
Roberta Flack, Lionel Ritchie. People in command of their craft.
You know what I mean?"

Penny took a drag on the Winston, thinking, get to the point,
señor, which is am I dirty or not? Did I have a hand in the shit
that went down with my unit or was I an innocent bystander?

Asbun said, "You resigned around the time they uncovered a
scandal in your Special Forces unit. Something about money disappearing from a secret defense fund, I believe." He looked up
from the file, crossed eyes on Penny who held his gaze and said
nothing because he remembered the oldest army rule of them all:
never volunteer. Asbun hadn't asked him a direct question; the
man had simply stated a fact, doing it in a way that made Penny
appear to be a man with something to hide. Which wasn't true.

Penny hadn't touched the missing money. Hadn't stolen a dime. But he'd still ended up getting burned.

Eyes on the file, Asbun turned the pages as he spoke. "Someone in your unit, it seems, was fiddling with expenses. Was it your commanding officer?"

Penny sighed, reminding himself he couldn't afford to get angry at Asbun, not if he wanted to work in San Augustín. Not if he wanted the big bucks that came with this job. So he didn't say anything to Asbun right away. He took his time grinding out the Winston and, by the time he'd finished, he was a little calmer.

"I'll tell you what I told a military court and a civilian court. I don't know who took the money."

"Ah, yes, that is what you told the authorities. You stated you were in ignorance of the entire affair, and yet you were quite close to your commanding officer, the one accused of taking the money."

Penny said yes, he was.

Asbun said, "The two of you served in Vietnam."

"Among other places. Colonel Neaman is a good soldier. And a good man."

"Is that why you refused to testify against him?"

Penny, an unlit Winston between his teeth, nodded. Hadn't said a word against the Colonel then. Wasn't about to do it now, either. Besides, the bastards who'd conducted the investigation hadn't really wanted Penny to testify. They'd wanted him to lie under oath, to help them nail Neaman. Penny didn't know who'd taken $810,000 of the unit's money. He'd only known it was missing and that Neaman, unfortunately, had gotten caught trying to hide the loss. Had Neaman taken the money? Penny didn't know. And he'd never asked.

But he knew a witch-hunt when he saw one. The investigators didn't give a shit if the 810 thou had disappeared through sloppy bookkeeping, vanished in a puff of smoke, or stuck to somebody's fingers. The investigators, traditional army people, saw a chance to get Neaman's head on a pole and put his unit out of business. It was out in the open now, the jealousy over Special Force's freewheeling ways. Time for a blood sacrifice.

Penny hung tough, kept his mouth closed and when the time was right, he did the only thing possible under the circumstances. He left the army.

And went straight into the private sector. And some nice money. Found work as a security adviser to corporations, celebrities, foreign businessmen. Was employed as a bodyguard and courier. And because he still loved the army, he trained commando units when asked and lectured at war colleges and think tanks. He'd left the army with the reputation of a man who was good at his job and could keep his mouth shut. There was always a place in the world for a man who knew how to leave things unsaid.

"Then we come to Manila and the incident involving your Senator Frances Machlis a few months ago." Asbun looked up from the file. "Violence rears its ugly head, it would appear."

Penny said, "I was in charge of the senator's security. My job was to keep her alive. And that's what I did."

Senator Fran Machlis was investigating an attempt by the *Mujin* corporation of Japan to secretly buy a major Washington D.C. bank, and the trail led to the Philippines, to a Manila-based syndicate of Filipinos and a Chinese financier who were fronting for *Mujin*. The syndicate also had some help from people in the Philippine government who'd been bribed to use their influence in Washington. The senator told Penny she intended to expose the syndicate's ties to *Mujin* and let the chips fall where they may. Her investigators had lined up several people in Manila who were willing to talk to her privately about this thing, and she was more than willing to listen. This Manila trip was important to her because her own re-election campaign wasn't that far off. Like any other politician, she was always struggling and scrambling for the right kind of headlines.

Second night in Manila. Penny, the senator, and two of her aides attended a reception at Malacanang Palace, official residence of Philippine heads of state. First lady Imelda Marcos hosted the reception, which included a tour of the palace, a complex of elegant state apartments and guest houses. Mrs. Marcos also sang "Don't Fence Me In." The first lady's vocalizing didn't thrill Penny or Senator Machlis.

Reception over, Penny and the senator's party returned to their hotel. But when the elevator stopped on the senator's floor and the door slid open, Penny knew something was wrong. He ordered everyone to stay on the elevator. Hold the door open. Keep quiet. No questions. When he stepped into the corridor the Browning was in his hand.

Almost every corridor light was out. Very tacky for a five-star hotel. Where the penthouse rented for two thousand dollars a night. And the exit door diagonally across from the elevator was open. Penny looked up and down the darkened corridor, getting more antsy by the second. He listened. Took a breath. Then whispered.

"Close the elevator door! Everybody down on the floor! Go, go, go!"

Penny dropped to the floor, thumbing off the Browning's safety and aiming at the exit doorway. He saw gun flashes in the doorway, coming from the left, and heard three shots whiz over his head and tear leaves from a potted palm and strike a standing metal ashtray. Then getting off four rounds himself, he aimed at the orange flashes in front of him, rolled to his right, and sent four more rounds into the doorway. Up on his hands and knees now, he quick-crawled toward the exit door, keeping low and to the right of the doorway, reaching the wall and crouching, waiting, Browning held shoulder high, hearing the elevator cable grind as the car moved down, and still smelling the marijuana the shooter had been smoking and hearing the senator's voice fade as she screamed his name. Penny still waiting. Keeping his breathing shallow. Waiting. A few feet away, just inside the exit doorway, someone coughed, then gave a long sigh and went quiet. Behind Penny, a door to a suite opened, sending light into the corridor. He yelled for whoever it was to close the door and call hotel security. *Now.* The door slammed. He waited in the darkness fifteen minutes before crawling through the exit doorway.

One shooter working alone and bleeding to death on the landing. Nobody special. Turned out to be a skinny, pock-marked hood named Carlos Rigodon, who'd taken two bullets in the chest and one in the leg and who died in the ambulance on the way to the hospital. Strictly small time, police told Penny. With priors working Manila sex shows with seven-year-old children; robbing patrons at cockfights; robbing tourists; drug dealing; peddling counterfeit jewelry. Throw in wife beating and receiving stolen goods.

Nothing on Rigodon's sheet about him being a shooter. Penny

thought, that was why he'd been picked to hit the senator. Hire an amateur, someone who's never done anything heavy before, and that way you'll keep the hit quiet before the fact at least. Except the shooter should have been warned that doing grass on the job tends to give away your position.

Did Carlos Rigodon have any ties to Senator Fran Machlis, Penny asked police? No, he didn't. Did Rigodon have ties to *Mujin* or the Filipino-Chinese syndicate being investigated by the senator? No again. But when Penny asked himself who had a reason for removing Fran Machlis from this earth at this particular point in time, the answer came up *Mujin*. Rigodon was simply a hired gun.

Senator Fran Machlis wasn't buying it. She was shaken by what happened, so she heard Penny out. But she wasn't ready to believe there were people ready to kill her merely over an investigation. Rigodon? In her opinion, nothing more than a common criminal, a small-time thug out for the quick buck. Business people, she said, did not go around shooting their critics.

Edward Penny begged to differ. He knew of a few corporations, American among them, that had created vacancies in the human race for reasons ranging from trivial to serious, though in the end all reasons came down to money. He'd been offered such work and turned it down. Others in his profession hadn't been quite so discriminating.

Proof linking Rigodon and *Mujin?* Penny had none. Had a gut feeling, though. Not enough, the senator told him. Not nearly enough. She would be forever grateful for his having saved her life. But she had a political career to worry about and this meant getting back to her investigations, something she wasn't about to let be derailed by a two-bit mugger. "Let's zero in on *Mujin,*" she said. Back to the vain pursuit of human glory. Penny was to let the matter drop.

Philippine authorities were similarly disinclined to seek out a connection between Rigodon and *Mujin*—no surprise to Penny. *Mujin* had a lot of money invested in the islands and money could purchase indifference. So why allow Senator Fran Machlis to poke around and perhaps stir up trouble? Because as an American politician she was too important to keep out of a country heavily dependent on American financial aid. In any case, people suddenly changed their minds about talking to her. Credit this new-found silence to Rigodon's death.

Asbun said, "So you are telling me the Philippine government covered up a murder plot against an American senator by a Japanese company?"

"I thought so at the time, yes. Still think so. But Senator Fran Machlis has a mind of her own."

"Like you. The man who did not betray his commanding officer. The man who refused to talk to the army investigators about the theft of the money. Would you say that you are a hard man to break, Mr. Penny?"

"Why do you ask?"

"Oh, I was just thinking. Some people say that they would never break under intense questioning. My experience has been that anybody could be brought around. Even a man like yourself, let us say. A proud man, a hero. Yes, even you."

"Or you," Penny said, slightly pissed at Asbun's need for territorial imperative and knowing he could do a number on Asbun's balls with the *tanto*.

Asbun smiled. "Even me. You are correct." Smile in place, he thought some more and again said, "Even me." Then, "You have admitted your need for money. Your cider business in France, your sick daughter in Oregon. Convenient to have such a daughter, wouldn't you say? She's your excuse to go anywhere in the world and do exactly as you please in a foreign country."

Penny's anger was so strong that he actually saw himself cutting Asbun's neck, slicing the carotid arteries, either of the two major arteries that carried blood to the head. Watch this swine bleed to death.

Penny lit another cigarette, took his time so he'd be calm when he spoke, then blew smoke at the ceiling and said, "My excuse for being in San Augustín, Colonel, is my friendship for Fabio. And yes, I do expect to be paid for my services. The same way you expect to be paid. I respect your right to question me. This is your country and I'm only a guest here. But when you use my daughter to criticize me, then I have to tell you I don't like it."

Asbun blinked, then leaned forward, one arm on his desk.

"Let me get this straight. You are telling me what you do not like?"

Penny stubbed out his cigarette in a stainless steel ashtray. "Perhaps it might be better if I told Fabio Ochoa and his father what I don't like."

He watched Asbun's nostrils flare and red spots appear on the colonel's cheeks, and he knew the man was infuriated over his last remark. Fit to be tied and foaming at the mouth, he was now rigid in his chair and staring at Penny from under hooded eyes, not liking what he'd just heard, obviously, but stuck with the truth of it: In San Augustín it was never a good idea to annoy *el Presidente* and his son.

Penny thought, I'm on his shit list now. Keep looking over your shoulder, Penny, my boy, because as soon as he gets the chance, the colonel is going to render you null and void. The man is walking around with one very large hard-on for you. But as long as Penny had Fabio for his rabbi, no problem. Twenty-eight-year-old Fabio. A big, good-looking army major whose daddy just happened to run the country. Fabio had been one of thirty foreign officers Penny had been training in the martial arts and small arms at Fort Bragg. Fun-loving Fabio, who spent his free time in North Carolina racking up speeding tickets in a new Ferrari, playing tennis at a local country club for outrageous side bets, and screwing a record number of blond cocktail waitresses.

He and Penny had become friends when Penny had saved Fabio's ass in a country and western club, the rescue having been necessary because Fabio had been coming on to the wife of a redneck wrestling promoter. After that Penny had gone on the Ochoa payroll as Fabio's off-duty bodyguard and earned every dime on the weekend trips to Atlantic City when Fabio carried a big bankroll and made a tempting target. On one visit to the casinos it took Penny all night to talk Fabio out of bringing an Australian showgirl back to Fort Bragg. "She can work as my chauffeur," Fabio told Penny, who told him no way. When the foreign officers' course ended, Fabio talked Penny into coming back with him to San Augustín.

In Asbun's home, it was Penny who now stood up, ending the interview by asking if there were any more questions. Asbun slowly shook his head, saying nothing, not looking at Penny but at a small toy on his desk, a monkey in striped pants and red hat, holding a pair of cymbals. As Penny left, Asbun picked up the monkey, wound the key in its back, then placed it on the desk in front of him and watched it bounce up and down and bang the cymbals together, doing it all very rapidly. Doing exactly what Asbun wanted it to do.

La Merced, San Augustín

January, 1985

Just after midday Edward Penny and Nick Maximillian stood in a small gymnasium, where they had been teaching unarmed combat, and watched six men enter through a pair of swinging glass and aluminum doors. The footsteps of the six echoed as they walked across a vacant basketball court and seated themselves in an empty grandstand facing the class. Trouble. The class, members of Ochoa's bodyguard, knew it. Penny and Nickie Max knew it.

Penny had gotten the word this morning, a warning from one of the bodyguards who said, "Asbun's coming to watch you teach today, but he's coming for a reason. He is bringing *El Indio*, the Indian, with him and this guy is a crazy son of a bitch." The bodyguard said *El Indio* he is a real good knife fighter, and he never loses. "He will challenge you in front of the class," the bodyguard told Penny, "and whether you accept the challenge or back down, it does not matter. He will attack you, anyway. What you do, Eduardo?"

Penny said thanks for telling me. And that's all he said. He wasn't going to get worked up about Asbun trying to fuck him over, since it wasn't the first time and probably wouldn't be the last. And he wasn't about to go running off at the mouth, telling the bodyguard how he was going to handle *El Indio* because that was what an amateur would do, and Penny was no amateur.

Penny had a couple of hours before *El Indio* showed up. By then he'd have figured out something. Shit, he'd better have figured out something. One thing was for sure: he wasn't running. The idea never entered his head. He knew something else, too; he could take the Indian and any fucking Indian Colonel Kentucky sent against him. If Penny didn't believe that, he belonged on the first plane headed north.

The bodyguard said, *"El Indio* is *loco,* crazy. Sometimes when he kills a man, he licks blood from the knife. Fucking crazy Indian, man."

Nickie Max said, "I'll tell you what you do. You get a piece and you shoot him in the fucking dick, that's what you do. We got us a head case here, and if you ask me, the guy's going to be coked up to his eyeballs. Couple of warning shots in the forehead, then get serious and finish him off and be done with it."

"Can't," Penny said. "Anybody can pull a trigger. A gun won't prove anything. At least not in this case."

Nickie Max said, "See, that's your trouble. Lately, you been thinking too much. You know what shooting the fucker proves? Proves you enjoy living, that's what it proves."

Penny said, "Asbun wants to embarrass me as a karate man. That's what I was brought down here to teach. And that's where he wants to see me fall on my face."

"You got that in one," Nickie Max said. "So why play his game? I think you're getting soft in your old age, you know that? You go play fucking Mary Poppins to a greaseball kid like Tómas. Then you let some wacko Indian come at you with a knife. Edward, my man, read my lips: Do unto others before they do unto you. Down and dirty. Ain't no other way. Don't be turning into no pussy, you dig?"

Penny pinched Nickie Max's cheeks. "I'm on top of things. I survived a lot worse shit than this, believe me. There are no problems, only opportunities."

Nickie Max said, "Sure. Know something? Being crazy keeps me from going insane, which is more than I can say for you lately. It ain't what you're doing that's the problem. It's what Asbun's doing that's got me worried."

Six visitors. Three were San Augustín army officers, authoritative in gray-green uniforms, pants tucked into riding boots, peaked caps, and Heckler & Koch P9 pistols. According to their collar and shoulder insignia, all three were attached to general staff and that made them important. People Asbun wanted to impress. Penny didn't recall having seen these officers before. He eyed Nickie, who shook his head because they were strangers to him, too. Penny looked at the three again. He found nothing comforting in their cold gazes.

And then there were the other three. Asbun, of course, stylish as always in a tailored navy blue blazer, pink silk shirt, and the customary blue suede boots. Mirrored sunglasses. José Cool.

As for the Indian he was *mestizo,* actually. Half Spanish, half Indian, fortyish, broad-shouldered and stone-faced in a red shirt, baggy gray pants, and black-and-white wing-tipped shoes. Penny watched him climb three rows above Asbun and the others, walk several feet to his right, and sit alone. After pulling a red bandana from a shirt pocket, he tied it around his head and leaned back with his elbows on the bench behind him, staring down at Penny through slitted eyes. He had a look that could crush a diamond.

Visitor number six was Herman Fray, a small, middle-aged man with oily skin, a hooked nose, horn-rimmed glasses with a hearing aid in one stem, and wispy black hair framing a bald crown. Wealthy and high-strung, he was usually seen in all-white clothing, and today was no exception. Suit, bow tie, suspenders, and patent leather shoes. All white from neck to tippy-toes.

Fray literally put his money where his mouth was. Three of his top teeth were gold and one of those was enhanced by a small, star-shaped sapphire. And of the 180 private planes at La Merced Airport, an astounding number for a country this size, three belonged to him. The rest, as Penny learned, belonged to drug traffickers whose ranks included some of San Augustín's oldest and wealthiest families.

Herman Fray was the country's most successful money changer, with a chain of *cambio* shops in four cities and a yearly turnover of *pesos* and dollars exceeding that of San Augustín's largest banks. It was no secret that the top government and military men in the cocaine trade relied heavily upon his services. Today he sat in the gymnasium and nervously fingered a diamond pinky ring, frowning as he chewed his bottom lip. When a door slammed above him on the quarter-mile track encircling the gym, he jumped as though he'd heard a gunshot. He was usually fidgety and on edge, the kind of man who'd drown in his own sweat.

Penny looked overhead at the running track. He tapped Nickie Max on the shoulder and pointed. He said, "What's wrong with this picture?" A dozen men, mostly American and European war freaks, were on the track, and none of them were jogging. All leaned on the railing, staring down at the six figures in the grandstand and at Penny. He told Nickie Max, "I do believe the word's out."

Nickie said, "Haven't got the slightest idea what you're talking about."

Penny, eyes on the overhead track, rubbed the back of his neck. Fucking war freaks. If they couldn't find action in Africa or the Middle East, and if they couldn't get paid for wasting people in Nicaragua, Honduras, or El Salvador, they could at least lean on a gym railing in San Augustín and watch the action for free. Now Penny started to feel the tension. All that was missing were small animals and frightened birds fleeing as they did when instinct warned them of an approaching earthquake, forest fire, or some other natural disaster.

On the track a muscular black man in dark glasses, yellow tank top and gray sweat pants gave Penny a shoulder-high clenched fist, then aimed his chin at *El Indio*. Penny nodded, then pulled a khaki towel from around his neck and dried his face. The black was Lydell Colmes, a former marine he'd known casually in Nam and who was still trying to make sense of his life. After Nam, Colmes had returned home to California, landing in prison for auto theft. That was when he'd become a Black Muslim, and was recruited by Iranians to fight in the Middle East. The last time Penny had seen him, prior to San Augustín, was two years ago in Beirut where Colmes decided he'd had enough of fighting with the Shiites and wanted to move on. Penny had given him five-hundred dollars, enough to buy passage aboard a Corsican freighter bound for Cyprus. Now Colmes was living in La Merced with a teenage whore in a shack near the railroad, surviving on her earnings and what he made by selling cheap jewelry and hand-rolled cigarettes made of tobacco and low-grade coca paste.

Nickie Max, eyes on *El Indio,* said, "Jesus, did they have to pick such a homely bastard? Look at his nose, his lips. Son of a bitch is so ugly I bet he has to sneak up on a glass of water to get a drink."

Penny draped his towel around Nickie Max's neck and said, "You look thirsty to me. Why don't you take a walk over to the Coke machine. Do you a world of good."

Nickie Max chewed his bottom lip and said nothing. Then he turned, walked to the edge of the mat and slipped his bare feet into a pair of straw sandals. On the way to the Coke machine he whistled B.B. King's *Nobody Loves Me But My Mother And She Could Be Jivin', Too*. The khaki towel still hung from his neck.

Penny clapped his hands to get the bodyguards' attention. Class was still on, he told them. He selected an opponent, a balding, thickset captain, and picked up where he'd left off. He said, "You eliminate your enemy's best weapons. If your enemy kicks, attack his leg. If he punches, attack his arm. Destroy his weapons," Penny told the class, "and you can win even when you have less ability than he."

Nickie Max stepped onto the mat in his bare feet, sipping a Coke and trying to look calm. He handed Penny the khaki towel which was rolled up. Keeping his back to the grandstand, Nickie said, "The Indian's on his way."

Penny said, "I see him." *El Indio* had climbed down from the grandstand and was walking toward the mat.

Around Penny, the bodyguards moved back to the far side of the mat. Penny watched Nickie Max move away, too. Except that Nickie, sly fox that he was, had one hand inside his *gi*. Penny guessed he was holding the .32 he sometimes wore in an ankle holster. If Penny lost, *El Indio* was a dead man. Bet on it. Bet on Nickie to try and take out Asbun, too. The three officers would then waste Nickie, and it would be a fucking mess all around. Penny had to win this thing or he and Nickie Max were in deep shit.

Penny's mouth was dry; his heart was pumping fast. Time to get down. He watched the Indian draw closer. Overhead, Lydell Colmes yelled, "Do it, bro'. Use that fucking Indian up!" More shouts came from the track, all of them telling Penny to put the Indian out of business.

Penny walked to meet the Indian, stopping several feet from the mat's edge. *El Indio* stopped at the edge, right hand behind his back. After a few seconds of staring at Penny he spat on the mat and casually brought his right hand around to his front. The hand held a long-bladed knife.

He put one foot on the mat, wiping the sole on the canvas and leaving black scuff marks, giving Penny the hard eye. That was when Penny reached into the rolled towel, pulled out a can of

Coca-Cola, and threw it, overhand fastball down the middle of the plate as he'd done the year he'd pitched three shutouts as an Arizona schoolboy. He put his body behind the throw, aimed high, and hit *El Indio* in the forehead, seeing the can bounce off his skull and fly straight up in the air. *El Indio* dropped down on his ass, sitting on the floor and shaking his head to clear it. Overhead, the war freaks cheered, stomped, clapped and yelled for Penny to go for it, finish that sucker off.

Penny stepped closer, ends of the towel held in one hand. Then he swung the towel like a baseball bat. Seeing *El Indio* raise an arm to defend himself, Penny clubbed *El Indio*'s elbow, not knowing if he'd broken it but damned sure he'd hurt the man real bad. The Indian fell back clutching his damaged left elbow and still holding the knife.

Penny hurled the towel with its two cans of Coke at the Indian and rushed him, grabbing the knife hand and breaking the little finger. *El Indio* dropped the knife. The pain was evident on his face, but he refused to cry out. He spat in Penny's face. Penny grabbed his right wrist and turned the Indian over on his stomach. Then, placing his left knee on the Indian's body, exactly where shoulder and arm meet, he pulled the arm up and to the left, breaking it. This time the Indian screamed. Nickie said, "All right. All right."

Nickie Max shot a clenched fist into the air and overhead the war freaks answered with whoops and yells. A couple of them chanted, "U—S—A, U—S—A." Penny climbed off the Indian and stepped back on the mat. He never looked at Asbun. But he winked at Nickie Max, who rushed over to him, tears in his eyes, and lifted him from the ground in one powerful, painful bear hug. On the track, the war freaks carried on as if Penny had just scored the winning touchdown in the Super Bowl.

Penny had won because he understood war. It was his life, his unending course of study. The object of war is not to die for your country but to make the other bastard die for his. That was George S. Patton telling it like it is and will always be.

Strategy. The Indian was an aggressive fighter, so take that away from him. Force him to fight a defensive fight. With two busted arms, he wouldn't be fighting any kind of fight in the near future.

Let Fabio handle the fallout, if there was any.

At the moment, Penny felt ten feet tall and covered with hair, and he was going to feel that way for a long, long time.

La Merced, San Augustín

February, 1985

Carnival time. Four days of pre-Lenten carousing and celebration. When the city's inhabitants disguised themselves in outlandish costumes and paraded through riotous, music-filled streets. When strangers were kissed, fondled, invited to dance, and hit with water bombs. When drunken, laughing groups of costumed celebrants wandered from house to house in search of parties and rum punch. When the rich and the poor staged their own costume balls, parties, and even their own parades.

Carnival time. When all consciences were put on hold. And restraint was a forgotten word. And nothing mattered but the pursuit of pleasure.

Second day of carnival. Edward Penny stepped from the back seat of a chauffeured Cadillac and onto the pavement. The heat hit him hard, a reminder that in San Augustín February was the beginning of summer. Ninety degrees at 11:15 in the morning.

He looked down *Paseo Metropolitano,* a cobblestoned walkway restricted to pedestrians. All seven blocks were decorated by fountains and flower gardens and contained the city's most elegant shops as well as its largest department store. The *paseo* led to the harbor and a small Baroque church built by Jesuits in the seventeenth century, which Penny liked because its dome was a small replica of the great dome of St. Peter's Basilica in Rome. He also liked it because there were no pedlars, beggars, whores, pickpockets, or street musicians. *El Presidente* Ochoa had ordered the *paseo* kept free of what he called "human lice and shit-coated vermin." The order was rigidly enforced because *el Presidente* owned most of the street.

Penny was bodyguarding Fleur Ochoa this morning. Baby-sitting, really. His job: follow baby around while she did some last minute shopping for carnival partygoing. He'd tried to lay the job off on some of *el Presidente*'s bodyguards, but Fleur Ochoa wasn't having any of that. She wanted her Eduardo, and if she had to go to her father to have her way, she would. Self-denial was not one of her strong suits.

Penny leaned against the Cadillac door and stared along the *paseo*. It looked festive enough. Banners, streamers, posters, bright lights. And music everywhere. Noisy as hell. Crowded, too. Jammed with costumed merrymakers and fun seekers, which could present a security problem. Carnival or no carnival, nobody was going to play grab-ass with *el Presidente*'s daughter.

Penny thought, how the hell do I get her in and out of this mob? She'd have to stay close to him, that was for sure. And to the pair of presidential bodyguards who'd be with them. Penny had ordered a third man to stay with the Caddy. Someone had to watch out for car thieves. And stop wackos from tampering with the vehicle.

Fucking Nickie Max. He should have been here with Penny, but at the moment he was seeing a doctor about a bad case of the runs. Penny had warned him never to drink unpurified water, raw milk, or eat uncooked vegetables. And to his credit, Nickie had listened. But on the first day of carnival, first fucking day, Nickie bought a rum punch in a hollowed out coconut from a street vendor, drank the whole thing at once, and now had the screaming shits.

To compound matters, Nickie had forgotten to take his daily tablet of *Doxycline,* the best thing for preventing stomach trouble in tropical areas. Talk about being paranoid. Nickie was now saying he might even have hepatitis and he was worried about a slight rash near his crotch, something he did not want to carry back to his wife in Thailand. Penny said, "You might have the trots and maybe a dose from a local hooker, but you don't have hepatitis." Nickie Max said, "Fuck it. I'm going to see a doctor, and maybe I'll even freeze my shit and sell it for popsicles."

Penny helped Fleur Ochoa out of the Cadillac, offering his hand which she squeezed and held onto longer than necessary. Bit of a flirt, our little Fleur. She smiled at him, batted her long lashes, and said, "Gracias, mi Eduardo." He watched her raise both arms to remove a blue ribbon from her ponytail, free her hair, and shake it loose, a little performance for his benefit. Look but don't touch, he told himself.

She wore a long-tailed raspberry-colored silk shirt studded in rhinestones and belted at the waist by a gold chain. Her studded white jeans were skin tight and buckled at the ankles, and her shoes were purple stiletto heels. She wore clunky gold jewelry, Penny called it hardware, and she smelled of evergreen and cinnamon. A bit too busty for his taste, but definitely an arousing, sensual young woman.

To take his mind off things he shouldn't be thinking about, Penny pulled his hand from hers and slid his sunglasses from the top of his head and down in front of his eyes. Fleur, however, took his arm, told him how handsome he looked today, especially with his tan. She invited him to a party at the cliffside home of San Augustín's leading actor. Penny could even bring the tall blond woman from the British Embassy, the one he had been seeing since he had arrived. What was her name?

"Sonja," Penny said, aware Fleur knew her name and wouldn't care if he brought her to the party or not.

Fleur said in Spanish, "You can come to the party with me. As my bodyguard, of course. Bring Sonja, too, of course. It will be a great party. Dancing, champagne. There will be a midnight horse race along the edge of the cliff. The riders will be blindfolded. Very exciting."

Penny told her he'd think about it, which was as polite a no as he could come up with at the moment. He watched her run a blue-tipped index finger down his left bicep, pouting with her little pink mouth as she watched her finger go down, then up, saying, "My father, he would like for you to keep an eye on me while he is away, I bet you." Penny said, "I don't bet," and asked himself how many men would turn down what Fleur Ochoa seemed to be offering. Seemed to be, because you could never tell with women as self-obsessed and frivolous as *el Presidente*'s daughter. Could be she was a tease, nothing more. Give the gringo a case of blue balls then send him on his way. If she was fucking around with other males no one was talking.

And where was *el Presidente* during these wild and wacky four days? In Spain buying breeding bulls for one of the three ranches he owned. Carnival no longer held any appeal for him. He'd be back in three days, when the whole thing was over.

Penny slipped his arm out of Fleur's and signaled Julio and Paco to stay close. He'd lead the way, Fleur would be behind him, and they could bring up the rear. Penny was supposed to have had the day off; he'd planned to spend it in the mountains with Sonja. Get away from the heat and the noise, just the two of them. Sure.

Penny took Fleur's hand and pushed his way forward, looking back once to make sure Julio and Paco were right on top of Fleur. They were. The *paseo* was a madhouse. There were people in clown costumes and T-shirts with powdered wigs and knee britches; people in caftans, in multicolored feathers and g-strings; in American cowboy outfits, Aztec and Inca dress and wearing tiaras on top of gorilla masks. There was music—guitars, bongos, steel drums, congas, timbales, maracas. And cassette players blasting out salsa, merengue, and the saddest of romantic boleros. Not to mention Van Halen, Madonna, Wham and Bananarama. Penny found it earsplitting.

Leave it to Fleur to do things the hard way. She'd insisted on making *Carioca* her first stop. This was La Merced's newest and most chic jewelry store. She proudly told Penny that the owner had planned to be closed but for her, *Carioca* would gladly open and the owner himself would be honored to serve the daughter of our beloved *Presidente*.

A block from the store, the mob began to thin out. Penny saw fewer fun seekers on this part of the *paseo*. Fewer dancers, fewer drunks. Fewer boozehounds shoving dripping wineskins in your face and demanding you drink up because *esta la carnival*. Penny was grateful for a smaller crowd, but he'd still have to stay alert. You never knew when some fool might try to tear off Fleur Ochoa's blouse, all in observance of the festivities.

Penny looked over his shoulder, saw her smile at him and he smiled back because it didn't cost anything. Underneath the glitz she was probably a scared kid who was just beginning to learn that life was a grim and dangerous business. She squeezed Penny's hand with both of hers, looking very young, very vulnerable. Her eyes said she trusted him and he thought, maybe it's a good idea I came along today. She opened her mouth to speak and that's when they heard a woman scream.

Penny looked toward the scream. He saw her, a young Indian woman, round-faced and dumpy, bright as neon in a beaded caftan and a headdress of blue-and-white feathers. She was pointing to something at her feet. Penny was going to pass her by.

But then he saw the thing on the ground move. Saw that it was a small boy. Shirt front wet, dark. Blood. Coming from a bad stomach wound. The boy was writhing among empty beer cans, discarded newspapers, and food scraps, and he wore a *Phoenix Sun* basketball T-shirt, white with a bright orange sun on it. Just like the one Penny had given to—

Penny raced toward the boy, their eyes meeting, the boy stretching a bloodstained arm toward him and calling his name. The boy was Tómas, Alicia's son, and he was dying. Fleur Ochoa was forgotten.

Penny pushed his way through a ring of costumed, silent bystanders and dropped down beside Tómas. Anger. Penny hadn't felt it like this in a long time. A very long time. He used one hand to raise the boy's head from the street and the other to lift one of Tómas's thin arms away from the wound.

A goddamn brutal wound. Wide. Deep enough for pinkish-gray intestines to be seen. Tómas whispered Penny's name. Whispered his mother's name. Clung to Penny's arm with small hands that were sticky with blood. "It hurts," Tómas said, and then his eyes glazed over and he died. Penny closed his own eyes, ready to kill over this, then opened his eyes. When he remembered Fleur Ochoa, it was too late.

He looked toward her in time to see a stocky man in an Uncle Sam suit and Ronald Reagan mask slash Julio across the eyes with a short-bladed knife, then shove him toward the small group of people surrounding Penny and the dead Tómas.

Julio had been brought along because he was big. So when he crashed into the spectators near Penny, it was like a defensive linebacker charging at full speed and hitting offensive guards who weren't looking. Shrieking, his hands covering his bleeding eyes, Julio was a loose cannon rolling over the deck of a ship. He hit the people looking at Penny and Tómas and several of them went down. The Indian woman landed on the squatting Penny, knocking the wind from him, dropping him on his back. As he shoved her aside and frantically tried to crawl over someone else, he saw Uncle Sam cut the throat of a screaming Fleur Ochoa, then disappear into the crowd.

Penny wanted to believe it wasn't happening to him. But he knew better. He felt sick enough to throw up. And he felt tired. He'd been tricked in spades. Faked right out of his shoes. Tripped up because of Tómas. As he ran toward the downed Fleur Ochoa, he remembered that Nickie had warned him about the boy becoming a problem, something Penny swore to himself would never happen. Well, it had. Had Penny ever been thrown off-balance like this before? Never. Never, never, never.

Paco. Almost as big as Julio. He'd been taken out, too. He lay face down near Fleur Ochoa, blood seeping from beneath his head. The guy who'd done this had been unreal. So unreal he was scary. *How could anybody be that good?*

Penny stepped over Paco's body, feeling the crowd pull away from him as he crouched beside Fleur Ochoa. The Browning was in his hand and useless unless he was going to kill himself. Her blood was bright. So very bright, which meant it was coming from the arteries. The killer had known exactly where to cut. He was no amateur. Penny, his eyes tearing, saw Fleur Ochoa blink twice and her body shook as though she were cold. Seconds later, she was dead.

Silence. Except for carnival noises and music coming from the other end of the *paseo*. And the shrieking of seagulls as they circled a fishing boat now pulling into the harbor. On either side of the *paseo* near Penny costumed revelers stood with their backs against store windows and fountains and quietly watched him touch Fleur Ochoa's hair. They saw him blink away tears. And they heard the harsh shouts and footsteps rushing toward them. Penny heard nothing. And he didn't see the three uniformed soldiers push through the crowd and aim automatic rifles at him. They ordered him to put down the *pistola* or they would fire. Not far away, a blinded Julio crawled toward the door of a posh men's shop, shouting, "I am blind. *Madre de dios*, give me back my eyes. I beg you, give me back *mis ojos*."

Tense and uneasy, Nickie Max stepped from the confessional in the church of Santo Domingo at sundown. He wore dark glasses, a priest's cassock with a Roman collar, and he carried a small suitcase in one hand. He had shaved his moustache and cut his ponytail. He looked around the empty church. The hand inside his cassock gripped the butt of a silenced Mark .22.

He stood back to a pillar in the quiet church until his eyes became used to the darkness. Until he was certain he was not being followed. Then he walked down a side aisle, under century-old ceiling paintings of Christ's trial and crucifixion and past stained-glass windows turned gold by a setting sun. When he reached a group of choir stalls that had been hand-carved by sixteenth-century Franciscan monks, he turned left and stepped into a small chapel lit only by several tall, white candles on either side of a wooden altar.

Getting too old for this shit, he thought. When he was younger the whole fucking world was a smooth track. Back then, he had energy to burn. Party hearty and bop till you drop. But those days were long gone, boys and girls. He'd lost some hair, teeth, and illusions. These days he lay awake at night worried about getting wrinkles on the brain. Worried that maybe he couldn't cut it anymore. That was life for you; always sticking it up your ass with no days off. Life was forcing him to prove himself once more. Prove he could stay alive. And save Eddie.

He looked around the darkened chapel for something to sit on. And sensed he wasn't alone. The adrenaline began rushing and his stomach, which had been bothering him for hours, suddenly felt worse. He started to sweat more. All systems go. He set the suitcase down on the stone floor and slipped his hand back into the cassock. Someone to his left, near the confessional. Nickie Max slowly pulled out the .22.

A male voice said, "Chill out, homeboy. You don't want to go wasting your friends, especially since you ain't got that many. How you doing on this festive occasion?" Nickie Max exhaled, took his hand out of the cassock and wiped it on his thigh.

Lydell Colmes and two men strolled out of the darkness near the confessional. In the soft candlelight Colmes said, "Damn, look at you. You suppose to be Michael Jackson or somebody? One a them Jehovah's Witnesses come round to people's houses and be saving their souls?"

Nickie Max said, "Stole this from a church near the *Verde* market. Had to do something. The fuckers are after me. After any merc, including you guys."

"Tell me about it," Lydell Colmes said. "Everybody's crawling into a hole and pulling the hole in after them. Right now's a bad time to be any kind of foreign military man."

"You guys sure you weren't followed?"

Colmes snorted. "We ain't exactly pussies. Nobody be following us. We made damn sure a that. We got our ass on the line, too, remember?"

Nickie Max looked at the other two men. One was Jürgen

Paderborn, a fortyish German, muscular and red-faced, with graying blond hair and a bulbous, battered nose. The other was Emil Osmond, a thirtyish American from Idaho, a large, mistrustful, bearded man with a low forehead and a glass eye.

Nickie Max thought, how the fuck can I save Eddie with only four men? Lydell Colmes was the only one he'd talked to about a rescue, and even he hadn't been that enthusiastic about the idea. All Lydell had said was he'd think about it and see who else he could scare up. Nickie had said, "Might be better if I told whoever you get what I have in mind. You just say Nickie Max wants to talk and let it go at that."

Eddie and his high standards. He wouldn't consider Lydell, Paderborn, and Emil Osmond as top of the line. They were losers, and he'd said so a thousand times. Well, Nickie Max was in no position to pick and choose. He had to improvise. Make do with whatever he could scrounge up. Shit, they'd all probably die anyway, Eddie included. Nickie Max could only give it his best shot. That's us, he thought. The A-Team. Just like on TV. Three white guys and a black asshole.

At least they were all pros. Lydell and Osmond had been around and so had Paderborn. The German had fought with West Germany's GSG 9 Commandoes, Rhodesia's Selous Scouts, South Africa's Special Services and he claimed to have been with "Mad Mike" Hoare on his disastrous Seychelles operation. Talk about things going wrong. Almost everyone who'd signed on for that one had ended up in a South African prison, including Mad Mike himself. Paderborn also trained terrorists in Libya and when the got drunk enough he'd sometimes dial a Tripoli number which he swore was Khadafy's.

Emil Osmond was ex-Special Forces, with merc experience in El Salvador, Lebanon, Guatemala and he'd fought with the Provisional IRA in Northern Ireland. The British had a murder warrant out for his arrest because of his role in the machine gunning of a Protestant church in Belfast, in which 18 people, mostly women and children, had been killed. Osmond was also wanted in the United States for questioning in two deaths that had occurred in a Florida training camp for mercenaries during an exercise which had featured live rattlesnakes. Osmond and Paderborn spent a lot of time together. Penny called them the Wacko Twins.

Nickie was about to speak when Paderborn lifted one hand in

a stop signal. The German said, "We're here, Emil and I, for two reasons. One: we need a place to hide and this is as good as any. Two: since your friend Edward Penny more or less is the cause of us having to run, we thought perhaps you might be able to help us get out of this godforsaken country."

Nickie Max said, "First things first. I want you to help me get Eddie away from Asbun."

Lydell Colmes said, "That all you want? Shit, I thought you wanted us do something impossible. Hey, you got somethin' wrong with your mind? Anyway, how you know Asbun got him?"

"I called the presidential palace," Nickie said. "I just wanted to let Eddie know I'd meet him back at the villa. Figured I'd leave a message. That's when one of the bodyguards told me the shit had hit the fan. Fleur's dead, he says. And Eddie's being blamed. Asbun's got him at his beach home. Guy tells me he likes Eddie, all the bodyguards like him, but they can't do anything. Everybody's scared of Asbun. Guy wishes me good luck and tells me to get the hell out of San Augustín as fast as I can."

Lydell Colmes said, "The man has a point. Beginning to feel a draft round here myself."

"Something else," Nickie Max said. "The bodyguard told me Asbun's claiming Fleur's death is part of a CIA plot to take out the whole Ochoa family. The president, Fabio, the sisters, the family dog. Ochoa's flying in from Spain and before he gets here Asbun's saying he'll have broken Eddie. You people have any idea what that means? Because if you don't, I'll spell it out for you."

They didn't have to be told. Emil Osmond said in a deep voice, "You're sure about him being at Asbun's place?"

Nickie Max nodded. "That's where Asbun takes his special prisoners. I believe what the bodyguard told me, but I figured out a way to make sure. Look, Asbun hates Eddie's guts. Everybody knows it. Now's his chance to get rid of Eddie and every merc in this fucking country. Asbun's gonna look like a big man. He's going to be the guy who broke the CIA plot."

Paderborn said, "So that's why we're being hunted like bloody rabbits."

Lydell Colmes said, "Plot? I don't know nothin' 'bout no plot."

"Whether you guys like it or not, you're being dragged into this thing," Nickie Max said. "Fleur Ochoa was the old man's favorite kid, and I don't have to tell you how crazy he is. When he comes back he's going to come down hard on every merc, every shooter, every soldier of fortune he can find. Asbun doesn't like us much, either. And now he's got the excuse he's been looking for to come after us with all of his White Knives. He'll kill us or drive us out of the country, take your pick. Any of you guys thinks he's in for a long and happy life around here, think again. The sooner you hightail it out of here, the better."

He paused, watching them think. And worry. Then he said, "I've been scheming on this thing and I've come up with a way to get us all out of the country, every one of us. A pretty easy way, if you want to know the truth."

Lydell Colmes said, "Sound like we just flap our arms and fly away."

Nickie said, "And we don't have to leave empty-handed."

Paderborn pointed to the suitcase. "Don't tell me that's full of money."

Lydell Colmes said, "Maybe my man's carrying around a supply of happy dust. Got him a couple of kilos put aside for a rainy day."

Nickie didn't have time to bullshit, so he crouched down and lay the suitcase on the stone floor, opened the snaps, and turned back the top. "Check it out." They did. Emil Osmond whistled. Paderborn grinned, and Lydell Colmes smiled and said, "Mercy, mercy, mercy." They stared at pistols, MCA-10s, C-4 plastique explosives, a pair of K-Bar knives, and smoke grenades. Nickie said nothing about the money and false passports for him and Eddie, which were hidden in a false bottom. He closed the case and stood up.

"Eddie's idea," he said. "'Always plan ahead,' he told me. First week we're in La Merced, he hides this case under the floor of the second confessional on the right. Figured it had to be safe in here."

He shook his head and whispered, "Warned him about that kid Tómas. Warned him."

Paderborn crouched over the suitcase and began stroking it. "Someone else knew about the boy. Someone very smart. And very, very good. You have to admire a man who is that clever and at the same time is such a skilled fighter."

Nickie Max stared down at the German and tried to keep his voice even, because he needed these guys and it didn't make sense to piss them off. But he said what he felt. "If you don't mind, I mean, if it's all right with you, I don't feel like admiring the man. He's the son of a bitch who put Eddie in Asbun's hands. I mean, I know we're in church and everything, but me, I got a hard-on for this guy."

Paderborn said, "I'm sorry. Penny is your friend and I should have been more careful in my choice of words. Again, I apologize."

Nickie Max said, "Asbun's going to torture him, then he's going to kill him, and he's going to make sure that Eddie dies hard. What I want is for you guys to help me get Eddie away from Asbun and out of the country. Help me, and I'll show you how to get your hands on some real money. Big bucks. And I've got a way for you to get it out of the country. It's a chance for all of us to do what we do best. And get paid for it."

Lydell Colmes said, "Don't want much, do you? Secret police after you. Army after you. And you say we got to go into Asbun's house, where he's surrounded by his own people—"

"Last thing they're expecting us to do," Nickie said.

Paderborn nodded. Smiled. And looked at Emil Osmond who nodded back. And didn't smile.

Nickie Max said to Lydell Colmes, "I don't know about these other guys, but you owe Eddie."

The black man looked up at a ceiling painting of the twelve Apostles and scratched his throat, wondering if there was a way to forget about the debt he owed that white man and if he couldn't forget about it, just how was he going to deal with the situation.

Nickie Max said to the others, "It's true, I'm asking you to help me because my friend is jammed up. He became my friend the way any of us make friends in our line of work." His voice broke and he stopped talking and tried to clear his throat. And that was when he sensed he'd gotten through to those men who were stone killers and didn't give a shit about anything or anybody, but who understood friendship in a way civilians never would, who knew that combat drew you closer in ways that couldn't be explained to someone who hadn't been there.

Lydell Colmes said, "Homeboy, you have painted a very black picture of things to come. Everything's darker than three feet up a bull's ass. You're right about Asbun. Colonel Kentucky is bad to the bone. We take him on, we better be ready to go all the way. Thing I'm interested in is your plan for us to depart this tropical paradise."

Paderborn nodded. "I second the motion. Emil?"

The big man stopped scratching his balls. "You make the call, Jürgen. I'll just ride with the tide and go with the flow. Ain't that what it's all about? Live by chance, love by choice, and kill by preference."

"Then from this moment on, let effort be your motto," the German said. He pointed to Nickie Max. "Look at him. See how determined he is. He's quite prepared to kill us all to save his friend from the White Knives. Admirable. Really and truly admirable. I'd almost follow such a man into battle for nothing. Almost. Forgive me, Mr. Maximillian, but you were saying something about big bucks."

Seven-seventeen P.M. Herman Fray followed Raul his bodyguard out of a restaurant in La Merced's Chinatown and into a narrow street jammed with carnival celebrants. Chinatown was a small area of tea parlors, herb shops, restaurants and stores selling goods imported from China, Taiwan, and Hong Kong. Fray found it crowded most of the time. As far as he was concerned, carnival made it a hell on earth. And difficult for him to get to his main exchange tonight and put in a few hours work.

Tonight Fray had had a rather upsetting experience in Chinatown. It occurred during dinner with two slim, polite Chinese gentlemen who had recently been taught an all-important lesson regarding drug dealing in San Augustín: *El Presidente* Ochoa always had the last word here, and to think differently was to take your life in your hands. The two Chinese gentlemen had been importing heroin from Taiwan and selling it throughout Central America for an astounding profit. Of course, they had the approval of *el Presidente* in return for one third of the profits.

Recently Ochoa had demanded sixty percent of everything, a request not open to negotiation. The Chinese had thought this highly unreasonable and so had their Taiwanese contacts, some of whom were members of that country's government. From Taiwan came word there would be trouble. Ochoa then sent his reply. Around Christmas a private plane exploded in flight, killing the son of one local Chinese drug dealer, along with the son's wife and baby daughter. Ochoa hadn't liked being threatened.

Fray hadn't been surprised when the Chinese had quickly given in and given Ochoa his sixty percent. And tonight over dinner the two Chinese had been friendly, accommodating, and predicted they would be moving more heroin in the future. Everyone involved was going to get richer, they told Fray. Then one of them said, "Isn't it sad about President Ochoa's daughter being murdered at this happy time of the year?" The Chinese knew how painful it was to lose a child. *El Presidente* had their sympathy.

With a sickening feeling in his stomach, Fray realized a frightening truth: The Chinese were telling him that *el Presidente* Ochoa, who had killed one of their children, had today been paid back in kind. Giving in to Ochoa and pretending to be beaten down had only been part of their strategy. The Chinese had no intention of allowing themselves to be slaughtered merely to fill someone's purse. Fray was as certain of this as he was of his own name.

The two Chinese then excused themselves, saying they had to attend a private party. As an afterthought, one of them said that at some appropriate time in the future he hoped *el Presidente* would be willing to sit down and discuss an adjustment in their current arrangement. There was an advantage in reciprocal concessions, the Chinese said.

Herman Fray walked out of the Chinatown restaurant frightened and excited by what he knew. Let this business with Fleur Ochoa end with the disposal of the American Edward Penny, who was now in Asbun's hands. Discretion was the better part of valor. Better for Fray to close his eyes to this situation, before Asbun or *el Presidente* closed them for him.

When Fray arrived at his exchange, he noticed that the two men on guard were not the ones originally assigned to his building. One was black, and the other was blond, German or Scandinavian. What in God's name was going on here? Fray didn't like this. Didn't like it at all. He turned to say something to Raul, turned in time to see a chubby man in a priest's black cassock step close to the bodyguard. Raul suddenly collapsed, as though he'd suffered a stroke or heart attack, and he would have fallen if the priest and a large, bearded man in the uniform of a San Augustín soldier hadn't caught him by the armpits and held him up.

No one in the crowd around Fray seemed to notice anything was wrong. He knew there was, especially when he saw the two door guards leave their post, take a quiet Raul from the priest and the large man, and hold him while the priest and large man sandwiched Fray in between them. The priest was in front of Fray and pressing a folded newspaper against his stomach. After looking around, the priest lifted up a corner of the newspaper and allowed Fray to see the silenced pistol he was holding. The priest touched his own ear. A terrified Fray got the message and with a shaky hand turned on his hearing aid.

The priest pressed his lips to Fray's ear and said in English, "We're going inside. I know the alarm system because I helped to install it, so don't do anything stupid."

The priest was Edward Penny's friend, the American they called *El Loco,* the crazy one. The madman with the hair-trigger temper. Maximillian. The one Asbun said could never be reasoned with.

Fray felt nauseous; his skin was suddenly cold and clammy. He began to suffer from shortness of breath. He knew what Maximillian and his friends were about to do. He didn't know how, but he knew what they had in mind. The money changer was close to tears.

He heard Maximillian say, "You know who I am?" Fray cleared his throat, knew he couldn't speak, so he simply nodded. He understood English and he spoke well because English was the international banking language. He understood every word Maximillian was saying just as he understood that the American would as soon kill him as look at him.

"We're going inside," Maximillian said, "and you're going to do exactly what I tell you to do. If you go near any of the alarms or try to warn anybody, I'll kill you where you stand. *Comprende?*"

"I understand."

"I hope you do."

Maximillian guided Fray out of the path of a fat black woman dressed as an Aztec and followed by several half-naked black children dressed mostly in rags. The American said, "Inside, you're to make two telephone calls. Just two. The first one is to Asbun. The other I'll tell you about after you make the first. All of us here, my friends and I, we speak Spanish, so be careful what you say. Get smart and you end up being a ghost. Move."

Fray hesitated. "You are going to Asbun's villa to rescue your friend, am I right?"

Maximillian said, "Wrong. *We* are going. We includes you. Remember that when you're on the phone to the colonel. You tip him off, and you're going to be caught right in the middle of whatever goes down."

Fray said, "I do as you say. You will have my complete cooperation. This I promise. But I must tell you that Asbun, he has guards at his home, and there are other men in that place as well."

"Men who are torturing my friend," Maximillian said. "Now let's cut the bullshit and get inside. Oh, here's a little something for you to think about. Your two guards? They're across the street in the park. They're in front of the bandstand but they can't hear anything because they're dead. See, anybody looking at them probably thinks they're drunk. But you and me, well we know different, don't we? You give me a problem and I'm gonna end your days right here and now, and I won't bother dragging your fat ass to the park. Nothing matters except getting Eddie out, and if you think I'm crazy, you are absolutely right. So you think on that, money man. Think on how you got a crazy man with a gun standing next to you. Now let's get the hell inside."

Herman Fray felt as though he were trapped in a coffin, still alive while being driven to his own funeral.

At 9:15 P.M. the money changer and the four mercenaries, all in a stolen police car, cleared a pair of electric gates at one end of a private driveway and began a slow climb up a gentle foothill leading to Efrain Asbun's villa. A silent Maximillian drove past mimosa and poplar trees, the folded newspaper on his lap, seemingly unaware of Fray who sat beside him. Fray, fighting a vicious migraine headache, kneaded his temples with both thumbs and stared through the windshield at a spectacular view of the Pacific Ocean, white-faced cliffs, and a full moon shining down on pleasure craft anchored beyond a coral reef. He did not want to die and would do anything at all to prolong his life.

If the three Americans and the big-nosed German were frightened, it didn't show. Fray saw them as unnaturally calm. Alert as eagles in search of prey, but calm. Yes, there was a tension coming from them, but it was not that of men who were anxious or apprehensive. It was the tension of those who were mentally responsive. Perceptive. Brisk in action. Fray, meanwhile, was so terrified that he could recall no stronger feeling in his entire existence.

The police car reached a crest, then rolled down an incline and slowed as it rounded a sharp curve. Its headlights picked up the villa's red tile roof and bougainvillea-covered walls topped by broken glass. Maximillian braked in front of wrought-iron gates. Fray was now the nearest one to the entrance. He would be the first person the guard would see. The money changer wiped his forehead with a damp handkerchief as Maximillian cut the motor and dimmed the headlights.

Inside the car the five men stared at the moonlight-covered, two-story building which had been constructed around a cobbled courtyard. All first floor lights were on; the top floor was dark. They heard water running into an unseen cistern. Mosquitoes whined around their faces. Not far away a guard dog snarled then barked rapidly, setting a second dog to barking inside the stucco villa. Booted footsteps raced toward the front gate. Fray felt the tip of Maximillian's pistol against his left rib cage.

At the exchange, Fray had watched the German kill his two clerks with a single shot each in the back of the head, doing it neatly and without hesitation as the others looked on with indifference, waiting with two pillow cases crammed with American dollars they'd scooped from the counting tables and taken from vaults unprotected by time locks. Maximillian had told Fray the killings were necessary; no one was to be left behind to warn Asbun or alert the authorities.

Fray had vomited right there in the office, on expensive gray shag carpet and on the trousers of his white suit. The black man had put an arm around Fray's shoulders, saying, "You shouldn't ought to get worked up like that 'cause it's just business. Something that had to be done." Later, the black and the big bearded man would kill the two guards manning the gates at the driveway leading to Asbun's villa. Something else that had to be done.

The killings had their effect on Herman Fray; he became more determined than ever to survive and to do that, he decided to make himself valuable to the mercenaries, so valuable that he would not only prolong his life but actually be allowed to live. This is how he prospered in San Augustín, making himself indispensable to power and he was going to follow the same course now. He had no other choice. What the mercenaries told him to do, he did without question and did it as well as his nerves and shaking hands would allow.

He made the two telephone calls they wanted, the first to one of the two pilots he kept on twenty-four-hour alert, the second to Asbun's villa. The pilot was ordered to go to the airport at once and prepare the Gulfstream III, Fray's largest plane, for a midnight takeoff from La Merced Airport. Destination: Mexico. No further explanation was necessary, nor did the pilot ask for one. Herman Fray did not have to account to aviation authorities, customs inspectors, or pilots.

The second telephone call. Fray's heart was in his mouth as he talked and he almost vomited again because this time he'd telephoned Asbun's villa with Maximillian and the German listening on extensions. Fray's reason for calling? One of his contacts at the American Embassy had heard a rumor that Edward Penny was in the hands of the White Knives. The contact wanted it known that Penny had no connection to the United States Government. Colonel Asbun was to not take seriously any protest the embassy might make regarding the arrest of one of its citizens. Edward Penny was just another soldier of misfortune who had gotten in over his head in Central America. He wasn't the first, and he wouldn't be the last.

Asbun, of course, hadn't come to the phone. He was occupied. The man who spoke to Fray said Asbun was downstairs with Penny in "The Choir," where everybody ended up singing whatever song the colonel wanted to hear. By tomorrow, the man said, Penny would be dead and the American Embassy could protest all it wanted to. The matter would be closed. Fray was told that most of the death squad wasn't at the villa; the members were out hunting for foreign mercenaries. Colonel Asbun wanted to rid himself of these lice as quickly as possible. Any who were picked up would be taken to *Soledad* prison on the other side of

La Mercéd. There weren't many White Knives at the villa. Just enough to deal with Edward Penny.

Fray hung up and said to Maximillian, "I tell you this in all sincerity because I know about Colonel Asbun. Always when he takes prisoners to 'The Choir,' he sends his family and servants away. They stay with friends and relatives, because Asbun does not want witnesses. He wants no one around who could testify against him at some future trial. One exception to this," Fray said, "is Asbun's father. He is very old, very sick, and Asbun takes care of him. He will be in the house."

A half mile or so from Asbun's villa, Fray asked Maximillian why he and the others didn't head directly to the airport. Why risk their lives to save a man who was either dead or certainly close to it, for Asbun and the White Knives were capable of quite harsh and cruel conduct. "You have money," Fray said, "and a plane awaits you." He himself would cooperate to the fullest extent in getting them past customs and other authorities. He would simply say the mercenaries were his bodyguards, protecting money belonging to *el Presidente,* money on its way to Mexico. Common sense said avoid the violent confrontation awaiting them at Asbun's villa, a confrontation that could cost Fray's life as well.

No answer.

He looked at Maximillian, the wild-eyed one, expecting him as the leader to say something, and what Fray saw was the face of a man possessed. Without looking at Fray he spoke with an intense, uncontained emotion. "Mister, if you can't figure it out for yourself, then nothing I say will ever clear it up for you."

It was, of course, a most confusing answer. No, thought Fray, it was a stupid answer and these ignorant men are not worth listening to. Stupid, stupid men bouncing back and forth between extreme audacity and the most unreasonable behavior. In their place Fray would have taken the money and fled the country. He would have avoided Asbun's villa as he would a leper colony. And he would have been correct because he was a smarter, more respectable man than those in the car with him. He was rich, a family man with prominent and powerful friends and he gave generously to the church and other charities.

Then he suddenly realized something: Maximillian's answer was confusing only to a man without honor, to a man like Fray.

Los Animales were killers and thieves but in their own way they
were men of honor. Perhaps this loyalty to a comrade was their
only point of honor but they were willing to risk their lives for it.
Fray, in his heart, knew he had no honor, that he willingly played
the whore for *el Presidente*, Asbun and anyone strong enough to
inspire fear in him.

Yes, he had always been more concerned with money than
principles and his morality had been measured solely in profita-
bility. As the car rolled through the night, he heard whispers of
despair say that he was a lesser man, *si*, a much lesser man than
these *animales*. The voice of the soul became louder and he was
shamed into silence.

Nickie Max followed Herman Fray out of the police car and into
the glare of the guard's flashlight. He shaded his eyes with one
hand; the other hand was under the folded newspaper held close
to his chest. He belched once and hoped he didn't have to shit
because coming into Asbun's villa like this was giving him another case of the runs.

He watched Fray, who was a couple of steps in front, move
toward the guard at the gate, smiling to the man as he held up a
bottle of rum in each hand. "For you, Ignacio, my friend," Fray
said. "If you cannot come to the carnival," Fray told him, "then
I, Herman Fray, bring the carnival to you." He jerked his head
toward the police car. "I have a case of rum in the trunk, enough
for every man in the villa, providing, that is, there aren't too
many. How many people are here tonight?"

Ignacio didn't answer, making Nickie antsy, so antsy that he
stepped to Fray's left and positioned himself for a clear shot. If he
had to clip the guard right here and now, fine. No problem. He
watched Ignacio shine the flashlight at the police car and that
took the light away from Nickie's eyes, giving him a chance to
check out Iggy. A tall greaser in his thirties, wearing jeans, tank
top, and straw sandals. Carrying a shotgun, an Ithaca 37 Stainless
handgrip 12-gauge with an eight-shot magazine. Enough weapon
to turn anybody into chopped meat.

From where he stood, Nickie Max could smell the beer on
Iggy, which meant the man had probably been celebrating carni-
val while on duty, a no-no if you had any brains. At the moment
Iggy was having one hell of a time controlling his dog, a slaver-

ing Doberman who was on his hind legs, clawing at the gate and barking loud enough to be heard in Argentina. Nickie was going to enjoy wasting this mutt.

As Nickie watched, Fray said to Ignacio, "I am here to pick up a package from Colonel Asbun which I must take to Mexico tonight. Like you, I am sorry to miss the carnival. But . . ." He shrugged. Smiled.

Ignacio relaxed. "I understand," he said to Fray. "Yes, I understand." His eyes were still on the car.

Fray looked at the police car then said, "My bodyguards. It would not do for anything to happen to the colonel's package."

The flashlight went to Nickie Max who didn't like that one bit and brought the newspaper up to protect his face from the glare. He heard Fray say, "He is no priest. He is my pilot, and he would fuck your sister and your dog and he would fuck you too if you bent over to pick up a dollar bill, believe me. He is dressed like that because of the carnival."

Nickie Max heard Ignacio laugh, and then the flashlight was turned off. Nickie blinked and shook his head to clear his eyes, seeing red circles and dancing pinpricks of light because the flashlight had messed up his vision, but somehow he made out Ignacio's form and saw the guard put down the shotgun, unlock the gate, then use both hands to pull back on the leash of the barking Doberman. Nickie heard Ignacio say to Fray, "Hey, you got enough rum for eight men?"

Fray said, "We have enough for eighty men," and laughed to show that he had just made a joke.

Nickie watched Fray put a smile on his face and step up to the gate, rum in hand. The money changer waited while Ignacio pulled the gate open with one hand and did his best to hang on to the Doberman with the other. When the gate was open, the dog calmed down a bit, but with Dobermans that didn't mean much. Nickie knew these were high-strung animals, always edgy and when they decided to attack, the bastards always went for the throat.

He heard Ignacio say the colonel's orders were to let no one into the villa, but Ignacio knew this didn't apply to Senor Fray. While the guard was reaching for the two bottles of rum at the end of Fray's outstretched arms, Nickie Max walked up to the gate, stuck the silenced .22 through a space in the wrought-iron

design, and shot the Doberman in the head twice, then shot Ignacio twice in the face and once in the chest. The guard fell to his
knees, remaining in that position with his head and right shoulder
against the gate. Fray, standing just inside the gate, dropped the
rum on the courtyard surface, a mosaic of pebbles, old bricks,
and local stones. His breathing became rapid, shallow, and he felt
his heartbeat quicken.

With the German holding Ignacio's flashlight, Fray watched
as Maximillian placed the suitcase on the car hood, snapped it
open, and removed a pair of hypodermic needles. Each needle
was attached to a length of string. Maximillian hung both around
his neck and closed the suitcase. Then both he and the German
removed their shoes and socks, placing them and the suitcase in
the front seat of the car. Without a word, the black and Osmond
also removed their shoes and socks and put them in the car. Fray
found this cold, silent efficiency to be quite intimidating.

At the gate, Fray stood surrounded by the mercenaries as they
stared at the courtyard and the villa. To their left several cars and
a single van were parked in front of a wall where a fountain
shaped like a lion's head spouted water into an eighteenth-century
cistern. To their right was a trio of hundred-year-old oak trees
ringed by a collection of pre-Columbian sculpture fragments.
Straight ahead was a white marble fountain in the middle of a bed
of hibiscus and bird-of-paradise flowers. The villa lay thirty
yards beyond the fountain.

Behind Fray, Maximillian and the German whispered to each
other and then the two stepped forward and he watched Maximillian point to an outside stone staircase on the right side of the
villa. It led from the ground to a second-floor terrace, which Fray
had said belonged to the master bedroom. Beyond the house and
still within the walls was a tennis court, swimming pool, and a
stable. The pool had a cabana which was sometimes used as a
guest house. But whenever Asbun and the White Knives "invited
someone to sing in the choir," the cabana was always empty.

Fray willed himself not to panic. His fear left him feeling
naked and ashamed. There would be nothing more terrifying, he
knew, than to take the first step toward the villa, to cross the
courtyard with the mercenaries as they moved closer to Asbun
and the White Knives. He was rooted to the spot by a terrible fear

that now possessed his entire being. He could not understand men like the *animales,* who appeared to love the very idea of danger.

Naked and shivering, Edward Penny lay on a metal cot in a large, low-ceilinged concrete room behind Efrain Asbun's wine cellar. His hands were cuffed behind him and his eyes covered by adhesive tape. His head was shaved; it bled where the straight razor had left deep gashes in the scalp. Behind the tape he saw only a red glow. Asbun had ordered light bulbs held near his eyes for a long time. Penny could still feel the intense heat.

The taste of blood was in his mouth, and he stank of his own vomit. Asbun had used electrodes on his teeth, and the pain had been incredible. It was as if a series of bombs were continually going off in Penny's head and he thought, Jesus, I can deal with that. With that. But then Asbun had used the beads, which were actually a string of small electrodes. Claudio, the little Red Brigade terrorist, forced him to swallow them, and when the electrodes did their job it was as if Penny's insides were being ripped apart by thousands of pieces of glass, cutting and slicing everywhere.

The pain was so horrific that he couldn't even scream, or move. He vomited and went into convulsions, and if he hadn't been tied down on the metal bed and handcuffed, he would have butted his head against the wall until he passed out. His insides felt like one single, horrible wound. The beads had also left him violently thirsty, and his fear of more convulsions was so great that he did what he'd prayed he'd never do. He wept.

There was some interrogation, though Asbun seemed to have already made up his mind about what happened with Fleur Ochoa and why. He asked Penny, who hired you to help murder *el Presidente*'s daughter and Penny said, no one. Asbun asked how many American mercenaries were involved in the plot and please reveal in detail the CIA's role in all of this. When Penny said there was no plot, Asbun touched his penis with a cattle prod and would not stop, despite Penny's screams.

Asbun said, I want a signed confession implicating Fabio Ochoa and the American mercenaries in Fleur Ochoa's death and in an attempted overthrow of *el Presidente Ochoa.* "Fabio brought you here, did he not?" he asked. "That's why I took you from the soldiers. You see, I do not trust Fabio to maintain the proper perspective on his sister's death where you are concerned, my friend. I will get to the bottom of this and present my findings to *el Presidente* on his return. I will show him that his son made a mistake in bringing men like you into this country."

Asbun removed his blue-tinted glasses and began cleaning them with a yellow silk handkerchief. "You are alone, *compadre*. All alone. Your friend the wild man, Maximillian, he is in prison with all the others. But you are a hero, am I right? So you must act like one. You must now rely on yourself, *compadre*, for you have no one else. No one at all."

A dazed Penny heard Asbun talking in Spanish to one of the White Knives, a tall Frenchman with a stye in one eye and wearing a pair of Mickey Mouse ears. The Frenchman then crossed the room and turned up the volume on a stereo. Giant speakers vibrated with the Bee Gees score from *Saturday Night Fever*. Penny tensed. The music was to drown out his screams. More torture on the way. He asked Asbun what he wanted to know. Asbun smiled and said nothing. He turned to go, then stopped and moved back to the cot, leaning down to put his lips close to Penny's ear. He said, "Well, *compadre*, there is one thing I want. I want you should ask me the question. Everybody who comes to the choir always asks me the same question, and I want to hear it from you. I want you to say—*will you please kill me?* That is what I want you to say."

Asbun stepped back and someone else sat on the edge of the metal cot. Claudio. The Italian said, "You are not Superman any longer, Mr. Edward Penny. You have gone from hero to zero. The elephant has turned into a mouse. Hello, Mr. Mouse. I think you have pissed on yourself, Mr. Mouse."

And as Penny began shaking from the effect of the electrodes inside him, and from fear, Claudio attached wires to his gums, nose, teeth, then to his nipples and over his heart, and finally to his penis. A needle was painfully inserted into his urethra. Jesus Christ, no.

This couldn't be happening to him. Not to him. He was ready to sign a statement, any statement, and he said so because he knew what was coming next. He'd seen it done to prisoners in Nam, to Palestinians in Lebanon, to black marketeers in Nigeria. The wires on his body were attached to a Tucker phone, an old battery-operated telephone used by armies in the field. Penny yelled, "Put whatever you want on a piece of paper and I'll sign it."

The first jolt of electricity slammed into his body, lifting him from the cot. His legs pulled hard against the ropes tying him down; he tore skin from both ankles, bloodying the ropes. A second jolt and he begged them to stop. *Begged.* Asbun, back to Penny, lit a black, twisted Cuban cigar and blew smoke at the air duct. Then he looked at the manicured nails on one hand and leaned down to speak to Claudio. He said, *"Mas."* More.

Nickie Max was in the house. He used a sleeve to wipe sweat from his forehead. It took him a few seconds but he finally worked spit into his dry mouth. His stomach felt ice cold, and he'd probably crapped in his pants and didn't know it. He thought, I'm getting too old for this shit.

Why the fuck was he here, anyway? Because he and Eddie had shared something in Nam, because they'd become like brothers over there, because that had been the best time of Nickie's life and he hadn't felt as good since. America sure hadn't cared about the men it sent over there. You had your buddies and that's all you had. That's why I'm here, Nickie Max thought. I'm here because Eddie would fucking do the same for me.

He checked guest bedrooms, a small study, a maid's room. All empty. He even looked in a linen closet. He closed the linen closet door, then opened it again and removed two folded pink sheets. One more room to go on this floor, then it was downstairs to link up with the others. By then Paderborn should have secured the rest of the house except for "The Choir." That's where Herman Fray came in. He was to take them down to the wine cellar which led to the "choir."

He stopped in front of the last room, which was near the staircase. He heard voices coming from downstairs and held his breath until he heard Paderborn say, check both windows, and then there was silence. Nickie tried to blink the perspiration from his eyes, finally giving up and wiping his face on one of the sheets. His nerves were about to come unfastened and he didn't care if he pooped in his pants or not. Just take care of business, he told himself, then shag ass out of here.

He opened the door and almost jumped out of his skin. Someone in the room. Shit. He felt it without knowing who or even where the bastard was. He was ready to kill, didn't matter who, and then he relaxed. Thank de good Lawd for moonlight. It shone through open rattan doors, shone on someone lying in a four-poster bed under white mosquito netting.

Nickie Max saw a small figure wearing a white night gown and leaning back against several pillows, head moving from side to side as it hummed tonelessly. Asbun's father. Looking like death warmed over. A very sick man, Fray had said. Too sick to harm anybody. Can't even get around by himself. Nickie saw two wheelchairs, a night table covered with bottles of pills and other medicines, and a second table containing food leftovers. He smelled the unemptied bedpan and the putrefying odor that went with being very old and very sick and the smell reminded him of his own father, who had rotted away for years until he'd done everyone a favor and died.

Nickie Max didn't need the flashlight; the moonlight was enough. He closed the bedroom door behind him, placed the flashlight and bedsheets on the floor, then held the .22 behind his back and crossed the room to the old man. He pulled back the mosquito netting and looked down at the shriveled, bald, toothless *thing*. The old guy had the bright eyes of the feeble-minded. The man wasn't just sick, he was senile or fucking close to it. He'd been looking over the balcony at the fireworks coming from the city and the yachts in the bay, smiling at the bright colors, humming some tune from carnivals he couldn't remember anymore, from when he'd been a whole lot younger and could dance the night away.

Asbun's father turned his toothless grin on Nickie, who thought, the music of your life has just about come to an end, old man. Nickie gave him a smile because the old man's mind wasn't entirely gone. No sirree. He recognized the priest's cassock and said, *Padre*. Stretched out his skinny arms to Nickie who shot him twice in the head. No witnesses. No fucking witnesses.

Nickie Max stepped from a circular stone staircase and into a cool, airy white living room whose rough cement walls were hung with pre-Columbian art. He walked across sand-colored tiles to an indoor circular fountain where Paderborn, Colmes and Osmond waited for him. He smiled at Herman Fray, who sat alone on a white leather banquette against a wall decorated with Aztec and Olmec masks. Old Herman still looked jumpy. Nervous in the service. Ready to leap out of his skin.

Paderborn said to Nickie, "The area is secured. We terminated the two guards. Found them in the kitchen, drinking beer and watching 'The Empire Strikes Back' on a Betamax. Extremely casual attitude toward security around here."

Nickie Max said, "That's what comes from having things your own way for too long."

Paderborn said, "Everything okay upstairs?"

Nickie Max handed him the two sheets and as the German submerged them in the fountain, holding them under the water with both hands, Nickie reloaded the .22 and said, "No problem." He said nothing about Asbun's father. All he told Paderborn was, "Everything's been taken care of." The German locked at him, nodded, then scratched his nose with a dripping forefinger and said, "That's nice." Then he turned his attention back to the sheets, which he continued to soak.

Herman Fray thought the business with the sheets was among the oddest things he'd seen the mercenaries do all night. It made no sense. But then neither did those two hypodermic needles hanging from Maximillian's neck like obscene medallions. The *animales* were out of their minds, all of them. Each one mad as a march hare.

He watched the German pull the dripping sheets from the fountain and hold them up for Maximillian's inspection. Maximillian then jerked his head toward Fray, who flinched and leaned back into the banquette, getting as far away from these maniacs as he could but not far enough. He visibly shook as the German walked toward him, then dropped the sopping wet sheets in his lap, saying, "Please carry these, if you'd be so kind." Then he ordered Fray to lead them downstairs to "The Choir."

Edward Penny lay on the metal cot, bleeding from his mouth, nose, and ears and shaking uncontrollably, feeling the piercing agony of the electrical shocks from the Tucker phone. He was still handcuffed, his eyes still bandaged. He felt his head being gently lifted, and he heard Asbun say, "Here, drink this, *compadre*." A glass was placed against his lips, tilted toward his mouth, and Penny swallowed deeply, then coughed violently, choking, spitting, gasping for air. He didn't see Asbun shake his head sadly, but he did hear the laughter of the others. The water had been mixed with soap.

Not far away from Penny a couple of men were singing along with Prince's *Raspberry Beret,* which was coming from the stereo speakers. Penny wept silently, feeling the same guilt and humiliation he had seen in other torture victims and never connected to himself. His body had failed him. And so had his instincts. He wanted all of this to be a nightmare, and he wished it would end now, *now,* so that he could wake up and be a whole man again.

But this was no bad dream. He had put all his faith in the skills he possessed, and that faith was now destroyed. His pride had always kept him at a distance from most men and because of that distance they had appeared as lesser men to him. Now he was the lesser man.

Asbun said, "Sentimentality. That is the problem with you, *compadre*. You tend to get soft-hearted at the wrong times. Your commanding officer, for example. I mean, you give up a perfectly good military career because you refuse to testify against that man. And the boy Tómas. Well, we don't have to talk about that, do we. You see, *compadre,* the truth is that for all of your training and skills, you possess the heart of a shop girl. A bleeding heart, they call it in your country. Oh, you can deal with the obvious, but you seem to have trouble with subtle things. Well, we learn by experience, isn't that so? No pain, no gain, they say."

Penny felt Asbun's hand on his shoulder. "I have won my bet," Asbun said. "I bet one of our generals two horses that I could break you. I made this bet on the day you disposed of *El Indio* in the gymnasium. Oh, let me say that your signature on a confession will not be necessary. The confession will be filled in after you are dead. And do you know something, *compadre?* I have ordered your friend Fabio placed under house arrest and now he awaits his father's pleasure for bringing you here in the first place. Well, it's time for what you in your country would call 'the old attention-getter.' Adios, *compadre.* You now get to answer that most important question, is there life after death."

Penny smelled gasoline.

And felt a new, soul-destroying fear.

Asbun said, "You cannot see, so I tell you what is happening. They are pouring the gasoline on the tire, which will then be placed around your neck. Oh, my friend, you are weeping. The great Edward Penny is weeping. I wish Fabio could see you now. But do not worry. We have taken photographs of our little session here this evening, and I shall make sure Fabio sees them."

He touched Penny's bleeding scalp. "You know something, *compadre?* You overestimated yourself. That is all I wanted to prove. Otherwise, I do not hate you. You are a man I respect and admire. Truly, I do. But you have your limitations, and I want you to realize this while you are able to think about it. I know what is on your mind now. You are thinking your values are gone. You are thinking there is no such thing as mercy in this world. You wish the pain to end. You even wish to live."

Asbun snapped his fingers, and Penny felt the ankle ropes being cut, felt himself being lifted from the cot and carried toward the gasoline smell. Too weak to resist, he could only plead with them not to burn him. Then he felt himself being lowered to the stone floor, felt cool air as a concrete wall slid up. Heard Asbun say, "We always have a problem with the smoke, you see. It goes out through air ducts and where the wall is. But we still have to use the fans. We have nice big fans for the smoke. I wish you could see them."

Penny smelled Asbun's cigar and heard him say, "You won't survive this session in 'The Choir,' but I tell you what you would feel if you did. I am an expert on such matters. Your emotions, they would be dead. You would not feel love, affection, those things. You would, of course, relive the hours you spent here, but they would be a frightening memory among many distortions and illusions in your mind, all brought on by this experience. Now you might find this odd, *compadre,* but I tell you there are people who look upon this experience as a fascinating one, so all-consuming, you might say, that they secretly wish to enjoy it again. Most of all, my friend, you would be a walking statistic. You would always be one of my victims, you see. Could you live with that? I do not think so. A proud man like yourself? No, I do not think you could live with that. So you see, it is better that you be put out of your misery. Oh, you have not asked me the question. Why don't you ask it now. Buy yourself a few more seconds of life, no?"

Penny said, Will you please kill me?

He didn't see Asbun smile and never saw the smiles of the others, but he heard their laughter, heard them congratulate Asbun, then he felt the weight of the gasoline-soaked tire around his neck, felt the strong blast of air from the fans, which were to drive the smoke outside, heard the roar of the fans and the sound of the stereo. He never saw Asbun touch his lit cigar to the tire, then leap back. The flames ignited instantly, and there was a bonfire around Penny's shoulders, devouring the flesh on his back, chest, neck, the flow of the flames visible through the adhesive tape. He screamed because the heat was so intense that he became crazed and twisted frantically on the stone floor, rolling around within the circle of flames.

Someone grabbed his ankles, jerked hard, and he was still screaming, not knowing he was clear of the flames because the hellish, racking pain was still with him. Someone ripped the tape from his eyes. *Nickie Max.* In a priest's cassock. He saw Nickie Max yank a hypodermic from around his neck and jab it in Penny's thigh, keeping his thumb on the plunger until all the morphine had been released. There was already a second hypodermic sticking in Penny's shoulder. Sticking in the blackened, bleeding flesh.

He heard Nickie Max yell, saw Herman Fray run toward them carrying dripping rags or sheets, and then Penny, drowsy with morphine, began losing consciousness, barely feeling the cool, wet sheets that were being wrapped around him as he slipped into fire and darkness.

Nickie Max, crouched over an unconscious Eddie, looked around "The Choir." The fans had been turned off, but the stereo was still going strong and the tire was still burning near the open wall which looked out on the tennis court. There was smoke in the large, concrete room. Not much, but enough to make Nickie's eyes water. All of the White Knives, except Asbun, lay on the floor, their bodies in the awkward positions assumed by the dead, who didn't have to worry about feeling comfortable or looking good. Nickie and the others had tiptoed down the stairs, following Herman Fray, coming through a thick steel door that had been

unguarded and unlocked, coming through in time to see Asbun
light the tire with his cigar and to hear Eddie scream, a sound
Nickie Max was going to remember as long as he lived.

Nickie's people knew what they had to do. Pick a target and
go for it. But don't waste Asbun. He belonged to Nickie Max.
Nickie almost had to laugh because the fans, two huge ones on
big metal stands, and the stereo, were making so much fucking
noise, nobody in the room had heard them come in. And four of
the White Knives had been clipped before Asbun and the other
two had even turned around to check out what was going on.

Nickie watched Emil Osmond and Lydell Colmes carry the
sheet-wrapped Eddie up the stairs. Nickie held out his hand. Paderborn placed the shotgun in it. Asbun, fighting for control,
smiled and rubbed the back of his neck. Shook his head in admiration. "I congratulate you, *compadre*. I mean, you did a real
bold thing coming here like you did. Balls. It took some very big
balls to do something like this." Anger, fear, confusion were in
his face, his words, but he forced a smile. He looked down at his
cigar, then at Nickie Max. He pointed with the cigar. "I can help
you, you know."

Nickie Max said, "No shit."

Asbun waved smoke away from his face, looked at the burning tire and took a step toward Nickie Max. The two men were
barely six feet apart. On the stereo Michael Jackson sang about
"Billie Jean." Asbun said, "I can guarantee you no trouble with
roadblocks."

Nickie said, "I could be wrong on this, but I don't think anybody knows we're here. I don't think there're any roadblocks to
worry about. Besides, we've got Herman Fray here to pave the
way. Got a police car outside. I'd say we've got that covered."

Asbun held up both hands. "Fine, fine. You got that covered.
Now, let's talk about medical care for your friend. He's going to
need it, you know. I can see that he gets the best."

"Right here in La Merced, you mean," Nickie Max said. He
looked at Herman Fray. Well, how about that. Old Herman was
chewing on his handkerchief. Talk about being uptight. Paderborn, arms folded, held a .45 in one hand and was grinning.
Enjoying the passing parade. Goofing on the whole thing.

Asbun said, "The best doctors in La Merced. I can have
them—"

Nickie Max, shotgun on his shoulder, shook his head sadly. "'Fraid not. See, we're going to try for Mexico. It's only a couple of hours away and Fray, here, he's going to lend us one of his planes. Aren't you, Fray?"

Asbun looked at Fray, who turned away. Practically had his back to his old friend and client. Nickie Max said to Asbun, "I guess Mr. Fray's turning shy in his old age. Anyway, Fray, he's going to radio on ahead to Mexico City once we're on the plane. Guarantees us there'll be an ambulance and doctor waiting when we land. No hassle. No questions asked. Fray says he's paid off half of Mexico, customs, cops, you name it. Says we have nothing to worry about."

Asbun frowned, thinking of a countermove. Looked up at the ceiling, then aimed his cigar at Nickie Max. "Tell you what, *compadre*. I am an important man. An important man. So you know what you do? You take me with you. A hostage. You need me, *compadre*. I am your insurance policy. May I ask you something? Are you sure about your friend staying alive until you get to Mexico City?"

Nickie Max looked at a still smiling Paderborn, then at Asbun. "Well, we've all had some experience with wounds, burns, that kind of thing, and we're pretty sure a man who's been burned bad can last five, six hours. Maybe even a day or two. I mean, without medical treatment. In any case, Mexico City's only three hours away, so we think we got a shot at saving him."

Asbun said, "I see, I see. Well—"

"The keys to Eddie's handcuffs," Nickie Max said.

"Right here in my shirt pocket."

"The *tanto*. Eddie's knife."

Asbun looked around the smoky room. "I think, I think. Yes, Claudio." He pointed. "The one lying near the table, the guy in the green-and-white Adidas. He said it was the best knife he'd ever seen."

Nickie Max said, "Eddie had it made special in Japan. One of those Japanese masters. Guy does nothing but makes knives and takes his time. Cost Eddie over a thousand dollars. Guy who made it has a five-year waiting list."

He looked at Paderborn then jerked his head at the dead Claudio. Watched the German walk to the Italian's body, pull the *tanto* from his belt, then walk to Nickie and hand it to him.

Nickie weighed the knife in his hand. Gripped it by the handle and said, "Yes, sir, Eddie's sure gonna be glad to see this baby."

He said to Asbun, "You got a car? I mean, a car that's yours and everybody knows it's yours. Say we bring you with us. It would look better if you were traveling in your own car, right?" He looked at the tire. Still burning. And smelling, too. But the smoke was thinning out a bit.

Asbun brightened. He exhaled and rubbed the back of his neck harder than ever because he was going to live. He knew it. He was the lucky one, not Edward Penny. One step at a time, he told himself. Get them to take me with them and we'll see what happens at the airport. He said, "There is a Silver Cloud Rolls Royce parked near the house. I suggest we use that one because everybody in La Merced knows this is my car."

Nickie underhanded the shotgun to Paderborn, then held out an empty hand to Asbun. He said, "I think it's better I drive. Give me the keys. Oh, don't forget the keys to the handcuffs."

Asbun walked toward Nickie Max, saying, "You won't regret this, *compadre*. I'm sure we can work out something to our mutual benefit." And Nickie Max said, "I'm sure we can," and when Asbun was close enough, Nickie grabbed his wrist, pulled and backhanded him across the stomach with the cutting edge of the *tanto*. Did it the way Eddie had taught him, which was to pull the blade toward himself. Always toward yourself. Asbun screamed, staggered backwards, and Nickie backhanded the *tanto* across Asbun's forearms. When Asbun turned his back, bleeding and screaming and trying to run, Nickie rushed forward, stuck the *tanto* between his legs, and pulled up and back, slicing into Asbun's testicles and penis. The colonel's scream became as high-pitched as a whistle. He staggered forward, fell facedown and continued shrieking, his legs close together. As the sound of a car horn came from the courtyard, Nickie Max said, "Shotgun," and Paderborn rushed to give it to him. Nickie dropped the bloodied *tanto* to the floor and shot Asbun in both knees. Then he used the toe of his foot to turn Asbun over on his back and shot him in both elbows. And as the car horn continued to sound, Nickie Max shoved the barrel in Asbun's mouth and said, ask me to kill you, you fucker, and he pulled the trigger.

12

AT NEARLY ONE in the afternoon, Edward Penny sat on a green carpet in Meyer Waxler's living room, shirt-sleeves rolled up to the elbows, and his seersucker jacket folded across his knees. Back resting against faded lavender wallpaper. Eyes closed. Browning in one hand. Handkerchief across the back of his neck to absorb the sweat.

He was also suffering from a bad case of stomach cramps, the worst since his session in "The Choir" with Colonel Asbun.

The sweating and stomach cramps had nothing to do with the temperature, which was in the eighties, or the lack of air conditioning in the old Edwardian house with its bay windows and pillared porch. They did, however, have everything to do with two hostage situations now facing Edward Penny. Life or death situations here in the house, something he'd never wanted to face again. Not after the deaths of Tómas, Paco, and Fleur Ochoa. Not after what had happened to him in "The Choir."

On the other side of the wall, at the top of a narrow wooden staircase, two black teenage males held Meyer Waxler's wife at gunpoint. Penny knew about her bad health, about the weak heart and the stroke which had left her paralyzed on her right side. Benita Waxler's age and physical condition, however, were of no interest to the blacks. All they wanted was for Penny to lay down his gun and show himself in the doorway because if he didn't, they were going to blow Mrs. Waxler's head off.

Second hostage situation.

This one was in the high-ceilinged living room with Edward Penny. Almost close enough for him to reach out and touch the two people involved. Less than eight feet away the old newspaperman Meyer Waxler was the prisoner of a black teenage girl. A very pregnant, very frightened girl in blue eye shadow, purple spandex pants, with glass beads woven into her corn-rowed hair.

Waxler, stocky and balding in a blue terry-cloth bathrobe, slippers and baggy gray pants, sat on the threadbare carpet in front of a walk-in fireplace. The girl was crouched behind him, left arm across his throat, and the point of a sharpened screwdriver pressed against the right side of his neck.

Penny watched the round-faced, toothy girl tighten her grip around Waxler's neck and all but cut off his air. Gasping for breath, the old newspaperman pulled at her arm and tried to call his wife's name. His glazed eyes, with their silent pleading, reminded Penny of Fleur Ochoa's expression just before she died. He pushed himself away from the wall and started toward Waxler, but stopped when the girl screamed, "Don't you come no closer 'cause I can stab this white man. I ain't lying. I do his ass and ain't nobody stop me, least of all you."

Least of all you.

How's that for an unkind thought, Penny told himself. Well, he could either prove the lady wrong, or learn to live with every word. Every ugly, unwelcomed word.

But then the blacks hadn't dropped by to bring him comfort or composure. They'd come for three small notebooks tucked away in his mobile telephone case. They'd also been told not to worry about him making trouble. *This one's easy, boys and girls, because you're going after a candy ass who's left his balls down south somewhere, who's over the hill and fading fast. Make it look like your everyday breaking and entering. Grab a few things from the house. Hell, you people know how it's done. Just make sure you get those papers. Anything else is on your own time. Have fun.*

Penny's stomach was becoming more queasy by the minute. Blame it on the August heat. Or maybe it was the fault of *The Dating Game,* now coming from the small television set on Waxler's desk. Or was his gut churning because he couldn't cut himself loose from sinister memories? But what about those few seconds when he'd remembered how good he used to be, when he'd trashed William, leader of the black toughs who'd forced their way into Waxler's home.

Young William, skinny and smartass, with his red goatee, mirrored sunglasses and low white Filas sneaks and his macho posing which hadn't been tested until today, when Penny had taken away his gun, sliced his right arm with the *tanto,* then reversed the knife and gone up the side of William's head with the handle. Now William lay bleeding and unconscious in front of Meyer Waxler's roll-top desk. Stomping that little shit had been a labor of love.

Penny was massaging the back of his neck, unconsciously trying to rub the bad pictures from his mind, when one of the blacks on the stairs called out to him. This one had a slight lisp. His high voice said he was also edgy.

"Yo, man. You in the room. I said hand Maureen your gun and step out here in the hall where we can see your ass. Be up to you this old lady she die or what. Just give us them papers and everybody be happy. Dig, how many times you gon' fuck up in your dumb life."

Penny thought, is there anybody in the western world who doesn't know I blew it in San Augustín? What had happened to him down there was a lot more serious than going into retirement without a hobby. But did he have to hear about it until the day he died? Maybe Nickie Max had the right idea. Eat a spoonful of shit in the morning and nothing worse will happen to you all day.

Good old Nickie. King of positive reinforcement. In the Mexico City hospital on Avenida Chapultepec, where Penny had spent three weeks in a burn unit, Nickie Max had appeared one afternoon with a bottle of San Marcos brandy, a couple of Big Macs, and words to live by. Since Penny had no appetite and felt lower than whale shit, Nickie Max had eaten, boozed, and talked for the both of them.

He said, "Viktor Poltava. The prick found your weak spot. Tómas. That was it, man. That fucking kid. You and Poltava, you meet again, you remember Tómas, know what I'm saying?"

Nickie Max. Drinking from the bottle and plucking the pickles out of his Big Mac and dropping them into an empty bedpan at his feet. Looking at a nurse's ass and asking her, do fries go with that shake? Then turning his attention to Penny, who lay in bed woozy with pain killers and staring through a window at the National Lottery Building. Penny feeling shamed by what Asbun had done to him. And only half hearing Nickie Max say, "You got to climb out of the coffin, dude. Ain't gonna be easy, but you have got to do it. You got to go to school on this one, babe. Learn from it."

Nickie Max saying, "Maybe this whole thing is a chance for you to do your absolute, humongous best. Find out what you really got, right? Could be up to this point you had it too easy. So now you got to bust your chops like us ordinary human beings. Except you got more going for you than we do. Tell you one thing: You let that kid make you forget the first rule, which is there ain't no rules. Not in our line of work. What counts is staying alive. Fucking Poltava, he don't play by no rules, so why should you? Look, my man, just remember who you are. Remember how good you are. Shit, you're Edward Penny, and you're my hero, and don't you fuckin' forget it."

Remember who you are. And climb out of the coffin.

In the living room, Penny listened to the blacks on the stairs argue with each other. Pushing for the last word, the lisper shouted, "Dig, I ain't worried 'bout the bitch. You be fuckin' her, not me. Maureen your problem, Jack. We don't get them papers, we don't get paid. Only thing I care about is the money."

Romance isn't dead, Penny thought. The lady with the sharpened screwdriver had a friend. Someone who cared, and that someone was the lisper's partner, alias the expectant father. Maureen and her champion. Both caught up in the foolishness and curiosity that was love. Penny was tossing this about in his mind when the lisper said, "Hey, in the room. Be cool now and give us them papers and nobody get hurt. We ain't 'spose to do nothin' to y'all. We promised the man we send you back to your woman in one piece."

Something new. Street gangs guaranteeing you a safe rip-off.

Unreal. Such spontaneous kindness, Penny knew, was rare in a world of innumerable pains and sorrows. He wondered who'd instructed these animals to exercise this great benevolence and why. The offer bothered him. Hell, it aggravated the shit out of him. Why?

Remember who you are and climb out of the coffin.

Back against the living room wall, Penny slowly pushed himself to his feet and dropped his jacket on the carpet. He heard the bells of an ice cream wagon as it cruised past the house. On *The Dating Game* bachelor number three admitted he did needlepoint. Penny used a forearm to wipe sweat from his forehead, then pointed the Browning at Maureen, aiming it at her head, feeling a sudden, wild glee when he saw her eyes practically pop out.

Still crouched on the floor behind Meyer Waxler, she pulled back against his throat, tightened her grip on the screwdriver and said to Penny, "You crazy or something?" He smiled at her. And pulled the trigger. Three inches to the left of Maureen's right foot, a jagged hole appeared in the faded green carpet. She screamed and threw up her hands, sending the screwdriver flying toward the ceiling.

Penny watched her fall backwards, feet in the air. When her feet came down, *The Dating Game* audience applauded. Penny fired again. Another bullet hole in the carpet, this one between Maureen's legs. The old attention-getter, as Colonel Asbun might say. Maureen's screaming climbed a couple of octaves.

Bawling and sniveling, she backed away from Penny on her butt and elbows. Meyer Waxler, lying on his right side and gagging, was forgotten. Penny had to forget him, too, because someone on the stairs yelled Maureen's name. That someone also started running toward the living room. Down the stairs three at a time. And into the hallway at top speed. A lovesick man on the move.

Penny positioned himself just inside the opened doorway. Waiting. How did he feel? A bit antsy, but no bundle of nerves. The old pump was a bit off. Racing a tad faster, but what the hell. However, the cold sweats had eased off and his mouth wasn't as dry as it had been just minutes ago. The footsteps were almost on top of him. Slipping the Browning under his left armpit, Penny wiped his damp right palm on his thigh, then took the gun in his hand once more.

From the stairway a voice yelled, "Nigger, get your ass back here!" The command was ignored. A second later the short, muscular black, who'd been wearing a red leather beret and a *Lakers* sweat shirt with the sleeves cut off, rushed into the room. He held a .22 in his right hand. Penny palmed the Browning and stepped behind him and as Maureen hollered, "Emmett, look out!" the black started to turn. And Penny slammed the Browning into his right temple. Not hard, but hard enough. Emmett dropped to his hands and knees, shook his head, and repeated the word shit, as though the word contained the answer to his new predicament.

Penny picked up Emmett's .22, shoved it in his belt, and said, "Get your ass over there, by Maureen." Emmett glared up at him and didn't move. Penny'd had enough attitude for one day, so he kicked him in the behind, sending the black sprawling. He said to Emmett, "That's your ass. Now no more clues. Fucking move before I put another hole in it." The black turned his head to look at him again. This time he saw something in Penny's eyes that made him turn away. And begin crawling toward Maureen.

"Emmett! Emmett!" The voice of the lisper coming from the stairs. The man holding a Luger to the head of Meyer Waxler's wife. Penny backed up until he was again just inside the living room doorway and yelled, "Emmett's resting. He's lying on the floor beside Maureen." He looked at Emmett and asked the lisper's name. Emmett, sitting and embracing his pregnant girl friend, never looked at Penny. But he said, "He name Marvell."

From the stairs. "Hey white man, I kill this woman you don't give me them papers."

Penny. "Marvell, I want you to listen carefully. If she dies, you die."

Silence.

"You hear me, Marvell? I said, if she dies, you die. That's not a threat, Marvell, that's a promise from me to you."

Penny heard a croaking sound from Waxler, who was having trouble speaking. The newspaperman held out a hand and was about to say something when Penny shook his head, then put a finger to his lips in a signal for silence. There wasn't any time for a second opinion. Then, "Hey, Marvell, let's work this thing out before a SWAT team gets here and ruins your day."

Silence. Then, "What the fuck you mean, SWAT team."

"Talking forty, fifty guys with shotguns, stun grenades and

bullet-proof vests. Guys who look forward to being interviewed on the eleven o'clock news after they've blown away a few perpetrators. These people are heavy duty, Marvell. They're not about to let some street kid embarrass them, know what I mean?"

"I got the bitch, Jack."

"I have three of your people, Marvell. And time's running out. Do we get together or not?"

Marvell said, "You was suppose to be a chump," which brought a smile from Penny, because Marvell sounded disappointed in the way events were unfolding.

Penny said, "Don't believe everything you hear. You might pass that on to the people who hired you to come after me."

"So what you got in mind? Tell you one thing. I don' want do no jail."

Penny said, what I have in mind is you give me Mrs. Waxler, and I let the four of you walk. And you don't have all day to decide whether or not to take the deal. Marvell said, how we work this thing and Penny said, to show you my good faith, Emmett, here, he goes out with William. Then you and me, we trade women. Maureen for Mrs. Waxler. Yes or no.

Marvell said okay, okay, but don't try no shit with me like you did with William and Emmett, 'cause I still got my gun, dig?

Penny tensed, remembering San Augustín, remembering that things usually go wrong when you least expect them to. He was only dealing with a man-child, but the man-child was armed, and he'd taken a hostage. Penny inhaled and forced himself to sound a hell of a lot more confident than he felt. He said, "All I want is Mrs. Waxler."

He said to Emmett, "Pick up William and take him outside." Emmett, still holding a weeping Maureen in his arms, looked at Penny and said, "I go, she come with me." *There're no rules,* Nickie Max said. *Not in our line of work.* Penny said, "Emmett, listen to me because I'm only going to lay this on you once. If you don't do exactly what I tell you to do, I'm going to turn my attention to Maureen. I'll start by making her take her clothes off. Every stitch. Then your lady and me, we're going to have a party, and you get to watch. You like that?"

A screaming Maureen buried her face in Emmett's shoulder. Penny watched him squeeze her tighter and stroke her hair. But Emmett's eyes were on Penny; his gaze offered much—concern for the girl, a desire to kill Penny, and a growing panic that he'd gotten himself in over his head. When he spoke, his voice was almost inaudible. "You callin' it, man. I do what you say."

Penny said, "The sooner you get started, the sooner you and Maureen can get out of here."

He watched Emmett detach himself from Maureen, stand up, and start toward William. Two steps, then Emmett stopped to stare at Penny, who said, "Don't even think about it. Just think about Maureen." Emmett turned from Penny who, with Meyer Waxler, watched in silence as he crossed the room and lifted the unconscious William from the floor. Blood from William's slashed arm, which had darkened the carpet, now dripped on Emmett's forearms as he walked across the living room. Penny thought, he ain't heavy, he's your brother.

He watched Emmett pause at the living room entrance to stare at a weeping Maureen and Penny tightened his grip on the Browning, thinking, the bastard's going to try something. But instead, Emmett stepped into the darkened hallway, disappearing from sight. Only when Penny heard Emmett's footsteps nearing the front door of the house did he step into the living room entrance, making sure to keep out of sight of the stairs. He heard the front door open and saw traces of sunlight in the hallway. Emmett and William were outside. Penny exhaled.

He said, "Marvell, you see that?"

"Yeah, I see it."

"Your turn. Bring Mrs. Waxler down to the bottom of the stairs. We'll make the switch there."

Silence.

Penny closed his eyes. Goddamn cold sweats were starting up again. He opened his eyes and said, "Marvell, I—"

"Yeah, man, okay, okay. I'm comin' down. But everything better be cool."

"It's cool. I'm telling you, it's cool."

"Yeah, well, I ain't too sure 'bout you, man. Nobody know where you be comin' from."

Penny let his head flop back against the wall and almost laughed out loud. But he had a grin that wouldn't quit, that filled the room, because he'd just been told he was dangerous. Hadn't heard that in a while. *I am a dangerous man. I fucking love it.*

He heard footsteps on the stairs and carefully peeked around the doorjamb to see Marvell, a big guy in black leather vest and do-rag, easing down the stairs, half-carrying, half-dragging a silent, dazed Mrs. Waxler with him, Luger pressed against her right temple. Meyer Waxler, on his feet, staggered toward the doorway, but Penny grabbed him by the elbow and pulled him back into the room, saying, "You'll kill her if you act stupid. Don't move."

Penny turned to Maureen and motioned to her with the Browning. "Over here," he said. She pushed herself to her feet, used the heels of her hands to blot tears from her eyes and walked to the doorway. He tapped her on the shoulder with the Browning. "Don't move until I tell you to. Something you should remember. I'm not the only one with a gun. Marvell has one, too, so if any shooting starts, you're just as liable to get killed by him as by me. So no sudden moves, understand?"

She nodded, her round face streaked with mascara. Penny said, "By the way, you want to tell me who sent you after the papers?"

Maureen said, "People at the travel agency call William. Tell him what to do. I don't know nobody's name. William, he be dealin' with the same man like before."

"What man?"

"William he call him 'the soup man' on account of his first name. That's all I know. You wanna know anything else, you axe William."

Soup man. Did Penny know him? Indeed, he did. Anyone working espionage knew the "soup man" and his travel agency.

But first there was a little business here that needed taking care of. And it involved a woman's life. Penny wished it didn't. Hell, he wished he was on the other side of the world, but he wasn't. The cold sweats were back in force, and he had a migraine that wouldn't quit.

Time to climb out of the coffin.

In a loud voice Penny yelled, "Let's do it, Marvell."

13

HANZO GENNAI, PRESIDENT of *Mujin*'s worldwide banking division, didn't like Americans. True, he'd done business with them for years, but as a people Americans could only be called barbarous and uncultivated. They hid behind technology and resorted to lawyers in the blink of an eye. As few bothered to do the necessary market research on Japan, they often attempted to force unsuitable products on the country. Hanzo was shocked at their inability to plan ahead, to think.

His business trips abroad usually meant traveling with several assistants. But this week only his wife Yuriko had accompanied him to New York, where he was to finalize *Mujin*'s purchase of Manhattan's Valencia Hotel for five-hundred million dollars. Hanzo's role in the hotel's acquisition, however, hid the truth about his coming to a country he detested. He'd actually journeyed to America to pick up Oliver Coveyduck's unfinished book, the one that could dishonor his mother and Warren Ganis. Viktor Poltava had brought the book to Ganis, who was to turn it over to Hanzo.

Reiko Gennai knew her son disliked America, that he was frightened by its violence and uncomfortable around its people,

303

whom he considered to be little more than grown-up children. Still she insisted that he go there, pick up the Englishman's book, and bring it to her in Japan. "I trust you and only you to deliver it to me," she said. Hanzo was the foundation upon which her life was built, she told him. Her dreams would continue through him and shine brightly long into the future.

He had bowed respectfully, thinking how shocked she would be to learn the truth. The truth was Hanzo cared nothing for her dreams. Nothing at all. And he knew only too well that her life was built, not on him, but on an insatiable hunger for power. With the Englishman's book, Hanzo saw the same old thing happening again. At his mother's command he was once more the errand boy. Not the most successful banker in *Mujin*'s history, but Reiko Gennai's highly paid slave. Cupbearer to the exalted empress. Playing the stooge turned his stomach, particularly since he hated his mother, a hatred which allowed her to occupy his mind more than anyone he loved.

When he'd finally decided to destroy her, to become the hidden sword at her throat, he'd simply viewed this action as right and appropriate. A fitting punishment for someone who'd oppressed him for as long as he could remember. She'd even come to overwhelm his father, once among the most feared and respected men in Japan. Anyone who challenged his mother was menaced or crushed. She had been established in blood, and in blood she ruled.

He'd heard people say she was gifted with magical powers; that she was *Mujin*'s guardian of wealth and power; that the company would prosper only so long as she was its shadow ruler. Superstitious nonsense, Hanzo thought. Claptrap stemming from an irrational fear of the *Empress*. Yes, she had boundless energy and strength to go along with her inborn intuition about almost everything. Yes, this gave her an advantage over most people. But it certainly didn't make her a conjurer, except to the empty-headed or half-assed.

Hanzo's view of his mother was infinitely more pragmatic. He saw her as an iron-fisted, scheming woman, too wrapped up in her own concerns to be interested in anything else. She was the center of her own circle. And the only passion of her life was power.

She was the most possessive of mothers, exhausting him with

her overbearing, unrelenting love. It was a love which had taken its toll on the reserved, withdrawn Hanzo. Under pressure to please her, he had developed ulcers, a nervous tic near his right eye, and he suffered from hives. He was also overweight and he'd started graying when he was nineteen. And there was his withered left arm, an ugly reminder of the *hell camp*, a kamika-zelike business course his mother had forced him to take.

Hell Camp was a program designed to improve the work habits of young Japanese businessmen. Reiko Gennai saw it as a confidence builder. Hanzo, on the other hand, found this so-called business training to be cruel and unfeeling. Twenty-five-mile endurance hikes. Shitty food. A work day that began at 4:15 A.M. And a cadre of the most sadistic instructors imaginable. To a young, terrified Hanzo, the camp had been unendurable. There were times during the thirteen-day course when he seriously considered killing himself.

Repelled by the military atmosphere, he twice attempted to run away. Better to abandon the training than to stay and be treated like some animal. His mother and the people at *Mujin* could talk about his being shamed and humiliated until their tongues turned to dust. All Hanzo wanted was to get away from this fucking place as soon as possible. The final decision, however, was made by his mother. And she insisted that he face the challenge; he must never run from anything. Her devotion to Hanzo, she said, allowed her to shape his destiny as she saw fit.

She ordered him to stay at the camp until he completed the course. And if anything, his instructors were to press him even harder. Should he fail to concentrate properly or show a strong spirit, Reiko Gennai authorized his teachers to physically strike him. Blame her for his withered left arm, a gift from one zealous instructor who'd delivered a very sharp blow with his steel baton, striking just the right nerve. Hanzo had survived the camp. But he'd lived in its nightmare for a long time.

And there had been the nightmare of losing Yoko, the only woman he had truly loved. Their short time together had been the happiest of his life. He'd never imagined that someone so lovely and charming could ever have been interested in him. Chunky, thick-lipped and crippled, he certainly was no pretty boy. Even his mother had pointed out that his wisdom far exceeded his beauty.

None of this had mattered to Yoko. Like him, she was awkward in the presence of others, preferring to keep her thoughts and feelings to herself. With Hanzo she'd seen beyond his shyness, finding an intelligent, sensitive man. A gentle person like herself. "We are one soul dwelling in two bodies," she told him. He called her his second self and said that until he'd met her, his life had been little more than a dark journey. When she agreed to marry him, he wept with joy.

At first it seemed that Reiko Gennai had gone along with her son's own selection of his bride. The two women had talked and his mother reported to a delighted Hanzo that Yoko had promised to obey him in all things. Yoko considered herself blessed to have a man like Hanzo. Her life would be spent trying to please him. "I must have her," he told his mother. "I cannot live without Yoko."

But on a visit to Japan, Warren Ganis met Yoko, and Hanzo's life was never to be the same. The American publisher became obsessed with the young Japanese woman; he was going to have her as his wife, and nothing or no one was going to stand in his way. Determined to get what he wanted, Ganis went first to Yasuda Gennai, then to Hanzo's mother. A day later, Reiko Gennai told her son that he wouldn't be marrying the woman he loved. Warren Ganis was to marry her, instead.

An emotional Hanzo appealed to his mother, pleading with her not to take Yoko from him. But Reiko Gennai insisted it was in *Mujin*'s best interests that Yoko be given to Ganis. The American was infatuated with her; thus she could easily gain his confidence and monitor his actions. Despite Ganis's long association with *Mujin,* the Empress felt it advisable to keep him under close scrutiny. Prudence, she said, was protection from uncertain events of the future.

Naturally, Yoko hadn't been too pleased with the change in marital plans. But the Empress had applied the necessary pressure, and she had agreed to the new arrangement. *Pressure*. Hanzo knew exactly what that meant. His mother had bribed or coerced Yoko's family into accepting a marriage with Warren Ganis. Until Yoko took a husband, she was obligated to obey her family's wishes. In any case, Hanzo was to consider the matter closed. Eventually he would forget all about Yoko, his mother said.

But he didn't. And he never would. He wept when he heard of her unhappy life in America; Ganis had learned of Yoko's unceasing love for Hanzo and systematically brutalized her for it. She began drinking and, to dull his own pain, Hanzo tried to drink, but stopped when his ulcers became troublesome. Even after marrying a wife chosen for him by his mother, he continued carrying a photograph of Yoko in his wallet. The memory of Yoko was his only true possession.

Her tragic life with Warren Ganis ended in an early death. For the grief-stricken Hanzo, any chance of future happiness was now gone forever. His dream of having Yoko come back to him had been written on water. Her passing also turned him into his mother's most implacable enemy. Yoko's fatal plunge from a Manhattan penthouse had been listed by police as accidental. Hanzo, however, soon learned the truth. Yoko had been murdered by Viktor Poltava. On Reiko Gennai's orders.

Yoko, the Empress told her son, had become a danger to Warren Ganis and therefore to *Mujin*. Mrs. Ganis had been both an alcoholic and a drug user. She'd taken lovers. Her behavior had been disgraceful and worse, she had begun talking too freely. Much too freely. Hanzo thought, Yoko's agony can only be laid at the feet of those responsible for this marriage. And that, dear mother, would be you and Warren Ganis.

A wise Hanzo held his tongue because as far as the Empress was concerned, the issue was *Mujin* and only *Mujin*. Sooner or later, she said, Yoko would have proven indiscreet and that would have caused the sky to fall. Reiko Gennai had hired Viktor Poltava to prevent this from happening. She was sure Hanzo would understand.

Understand.

Did his mother understand what it took for him not to kill her on the spot? But he listened to her in silence, and when she finished, he forced himself to leave her presence calmly. *In silence.* Without a bloody word. Outside, he climbed into his car, a thirtieth birthday present from Reiko Gennai, and raced out of Tokyo, heading north toward the mountains. Driving recklessly. Not giving a damn about exceeding the speed limit. Refusing to stop when he sideswiped a small truck laden with tomatoes.

In a lakeside lodge belonging to *Mujin*, he wailed aloud with grief and became ridiculously drunk on vodka and scotch. When he didn't weep for Yoko, he cursed his bitch of a mother. Then Hanzo went outside, removed a tire iron from the car trunk, and as the lodge staff of four watched from the porch, he attacked the car in a white-hot fury, smashing the headlights, the hood and moving on to the windshield, doors, side windows, and finally the taillights, annihilating the car as he now wanted to annihilate his mother. And Warren Ganis.

New York

August, 1985

It was exactly 9:43 that morning when Hanzo Gennai, sipping warm milk to soothe his ulcers, entered the private screening room in Warren Ganis's Fifth Avenue apartment. The dim, plush room was empty. Hanzo was minutes early for his meeting with Ganis, now being attended to by his Japanese masseur in the gymnasium next door. Flinching from the bitter blasts of the air conditioning, Hanzo took a seat in a row of leather club chairs. The room was cold enough to freeze a saint's heart. Americans and their damned technology.

For a few minutes he sat staring in the direction of the screen, now hidden behind a gold curtain decorated in a Chinese design of moored boats and curved bridges. Then he turned his attention to several paintings hanging from the upholstered walls. One in particular caught his eye. It was a small canvas brightened by a tiny light atop its frame. He left his seat and stood in front of it.

Rather good, he thought. A depiction of the ancient Japanese tea bowl, nothing more. The bowl was reddish-black, but the artist had managed to capture an opaque white glaze at the top, creating the impression of gently falling snow. Not too clever, not too cute. Hanzo was impressed.

The artist was Ganis's wife Aikiko Shaka. A gifted young woman. And quite beautiful. No wonder Ganis was so enamored of her. According to Hanzo's mother, the publisher's feeling for his young wife teetered on the edge of desperate madness. "To Ganis, loving her is the same as staying alive," the Empress said. "As for Aikiko, her responsibility is to flatter him so that he does not notice he is getting old."

Hanzo touched the painting, feeling its brushstrokes with his fingertips, wondering how Ganis would react if told his wife was being unfaithful. And that Viktor Poltava was going to kill both Aikiko and her paramour.

Two days ago in Tokyo, Hanzo had followed his mother's instructions and sent a coded message to Poltava's bank in Geneva. There was no other way of contacting him, since the killer rarely spent two nights in the same place. Twenty-four hours later, Hanzo received a coded cable from Montreal instructing him to promptly wire one million American dollars to a numbered account in the Cayman Islands. *Oni* had agreed to kill Warren Ganis's wife and her lover, an American named Edward Penny.

The decision to liquidate them came after Hanzo and his mother had listened to tapes of their private conversations made by an American wiretapper. The wiretapper, Aristotle Bellas, was a greedy man and because he'd attempted to blackmail the Empress, he was now living on borrowed time. But he'd lived up to his reputation as a master of his craft and had delivered very damning evidence confirming Aikiko's treachery. *Warren Ganis was being betrayed by the wife he loved so passionately.* Hanzo was elated. Sometimes the gods were kind.

A sordid little flirtation has become an immediate danger, the Empress said. Warren's wife had stupidly involved herself with an investigator employed by a powerful American senator. An investigator now prying into *Mujin* and the past history of Warren Ganis. Aikiko's thoughtless behavior was most unforgivable.

Reiko Gennai said, "I do not propose to agonize over what she may or may not have told Penny about *Mujin* and Warren. As of now the matter is in the hands of Poltava. Let him interrogate the lovers, then report to me."

"Ganis will hate losing the wife he loves so dearly," Hanzo said. He could barely suppress a smile.

"Warren's attachment to his wife threatens us all," Reiko Gennai said. "And since he readily accepted the elimination of his first wife as a safeguard, I see no reason for any objection to my defending him once more. True, Aikiko's infidelity will be a bitter pill for him to swallow. But life is the art of avoiding pain, and there will be less pain for all concerned—Warren included—if his wife and her lover leave this world for the next."

Then his mother had looked at Hanzo for long seconds before finally whispering, *Aikuchi. Hidden Sword.* Hanzo thought his heart would stop. His gastric ulcers flared up. He bit down on his tongue to keep from crying out. He was ready to leap from his chair. To start running for his life.

Reiko Gennai put a hand on his shoulder, keeping him in place. Hanzo went rigid. His mother's eyes narrowed. Then, smiling, she placed her face close to his and whispered, "Consider the possibility that Aikiko and Penny are working with *Aikuchi*. Wouldn't it be interesting," she said, "if the two of them actually were *Aikuchi?*"

Closing his eyes, Hanzo squeezed the seat of his chair and waited for the dizziness to pass. Then he opened his eyes and caught himself just in time. Because so great was his sense of relief that he wanted to shout like a madman. And he wanted to laugh in his mother's face because this business about Aikiko and her American lover being Hidden Sword was craziness. Sheer idiocy. And yet . . .

Hadn't his dear mother taught him to take advantage of others' mistakes? Hadn't she developed in him a strong sense of self-preservation? Hanzo remained silent and gave his mother his full attention.

She said, "An intriguing possibility, don't you think?" Hanzo watched his mother wet her lips, an indication she was focusing her complete attention on a subject. "Due to Warren, our dear Aikiko has valuable contacts and invaluable information. To start with, she has access to the special computer in Warren's home, the one which links him to us here in Tokyo."

Hanzo said, "Warren also has a bank of telex machines and stock tickers in his home."

"Exactly," said his mother. "Aikiko and her lover have access to any amount of information that could harm Warren." The Empress's eyes brightened. She was warming to the task of supporting her assumption.

She said, "Consider this. Through Senator Frances Machlis, Penny gained access to Coveyduck and Waxler. And did not Poltava inform us that Penny had attempted to warn Coveyduck?"

Hanzo nodded. He appeared outwardly calm. But inside his nerves were being torn apart. "I'm listening," he said.

His mother said, "The Frenchman Serge Coutain passed information to Coveyduck, information that could easily have been furnished by his friend Penny. Anything posted from Switzerland by Coutain and destined for Meyer Waxler probably emanated from Penny as well. And from Aikiko, too, of course. Aikiko, who has charmed a senator's private policeman into helping her start a new life. As Hanako did with the Frenchman Coutain. It appears neither woman is interested in the privileged existence I have given them. Both are little more than starving dogs whom I made prosperous, and who now turn on me."

Another nod from Hanzo, who said, "But the tapes mentioned that Waxler was getting information by mail from Japan. Would that not rule out Coutain?" His heart was in his mouth, but he had to at least give the appearance of having an open mind. Mustn't look too eager to swallow his mother's theory.

"You forget, my son," she said, "that Coutain did quite a bit of traveling on business. That's how he met Hanako. Remember, he met her in Hong Kong then pursued her to Tokyo. I regret not having had Poltava interrogate Coutain at length. We might have gotten on to Penny and Aikiko much sooner."

Hanzo agreed. His mother said, "Aikiko and Penny could easily post information to someone in this country, who would then send it back to America."

A smiling Hanzo said, "Didn't Helen Silks's last report on the senator note a growing friendship between Aikiko and Edward Penny?" Reiko Gennai narrowed her eyes, and nodded in agreement. But when his mother pointed out that there was no mention in Helen's letters about Aikiko and Penny coming after the Gennais, the nervous tic near Hanzo's right eye flared up. By all the gods, he did not want her to abandon this theory. Not now. Not when she could protect him by targeting someone else.

Reiko Gennai said, "Nor is there is any mention of *Mujin* or Warren on the Aikiko and Penny tapes." She licked her lips, thinking.

A desperate Hanzo said, "Blame it on love, the reason of all unreasonable actions. Perhaps they were too wrapped up in each other to consider more serious subjects. Perhaps Penny felt it wise not to discuss *Mujin* over the telephone. Remember, he is trained in security matters. And regarding Helen Silks's perceptions, she's disappointed us once or twice in the past. Therefore her failure to notice the true relationship between Aikiko and Penny until now does not surprise me."

His mother looked at Hanzo for a long time, causing him to

feel uncomfortable, and he wondered if he'd said the wrong thing. Then she smiled and touched his cheek, saying there was merit in his words. Her eyes were bright and he could feel her pride in him. Hanzo wanted to run and hide, to get away from her eyes. His mind was distorted by guilt; if he wanted to avoid giving himself away, he would have to leave her presence soon.

Squeezing his hands, the Empress said, "We're closing in on Hidden Sword. We'll soon taste the blood of that stinking Judas." With a child's enthusiasm she brought Hanzo's hands together and said, "I am so very anxious to read Poltava's report on Aikiko and Penny, aren't you?" Without waiting for his answer she said, "I feel better than I have in a long time."

Even Hanzo had to agree she suddenly looked younger; her *Aikuchi* theory had apparently lifted a huge weight from her shoulders. She said to him, "I take my strength from knowing that you will be the next president of *Mujin*. Hanzo, my son and dearest friend in all the world." Her eyes misted, and so did his. Both began to weep. A confused Hanzo, however, didn't know whether he wept for his mother or himself. Or Yoko.

In the screening room, Hanzo swallowed the last of his warm milk and turned from an Aikiko Shaka painting of purple irises to look over his shoulder. He was shivering. Not from the air conditioning, but from a feeling that he was being watched. The feeling was so strong that his stomach began to knot. Since being kidnapped in Hong Kong, he'd been able to sense when he was being observed. Hong Kong had taught him to anticipate evil.

But the screening room was empty. Hanzo was alone.

Perhaps someone was hiding in the projection booth. Located near the entrance to the screening room, it also should have been empty. Ganis had selected the screening room for his ten o'clock meeting with Hanzo, claiming this was the most isolated area of his forty-room triplex and offered the most privacy. Hanzo stared at the booth, seeing only the glint of projector lenses in two of its three small dark windows. *He was being watched. He was sure of it.*

The entrance to the projection booth was in the hallway. In a panic, Hanzo dropped his empty milk glass on the leather chair next to his and raced across thick gray carpeting to the screening room entrance. Outside, he ran along the hallway to the projection booth, opened the door, and switched on the light. The booth was empty.

In the small, low-ceilinged room, Hanzo saw two projectors, a high wooden stool, and a workbench containing a projector zoom lens, empty take-up reels, and a week-old copy of the *Hollywood Reporter*. The top of a battered wooden desk was covered by cans of film, a digital clock, a Mickey Spillane paperback, a note pad, the sports section of the *New York Times,* and an overflowing ashtray. A red telephone intercom, connecting the booth to the screening room, hung on the wall between the projectors. The booth smelled of machine oil, stale cigar smoke, and stale coffee. And it was empty.

Still edgy, Hanzo returned to the screening room, flopped down in his chair, and leaned back to think. He shoved his right hand in his jacket pocket and fingered a tiny locket which was on a gold chain. It had belonged to Yoko and was a *katami,* a keepsake given him by her parents. In accordance with *Shijuku-nichi,* the forty-nine-day service, they had waited forty-nine days after Yoko's death to celebrate the entrance of her spirit into paradise. On the forty-ninth day, the family had also distributed her personal effects to relatives, friends, and acquaintances. Dressed in dark mourning clothes, Hanzo had attended the service which had been held in the home of Yoko's parents. He'd lit candles, burned incense, and prayed that Yoko's spirit would be reincarnated into a better and more beautiful life. Warren Ganis had not attended the service, choosing instead to remain in New York.

Now Hanzo looked over his shoulder to see the silver-haired, handsome Ganis enter the screening room dressed in a white kimono, clogs and carrying a Mark Cross attaché case with his initials embossed in gold. The banker was secretly pleased to see that the American had gained weight since their last meeting a few months ago. According to the Empress, the vain Ganis now wore corsets to flatten his waist. Hanzo stood up and they greeted each other in Japanese, bowing as they spoke. He could smell the scented oils used by the masseur on Ganis's pampered flesh. The aroma of an aging whore, he thought.

Neither man cared for the other. Ganis saw Hanzo as little more than a glorified bookkeeper, one fortunate enough to have a mother like Reiko Gennai. Hanzo saw the American as self-centered, with a vulgar heart that no amount of money could beautify. And, of course, there was Yoko, who represented hatreds and injuries between the two men that would never disappear.

They sat in adjacent rows, one in front of the other. Ganis placed the case on his lap, thumbed open the locks, and turned it around to let Hanzo see the contents. Ganis said, "The manuscript, Coveyduck's notes, and correspondence pertaining to the book. All here. No copies. Though why your mother would even think I'd want a copy of this shit is beyond me. I wouldn't want to take the slightest chance of anyone seeing this."

He closed the case and handed it to Hanzo, who glanced at him before deliberately opening the case and looking inside. Heart beating wildly, he said, "Has Aikiko seen any of this?"

Ganis snorted. "What the hell kind of question is that? Of course she hasn't. What kind of fool do you take me for? She knows enough about what goes on, believe me. There's no need for her to know any more. Look, what you've got there could easily ruin me, so I'd appreciate your not letting this case out of your sight until you get back to Japan." Hanzo thought, as usual he speaks with the arrogance of one convinced of his own importance. Thank you, my friend, for giving me a second chance to destroy you.

As Hanzo reached for the top piece of correspondence, his hand started to shake, so he gripped the attaché case with both hands and read silently. His final letter to Coveyduck. The one in which Hanzo as *Aikuchi* accused his mother of ordering the murder of Serge Coutain and of forcing *Mujin* wives who displeased her into heroin-addicted prostitution. The letter in which he linked his mother and Warren Ganis with Viktor Poltava. An unsettled Hanzo slammed the case shut.

Misunderstanding Hanzo's show of nerves, a surprisingly sympathetic Ganis said gently, "Yes, I know. It does place your mother at very high risk. You and I aren't the best of friends, but we do agree on one thing, and that is our loyalty to the family. I don't know how many times I've told her to do something about Tetsu Okuhara. He has to be *Aikuchi*. Outside of you, only Okuhara's got any real chance of succeeding your father. No one else stands to gain as much from our troubles as that bastard. He's always been too clever for his own good, that fucking Okuhara. And to think he's Yasuda-san's godson. Your father gave him everything, and Okuhara pays him back by trying to destroy his family. As far as I'm concerned, no punishment is too severe for someone like that."

Ganis spoke about Hanzo's father, about their early days together, and about how much he loved the old man. All of this trouble started, he said, when Yasuda-san became ill and jackals like Okuhara decided to make a power grab. Hanzo thought, there'd been no better time for me to get back at my mother and Ganis. He'd never wanted to be company president, preferring the banker's life where he knew exactly what was expected of him.

Fingers drumming nervously on top of the case, he said, "Where's Poltava?"

Ganis rubbed his freshly shaven chin and grinned maliciously. "I thought you found his presence unnerving, to put it mildly."

"Is he here? In the house, I mean."

"I know what you mean. Why are you so interested in Viktor all of a sudden? Do you have a message for him from your mother?" His mocking tone was not lost on Hanzo.

The banker kept his eyes on the attaché case. "I carry no message. I simply wondered where he was. He likes to move around, and it occurred to me that he might be staying with you. Temporarily, of course. I asked out of curiosity, nothing more." And because everything in me shouts that I am being watched, Hanzo thought.

He glanced at his watch, then rose from his chair. "Thank you for the milk. I'm supposed to call my mother and let her know I have possession of the material." He tapped the attaché case with one hand. "Then I have an eleven o'clock meeting to close the hotel deal."

Ganis rose, shoving his hands in the sleeves of his kimono. "Use the telephone in the computer room at the end of the hall."

Hanzo thanked him and asked, that, as usual, the room be cleared of all personnel while he was talking to his mother. Ganis nodded in agreement. Hanzo asked if Poltava had done anything about the wiretapper and the newspaperman, the other two people his mother wanted eliminated. Ganis said Poltava was the closed-mouth type, but he'd indicated that his business here in America would be concluded within the next couple of days. "Make of that what you will," Ganis said.

The two men talked briefly, then bowed to one another in

farewell. Seconds later Ganis was alone in the screening room, staring at the door that had just closed behind Hanzo. Then the publisher walked to the center of the back row, sat down in the middle chair, and thought for a few seconds. Then, leaning forward, he picked up the telephone receiver from the control panel directly in front of him, pressed a button on the panel, and put the receiver to his ear. Inside the projection booth someone picked up on the first ring. Ganis took a deep breath, exhaled, and said, "You heard?"

"Yes," Viktor Poltava said, then hung up the intercom.

14

TWENTY-FIVE HUNDRED YEARS *ago Sun Tzu appeared at the court of Ho-Lu, King of Wu, who had been impressed by his book on the art of war. The king said he had read all thirteen chapters and asked if Sun Tzu could illustrate the control of troops by conducting a test with women. When Sun Tzu said yes, the king ordered 180 of his concubines to participate in the experiment.*

Sun Tzu divided the women into two companies, assigning the king's two favorites as leaders. All women were given spears. Sun Tzu then asked if the women knew where the right and left hands were. They replied yes. They were asked if they knew where the heart and back were. Again, the women said yes.

Sun Tzu said, "When I give the order front, face in the direction of the heart. When I say right, turn toward the right hand. When I say left, turn toward the left. The command rear means to face toward your back." The women said they understood. As Sun Tzu spoke to them, an executioner appeared and began to lay out his weapons.

Three times did Sun Tzu repeat his instructions, then he struck the drum and gave the command, "Right." The women only laughed. Sun Tzu said, "If the instructions are not clear, it is the commander's fault. But when they have been made clear and are not obeyed, the officers are at fault." He ordered the execution of the two women who had been appointed leaders.

The king was alarmed and sent a messenger to tell Sun Tzu not to kill the women. Sun Tzu replied that he had received the king's commission as commander and while in the field, the commander need not obey all of the king's orders. Sun Tzu then had the two women executed as examples to the rest and picked two more women as company leaders.

Again he struck the drum to signal the start of the drill. This time the women faced right or left, rear or front, performing each command with precision and in silence. Sun Tzu then sent a messenger to the king, telling him that the troops were ready for his inspection. They would, he said, obey all commands even at the risk of their lives.

The king, however, sent back word that he had no interest in inspecting the troops. The deaths of his two favorites had left him inconsolable with grief. Sun Tzu was free to end the exercise and go about his business. Instead of leaving, Sun Tzu said, "The king prefers only empty words. He is not capable of translating these words into action. He is interested in theory, not the real thing."

With that the king realized Sun Tzu's abilities and made him a general. In this capacity, the famed strategist defeated the state of Ch'u, led an army into Ying, and made himself feared in the states of Ch'i and Chin. It was noted that the glory of the King of Wu owed much to the proficiency of Sun Tzu.

Manhattan

August, 1985.

Ten-forty-five A.M. Viktor Poltava was a careful driver. When Hanzo Gennai's limousine ran the red light at Fifth Avenue and Sixty-fourth Street, Viktor stopped, halting his motorbike between a hansom cab and a hot dog cart being pushed by a dwarfish Vietnamese. As the limousine sped past Central Park on one side and old mansions turned into consulates and private schools on the other, a brief frown crossed Viktor's face. The frown, hidden by a crash helmet, disappeared when he saw the limousine brake for a red light two blocks away. Hanzo had an imbecile for a driver.

Minutes ago the banker had walked out of Ganis's apartment building carrying two attaché cases. One, in his good hand, contained Coveyduck's manuscript; the other, hanging from the wrist of his withered arm, held business papers. Viktor had been across the street, sipping a Coke and sunning himself on the wide staircase in front of the Metropolitan Museum of Art. Waiting for Hanzo, whom he was going to kill sometime during the next three days.

Hanzo had appeared jumpy, causing Viktor to smile. The banker looked like a man waiting for a bomb to go off. Maybe the telephone call to Mother in Tokyo had left him with the shakes. The Empress could throw the strongest man off-balance, and Hanzo was far from sturdy. Viktor thought, maybe sonny boy's sweating because he knows he can't turn the Coveyduck stuff over to his mother. She would read one page, then string him up by the balls.

But if Hanzo wanted to get back at Mother, and Viktor was certain he did, he'd have to do something with the material. His decision, however, would be an irreversible one. Hanzo, alias *Aikuchi*, was playing a dangerous game. He was walking a tightrope without a net. And his first mistake would be his last.

Experience had taught Viktor that self-interest prevented people from seeing the truth. Take Warren Ganis. He'd had the Coveyduck material in his possession for over twenty-four hours, yet he'd barely glanced at it. "Conjures up unpleasant memories," he'd told Viktor, who'd thought him a pathetic old coward. And a fucking fool for thinking the past could be ignored.

As for Reiko Gennai, she had been too close to the forest to see the trees. Her only son was Mother's little darling, and in her eyes he could do no wrong. The Empress preferred to rely exclusively on her preconceived preferences, and heaven help anyone who disagreed.

Early on Viktor had noticed her habit of excluding all viewpoints but her own. With a bit more objectivity, Mrs. Gennai might have seen that *Aikuchi* could only have been Hanzo. Instead their relationship had placed sonny boy above suspicion. Was there a mother alive who saw her child as anything but a beam of sunlight from the infinite?

Viktor's examination of the Coveyduck material had convinced him that *Aikuchi* was not merely a *Mujin* insider, but a highly placed one at that, a man burning down his home in order to destroy a rat. Such men, he knew, had a great deal of hatred in them, the kind of hatred Viktor once felt toward the man who'd killed his grandmother. His research on the Gennai family, combined with his knowledge of informants, had yielded just one candidate for the role of *Aikuchi*. Just one man whose hatred of Reiko Gennai had made him reckless enough to take her on. Who had access to everything necessary to bring her down. And that was Hanzo Gennai who, in attempting to destroy his mother, had finally become the man she'd always wanted him to be. The irony was not lost on Viktor.

Did Hanzo's plans call for eliminating Viktor or manipulating him in any way? Who could say. One thing was certain: Sonny boy wanted Mother to suffer the greatest agony possible, which meant the slow death of public disgrace, followed by a criminal trial of some sort. He might even consider sacrificing Viktor. A man who would give his dear old mum the chop would do anything. Viktor's very own survival seemed to call for removing sonny boy.

But in deciding to kill Hanzo, he'd let himself be guided by Sun Tzu. Excellence in warfare was Viktor's only standard, and that standard must never be lowered. As he saw it, the Empress either wanted to win for *Mujin* or she didn't. He had no time for dilettantes, for dabblers and hobbyists. War, Sun Tzu had written, is a matter of life or death, a road to either safety or ruin. There was no middle ground. As commander in the field, Viktor was free to conduct this war as he saw fit, and he had decided that victory was impossible while Hanzo lived.

Sonny boy was the problem. Not Coveyduck, not the Jew Waxler. And the idea that Edward Penny and Ganis's wife were *Aikuchi* was absurd. But if the Empress wanted Viktor to punish Penny and Mrs. Ganis for having it off, well, business was business. He would interrogate the lovers, then dispose of them and pass on his report. As Edward Penny would soon learn, Reiko Gennai did not approve of outsiders poking *Mujin* wives. Mr. Penny would also learn that history repeats itself. Viktor was about to defeat him again.

The couple was about to become casualties in Hanzo Gennai's

war against his mother. Penny, Mrs. Ganis, Coveyduck, Waxler. Even Bellas the wiretapper. Nothing more than branches on a tree, all of them. Hanzo was the root which gave the tree life.

For Reiko Gennai, the choice was her son or her kingdom.

Back at Ganis's apartment Viktor had casually asked the publisher what the Empress would do when she discovered *Aikuchi*'s identity. Ganis said, you must be joking. She'll turn the matter over to you, of course. And you'll do what you usually do in these cases. Viktor said, you mean she'll order me to kill him.

Any talk of killing left Ganis uncomfortable, so he dismissed the subject with a wave of his hand and said, "Of course she'll want you to dispose of *Aikuchi*. *I* want you to dispose of *Aikuchi*. Now if you don't mind, can we talk about something else?"

Viktor thought, we could talk about your wife and her lover, who I've been paid to dispose of. Instead a calmly persistent Viktor said, "I assume I have your permission to kill *Aikuchi*."

Barely concealing his irritation Ganis said, "Yes, you have my permission to kill *Aikuchi*," nodding his head with every word as though explaining something to a recalcitrant child.

Viktor smiled. And changed the subject.

When the stoplight turned green at Fifth Avenue and Sixty-fourth Street, Viktor shoved his right foot down on the motorbike's starter pedal, then drove across the intersection. He passed an orange school bus and was picking up speed when a U.S. Mail truck cut directly in front of him. To avoid a collision he quickly hit the brake pedal, then squeezed the brake control on the right handlebar. The truck missed the motorbike's front wheel by less than a foot.

An angry Viktor thought, you bloody maniac. Everyone in this damn city drove as if they were being chased by a policeman. This was his eleventh trip to New York, and he still disliked the place. Nor did he care for the unsmiling, driven people who lived here. New York was a city that would make a stone sick. Seconds later, Viktor passed the mail truck in time to see Hanzo's limousine turn left on a town house-lined side street. He smiled. Sonny boy was really quite predictable.

Hanzo was due at the Valencia Hotel at 11 A.M. to meet with the owners and various lawyers to conclude arrangements for purchase of the hotel. The Valencia was on the corner of Fifth Avenue and Fifty-fifth Street. And according to Viktor's watch,

Hanzo had less than ten minutes to get there. So why was he making a detour when he should be going straight ahead?

Viktor knew the answer to that one. Being the jittery type, sonny boy couldn't wait to do something with the Coveyduck stuff. He had to make his move now. Like everyone else in this world, he was acting according to his nature. As Viktor had known he would.

Yes, he could kill Hanzo now, but Viktor dismissed the idea as stupid. There'd be no time to work out an escape route. And Hanzo's murder would generate a great deal of publicity, making it difficult for Viktor to operate here. If possible, sonny boy's death had to look like an accident.

Meanwhile, it was wiser to cancel all or at least some of the others first. Bellas and his daughter. Waxler the Jew. Penny and Mrs. Ganis. Then Viktor could turn his attention to Hanzo, scheduled to be in New York for another three days. Better to eliminate him in America than try it in Japan, where Hanzo was better able to defend himself. And could call on the Empress for help.

On Fifth Avenue and Sixty-second Street Viktor turned left, moving in light traffic and following Hanzo's limousine across Madison Avenue, then Park Avenue with its luxury apartment buildings and wide street separated by planted road dividers. On traffic-clogged Lexington Avenue the limousine turned right and slowed down before parking at a bus stop. Viktor thought, stupid, stupid. He stopped the motorbike at the corner, wondering how long Hanzo's moronic driver could continue to defy New York's traffic laws.

He watched Hanzo step from the car and stand on the sidewalk with Ganis's attaché case under one arm and a small piece of paper in his good hand. Hanzo looked at the paper then stared up at a row of shops located on the second floor. Checking an address, no doubt. Viktor wasn't positioned properly to see the shop fronts, but he did see Hanzo cross the sidewalk and vanish through a doorway. Sonny boy was definitely up to something.

Viktor found Lexington Avenue practically claustrophobic. Narrow and bustling, it was crammed with high-rises, department stores, modest shops, and fast food stands. Car horns blared, and the smell of exhaust fumes hung heavy on the August heat. Viktor watched a black policeman walk over to the limousine and use his nightstick to motion the driver to get moving. The driver slid across the front seat, rolled down the passenger window, and revealed himself to be a slight, bearded hispanic. But before he could say a word, the cop slowly shook his head and tapped the car hood with his club. The conversation was over before it had even begun. Viktor watched the limousine pull away from the bus stop.

Now he slowly moved into the bus stop, looking to his right at the second floor. He smiled when he saw the faded gold lettering in the third window from the corner. *S & E Photo Copiers*. Now wasn't that interesting. Chuckling softly, he continued down Lexington Avenue, on his way to kill the wiretapper Bellas and his corpulent daughter.

Twelve hours later, in the basement of a red-brick, two-family house in Queens, Aristotle Bellas finished packing a suitcase with equipment needed for the police station job. Then he swallowed the last of his *mavrodaphne,* drinking the sweet, strong Greek wine from a cup as his grandfather used to do. "Keep it away from her nose," Grandfather had said of his nagging wife, "and she thinks it's coffee." Wine in a coffee cup. For a boy, it had been the most delicious of forbidden fruits. Not in a class with sex, but close.

Sex. There'd been none while he and Sophie were hiding out in cousin Andreas's house. They were in Greek Astoria, largest Greek neighborhood in New York, where you could get all the *moussaka* and roast lamb you wanted, but try and find some black pussy when you needed it. Half a million Greeks living just fifteen minutes from Times Square, with a handful of Italians but no jigaboos to speak of. Definitely no hookers to be had, not in a neighborhood where your rear window looked out on the back of St. Demetrios Greek Orthodox Church.

Another problem: Aristotle Bellas couldn't get used to living with so many people. In Manhattan it was just him and Sophie in a nice ten-room apartment on Riverside Drive, facing a park and looking out on the Hudson River. Here in Queens there was a house full of people and the noise was enough to drive you bananas. He and Sophie had tried working on their equipment in Andreas's basement, but they hadn't gotten much done. If it wasn't Andreas's wife Julie coming down to use the washing machine, it was screaming kids running in and out and slamming doors.

The noise bothered Aristotle Bellas almost as much as not getting laid. There was Andreas and his family, which included three very loud kids under twelve. There was Aristotle Bellas's eighty-eight-year-old maternal grandmother, half blind, half crazy and still mourning her wine-drinking husband who'd died fifteen years ago. And there were the cousins, young guys, two illegals who spent all their time in front of the television set trying to learn English. One played a *bouzouki* and that wasn't half bad, except the son of a bitch only knew three songs.

When Bellas had skipped out on Edward Penny three days ago, he hadn't been thinking about noise. He'd been thinking about staying alive and fuck everything else. *Oni*. The man was unreal. You didn't reason with somebody like that. You just started running and prayed he'd never find you.

Bellas also prayed he'd eventually get his address book back. He needed it more than Edward Penny did. On the other hand, the loss of the Greek's notebooks could be a bigger problem. Penny had certainly read them by now and probably wanted to ask Bellas a few questions about Japanese corporations and Viktor Poltava. There was also the thing between Penny and Ganis's wife, which the Greek had stumbled across. Penny wasn't going to like anybody checking out his love life.

Bellas should have listened to Sophie. "Forget about blackmailing Reiko Gennai," she'd said. "Japanese women aren't like other women," she'd told him. "They've been around a long time and they know how to survive." Bellas had ignored her. Hell, he'd had his reasons.

His overhead was climbing. Sure, he designed most of his own stuff, but he only worked with the best material and none of it came cheap. His apartment was going co-op and even with an insider's price it was going to cost him six figures. And then there was the stock market, which had been busting his balls. He was in so deep he didn't even want to think about it. He owed enough money to put his broker into happy retirement.

He told Sophie he had to go for it, that what he had on Mrs. Gennai was so strong, she'd pay up in a second. If she didn't, the exposure would finish her. And Bellas had copies of the tapes, so how could she hurt him? The woman would be stupid to try anything, is how he figured it. He figured wrong. Sophie had known what she was talking about. Mrs. Gennai was not like other women.

In the basement he picked up a telephone scrambler and examined it before putting it in the suitcase. He was damn proud of this baby. This time he and Sophie had outdone themselves. Best portable scrambler ever invented, even if he had to say so himself. Wasn't on the market yet because they'd just completed the prototype. It was functional, but Bellas was a perfectionist. He'd told Sophie no marketing until they cleared up a trace of static in the mouthpiece.

Static aside, the fucking thing worked like a charm. Connect the scrambler to your phone and it made every word out of your mouth sound like gibberish. Unless, of course, the listener owned a mated unit to convert your speech into something understandable. Damn thing was light. Weighed a little over three pounds, was battery-operated, held thirty codes, and automatically switched back and forth between high and low tones. Sophie had even worked out a precision timer which switched codes every four seconds. Cops, drug dealers, Wall Street guys, wives cheating on their husbands. Everybody and his brother would want one. Talk about being rich. Bellas was going to end up farting through silk.

He checked the other items in the suitcase. Wire locator, tap detector, tools. All there. He closed the case and looked at his watch. Ten-twelve P.M. Time to get cracking. He picked up the case and walked to the stairs, yelling for Sophie to back the van out of the garage and have it waiting in front of the house. She said, "Okay, Papa." Then she said something he couldn't understand, meaning she was stuffing her face again and couldn't talk while chewing. Bellas smiled, remembering she once said she ate to take her mind off food.

He reached the kitchen in time to see her shove more *baklava* in her mouth, then pick up her suitcase and go out the back door. Sophie was sensitive about her weight. Hadn't stepped on a scale in years. Not since somebody had seen her do it and called her God's Little Acre. She was no beauty like her mother Irene, dead of kidney failure ten years, God rest her soul. But Sophie was a sweet kid and a lot smarter than most men. Because of her the business had expanded, and they were coming up with new stuff every year. Bellas was damn proud of her.

He opened the fridge door and picked at what was left of the *baklava*, thinking, cops, they'll use you every time. Bellas was working tonight because the precinct captain needed a favor. The Greek found the request to be an offer he couldn't refuse.

It wasn't that Captain Aronwald hadn't done anything for Bellas. Right now he had a squad car driving by the house two, three times a day and once on the night shift. Bellas hadn't told him why he needed help. All he'd said was, "I'm jammed up." Nothing more. Let Aronwald think it was shylocks or bookies, some shit like that. These were Bellas's reasons for holing up at Andreas's place in the past. Hell, he definitely owed Aronwald, but couldn't the bastard have waited until tomorrow?

Not so, said one Detective Rembuli, who'd called fifteen minutes ago to say that Captain A. had a problem. He needed something done tonight. Something that couldn't wait until tomorrow. Bellas remembered last year's rush job for Aronwald. Divorce work. Aronwald's. A messy end to a fifteen-year-old marriage, and it was about to cost the captain a bundle. Aristotle Bellas had come through, getting enough on Mrs. Aronwald to turn her demands for alimony into a joke.

Rembuli told Bellas that Aronwald's problem had to do with an investigation now going on at a Brooklyn precinct, where cops had been accused of stealing confiscated drugs and drug money. Bellas knew about it. The damn thing was in all the papers and all over TV. If all the cops who got sticky fingers around drug dealers were laid end to end, the line would reach from here to the moon.

Rembuli said that the captain had gotten the word from an informant. Aronwald's station house was bugged, and Internal Affairs was behind it. Bellas immediately said, "I didn't have anything to do with it." Which was true. Rembuli said the captain wasn't accusing him of anything. All the captain wanted was a little help, and he wanted it right away.

Internal Affairs, Rembuli said, was convinced that Aronwald and some of his people were just as dirty as the Brooklyn guys. Indictments might be handed down. Rembuli was calling from a public telephone and told Bellas not to call the precinct until after he'd made a sweep. Nobody at the station house trusted the phones anymore. Aronwald wasn't even sure he could trust his own people. He wanted Bellas and Sophie to sweep the precinct tonight. Aronwald's office, telephones, the holding pen, closets. Everything.

In his cousin's house, Bellas stuck his head in the living room and said good night to Andreas, who was in front of the TV set translating *Wheel of Fortune* for the illegal cousins.

Outside, the weather was still hot and sticky. August. Worst time of the year in New York. Even winter was better. At least you had cool air to breathe. Bellas was wearing a summer jacket but no tie, not this time of night. Ordinarily he made sure he looked neat, like a businessman and not some scuzz who made a living taping heavy breathers. He looked up at the sky. Plenty of stars. Forget about rain. Then he noticed the van wasn't out front. Where the hell was Sophie?

He walked down the stairs, then to his right across the small, parched lawn and to the side of the house. The garage door was up. And the van was still inside, motor running. The van door was open on the driver's side. Bellas had the use of the garage until Andreas took delivery on a new Chevy next month.

Stepping over a folded lawn chair, he kicked a black-and-white soccer ball out of his path and entered the darkened garage. He walked along the driver's side of the van, stopping to slide open a side door and place his suitcase inside. After closing the side door, he stepped up to the open driver's door, slid behind the wheel and looked at Sophie in the dashboard light.

She was sitting on the passenger side, head leaning against the window, hands in her lap. Sleeping. Bellas smiled. The past few days had been hard on her. There'd been the pressure of knowing that *Oni* was in their lives. And the stress of having to share a room with Grandmother, who snored and wet the bed and expected Sophie to wait on her hand and foot. No wonder the girl was tired.

Bellas closed the door and looked to see if he'd awakened Sophie. He hadn't. He turned away and had his fingers on the key she'd left in the ignition when he froze and snapped his head in her direction. *Blood. On the front of Sophie's jump suit. On her neck and left shoulder.* A startled Bellas reached for his daughter. And that was when Viktor rose up from behind the front seat and with his belt knife cut the Greek's throat.

When he had wiped the knife on Bellas's jacket, Viktor reattached it to his belt, then pulled the stocky Greek in the back with him and dropped his body on top of the two suitcases. Something fell out of Bellas's jacket pocket. Viktor picked it up. A folded copy of today's *Wall Street Journal*. He smiled. Bellas was dead because he hadn't been able to keep away from the stock market.

Since coming to his cousin's house, the Greek had telephoned his broker faithfully. But he'd kept his hiding place a secret, a useless precaution as fate would have it. For on his arrival in America, Viktor had studied information on Bellas collected for him by Warren Ganis, then ordered the publisher to put an immediate tap on the broker's telephone lines. Three hours later Viktor had learned exactly where the Greek and his obese daughter had gone to ground. The stock market had been Bellas's vice. And as Colonel Feltsman had once told Viktor, your vices might abandon you, but you never abandoned your vices.

Behind the wheel, Viktor placed the saddlebags from his motorbike on the seat between him and the dead fat woman, then switched on the ignition. He slowly backed the van out of the garage, stopping at the end of the driveway to allow two cars to pass before he entered the street. He'd only gone a few yards when he saw a police car heading toward him on the fat woman's side. Viktor slowed his breathing and reached inside the saddlebags for a grenade.

But the police car passed by with only a friendly tap of the horn. A smiling Viktor took his hand from the saddlebag and tapped his horn once. He whispered, "Detective Rembuli at your service." Viktor's eyes were extraordinarily bright.

15

Washington, D.C.

August, 1985

BECAUSE IT WAS early morning, the Brussell Gallery of Art was empty, and Edward Penny had the cafeteria to himself. He sat in a wrought-iron chair and watched a miniature waterfall spill into a reflective pool. The sound of the water was restful and cleansing. Penny took a sip of black coffee and closed his eyes.

He opened them in time to see Aikiko and a security guard approach the cafeteria entrance. When Aikiko gestured that Penny was with her, the guard—a fat, heavy-faced young black —looked disappointed, as though life had just failed to satisfy certain hopes and expectations. As the guard glared at him a smile crossed Penny's lips, lasting only seconds. The guard was testy, Penny knew, because he'd just been prevented from exercising his power. Men went to war because women were watching.

The guard, one Olonzo Screen, presided over security on the first floor's west wing, where his orders were to question anything out of the ordinary. You see some dude sitting in an empty cafeteria twenty minutes before the gallery opens, you check him out. Rules were rules. Except this dude happened to be with a Japanese woman whose paintings were going to be shown here next Tuesday. People like her didn't have to explain shit to some nigger making $3.75 an hour and carrying an unloaded gun.

Aikiko took a seat beside Penny and looked straight ahead at the waterfall. They sat in silence. Penny drank the black coffee he'd brought with him. Aikiko slowly stroked the back of her left hand.

Penny finished his coffee and placed the empty Styrofoam cup on the floor beside his cellular telephone case. Then he examined Aikiko's face for signs that she knew why he'd come to see her. A goddess, he thought, with a beauty that was both remote and accessible. For the past ten days she had shaped his life, but in the end she was beyond his understanding. I can know what she isn't, he thought, but I can never know what she is.

He saw no indication of her thinking. The dark eyes and the sensual mouth held no more expression than the flagstone floor beneath their feet. Aikiko could have been eaten up with guilt or wondering whether or not to serve Perrier at the opening night buffet. He watched her stroke the back of her left hand, and when she stopped, he waited for her to say something. Instead she bowed her head and remained quiet. A silent goddess. A woman who was intimate and immediate, yet so distant, so apart in space and time.

Penny said, "Yesterday, when I went to see Meyer Waxler, you sent some black hoods after me. Let me rephrase that. You arranged for a man named Campbell Espry to do it. Mr. Espry said he promised you the blacks wouldn't hurt me. Pardon me if I'm not grateful."

Penny spoke in English; speaking Japanese meant he and Aikiko were close, a feeling he could no longer afford. Did he still love her? Probably. Like war, love was easy to begin but goddamn hard to stop.

The black kids called Campbell Espry "Soup Man" because of his first name. Espry ran a travel agency over on Eighth and F Streets. Although Espry said he was no longer with the CIA, everyone knew he was still doing work for his government friends and for people like August Carliner.

Penny put his hands behind his neck and grinned. "When I

showed up at Campbell's travel agency I was not in a good mood. The run-in with those four kids had changed my behavioral pattern. You might say it caused me to revert to my old self, to resume what could be called a tendency toward belligerent and pugnacious behavior. Surprised the hell out of Campbell. He'd heard I'd become a pacifist."

"What did he tell you?" Aikiko said.

"He told me he's working for the Japanese. Like you, Carliner, your husband. Whole damn world's working for *Mujin*. Change that. Everybody's working for Reiko Gennai, who's got a stranglehold on the company and doesn't want to let go. I hear she's received a bit of help from your husband over the years."

Aikiko said, "Things are not always what they seem." Later Penny would remember the incredible sadness in her voice when she spoke those words. But at the time he felt no sympathy for her. She'd hid herself from him even while lying in his arms. Whatever he and Aikiko once had was now as flat as piss on a plate.

Penny looked up at the cafeteria ceiling. "Things are not always what they seem. The mystical far east and all that shit. Well, tell that to an Englishman named Oliver Coveyduck. He's dead because Reiko Gennai is afraid of a book he was writing. Tell Coveyduck things aren't always what they seem. Tell him he's not really dead, that Viktor Poltava didn't break his neck then burn down his home to hide the killing. But why am I telling you what you already know? You know Mrs. Gennai's hired Poltava to stop people from digging into your husband's past. I bet you even know when Poltava's due to arrive in this country."

"He's here."

There was a long silence. Penny's face assumed a dark, worried look. Finally he said, "Are you sure?"

Aikiko waited awhile before answering, then said, "My husband is terribly afraid of him. Whenever they are to meet, Warren becomes tense in a certain way. It is not the tension of business. His stomach gives him much trouble and he must see his special masseur twice a day. He always sends me away so that I do not have to see Poltava. He does not say why he sends me away. And he thinks I do not know. He tries to protect me."

Penny rose from his chair, walked toward the waterfall, and

stood with his back to Aikiko, thinking. Then he turned to face her. "When did Poltava arrive?"

"Over the weekend, I think. I was supposed to return to New York Saturday for a dinner party. Warren had planned to entertain some people from the publishing company he is trying to buy."

"Butterfield Publishing."

"Yes. But he telephoned to say he'd canceled the party and that I could stay in Washington longer if it pleased me. I understood what he meant. I told him there is much work for me to do here. He seemed relieved."

Touching a paint stain on her smock, she permitted herself a small smile. "I am touching up a rather complicated watercolor which the gallery feels will be the centerpiece of my exhibition. I fly to New York this afternoon—"

"Why?" Penny tried not to appear worried. But the uneasiness was in his voice. *Viktor Poltava was here*.

Aikiko heard his concern; her face brightened for a second, then the expression vanished. "The gallery insists that I exhibit three hanging scrolls which also include *haiku* verses I've written. Unfortunately, the scrolls are in New York."

When Penny asked if she couldn't have them shipped to the gallery Aikiko said she preferred to hand-carry them herself. It wasn't something to be done over the phone; she had to choose the scrolls personally, and rather than have them packaged poorly, it would be wiser to be her own messenger. This was her first American show, and nothing must go wrong. Penny, giving in to bitterness, said, "It's all gone wrong with us."

Aikiko said, "Campbell Espry did not tell you everything."

"You asking me or telling me?"

"Please believe that I never meant to hurt you in any way. I did not say everything to you because I did not want to lose you. You are a special man, someone I need in my new life."

Penny said, "New life? I have a feeling your husband might want to hear this. Don't worry, he won't hear it from me."

She looked at the floor. "Do you know what Mrs. Gennai does to *Mujin* wives who try to leave their husbands? Do you know what I risk by loving you?"

The fear in her voice stopped Penny cold. Meyer Waxler had told him about Mrs. Gennai's approach to discipline. *Oni*. Penny felt sick with shame. He'd been thinking about Aikiko's so-called treachery, about what she'd done to him. Hadn't given a thought to her safety. Not one goddamn thought. How long would she live after the Empress heard tapes of their telephone calls made by Aristotle Bellas? *How long?*

Penny said, "Meyer Waxler told me how Mrs. Gennai handles company wives who won't stay in line."

"My husband has mentioned Mr. Waxler a few times. They do not like each other."

"You're right, they don't. How did you learn about the punishment?"

"Two years ago she showed me a film of a woman being tortured." Aikiko closed her eyes, remembered the horror and dropped her voice to a whisper. "In the film a half-naked man wearing a demon mask and claws did things to a woman—" Aikiko covered her face with both hands, unable to continue.

"Poltava," Penny said.

Aikiko nodded. Penny saw that she was weeping. Her tears. His shame. Any animosity he felt toward her was gone. He left the waterfall, crouched beside her chair, and took her in his arms. She was the first to break the silence. She said, "Mrs. Gennai is a powerful woman. To break free of her, I needed the protection of someone quite strong, someone who was not afraid of her."

Penny looked into her eyes, waiting.

"He promised to protect me," she said. "In return, I had to help him take the company away from her."

Campbell Espry did not tell you everything.

Penny thought, damn right he didn't. Soup Man was a player, a pro. He wouldn't hand over the entire package unless you leaned on him real hard. Penny had scared him, but he hadn't scared him enough. Soup Man had not been entirely straightforward and aboveboard. He'd held out the identity of the man he and Aikiko were working for. The man who'd promised to protect Aikiko from the Empress.

"I have to know his name," Penny said.

"Tetsu Okuhara."

Surprise. Penny frowned. For some reason he'd been expecting the mystery man to be Hanzo Gennai, the Empress's son. Tetsu Okuhara. Yasuda Gennai's godson and, according to Meyer Waxler, the *Mujin* executive with the most smarts.

Aikiko said, "Yasuda-san wants his godson to succeed him,

but Mrs. Gennai is opposed to this. She prefers that her son be president, and she will do anything to bring this about. Warren says Okuhara-san is the only person Mrs. Gennai fears."

Aikiko dried her tears with a handkerchief. She said, "Okuhara-san told me that Yasuda Gennai was ill and did not have long to live. It was important, he said, that Mrs. Gennai's influence at *Mujin* come to an end. He said she was out of control and unless she were stopped, she would destroy everyone. He knew I was unhappy with Warren. Okuhara-san knows many things. He told me there was a way out. The way out, he said, was the information passing through Warren's hands almost every day."

"Did he tell you how much danger you'd be in?"

"As long as Mrs. Gennai is in power, all *Mujin* wives are in danger. Our lives literally hang by a thread, one she can break whenever it suits her. This was my chance to be free of her."

"And be free of your husband at the same time."

She bowed her head.

Penny spoke in Japanese. "You married a man you do not love. Why?"

Aikiko drew him closer. Her voice was muffled against his shoulder. She, too, spoke in Japanese. "Warren saw my photograph in a Tokyo magazine. He was very impressed, he told me later. At the time I worked as a model to pay for my art studies. He had Mrs. Gennai investigate me."

Aikiko dug her nails into Penny. "My mother had died not too long before Ganis entered my life," she said. "The cause of her death had been listed as heart failure, but Mrs. Gennai said this was not true. She said that my mother had been slowly poisoned to death."

Aikiko looked at Penny. "My father had done it over a period of time to make it seem a natural death."

"Why did he kill her?"

Aikiko looked away. "He wanted our home and property. Everything belonged to my mother. She had planned to draw up a will leaving it all to me upon her death. She never got to do that. My father had a second reason for killing her. He wanted me."

Penny exhaled. Then, "I'm sorry. Really, really sorry. How long—" He left the sentence unfinished.

"It started when I was thirteen. He said he had given me life, therefore I belonged to him. He had created me, and I was his creature. He said no man could love me the way he could because he was my father and we were of the same blood, the same flesh. I did not know how wrong it was, I did not—"

She shook her head violently, then began to weep almost uncontrollably. Penny quickly took her in his arms, clung to her, stroked her hair and rocked her gently. After a while Aikiko said, "It went on for seven years. Seven horrible years. He controlled my life. I had no friends. I had my art. Just my art."

"Did your mother know?"

"Not at first. When she found out she blamed me for leading him on. That was the worst part. Her accusations, her insults. Eventually she began to hate my father even more than she hated me. That's when she threatened to leave her property to me."

Penny said, "Wasn't there someone else you could talk to?"

"In Japan the family is considered more important than any one of its members. One must never disgrace it. Nor must we disgrace the national family, for we are taught that all Japanese belong to a single tribe. We are a special race, one apart from all other races. From childhood we are taught that Japan is even more important than our families. My father convinced me that to discuss our relationship outside of family would be to dishonor our name and our country."

"Jesus. Excuse me for saying so, but your father was a shit."

Aikiko permitted herself a small smile. "It took me a long time to see that. In Japan women must obey men in all things. We do as we are told. Even in the twentieth century this idea remains undisturbed. Japan has always been a man's country. Women are taught to submit, to yield, to never question. Apart from my mother, I told no one what my father was doing. It did not seem proper to bring this matter before strangers."

Penny said, "Under those circumstances even Warren Ganis must have looked good."

"One man had put me in hell. Another could release me. We have a proverb: To remove a thorn from your flesh, use another thorn."

"Use a thief to catch a thief, we say."

"*Hai.* Warren wanted me and was determined to have me. My father protested, but Mrs. Gennai confronted him with what she'd learned about my mother's death. And about the relationship between my father and myself."

"So he went along with the marriage."

"He was threatened with public disgrace and with prison. In the end he received money and a job at *Mujin.*"

Penny said, "What happened to him?"

"I did not love Warren," she said. "I tried, but I could not. I was most unhappy, and the only person I felt I could open my heart to was my father. He said he would help me as best he could."

Penny knew what was coming next. He waited.

Aikiko said, "He had become a heavy drinker and was himself a most unhappy man. He blamed himself for what had happened to me, so he did the one thing he thought would free me. He committed suicide by swallowing the same poison he had used on my mother."

Penny nodded. "He figured if he were gone, you could leave Gannis."

"*Hai.* But Warren is very possessive. When he suspected that I might want to leave him, he said he loved me terribly, more than any woman he'd ever known. He vowed never to let me go. I would stay with him, he said, until one of us died."

Stroking her hair, Penny said, "That's when Reiko Gennai arranged for you to see the film of Viktor Poltava torturing a *Mujin* wife. If I didn't hate your husband before, I hate the son of a bitch now."

A suddenly alarmed Aikiko took his face in her hands. "She must never find out about us. Never. If she does, we will be killed. Poltava—"

Aikiko stopped. She saw it in his eyes. She said, "Mrs. Gennai knows about us, doesn't she." She suddenly clung to Penny with all her strength, digging her nails into his shoulders, sobbing uncontrollably. He tried to calm her, telling her that the two of them were together, that nothing else mattered. Her love had made him want to live again, he told her. Aikiko would always be a part of him. Her love was all he had.

The cellular phone rang.

Penny reluctantly moved away from Aikiko, opened the case, and placed the receiver to his ear. "Penny," he said.

At the other end a very tense Bob Hutchings said, "Trouble at the house. Guy tried to break in. We got him—"

"Hold him. On my way," Penny said, thinking it couldn't be

Poltava. Or could it? Could they have gotten that lucky? But if it wasn't the demon, then who the hell was it? Penny hung up the receiver, slammed the case closed, and reached out to touch Aikiko's tear-stained face. He thought, if the demon hasn't come today, he'll come tomorrow. And he'll kill the two of us unless I get awfully lucky and kill him.

Penny kissed Aikiko, then picked up the cellular phone and hurried from the cafeteria, the taste of Aikiko's tears still on his lips.

16

WHEN REIKO GENNAI knelt beside her dying husband, it was dawn.

Outside the bedroom a heavy rain beat against the *ama-do,* thin wooden shutters used as storm protection. And with the deluge came an eerie glow from a nearby grove of cherry trees. The glow sprang from car headlights whose harsh brilliance lit up the darkness and shimmered in the rain. These were the cars of reporters who had begun their death watch in the afternoon, when Yasuda Gennai had been taken from the hospital and brought home to die among the spirits of his ancestors. It was the journalists' claim that they had come to witness the passing of a king. But to Reiko Gennai they were vultures, waiting to feed on dead flesh. Scavengers out to advance themselves with no regard for principles or consequences.

In the bedroom she took an incense stick from a black lacquered box on a small writing desk. After touching the sliver of fragrant wood to the flame of candle resting on a low night table, she placed it in a duck-shaped incense burner. The duck's body served as the burning chamber, while the smile and fragrance came from its bill.

This second-floor bedroom was her favorite room in the villa. Medieval storage chests, an oak floor, rice paper walls and sixteenth-century bronze lanterns gave it the look of an ancient Japanese temple. Here she restored her peace of mind through long hours of silent meditation, or by staring down at the moss-lined pool in her tea garden. Here she reaffirmed her courage and saw the possibility of everything.

Her life with Yasuda-san was about to come to a close. But because she would control its next president, her son Hanzo, Reiko Gennai's domination of *Mujin* would continue. If fate must descend upon her, let it happen in this room.

A folding screen decorated with hawks and dragons had been placed around Yasuda Gennai's bed. It served as a wall, hiding Reiko Gennai from two men in the bedroom. One, a former sumo wrestler, held a two-way radio in one huge hand as he stood arms folded in front of a sliding door leading to the corridor. The second was an elfin little man in his eighties, whose lopsided expression was caused by the loss of his left eye as a child. He was Oda Shinden, Yasuda Gennai's personal physician and a man of exceptional medical ability and intellectual power. In the opinion of many, he was also slightly mad.

Descended from a noble Kyoto family, he insisted on living his life by the ancient code of *Bushido*, the Way of the Warrior. Despite abolition of the privileged samurai class over one hundred years ago, Shinden still allowed the warrior code to dictate almost every aspect of his existence. The essence of that code was absolute loyalty to the feudal lord, a willingness to die in the lord's defense, and an adherence to a sternly refined course of etiquette governing a samurai's every action. The code also demanded that a samurai commit suicide rather than be dishonored by failure.

Because of his fixation with traditional Japanese beliefs Oda Shinden had chosen to spend his entire working life with *Mujin*. The company's feudal climate, with its dictatorial rule by a single clan, matched the self-discipline and obedience drilled into him by an aristocratic family. He saw *Mujin* as an incarnation of Japan's old imperial system, an ideal to be preserved at all costs.

Its leaders became his feudal lords; over the years he would serve each with extraordinary ability and unswerving loyalty. The *Mujin* leader who received his most single-hearted allegiance, however, was Reiko Gennai.

1943. On *Mujin*'s orders, Oda Shinden delivered an emotional rallying speech to the National Patriotic Women's Association. His purpose: to strengthen resistance to upcoming American bomber raids. Men were at the front, he said. It was up to women to become active in civil defense, to fight fires, identify planes, dig bomb shelters and make firebreaks by razing their own homes if necessary.

Women faced a difficult task, no doubt, but as long as they retained a great spirit of loyalty and patriotism, Japan could never be defeated by America and Britain. National unity and pride will surely carry the day, Shinden told them. Weeping with emotion, the women interrupted him several times with applause and cheers, for he was an impassioned and soul-stirring speaker.

After his talk an attractive young girl captured Shinden's attention with penetrating questions concerning his knowledge of America's war machine. Her queries amounted to an interrogation, a probing cross-examination of his every answer. The doctor was hard put to hold his own. But surprisingly, he seemed to enjoy the battle of wits with the outspoken youngster.

Instead of being offended he encouraged the girl, responding to her challenge with a courtesy and good humor that amazed onlookers. She was a nobody, after all, while Oda Shinden was a man of importance and significance. Yet he remained gracious, gently poking fun at the girl's imperial manner. She was, he said with a twinkle in his one eye, a little empress. But a scowl of disapproval on her pretty face indicated that she did not enjoy criticism. Her name was Reiko Dazai. She was sixteen.

He later learned that she came from a good family, one descended from minor nobility and which was quite patriotic. In subsequent talks with Reiko he found her to be quick, hardheaded and, for one so young, surprisingly farsighted. Her love of the homeland appealed to him most of all. It was she who had insisted that Shinden end the meeting at the National Patriotic Women's Association by leading them in a well-known patriotic song, one taunting the American aircraft. *Come on enemy planes. Come on many times.*

Reiko claimed descent from Chacha, concubine of the great Hideyoshi, the sixteenth-century military genius who had united Japan. And while an investigation by Shinden eventually disproved this claim he still found himself captivated by her, seeing in Reiko the daughter he would never have. He had taken a vow of celibacy, viewing it as a means of fully developing his mental, physical and spiritual powers. A true celibate, he believed, could do the work of twenty men.

Reiko was the daughter of Ikuo Dazai, a legal scholar and government worker. Dazai was also a descendent of samurai. Shinden found him to be active and industrious, a man who was very careful not to waste what little his family had. These traits made him something of a busybody who often irritated neighbors and friends with his so-called good intentions.

My daughter, Dazai told Shinden, has been born with an old soul and is wise beyond her years. Unfortunately, she is also inflamed with ambition and has an insatiable desire for honor. Young Reiko was driven by the need to be first, a trait her father found less than admirable. And she was a bossy little thing, ordering her parents and brother about as though they were her children. Her brother, serving with the navy on Okinawa, claimed she was more despotic than his officers. Oda Shinden listened carefully, his one eye focused on Ikuo Dazai's face with a disturbing intensity.

Three weeks after their first meeting, when Oda Shinden had completed his investigation into her background, he visited Reiko at her home and asked if she believed in destiny. She said yes, but only in her own destiny. He then asked her if she were willing to trade the known for the unknown, to leave her family and place herself under the total control of those who ran the *Mujin* corporation. If so, then men and women of great power would shape her destiny. Instead of waiting for her future, she had a chance to choose it.

Shinden said, "The opportunity to possess the wealth and power of an empress can be yours. But in return you must vow total obedience to *Mujin*. Nothing less will be acceptable. You must be able to do without freedom for a time, but this will prevent you from frittering away your energy on useless things. You will join a kingdom without boundaries, one so powerful that even kings are forced to bow down to it.

"But be warned," Shinden told Reiko. "Once in, never out. Because women occupy a special position at *Mujin*," he said, "none are allowed to leave the company after joining. Do you understand what I am saying to you?" Reiko nodded.

"Think carefully before you decide," Shinden told her. "You are responsible for your own fate. When you pour the wine, you must drink it."

He watched Reiko close her eyes and think before asking, "Will I have a chance to rule this kingdom one day?"

Shinden said, yes. Many women before you have done so. But to achieve this you must work three times as hard as any man. However, it has been done.

When she lifted her head to look at him, her smile was cold and triumphant. "I am ready to go with you," she said. Shinden said he would leave the house while she bid farewell to her family. But Reiko shook her head. "That won't be necessary," she said. "If I am to be an empress, I must learn to be decisive. I trust you to make the proper arrangements with my parents."

Shinden had brought a young Reiko to *Mujin* years ago. He was still certain that in her he had chosen well. She is my child, he thought, and in her I have given birth to *Mujin*'s future. He was more certain of Reiko than of any woman he had ever brought into the company.

Behind the folding screen Reiko Gennai stared down at her dying husband who lay on a *futon*, a mattress stuffed thick with cotton wool. Despite the warm night he was covered with a quilt and blanket. He also wore gloves. A respirator mask connected to an oxygen tank covered his nose and mouth.

His eyes were closed, but Reiko Gennai wondered if her husband was asleep or merely pretending to be. Count on him to play the fox even at death's door. It was not enough to be astute, he'd often told her. One must be cunning, as well.

Yasuda-san has only minutes to live, Oda Shinden had said to Reiko Gennai. Squeezing her hands, the one-eyed little man whispered, "Be quick. Act boldly. Your strong spirit will triumph over fear and despair."

Reiko Gennai remained outwardly calm, but inside she was more uneasy than she'd been in a long time. For she knew that her future would be decided this night at Yasuda Gennai's bedside. She had come to this room to find either destiny or sorrow.

After tonight she would achieve the highest glory or be overthrown.

Her husband slowly opened his eyes and stared at her. There was a flash of recognition in his gaze, along with something else. Reiko Gennai understood. She, not he, had realized that one could have power or happiness, not both. Therefore in the end he had been forced to give way to her. And the deepest love had turned into the deepest hatred.

For her part, she had stopped hating him. Instead she had become indifferent to this man she had once worshiped. Now he was shrunken and withered, no longer able to have his way in this world. Truly an object of pity, she thought. And pity was the only charity she felt inclined to give him. To Reiko Gennai, he looked like a wizened monkey. Not so much ugly as uninteresting.

Rain pounded the bedroom shutters as she reached inside a black lacquered box on the writing table and removed two sheets of paper. She glanced briefly at one, then leaned forward and held both in front of her husband's face. He blinked several times. And when his eyes widened in panic, she smiled.

One sheet contained several sentences in Japanese characters. Yasuda Gennai had painfully drawn them himself just hours ago. *Honor my last request,* he had written to *Mujin*'s officers, *and choose for your new leader my godson Tetsu Okuhara. I have charged him with ending my wife's influence at this company to which I have given my life's blood. Only Okuhara-san is strong enough to bring about a new era at* Mujin. *Honor my godson,* Yasuda Gennai had written, *and you honor me with eternal peace as I go to live among the spirits of my ancestors.*

He'd signed the page with both his *jitsu-in,* a registered personal seal, and his *mitome-in,* the family seal. The smaller sheet of paper was the government certificate that had to accompany any document containing the registered seal. Seals were the legal method of identification. A signature had no official recognition.

Yesterday Yasuda Gennai had handed the paper and certificate to a buxom, middle-aged nurse who had gone out of her way to befriend him and make his hospital stay as comfortable as possible. He'd been forced to live with guards at his door, placed there by his wife with orders to admit only hospital personnel. She had also instructed the switchboard to turn away all telephone calls. The great Yasuda Gennai must be allowed peace, she'd said.

Thus in his painful final days the sympathetic nurse Kojima had emerged as his only bright spot.

She had been more than a confidant. Nurse Kojima had served as an occasional messenger between Yasuda Gennai and his god-son Tetsu Okuhara. Yesterday, in return for a handsome reward, she had promised to deliver to Okuhara the paper containing Yasuda-san's final statement. And, indeed, nurse Kojima had discharged this errand as she had previous ones. She had taken the paper directly to Oda Shinden.

Instead of reading it then returning it so that she could complete her mission, the one-eyed little man had kept the paper. But, as usual, he praised her for a job well done. Nurse Kojima, however, had insisted that it was she who would forever be in his debt. His influence alone had prevented medical authorities from ending her career due to her unfortunate role in the death of a small boy three years ago.

In the bedroom, Reiko Gennai held the two pieces of paper over the candle flame. They caught fire immediately. She held them by a corner for a few seconds, then dropped the burning papers onto a silver tray on the night table. When they had curled into blackened bits, she leaned over her husband and removed his gloves. His fingers were clubbed, thickened and round at the tips with long nails curving over the ends. A sympton of severe lung disease, Oda Shinden had told her.

As her husband watched helplessly, Reiko Gennai pulled the small writing table toward her. Made of hand-carved silver and only centimeters high, the table's surface was decorated with flying cranes executed in inlays of gold and silver. There were two flat gold and lacquer boxes on the table. One contained *shikishi*, thick, square writing paper. The other was a *suzuri-bako*, an ink-stone case for instruments used in writing with a brush. Both boxes belonged to Yasuda Gennai, who'd last seen them when he'd written the plea on behalf of Okuhara-san.

Reiko Gennai slid the top from the inkstone case to reveal a writing brush, an inkstone, an ink stick, and a small water dropper shaped like a dragon. Picking up the water dropper, she poured a trickle of water into the depression of the inkstone, then rubbed the inkstick along the stone's abrasive surface, mixing it with the water. When she had produced liquid ink, she removed a sheet of paper from the stationery box and placed it on the table.

Now she rose, lifted the table, and fitted it over her husband's waist as though it were a breakfast tray. Then she walked around the *futon* and, with the oxygen tank to her back, leaned over the table to uncap the writing brush. Made from carved ivory, the brush was over four hundred years old and had been used by a Chinese emperor during the Ming period. It had been a gift to the Gennai family from the Emperor Hirohito.

Reiko Gennai dipped the tip of the brush into the ink and, when it was thoroughly wet, she fitted it to her husband's fingers. Placing her lips to his ear, she whispered, "Write as I tell you. 'I, Yasuda Gennai, do make this last request of my fellow officers at *Mujin* that they honor my beloved son Hanzo by choosing him as—'"

The dying man's eyes widened. With an effort he spread his misshapened fingers, letting the brush fall onto the paper. He shook his head slowly.

His wife picked up the paper, looked at the ink blot left by the brush, then tore the paper in half and tore it once again. Setting the torn bits aside, she removed another sheet of thick paper from the stationery box and lay it on the writing table. Again she wet the brush. Then, reaching to the left, she turned off her husband's oxygen.

Eyes bulging, a terrified Yasuda Gennai raised both hands in a desperate, silent plea. His face reddened. His chest rose and fell rapidly. After five seconds Reiko Gennai turned the oxygen back on, leaned over, and whispered, "Write as I tell you." Again she fitted the brush to his trembling fingers. This time she guided his every stroke, dictating to him, patiently steering him through every character.

Finished, she lay the brush aside and reached for his black lacquered seal box. Opening it, she removed his seals, along with a patty of cinnabar. Shaped like thin carrots and made of jade, the seals had been engraved by a master artist. Reiko Gennai pressed the engraved end of the official seal into the cinnabar, a waxlike substance known also as "dragon meat." Then she affixed the engraved end to the paper, leaving behind a bright red imprint. She did the same with the family seal.

Finally, she read the paper one last time. Satisfied, she set it aside and stared down at her husband. He was frightened and defiant. She saw in his eyes the strong desire to live. So long as he drew breath, he would do his best to prevent Reiko Gennai from having her way. It was a dazzling concentration of courage.

His eyes said he would begin by hanging on one minute longer. Then one minute more. He had both the inspiration of a great name and his hatred for her. A minute longer. Enough such minutes could destroy her plans.

Reaching over, she removed the writing table from him and placed it on the matted floor to her left. Now sitting upright, buttocks on her heels, she stared down at this man who had been so much a part of her life. A glance at the paper she had forced him to write, then she closed her eyes. Seconds later she opened them. And turned off Yasuda Gennai's oxygen.

17

August, 1985

IN THE GARDEN room of Senator Machlis's home, Edward Penny
sat under a French chandelier and stared at Nickie Max's back.
Nickie was the early morning intruder who'd just sent Penny
speeding from Aikiko's gallery back to the Georgetown house.
Nickie Max, who'd shown up after a twenty-four-hour-flight
from Thailand looking flat out ugly and mean.

Nickie Max, who'd appeared two hours earlier and gotten
pissed when told that Penny wasn't here. Who'd been informed
he couldn't wait around no matter how urgently he had to see his
old friend. Nickie Max had developed an attitude, and it had
taken four men to stop him from forcing his way inside.

Nickie Max. Lying handcuffed and weeping on the kitchen
floor when Penny'd finally arrived. Nickie Max, who'd come to
Washington to ask Edward Penny's help in killing a man.

In the garden room Nickie stared through an open floor-to-
ceiling window at the wide-column arbor which was a part of the
garden. One hand massaged the back of his neck; the other held a

347

glass half filled with Fran Machlis's best brandy. When a rose-
wood and mahogany mantel clock began striking twelve noon, he
swallowed the rest of the brandy and turned around slowly.

Penny saw a man whose nerves were stretched tight. A man
under a great deal of pressure. Eyes red-rimmed. Face pouchy
and unshaven. Baggy clothes he'd probably slept in for a week,
with running shoes that were so beat-up they looked like a gray
fungus. More gut and less hair than he'd had five months ago,
when Penny'd last seen him. Nickie looked like hammered shit.
And he spoke in a voice hoarse with fatigue and despair.

He said, "The guy's a Japanese. Name's Waseda. Works for a
heavy dude in New York named Warren Ganis. Past couple years
I've been supplying them with Asian art. Ganis collects the shit.
Doesn't care where it comes from or what it costs. Has to have it,
and that's all that matters."

Nickie swallowed more brandy. "Waseda's the guy I deal
with. He flies over to Bangkok four, five times a year to pick up
stuff. He's a sick fucker, Waseda. A big reason he comes to
Thailand is for the sex. Bangkok's heaven on earth if you're a sex
freak. You want it, you got it. Waseda, he's a chicken hawk.
Likes to fuck kids. Girls, boys, he ain't particular. Just likes 'em
young."

Nickie emptied his glass. "Couple times he said something
about my daughters, and I told him I didn't like that kind of talk.
Once he offered me money if I would let him fuck my kids and I
just flipped out. Fucking decked him. Went upside his head. I got
two beautiful daughters, man. Oldest one's twelve, other's nine,
and ain't nobody gonna say that kind of shit in front of me."

He looked down at the Kashan rug. "Japanese people, man.
They're fucking arrogant. They really think their shit don't stink
and when it comes to women, I mean, they've got no respect.
They think they should be able to fuck any woman alive. I've
seen Japanese men come to Bangkok on these sex tours they
have. Air fare, hotel, and all the sex you want. Everything's
included in one neat package. Goddamn Japanese, they treat the
women like dirt."

Penny watched as Nickie Max stepped over to a driftwood
coffee table, picked up the decanter, and refilled his glass. Nickie
said, "Waseda. He was just biding his time, man. Just waiting for
the opportunity to get back at me for knocking him on his ass.

And I fucking gave it to him. Played right into his hands."

He emptied half of his glass at a gulp. "Had a deal going with Waseda and Ganis for some Korean scrolls and Ceylonese sculptures. I needed the money. A lot of what I got from Herman Fray in San Augustín went for your hospital bills in Mexico City. And if you remember, I had to grease a few Mexican cops to leave us alone until Senator Machlis could step in and get us away from them fucking bean eaters."

Penny said, "I remember."

Nickie said, "Anyway, I tell Waseda I'm upping the price on this shipment. Hell, you can't do business in Thailand without paying off people and I mean a lot of people. My wife's Thai and I also give money to her relatives. Shit, they're all poor and like everybody else over there they think all Americans are millionaires. So what happens is, Waseda, he gets pissed, says I broke my word to him about the price and nobody's supposed to do that, I guess, because he's fucking Japanese. So he says he's gonna teach me a lesson."

Nickie blinked tears from his eyes. "The guy rapes my daughters. First he has the cops pick me up. Tells them I threatened to kill him. Fucking cops know better, but Waseda, he greases a few palms and I'm in the slammer while he rapes my kids. I've come halfway around the world to kill him, and nobody's going to stop me. Don't care if I have to die for it. I'm willing to die ten times if it means I take his ass with me."

He turned his back to Edward Penny and stared out at the garden again.

No mouthing off here, Edward Penny thought. No posing, no macho bullshit. Nickie Max meant every word he'd said. Some guys might dare you to spit across the line or knock the chip off their shoulder. Then maybe, just maybe they'd get physical. Not Nickie Max. No threats, just promises. When push came to shove, bet on him sticking it to you in spades.

And that was the problem because this time he was facing some heavy-duty people. The kind who played hardball and didn't like to lose. Nickie Max was in over his head. And only Penny knew how deep. Going after the Japanese guy meant taking on Warren Ganis. Meaning there was a better than even chance of running into Viktor Poltava. Ain't nothing so bad it couldn't get worse, Penny thought.

He leaned back in a wicker armchair. "The guy who attacked your kids. What's his name again?"

Nickie Max said, "Waseda. Ioko Waseda. I call him Iggy."

"And he works for Warren Ganis?"

"Yeah. Past couple years I sent a lot of stuff to Ganis through Waseda. Some of it I came across myself. Some of it's from people I put him in touch with. Chinese bronzes, limestone Buddha heads, Thai carvings, Japanese porcelain jars, Korean wood carvings. Ganis is queer for anything Asian. You name it, the man owns it. Thing is, most of the shit he has is stolen. Hell, I oughta know."

"And Waseda was the middleman, the guy who actually gave you the money."

Nickie said yeah, threw back his head, and swallowed the rest of the brandy. Penny stood up, crossed the room where he refilled Nickie's empty glass and handed it back to him. He said to Nickie, "Waseda did this because you tried to raise the price?"

Nickie Max said, "People like me, westerners, we don't pay off they put us in jail and throw away the key. They don't mind you dealing in stolen art, drugs, gold, whatever. You make money selling jock straps to parakeets, fine. Just make sure those in charge get theirs. Shit, I must be paying off at least half a dozen people.

"I like living over there because it sure beats plowing a farm and staring at a horse's ass twelve hours a day. But I tell you, every time you turn around somebody's got his fucking hand out. Sticky-fingered gooks coming at you out of holes in the ground. I needed the bread," he told Penny, "so I upped the price and Waseda, he didn't like it. Basically the man just wanted to get back at me for punching him out."

Penny watched Nickie finish his brandy. No wonder he looked wasted. Three drinks on an empty stomach, jet lag, and almost no sleep for three days. And on top of it all, a problem that wouldn't go away until he killed a man.

Nickie said, "I gotta sit down," and he staggered over to a large glass-topped table where he collapsed in an American country chair. Then it was head down on the table for a few seconds before suddenly sitting erect as though jerked upright by invisible wires.

Penny said, "If you're thinking of tossing your cookies, that table cost eight-thousand dollars."

Nickie Max forced a smile. "When you're gonna barf, do it in a class place, I always say. Only kidding. I'm cool. Just let me rest awhile."

"When's the last time you ate?"

"I'll be all right. Look, man, I don't want you involved in this thing. You got yourself a nice set-up here. Nice job, nice place to stay. You're working for an important lady, and you two get along. All I need's one or two things from you, then I'm outta here."

"You need a piece, right?"

Nickie shrugged. "Yeah, well, it ain't cool to try and bring one into the country. Also, maybe you can lend me a few bucks. I'm good for it. Cost me everything I had to buy my way out of jail and get my passport back."

Penny left the wicker chair and sat down at the glass-topped table across from Nickie Max. "Waseda fixed the cops?"

Nickie Max nodded. "Better believe it. That's how he got to my kids. Shithead has me arrested. Then one of the cops, guy named Chakri, he goes and gets my kids. Tells my wife I asked for the kids to be brought to me. Same time Chakri says only two people from the same family can visit at one time. Fucking bullshit. Can't blame my wife. I mean, over there when the cops say do something, you do it or it's your ass. Chakri, he takes my kids to Waseda and . . ." The sentence went unfinished.

Nickie Max stared down at his reflection in the glass-topped table. "Remember that Turkish saying Charlie Sullivan used to lay on us all the time? 'To whom can you complain when the judge is fucking your mother.' That's how I felt. I mean, I couldn't even ask the cops for help, and all on account of Chakri. He's definitely on my list. Only reason I didn't whack him first is I wanted to make sure I got Waseda. But I ain't forgetting Chakri. One of these days, man. One of these fucking days. Did I tell you he owns a piece of that whorehouse where Hanako's working? They say she hardly ever takes off that silver fox mask she wears."

He cocked his head and listened. "What the fuck's that?"

Penny looked over his shoulder. "Having some changes made

in security. Installing new locks, new alarm system. Getting rid of the hedges so nobody can hide behind them."

"Noticed something going on when I came in. Or I should say when I was dragged in by your troops. The fuck's going on around here? John Hinckley get loose or what?"

Penny folded his hands on top of the table, sighed, and said, "That's what I wanted to talk to you about. Your problem and my problem. I—"

Nickie held up both hands. "All I want is for you to get me a piece and maybe lend me a few bucks. After that, I'm outta here. I don't want to bring you down with me. After today, you stay clear of me."

Penny stared at him for a long time. Then he said, "I'm only going to say this once, and I want you to listen. If it wasn't for you I'd be just another crispy critter buried in a stinking San Augustín jungle somewhere. You put your life on the line for me. We both know that if it had gone wrong, Colonel Asbun would have done a number on you and the other guys, and we wouldn't be sitting here having this conversation. I owe you, and we both know it. Yeah, I'm going to stay clear of you, all right. I'm going to stay clear of you like you stayed clear of me in San Augustín."

Nickie looked down at the table and shrugged. "I'm telling you, you don't have to do anything for me. You done enough for me already." His tears started again.

Penny said quietly, "No, I haven't. And I don't think there's any way I ever can. But I sure as hell am gonna try."

They sat quietly across from each other, listening to sounds of workmen moving in and around the house, listening to the telephone ring, hearing a radio just outside the window broadcasting a Baltimore Orioles-Red Sox baseball game. Nickie Max finally broke the silence. After three attempts to clear his throat he whispered, "Thanks."

He lifted his head, used his shirttail to wipe tears from his eyes, and smiled. "Shit, nobody ever said I was smart. What's your excuse?"

Tapping his temple with a forefinger, Penny grinned. "Too many Twinkies. Fucks up the brain."

Then he put his arms on the table and stopped grinning. "Listen up, wild man, because I'm going to tell you a few things that will make your hair stand on end."

Nickie Max touched his balding pate. "What's left of it, you mean."

Penny said, "When I mentioned your problem and my problem, I meant exactly that. They're not separate. First, I'm going to have the cook rustle you up an omelette and some black coffee. As of now you've had your last drink until I say you can start again. Both our lives just might depend on your being sober."

"You shittin' me?"

"No, I'm not. The other thing is, what I'm about to tell you goes no further. I don't even want you to say anything to the people you're going to be working with."

Nickie Max frowned. "Did I miss something? What work and when did I get hired?"

"You got hired the minute they dragged your ass through the door. And you'll be working security here with me. Believe me when I say you're gonna earn your money."

Nickie Max looked out at the garden. "That's what all the hammering and banging's about? What's the problem?"

"Viktor Poltava."

"Jesus."

Penny nodded. "Viktor fucking Poltava. I'm going to the kitchen to get you something to eat. Don't move. And don't puke, either. You have a suitcase?"

Nickie nodded. "If you can call it that. One of your guys took it. Probably checking for nuclear warheads or something. Belongs to my wife's uncle. He uses it to carry chickens. You wouldn't believe the smell. Got a shirt, couple pair drawers, razor, my wife's picture. Thought I might not see her again, so I brought it with me."

Penny said, "I'll fix it up with the senator for you to stay here. Right now there's nobody I'd rather have watching my back than you. Have to do something about getting you a temporary pistol permit. Sit tight. Be back soon."

When Penny returned he brought black coffee. He poured cups for Nickie and himself, then said, "I've left word we're not to be disturbed unless it's the senator. Now listen up. You've heard of the *Mujin* corporation. Well, I'm going to tell you a few things about the company you don't know, starting with some things about a woman named Reiko Gennai."

Penny left out nothing. His relationship with Warren Ganis's wife. The relationship between the senator and Helen Silks. The attack at Meyer Waxler's house. Aikiko's secret arrangement with Tetsu Okuhara. The death of Oliver Coveyduck. And Viktor Poltava's role in all of it. A fascinated Nickie, hanging on his every word, could only pick at an omelette, cottage cheese, and an English muffin.

Penny was still talking when a slim Salvadoran maid stood in the doorway and said a Mr. Georges Cancale was calling from France. He insisted it was quite urgent. Did Mr. Penny wish to speak to him? Mr. Penny did. And he would take the call here.

When the maid hung up the extension, Penny placed the receiver to his ear and began speaking in French. He and Cancale spoke for fifteen minutes, then said good-bye. He returned to the table, poured more coffee for himself and Nickie, then said, "Time for an update. I'd asked George to poke around Serge Coutain's place the same time I asked you to check the whorehouses in Bangkok for Hanako. Like you, George found something. He found some grains of bleached rice and a few sesame seeds in the hayloft of Serge's barn."

"I'll take your word this means something," Nickie Max said.

"I've been doing a bit of reading lately."

"So what else is new? Omelette's pretty good, by the way."

"Glad you like it. I'm not talking about books. I'm talking about reading Viktor Poltava's file. Hutchings, the big guy you ran into out front? Ex-Secret Service. He used one of his old contacts and got me the FBI file on Poltava. Last year Poltava killed a guy in Paris, someone who tried to turn him in for the Count Molsheim murder."

"I read about that," Nickie Max said. "Poltava cuffed the dude's hands behind his back, then ran a wire from the cuffs to the man's nuts. Man ended up cutting off his own balls."

"That's right. The FBI file said Poltava sat in the room eating and watching him die."

"Viktor always was a fun guy."

"Which brings us to Count Molsheim. He was jogging in a Paris park when he got hit. Poltava leaped out of a tree and cut his throat."

"Like I always say, jogging's bad for your health."

Penny said, "Even though he came from a wealthy family, the count was one of those people for whom too much is never enough. He was involved with a Singapore group running guns to Iran, and apparently he was overcharging everybody involved. So Viktor Poltava was hired to teach the count that greed can be a drawback to a long life. Anyway, the point is this: in the room where the informant got killed and also near the tree where Molsheim got his, Paris police found the same thing. They found a few grains of bleached rice, along with some sesame seeds."

Nickie Max nodded. "Same stuff Georges found in Coutain's barn. The kind of food Poltava eats when he's waiting around to clip somebody."

"Our boy Viktor's devoted to the old *ninja* diet. It's something he picked up from his grandmother. Georges turned the seeds over to the Deauville police who are going to pass it on to the Paris cops. Which brings me to Helen Silks."

"The senator's main squeeze."

"Georges tells me there was a party at the farm the night Serge got sick and went into a coma. The night the colt was killed and Hanako disappeared. And guess who was one of the guests at that party?"

"Helen Silks. Miss Lickety-Split, herself."

Penny sipped some coffee and said, "I read it this way: she was the inside man. She got Poltava onto the property. Got him past security. Probably in her car. Maybe even as her date, who knows. All she had to do was get him near the barn. He took it from there."

Nickie Max speared a chunk of mushroom omelette, looked at it and said, "She could have clued Poltava in on the alarms and the generator, and told him where Serge and Hanako were sleeping." He shoved the egg in his mouth and said, "The broad's a fucking sweetheart. The senator know what her girl friend did over there?"

"No. Haven't had a chance to clue her in on the stuff I've gotten from Georges. The lady puts in fifteen-hour days, beginning with breakfast meetings at eight in the morning. I've told her to stay away from Silks, and all I can say is I hope she's doing it."

Penny stood up, walked away from the table, and stood in front of the fireplace. Back to Nickie Max he said, "Let's talk about your problem. Or rather, our problem, seeing as how we're dealing with the same people. Warren Ganis, Waseda, Reiko

Gennai, Aikiko." He turned around. "And Viktor Poltava."

Nickie Max burped and scratched his paunch. "Thing is, you never know with fucking Poltava. I mean, we know he's coming after you, but we don't know when he's coming. We don't know where he is, either. With this guy you don't know shit."

"What if we knew when he was coming for me? And what if we were waiting when he showed up? We could take him out before he knew what hit him."

Nickie Max stopped scratching. He grinned. "Love it. But how the hell is that possible? I mean, the only guy who might know where he is is Warren Ganis, and how do you get him to open up? And what happens when Mr. G. learns you got something going with his wife?"

Penny looked down into his empty coffee cup. "I still think about San Augustín a lot, about being in that cellar with Asbun and the White Knives. I was dead meat until you showed up. I'm only here because you had the balls to do the last thing anybody expected you to do."

Nickie chuckled and shook his head. "Tell you the truth, none of us knew what the fuck we were doing."

"The point is, you did it. You won big because you gambled big."

"With me the trick is not to think too much. Like they say, think long, think wrong."

"Paralysis through analysis."

Nickie nodded. "That's about it. I'm getting some strange vibes. Like maybe you've got something weird planned."

"No more weird than what you did down in San Augustín. In fact, it's exactly what you did in San Augustín."

"I don't understand."

Penny said, "Poltava's after me and Aikiko Ganis. And you want to get Waseda."

"You're on a roll. Keep going."

"So it's time we returned to the gospel according to Nickie Max. We change the course of direction of the action in progress."

"You want to put that in English?"

"We attack first," Penny said. "No waiting around for anyone to come to us. We go after Waseda and Poltava at the same time.

We solve two problems at the same time. Kill two birds with one stone."

Nickie held his smile for a long time before saying, "Beautiful. Fucking beautiful. Don't know how you gonna do it, but all I can say is, I love it. Fucking love it."

"The plan won't work if you use too many people. It's you and me, nobody else. If either one of us messes up, it's turn out the lights, the party's over. Poltava will be on us like ugly on an ape, and we'll both be stone dead before you can pick your nose."

Nickie said, "When do we go?"

"Don't you want to know—"

"All I want to know is when."

"Tomorrow night."

"Jesus."

Penny saw Nickie's eyes narrow, saw him rub the top of his head. Thinking. Not doubting, because Nickie believed in Penny. Believed in him when Penny'd stopped believing in himself. No, Nickie Max was simply being professional, tossing the odds around in his mind, then seeing something in Penny's face. Seeing the old Eddie. Seeing a man who was tougher than cheap steak. And smarter than a tree full of owls.

Nickie Max smiled, showing nicotine-stained front teeth. "Iggy's mine. You got to promise me he's mine."

At 5:33 that afternoon Edward Penny and Nickie Max watched from the wisteria-shaded front porch as a limousine carrying Aikiko Ganis rolled out of the cobbled driveway. After pausing to allow a Rolls Royce Corniche the right of way, the limousine turned left. Then it was gone, hidden behind beech trees lining the street of expensive Victorian and federal mansions. Aikiko Ganis was on her way to Washington National Airport, where a night flight would take her to New York to pick up her scrolls.

"I've got to kill Viktor Poltava before he kills us," Penny had said to her. "There's no other way. And I'm going to need your help. I want to get together with your husband. But I don't want him to know I'm coming. I want to surprise him. Just get us together, and I'll take it from there."

A brief hesitation, she'd been packing, then she'd said,

"When do you want me to do it?" Penny said, "It'll take me a day to get ready, so make it tomorrow night. Will he be in Manhattan or in New Jersey?" "At the Fifth Avenue apartment," she said. "Where my scrolls are. We're dining in tomorrow night, just the two of us." "Tomorrow night's perfect," Penny said. "All you have to do is get Nickie and me in the apartment. We'll take care of the rest. Your husband's the one person I know of who's in contact with Poltava," Penny told Aikiko. "I'm going to force him to bring Poltava out in the open so Nickie and I can kill him. It's the only chance you and I have. I'll tell you how to get us into the apartment, but first I want to know the number of people on your husband's staff. And what kind of security."

"Two Haitian maids," she said. One full-time butler, one part-time butler, both Jamaican cousins. An Austrian chef, whose wife served as housekeeper. And a former Green Beret who was both bodyguard and chauffeur. There was also a Japanese named Waseda, who worked for Warren Ganis as private secretary and personal assistant.

Then she said, "My husband would not kill me. I know this. Do you plan to kill him?" She seemed concerned, and Penny remembered the compassion he'd received from her and for a few seconds he was jealous that she should feel that way about any-one else. He wanted to tell her that you couldn't weep for every-body, that she would have to choose and do it soon. Instead, he said he would not kill Warren Ganis. But he said nothing about Waseda.

Penny and Nickie Max watched Aikiko's limousine disappear behind the beech trees. On the lawn in front of them a Hispanic workman loaded the last of the chopped hedges into a wheel-barrow. Inside the house someone tested the new alarm system by ringing it in three short bursts, waiting several seconds, then ringing it again.

Nickie Max said, "Well, what do you think?"

Eyes on the empty driveway, Penny said, "There's this Ari-zona story, old as the hills, I guess, about an Indian who would go up to women and say 'chance.' Just that one word, chance. Finally one girl gets real curious so she goes up to the Indian and says 'hello.' He says 'chance' and she says, 'I thought all Indians said 'how.' Indian says, 'Lady, I know how. All I want is a chance.'"

Penny put an arm around Nickie Max's shoulders. "That's us, my man. We know how to deal with the demon. I'm just hoping a certain lady gives us the chance."

18

Washington, D.C.

August, 1985

FRAN MACHLIS RETURNED to the Senate office building at 5:45
P.M. and stepped into the office of Regina Peck for a drink. Her
administrative assistant handed her a gin and tonic, then began
reading a list of fifty-two telephone calls received during the senator's absence. The list contained three check marks. These, Regina said, are *primo*.

The *primos* were calls from the New York representative of
the Teamsters union, a major Jewish political action committee,
and the president of an east coast bankers association. To Regina,
thirty-three-year-old failed novelist and former editor of a Brooklyn Jewish weekly, *primo* didn't mean first in time or sequence. It
meant potential campaign contributions. And as Fran Machlis
knew, a politician seeking reelection was wise to rank money
right up there with oxygen.

In any election the odds favored the incumbent. Unlike her
opponent, Fran Machlis was already in office, allowing her to get
the credit for any federal money dispensed to New York State.

She could sponsor bills, service constituents, and enjoy free mailing privileges. With victories in two senatorial races, she was a proven vote-getter, and good vote-getters usually won every time. Win once and you could be expected to win again. More members of Congress retired or died than lost elections.

At almost any time this month, Fran Machlis could have taken advantage of the district work period, which allowed members of Congress to return home and toil out of local offices. This was a chance to meet mothers concerned with day care, to talk with police groups anxious to avoid lay-offs, to present prizes to twelve-year-old winners of spelling bees, to lunch with *New York Times* editors in the paper's private dining room. It was a chance for Fran Machlis to serve her constituents and insure herself a place in their hearts come next election.

But instead, she'd chosen to remain in Washington where she'd deliberately kept herself busy to the point of exhaustion. She'd spent time on Capitol Hill conferring with a fellow member of the Senate Banking Committee, then with colleagues on the Senate Appropriations Committee.

The day's activities had also included lunch with Washington's mayor, a rather dynamic black man who enjoyed being the center of attention but whose sense of humor barely concealed a quick temper and suspicious nature. Then it was back to her office to accept an award from an antidrug organization before dashing out to a reception for a new under secretary of state whose appointment she'd been instrumental in bringing about. She'd even found time for a swim and sauna at the Senate gymnasium.

Fran Machlis could have postponed or even avoided a few of these chores. Today's so-called grandness of effort, as she so well knew, had been nothing more than an attempt to avoid Helen Silks.

She'd first met Helen Silks at a dinner party given by Warren Ganis and found herself carried along by a sensual power surpassing anything she'd felt in years. Worn down by fifteen-hour workdays and feeling increasingly lonely, she was unaware how susceptible she was to the wrong kind of persuasion or temptation.

Only once before she'd known such a love, and she'd not allowed herself to ever feel it again. Then she'd been a restless thirteen-year-old facing another boring summer camp in Dutchess

County, New York. Boring until she'd met a fellow camper, a lean, green-eyed Brazilian named Ida Domitila Carlota Xavier.

Ida, the eighteen-year-old daughter of a millionaire who owned a third of his country's tin mines and its most popular soccer club. Ida, who wore a diamond ring in one lip of her vagina, who one night in their tent stripped Fran Machlis nude and introduced her to carnal pleasures that made the summer rush by much too fast. Ida, who fused ideals of pleasure into her body that would lie dormant until Helen Silks.

Fran Machlis had told no one about Ida. Not her friends, her husband, her two daughters, not even Edward Penny. Nor had she ever gone to bed with another woman. But somehow, Helen Silks had discovered a hidden fire in her and, as Fran Machlis knew only too well, hidden fires were the fiercest.

Senator Machlis stood in front of her office window, holding an empty glass and staring south at the Capitol Building. Helen Silks had telephoned four times, leaving a number but no message. Fran Machlis had not returned the calls, nor did she intend to. Edward Penny was right. Better to cut your losses all at once. *Loss is nothing else but change, and change is nature's delight.* If that's true, Fran Machlis thought, why aren't I feeling more delighted? Why do I feel like swallowing a bottle of valium and throwing myself out of this damn window?

She'd been had. Exploited, manipulated, and played for a sucker. In the words of Edward Penny, she'd been jerked around. And she didn't like it. On the other hand, how can you lose what you never had?

Did she owe it to Helen to hear her side of the story? Perhaps there were reasons for what Helen had done, reasons Fran Machlis could understand, thus allowing her to forgive. Get real, Frances. Any excuse to have Helen make love to you again is more like it.

She turned from the window and looked at her desk, at tonight's party invitations laid out for her perusal. Not much to choose from. These days the fizz had gone out of Washington's social scene. Embassy parties, the essence of the town's so-called glamour, had come face to face with the real world of fading economies, terrorism, weakened currencies, and puritanical revolutions. It was too expensive to entertain. The town had gone from caviar to peanut butter, and it was a damn shame.

Fran Machlis decided on a reception at the Swedish Embassy, followed by a visit to a party at the French embassy. Both still managed to entertain fairly well in this age of penny pinching and retrenching. Anything to keep her mind off Helen. Anything to keep the two of them apart.

Her suite of offices was still humming. The phones hadn't stopped ringing since she walked in. The sound of twenty-two staff members hard at work. They'd be going strong until ten tonight. Several wanted private audiences, but she'd had them wait while she spent time alone in her private office. Time thinking about Helen.

She sat down at her desk and stared at her three phones. All buttons lit up as usual. Was one of them Helen? She closed her eyes, remembering their last night together, remembering their bodies together. *Their bodies*. Remembering Helen's laughter as they lay in each other's arms and both quoted Madame de Sèvigné. *We make love like animals, but a bit better*.

A knock on the door and Fran Machlis opened her eyes. "Yes?"

Regina Peck came in with a sheaf of typewritten pages and laid them on the desk, saying, "These just came over by messenger."

Regina turned to leave, stopped, and held up one finger. "Oh, your friend Helen Silks?"

Fran Machlis held her breath. Waited.

Regina said, "She's on the line again. Sounds perturbed, to say the least. Says she absolutely, positively has to speak to you. Thinks we're deliberately refusing to pass on her messages. I notice she's not on the call-back list, so I put the question to you: Is there anything I should know?"

Fran Machlis shook her head. "She's a friend of Warren Ganis's. He wanted me to see what I could do about some visa trouble she's having with Japanese immigration. She spends a lot of time in Tokyo."

"What are we going to do about it?"

"Nothing. I told her to reapply, then drop me a line. She wants me to write the letter for her. I don't think that's wise. Not at this point, anyway."

"I agree. So what do I tell her?"

Fran Machlis looked at the nails on her left hand. "What line is she on?"

"Four-six. Your private line. The one only you and I are supposed to use."

Fran Machlis looked at the phone. Thought about picking it up. Wanted to pick it up. She said, "Tell her I'm unavailable at the present time. If she asks when I will be available—" The sentence went unfinished.

Regina Peck said, "Leave it to me. What about tonight?"

"The Swedes and the French," Fran Machlis said. "Have the car ready downstairs in fifteen minutes."

When Regina left, Fran Machlis inhaled and picked up the receiver. Held it to her ear. Closed her eyes. Imagined she could almost hear her heart pounding in her chest. And then she pushed the button. When she heard Helen begging to be put through to her, she slammed down the receiver, covered her eyes with her hands, and wept.

19

EDWARD PENNY AND Nickie Max entered the lobby of Warren Ganis's apartment building shortly after sundown. Both wore summer suits, Penny in olive drab gabardine, Nickie Max in off-the-rack wool and polyester. A clean-shaven Nickie also sported a powder blue handkerchief and matching tie. Both carried new attaché cases.

With the temperature hovering near ninety, getting Nickie Max into a tie hadn't been easy. It was hot enough to fry spit, he said, so why the fuck choke himself to death? Penny insisted that he wear the tie. It was part of the game they were running on Warren Ganis. They had to look like capitalists. Which is what every American hoped to be before he died.

In the lobby Penny handed a business card to the doorman, a tall Yugoslav fellow with hairy ears and a haunted look. "Mrs. Ganis is expecting us," he said. "We're from the Brussell Gallery, and we're here about the scrolls." The Yugoslav read the card carefully, fingering it as though testing the paper for quality.

When he looked at the blank side, Nickie Max's eyes turned up in his head.

Finally the doorman, made perennially surly by kidney stones and a promiscuous fifteen-year-old daughter, moved to a wall telephone, dialed the penthouse and waited.

Turning his back on the glitter of the lobby's Art Nouveau mirrors, Penny stared across Fifth Avenue at the Metropolitan Museum of Art, whose rear and west wing pushed into Central Park. What he saw bothered him. Bothered him a lot. Streams of people were entering the museum at an hour when it was supposed to be closed.

Larger numbers of people were also filing into Central Park, many carrying blankets, picnic hampers, drink coolers, and flashlights. On their way to an outdoor show and planning to watch it in comfort. Suddenly tense and uncomfortable, Penny began to chew on a thumbnail. Too many people near the apartment building. They could get in the way. Some could even get wasted. Penny began feeling some very bad vibes.

And then Nickie was at his elbow, whispering, "Where the fuck did all these people come from?" Penny asked the Yugoslav, whose metal nametag read Josip Dushan. Placing a hand over the mouth of the receiver, Dushan said the museum stayed open late once a week. A disgusted Nickie Max said, "Don't tell me. Tonight's the night, right?"

Penny asked what was happening in the park. "Free opera and free Shakespeare," Dushan said before turning his attention to the telephone. "Penthouse? Josip downstairs. There's a Mr. Wallach and his assistant here from the Brussell Gallery in Washington. They say they have to see Mrs. Ganis about some scrolls. Yes, I'll wait."

Penny was eyeing the crowds when behind him Nickie Max whispered, it's your call. I'll play it any way you like.

Penny turned to stare at the fluted, tapering legs of an Art Deco couch in front of a lobby wall. The crowds were distracting. He had to concentrate. His palms were sweating again and not from the weather. Fucking migraine was creeping back, too; it was as though someone were pushing pieces of broken glass into his brain. He closed his eyes against the pain. When Nickie Max touched his arm, Penny opened his eyes.

Both looked at Josip Dushan, whose back was turned and who

still had the receiver pressed to his ear. Finally, Dushan hung up and turned to them. Pointing to the bank of elevators he said, "First one on the left."

Edward Penny felt Nickie Max's eyes on him, felt he was expected to say something. Instead he looked at the crowds across the street, stroking his bearded chin with a thumbnail, and hardly seeming to breathe. Then without a word, he turned and walked toward the elevator. Nickie Max quickly followed.

At the penthouse door they were greeted by a slim light-skinned Jamaican in black jacket and bow tie, with processed hair and the barest touch of eye shadow. He, too, was given a business card, but unlike the Yugoslav he refused to look at it. Instead he held it between thumb and forefinger as though it were a dead rat before slipping it into his handkerchief pocket. With his pinky in the air, Penny noticed.

From a marble foyer, the Jamaican led Edward Penny and Nickie Max up red carpeted stairs and through an ante room which appeared to be a showcase for a collection of seventeenth-century Japanese clocks. A right turn and then the three were walking along a gray carpeted hallway lined with shelves of Japanese pottery and sword-guards. In the middle of the hallway, the Jamaican stopped and, with a white-gloved hand, opened a cherrywood door leading to an air-conditioned book-lined study.

Then in a crisp British accent he said, "Kindly wait inside. Mrs. Ganis will be with you shortly. Would either of you gentlemen care for a drink?" On behalf of Nickie Max and himself, Penny refused. The Jamaican left, leaving behind traces of an Yves St. Laurent cologne. Nickie said, "Wake tutti-fruit up in the middle of the night, and I bet he talks just like the rest of us."

Penny looked around the study. Very plush, very comfortable. And air-conditioned, thank God. Unfortunately, there wasn't time to check out the expensively bound books. Or admire the nineteenth-century portrait of a Hong Kong merchant hanging over a gilded pier table. He did, however, give more than a passing glance to a black oak antique desk which dominated the room. Magnificent. It would probably cost him a year's salary. Two lovely Japanese folding screens near a fireplace looked to be even more expensive. Warren Ganis had taste to match his money.

Nickie Max pointed to some Japanese bronzes and nineteenth-century Chinese porcelain. "Guess who sold him those little suckers," he said.

Penny led the way to the black oak desk, placed his attaché case near a green-shaded banker's lamp, and said, "Let's do it." A grim Nickie Max followed, setting his case down near the intercom and humming *Flintstones, Meet the Flintstones* under his breath. The result was more a funeral hymn than the theme for a TV cartoon show.

Opening his case, Penny removed a pair of surgeon's gloves and put them on. Then he pulled his Browning from its shoulder holster, took an eight-inch silencer from the attaché case, and screwed it onto the gun barrel. Working even faster, Nickie removed a Beretta 92SB and silencer from his case, then attached the two. Did it all with a hard, unblinking stare. His "ready for the bughouse" look, Penny called it.

Each man took a ski mask from his case, jammed it into a jacket pocket, and closed the case. Nickie exhaled, then looked up to find Penny staring at him. No problem, Nickie said. I'll be okay. Just want to get the Iggy part over with, is all. Penny nodded, then gave him a thumbs-up signal. Nickie grinned. Ready to rock and roll, he said.

A noise at the study door drew their attention. Penny jerked his head toward the Japanese folding screen decorated with scenes of Mount Fuji. Nickie nodded. Picking up his case and the Beretta, he raced to the screen and stepped behind it. Penny remained at the desk. He closed his attaché case, hid the Browning behind his back, and casually leaned against a high-back leather chair. Doing my best to look cool, he thought. Doing my best not to look like a man with his heart in his mouth.

He took a deep breath as the study door opened. Behind his back he eased the safety off the Browning with his thumb.

Aikiko.

He exhaled. Seconds later she had crossed the room and thrown her arms around him. Still keeping the Browning out of sight, he held her with one arm.

She spoke in Japanese, her words barely audible. "I am afraid, so afraid. Warren is very clever. Tonight I sat at the table expecting him to say, 'I know what you and your friends are planning to do. *I know.*'"

Penny said, "It'll be over soon. Hang on just a little bit longer."

He thanked Aikiko for telephoning him at Fran Machlis's Manhattan home less than thirty minutes ago. The call had been a warning. We're about to sit down to dinner, she'd told him. With Waseda. And then she'd quickly hung up.

"Where is your friend?" Aikiko said.

"He's here. Don't worry about him. I couldn't be sure who might be coming through that door. So as a safety precaution, I had him temporarily disappear."

Penny said, "Let's talk about Viktor. Everything depends on his being in New York. If he isn't, all I can do is squeeze his whereabouts out of your husband, then go after him as quickly as possible. Unfortunately, he could be in Washington."

"I believe he is still in New York."

"What makes you say that?"

She stared at him. "You have not heard?"

"Heard what?"

"Mr. Bellas and his daughter. It was on the television news this evening. They are dead."

"Viktor?"

She shook her head. "His name was not mentioned. Their bodies were so badly burned that police have been unable to determine the cause of death. Some boys were playing near an abandoned factory in Queens and found a van with the dead father and daughter. Police feel the killings may have been ordered by someone in the underworld."

Penny disagreed. "This thing has Viktor's mark all over it. He's a magician, our Mr. Poltava. He's very good at making you see what he wants you to see."

Penny said, "Viktor put one over the British police when he murdered Coveyduck. Now he's done the same with the American police. Instead of looking for him, they're looking for a homicidal Colombian drug dealer or a bloodthirsty Mafia don. What was your husband's reaction to what happened?"

Aikiko said, "He and Waseda were here in the study watching the evening news together, just the two of them. I had to meet my husband in order that he escort me to dinner. He is very insistent on certain formalities. Unfortunately, I was not close enough to hear what they said. But I do know that Warren appeared tense. It was as though he were about to meet with Viktor."

"Think," Penny said to her. "Did you hear anything at all? Anything."

She closed her eyes, then opened them and leaned back to see his face. Holding up a forefinger she said, "I heard one thing. Warren mentioned something about tapes. 'Hanzo Gennai had better be careful with the tapes,' he said. Both agreed that nothing must prevent the tapes from being returned to Japan. That is all I can tell you."

Penny thought, it had all started with those tapes. Tapes which threatened to ruin Fran Machlis. Tapes which had killed the Bellases and brought Penny into conflict with the Empress, and pushed him into going after the one man he feared.

"You say Hanzo Gennai's in New York," Penny said.

She said Hanzo was staying at the Valencia Hotel, which had just been purchased by *Mujin*.

Penny nodded, then gave final instructions. Now Aikiko must return to the dining room, he said. He touched her cheek and said what he had put off saying until now.

She couldn't stay with her husband after tonight, he told her. When Penny and Nickie left, she'd face a new danger. Her betrayal of Warren Ganis would be known to him almost immediately. There would be no forgiveness. Even if Ganis wanted to forgive, the Empress would not allow it. "Decide now," Penny told her. "Walk out of this apartment now. This instant. Or remain behind and die."

She bowed her head. "I will go."

Penny said, "When Warren Ganis starts for the study, leave the apartment immediately. Don't stop for anything except a handbag. Head straight for the airport. And don't look back. Whatever happens, don't look back." She was to stay in Georgetown until he came for her. If he didn't come back, she was to tell the senator everything and ask for protection.

Aikiko brushed away a tear. "Does the senator know of your plan to trap Poltava?"

"No. I told her Nickie and I came here to run a security check on the Manhattan house and her district headquarters. We arrived around eight this morning and haven't stopped since. I figured if we told her why we really came to New York, she'd worry herself sick. Perhaps bring in police and the FBI. Viktor's as smart as they come. If he smells a trap, he'll back off. Our best chance is to use as few men as possible."

Aikiko said, "What happens if you do not kill Viktor?"

Penny held Aikiko close. Thinking about failure would only weaken him, so he fought against it. And to sympathize with Aikiko any longer would be to remember his own fears. Even the waiting was beginning to unnerve him. It was the wrong time to give himself to anything except the killing of Viktor Poltava.

He gently pushed Aikiko away, then watched her turn from him and cross the room. At the door she paused, head bowed and her back to him. He waited for her to speak. But instead she opened the door, stepped into the hallway, and was gone.

When Aikiko returned to the dinner table in tears, Warren Ganis was enraged. "They want to talk to you," she said.

Ganis said, "We'll have our talk, and they'll remember it for the rest of their stupid lives." The boys from the Brussell Gallery were about to become troubled in mind, if not pained in body.

Through experience he'd learned that for all of its ostentatious and mannered behavior, the art world was a jungle. God knows, he'd had his share of problems with the bastards who infested it. The sort whose idea of an even-handed policy was pulling one knife out of your back while sticking another in.

Think smart on this one, he told himself. Come up with a way of leaving these two fast-buck artists sucking wind. He smiled. It was a duty and a joy to use his power on Aikiko's behalf. Before he finished the two shitheads in his study would learn that the ax of power could cut quite deeply.

The Brussell boys had dropped by the apartment to pick up Aikiko's scrolls, or so they said. We'll save you the trouble of taking them to the gallery, was their line. Well, this particular act of Christian charity had a very long string attached to it. Aikiko's scrolls had not been uppermost in their minds.

According to her, the two wanted seventy-five-thousand dollars or her show would be canceled. The money wasn't for them, of course. Promotional expenses were continually rising, and the gallery's budget could only go so far. It was only fair that she do her share toward helping her own career.

Warren Ganis stood ready to deal with the Brussell Gallery crew or anyone else who imagined they could take him for a ride

by blackmailing Aikiko. Nothing incensed him more than an attempt by small minds to make him the object of grand scale
thievery. It was a line of conduct he neither appreciated nor forgave.

In front of his study he adjusted his tie, patted his silvered
hair, opened the door. He stepped into the room, turned to shut
the door, and froze at the sight of a bearded man standing just
inside the study. The man, dressed in olive drab gabardine, put a
finger to his lips in a signal for silence. Then he quietly closed
the door, stepped forward, and pointed a gun at Warren Ganis's
head.

Seven-forty-seven P.M. Two men stepped through the study door.
One was Ray Tooky, Warren Ganis's chauffeur-bodyguard, an
intensely private individual in his late thirties, with an aptitude
for combining worry and determination. Gangly, blond, and
balding, he wore his Special Forces cap badge on a snakeskin
belt hand-made for him by a Montagnard woman he had lived
with in Vietnam's Central Highlands. Having heard Tooky whisper her name during sex, his wife had recently filed for divorce.

With him was Ioko Waseda, a small, bespectacled, round-
faced man in his midforties, whose air of cold, unfeeling superi-
ority had made him the most unpopular member of Warren
Ganis's household.

Inside the study Tooky followed Waseda toward Warren
Ganis, who waited for them behind the black oak desk. Halfway
across the room the bodyguard slowed down and shook his head.
Jesus, what now? The old man appeared ticked off. Sitting tight-
lipped in his high-backed leather chair as though he had a poker
up his ass. Looking like he'd just bitten into an apple and seen
half a worm.

Ray Tooky had been relaxing in his room watching the Jets
and L.A. Raiders in some pre-season action out of Canton, Ohio,
home of the football hall of fame. Headphones on and listening to
Hank Williams, Jr., the only singer worth a shit. Thinking the
only way he could pay his wife's lawyer would be to cash in his
life insurance policy. At the start of the third quarter, with the Jets
up by twelve, Ganis had buzzed him on the intercom, saying go
down to the garage and bring the car around front. Then get

Waseda and bring him to the study. What I need, Tooky thought, is an unlisted number.

Seems Mr. Ganis had just agreed to lend some Japanese bronzes to a couple of guys from his wife's art gallery down in Washington. They'd dropped by the apartment tonight, though Tooky hadn't seen them. He and Short Eyes were to carry the bronzes down to the car. Without breaking anything. Then Ray Tooky was to drive the two art guys to LaGuardia Airport for a night flight to D.C.

The last thing he felt like doing was driving around in weather hot enough to melt your eyeballs. For some reason the limo's air conditioning didn't work too well in the front. When the plastic shield separating the passenger seat from the driver seat was in place, the front stayed lukewarm. The back turned cold enough to freeze the stink off shit.

But if Mr. G. wanted Ray Tooky to make an airport run with some artsy-fartsies, consider it done. Now wasn't the time to be short-fused. Tooky needed a paycheck because he was under a court order to send $75 a week to his wife in Atlanta as child support for a nine-year-old step-daughter. Which is what he got for adopting the kid. And what were you before you got married, Mr. Tooky? Happy, man. Fucking happy.

In the study he watched Mr. G. rub his hands together then place them palms down on the desk and begin a nervous tapping with his right thumb. The old man looked antsy. Keyed up about something. He looked ready to wet his pants.

Waseda said something in Japanese, which Tooky didn't understand since he didn't speak the language. Waseda then started to laugh, but then he was half in the bag from too much rice wine at dinner. Mr. G., though, didn't laugh. Didn't even answer. Ray Tooky looked around the room for the two art guys and didn't see them. Which is when a red light went off in his head.

Too smart, too late.

They stepped from behind one of the wooden folding screens, moving quickly and keeping out of each other's way. Two guys —one tall, one short and round. Mutt and Jeff. Wearing suits, ties, dark blue ski masks. Both carrying a silenced handgun. A couple of pros.

Too dumbfounded to even blink, Ray Tooky could only force a very thin smile, thinking, I walked right into it. His prick might as well be growing out of his forehead because then his balls would be in his eyes and he'd have an excuse for being blind.

The Smith & Wesson, along with the .32 he usually wore in an ankle holster, were both a long way from the study. They were in his room, in a locked metal box beneath his bed. In there with some Colombian weed, his service medals, and a tuft of the Montagnard woman's pubic hair. And anyway, he hadn't figured on carrying a piece until he'd actually started for the airport.

Two tours of duty in Nam, three times wounded, and now Ray Tooky was thinking maybe he'd used up all his luck. Shit way to go, getting suckered like this. Getting caught up in some-one's dark and crooked ways, because the two guys in ski masks had had help from the inside. How else could they have gotten into the apartment then moved around without arousing suspi-cion? There was a third party in this thing, and Tooky blamed himself for not knowing who. The feeling left him more embar-rassed than scared. More ashamed than terrified.

Mutt and Jeff positioned themselves behind Ray Tooky and Waseda, with the tall one doing the talking. He ordered Tooky down on his knees, fingers locked behind his head. Then he cuffed Tooky's hands behind his back and pushed him down to the deep pile carpeting on his side. The short, round guy, mean-while, never let his attention stray from Waseda. The Japanese man started crying and didn't stop. Reminded Ray Tooky of some gook in Nam who'd just had his hut burned down, the way he stood hugging himself and moaning, the tears streaming down his round little face.

Lying and staring at a wall of books, Tooky looked for a sign indicating how close he was to dying. When it came he almost missed it. The tall guy began patting him down to see if he was carrying. Unbuttoning Tooky's jacket. Checking his belt, small of his back, both legs, sides of the body. Finding nothing.

But at the sight of Tooky's Special Forces badge, the tall guy froze. Their eyes met. And relief washed over Tooky like an ocean wave slapping his butt on a hot day. He thought, bless the good lord, another fucking snake eater. Tooky almost sat up and shouted for joy, but he forced himself to lay still. His heart stopped flip-flopping because as sure as Took's asshole pointed to the ground, the dude in the gabardine wasn't going to smoke him.

However, the snake eater did take a roll of adhesive tape from a jacket pocket, tear off a couple of strips, and cover Ray Tooky's mouth. Then he pulled Tooky's jacket off the shoulders, injected him in the arm with a hypodermic, and whispered, what you don't see, you can't say. The shot's just to put you to sleep. Tooky started to say, what outfit, buddy, but there was the tape and anyway he began to nod out. Last thing he remembered was the snake eater loosening his belt and tie, making him comfortable.

Penny put the needle back in its case and dropped the case in a side pocket. Then he took off his ski mask. Nickie Max did the same. At the sight of Nickie Max, Waseda whimpered and backed toward Ganis's desk. Nickie, gun hand at his side, simply watched him. When Waseda's hip touched the desk, Nickie said, nice to see you again, Iggy, and shot him in the head and throat.

Waseda fell back across Ganis's desk, knocking the banker's lamp to the rug. As Ganis leaned back in his chair, eyes bulging, fingernails gouging the spotless blotter, Nickie stepped closer and shot Waseda in the chin and left eye.

Waseda abruptly sat down on the rug, one leg under his buttocks, his right arm pulling a carriage clock and wedding pictures of Ganis and Aikiko to the floor with him. He remained with his back to the desk for a few seconds, then slid to the rug where he lay with his face inches away from pieces of the broken green lampshade.

Nickie walked to the desk and aimed his pistol at Ganis's left temple.

Penny said, "I promised not to harm you. But my friend didn't. I want you to telephone Viktor Poltava, and I want you to do it now. If you refuse, my friend will kill you."

20

New York

August, 1985

APPROXIMATELY TWENTY MINUTES after Edward Penny threatened Warren Ganis's life, Viktor Poltava exited the subway at West Seventy-second Street in Manhattan, emerging by the Dakota Apartments, the nineteenth-century mansion where John Lennon was murdered. He stopped to adjust oversized dark glasses and touch a Steyr GB at the small of his back. The Austrian pistol held eighteen rounds, was a semi-automatic, and should safely see him through the night.

Viktor found the noise and filth in New York's subway to be overpowering. He'd ridden in a graffiti-splattered car seated across from an obese bag lady who chain-smoked in obvious defiance of a city ordinance. A gigantic young black man in a business suit, apparently a crazed evangelist, had clung to a pole in the center of the car, preaching the gospel of Jesus at the top of his voice. New York truly was a dismal place. A nightmare in stone.

Viktor couldn't wait to return to Hong Kong and ride the

lovely old tram a thousand feet to the top of Victoria Peak. The view from the tram, with its green, cast-iron cars and mahogany slatted wooden seats, was magnificent. You could look across Victoria harbor and see as far as Macau and China. A stroll through the peak's bamboo forests to the sound of blue magpies and sparrow hawks was heaven itself.

Unfortunately, Viktor's plans for Hanzo had kept him in New York, a city which seemed to grow more shabby and sinister with the years. It would require more than the social graces to smooth one's way through this particular world.

Now he was on his way to see Warren Ganis at Ganis's request. From a safety standpoint Viktor had to question the publisher's insistence upon a crisis meeting tonight in front of his Fifth Avenue apartment building. Uncomfortable with the unforeseen, Viktor much preferred a prescribed and detailed course of action, one set in motion by him. To be surprised was to be destroyed.

Why this coming together on such short notice? Because in a very tense telephone call Warren Ganis had demanded that the Bellas tapes be brought to him immediately. Under no circumstances was Viktor to give them to Hanzo Gennai. Instead Ganis would catch the first flight to Tokyo and personally bring the tapes to the Empress.

Keeping all thoughts about Hanzo to himself, Viktor asked why had Reiko Gennai turned against her son. The question seemed to get Ganis's back up. "I'm not at liberty to discuss the matter," he'd said. Like Viktor, he did as he was told. In any case, he couldn't stay on the phone explaining his actions. He had dinner guests who could not be ignored.

And who might they be, Viktor asked. My attorneys, Ganis said. We're working on the Butterfield deal. That's why you and I can't meet in the apartment, he said. I'll be downstairs, waiting in my limousine. Get here as soon as you can. Simply hand me the tapes and be on your way. Then Ganis had hung up without waiting for a reply. Viktor had laughed, wondering who was more afraid of him—Ganis or Hanzo.

Viktor entered Central Park, intending to walk across to Fifth Avenue. Ordinarily he would have traveled along the east side by subway or motorbike. But tonight he varied his route somewhat, leaving the motorbike in a garage at 42nd Street and 12th Avenue and taking a west side subway. He didn't expect to be followed, and he wasn't. Still, one must be on guard against the deceptions and evil intentions of others.

In the approaching darkness Viktor made his way through a park bursting with people. He wondered about the absence of cars until he saw a sign noting a ban on motorized traffic during summer evenings. Cyclists, however, whizzed dangerously close to him, and on another occasion he had to do a bit of fancy stepping to avoid a lanky youngster speeding toward him on a skate board.

He avoided the open spaces, keeping away from the park mall, and the area called Sheep Meadow, where tonight thousands were enjoying free opera, *Tosca* by the sounds of it. Dodging roller skaters, drug dealers, joggers, and homeless panhandlers, he headed north, making his way along footpaths and bridle paths until he reached the Ramble.

Here he began walking east along mazelike paths, past elm trees and twisting streams, enjoying this little bit of untamed nature. The area contained far fewer people, resulting in a tranquility readily welcomed by Viktor. However, too many of the men around here this time of night were queers, the sort of people who made him bloody uncomfortable. Men lusting after men would always be a mystery to him.

He exited the park on East Seventy-ninth Street and walked one block up Fifth Avenue to the Metropolitan Museum of Art. At the spraying fountain in front of the museum, he purchased a hot dog from a young Puerto Rican, then walked to the museum's wide staircase. Pausing briefly to stare at a mime performing for people seated on the stairs, he took a bite of the hot dog and climbed the staircase. Not once did he look across the street at the limousine parked in front of Warren Ganis's apartment building.

At the top of the staircase, he stood alone near one of the four marble pillars at the museum entrance, brushed crumbs from his shirt, and took another bite of the hot dog. Down on the sidewalk the mime, a small fellow in a striped shirt, white makeup, and red lipstick, pretended to be climbing a rope. Viktor, eyes on the limousine, finished his hot dog and wiped his hands on his thighs.

He watched a blue-and-white police car cruise by the limousine without stopping. It was impossible to see inside the limo from here; side windows were tinted and the night was getting darker by the minute. But Viktor did see signs of someone in the driver's seat. One person.

He watched well-dressed men and women leave and enter the building. The uniformed doorman chased away a disreputable looking panhandler, helped a woman carry packages into the building, and hailed taxis for departing tenants. No one came near the limousine. No one entered or left it.

Viktor rose, stretched both arms overhead, and touched the tape cassettes in his back pocket. He watched the mime's assistant, a slight, young blond girl, begin to pass the hat among those watching the performance. Strolling players. Dancing dogs, someone once called them.

He took some coins from his pocket, walked down the staircase and, when he reached the girl, he dropped the coins into the cheap cloth cap that was her collection plate. She thanked him, showing a mouthful of braces and a vacant smile.

At the bottom of the staircase he briefly eyed the next scheduled street performer, a young man who was a fire eater. A smiling Viktor shook his head, then waited for a pair of buses to pull away from the curb. When they did, he stepped into the street and walked toward the front of the limousine.

In the back seat of the limousine, Edward Penny, the Browning on his lap, wiped perspiring hands on his thighs then stared at his palms. The right hand shook slightly. His heartbeat had quickened. And the pain in his head was getting worse. Bit of abdominal pain, as well. With his right hand he began kneading the back of his neck, wanting Viktor to show up and hoping he wouldn't.

Nickie Max sat on his left, looking through tinted windows at the Fifth Avenue side, hands in his lap, the Beretta resting on one forearm. Penny was checking the museum side. Ganis was to point out Viktor, who apparently had changed his appearance somewhat. As soon as the demon came within range, Penny and Nickie were going to take him out. No muss, no fuss. Just wax Viktor's ass as quickly as possible.

Inside the car, silence. There was nothing to say. There was only waiting. With its boredom and tension.

"We're waiting for my driver," Ganis had told the doorman. The Yugoslav then bowed deeply, since Mr. Ganis was an excellent tipper and thereby entitled to park in front of the building until the next ice age if he so desired. Money was power and the sum of all blessings.

Before leaving the apartment Penny had Ganis lock the study door. In Nickie Max's words, Tooky could use the rest and Iggy wasn't up to seeing visitors. Nickie also told Ganis, "Waseda was your boy and I'm wondering if he hurt my kids because you told him to."

Ganis, on the verge of tears, denied having ordered Waseda to do such a thing. He denied even knowing about any attack on the two girls. But Nickie shook his head. He wasn't interested in excuses. All he said was, fuck up once, just once, and it'll be me who blows your dumb ass away. Know something? I sort of hope you do. I'd sleep a lot better knowing you were dead.

In the limousine Penny was checking the safety on the Browning, making sure it was off, when he heard Nickie Max say, holy shit. Penny looked at him, then past him to the front of the apartment building and said, "Jesus, I don't believe it."

It was Aikiko, walking out of the lobby with a small suitcase probably packed with things she couldn't bear to leave behind. Things she'd spent time packing. Valuable time. Nickie said, I thought she'd left. Penny leaned across the back seat, a hand on Nickie's shoulder, as angry as he'd ever been in his life because Nickie was right. Totally, positively, absolutely right.

Aikiko should have left a long time ago. What the hell was she doing here now?

Viktor. Still crossing the street. Taking advantage of a red light that had stopped Fifth Avenue traffic. Now only feet away from the limousine and able to look through the front window at Warren Ganis. Seeing the publisher sitting alone up front, hands gripping the steering wheel and looking terribly, terribly frightened.

Ganis was staring at the Fifth Avenue side, away from the museum, perhaps looking in the direction he expected Viktor to come from. Viktor took one more step, then froze. Because he saw Mrs. Ganis walk from her apartment house lobby, escorted by the doorman who took a single suitcase from her and pointed to the limousine. She shook her head. Refused to look at the limousine. *Refused to look at her husband.*

As Viktor watched, Warren Ganis started to call out to his

wife. Then he changed his mind. Or had it changed for him. The publisher straightened up and turned from his wife as though someone behind him was directing his actions. Directing him to look forward. Viktor took one step backward. Then another.

Ganis recognized him.

As the publisher said something over his shoulder, Viktor turned and ran, dodging cyclists, hearing the sudden shrieking of brakes, the cursing of motorists.

On the sidewalk in front of the museum he quickly glanced over his shoulder in time to see the limousine's back doors fly open and two men leap out. One was tall, bearded. The other was short, stout and Viktor recognized him. He was one of two men Viktor had stalked in San Augustín before arranging the incident with *el Presidente's* daughter.

And now they were stalking Viktor.

Filled with an unspeakable rage, he ran for the park, heading for the darkness and the crowds. And as he ran, he heard Warren Ganis call to him, "Viktor! They forced me to do it! They forced me!"

21

FOUR HOURS AFTER the attempt on Viktor's life, a haggard-look-
ing Warren Ganis sat in his study and let his private line ring. He
wept silently, his face buried in his hands.

Finally he reached for a small brown bottle on the black oak
desk, opened it, and shook three tiny pills into the palm of one
hand. After placing them on his tongue he swallowed half a glass
of mineral water. Then he flopped back in his chair, closed his
eyes, and listened to the ringing for a full five minutes. Finally,
opening his eyes, he stared at the phone, picked up the receiver
and said calmly, "Yes, Viktor."

"You betrayed me. You—betrayed—me," Poltava repeated,
spacing out the words.

"They threatened to kill me if I didn't do exactly as they
ordered. I watched them kill Waseda here in my study, so I had
every reason to believe they meant business. I also cooperated for
fear harm might come to my wife. It's as simple as that. I apologize for what happened to you, but at the time I had little choice
in the matter."

"Ended up running for my life. All because of you, you

bloody bastard. If you'd been standing in front of me, I'd have killed you on the spot. Where were the police?"

Ganis shook his head. "There were no police. Just the two men in the limousine with me."

"Two men? Just two fucking men?"

"Yes."

"Did you tell them where I was staying? Not that I intend to go back there, but did you tell them?"

"I told them, yes. When one dug his pistol into my temple I told him everything he wanted to know."

"You know what happens to people who betray me."

Ganis bowed his head and sighed. "I know, Viktor, I know. You'll have to excuse me, but at the moment I have other things on my mind." He swallowed, cleared his throat, and said, "Did you know that Yasuda Gennai is dead?"

Viktor was quiet. Then, he asked, "When?"

"Last night. I've just finished talking to Reiko Gennai and she—"

"Did you tell her what happened tonight?"

Warren Ganis placed a hand over his eyes. "Yes." He sounded exhausted. "I needed her help in disposing of Waseda. Bringing in the police wouldn't have been wise. As noted by my two visitors, I was in no position to discuss stolen art with the cops. Reiko Gennai had local *Mujin* people come for the body. I have no idea what they did with it, and at this point, I don't much care."

"Why did they kill Waseda?"

Warren Ganis told him.

Viktor said, "Well, I guess we can safely say your late assistant has ill-used his last adolescent. No great loss, really. The man truly was a swine. I take it Mrs. Gennai has informed you of your wife's affair."

"She has, yes."

"Did she mention the man's name?" Viktor seemed amused.

"Yes. He works for Senator Fran Machlis."

"That is, when he's not fucking your wife. His name is Edward Penny, and his fat little friend is Nicholas Maximillian. You got your first look at them tonight. I recognized them from San Augustín. Penny also put the authorities onto me in England last week when I was there to do Coveyduck. That's twice he's nearly

polished me off. I think it's time I chucked a turd in his direction
for a change."

"You never mentioned that Reiko Gennai had ordered you to
kill my wife."

"You never mentioned that Edward Penny was waiting in your
limousine to send me to a better world. As for your wife, I suggest you discuss her with the Empress."

"I have. I've told Reiko that if anything happens to Aikiko,
I'll give her cause to regret it. I pointed out that I'm capable of
doing *Mujin* as much harm as good."

Viktor chuckled. "Rattled your saber, did you? The loving
husband defending his straying wife. Truly heartwarming."

Ganis massaged the corners of his eyes with a thumb and
forefinger. "I meant what I said. I love Aikiko very much, and if
anything happens to her, anything at all, Reiko Gennai is going to
be one very sorry woman."

"Which means you're threatening me, as well."

"Take that any way you choose. I really don't care. I'm not
fooling myself that I'm a match for you, particularly in your line
of work. But I have weapons of my own, and I know how to use
them."

"My, my. Well, it is easy to be brave from a safe distance. If I
didn't know better, I'd say you inherited a bit of Yasuda Gennai's
fighting spirit."

Ganis, his face wet with tears, took a handkerchief from the
pocket of his kimono. "I knew him for almost fifty years. Everything I am, everything I have or ever will have, I owe to him. I
wish I could have told him how much I loved him."

"I wonder if his widow shares your grief. My impression was
the sooner he passed away the happier she'd be. If she allowed
herself to be swayed by passion, it certainly wasn't in his direction. Well, it hasn't been your night, has it? Your patron dies,
you've insulted the Empress, and you haven't exactly endeared
yourself to me. Oh, and your wife's left you. She has left you,
hasn't she? When last seen she appeared to be ignoring you and
striking out for new shores."

"My wife is my business. One way or another, I'm going to
get her back. You just remember what I said. If anything happens
to her—"

"My friend, my friend. I've just decided that you don't need

Viktor Poltava for an enemy. You already have more than your share. You have yourself, you have your wife, you have the Empress. I doubt if you'll last out the week."

"Good-bye, Viktor. I'll fight you as best I can."

Poltava chuckled. "Wonderful. That thought will be uppermost in my mind as I go about my business. What is the saying you have here in your country? Ah, yes. 'Have a nice day.'"

22

Washington, D.C.

August, 1985

EDWARD PENNY, A cup of herbal tea in hand, stood in front of French doors in the music room of Fran Machlis's home, staring out at the wide column arbor leading to the garden. The arbor was a thing of beauty, an open framework of rustic wood covered in roses, honeysuckle, and pea vines.

It shaded the music room and the library, making drapes and shutters unnecessary. But as Penny had told the senator, the arbor allowed intruders to approach the house without being seen. Tear it down, he'd said. For your own sake, tear it down.

Fran Machlis had refused. The view through the French doors was enchanting; she wanted it kept that way. Penny could make security changes elsewhere in the house but the arbor was off limits. One of my daughters took her wedding vows there, she told Penny. Two presidents had attended garden parties at the house and walked away praising the arbor.

Fran Machlis did some of her best thinking there. She considered the arbor an endangered species, one worthy of protection

Nor would she permit Penny to remove the French doors and install something stronger. Just wire the doors and let it go at that.

All of this had occurred a few days ago, when Penny had learned that the senator *might* be on Viktor Poltava's hit list. At the time he'd had no hard evidence to back up his claim. All he'd had were some lines scrawled by Aristotle Bellas in a $1.35 notebook. Not reason enough to flatten the arbor, the senator had said.

In the music room, Penny turned to stare at Nickie Max who sat at an upright piano, using one finger to pick out Billy Joel's *Just The Way You Are*. A bronze bracket clock chimed twice, indicating the half hour. The time was 5:30 P.M. on one of the hottest August days so far.

Nickie Max, his back to Penny, said, "She's due here in an hour. How we gonna work this thing?"

He was talking about Fran Machlis. He was also asking if Penny had decided to tell her what happened with Viktor Poltava in New York almost twenty-four hours ago. They hadn't told her or the police anything. On Penny's orders, Aikiko had also remained silent. She'd also said nothing about having left her husband.

Telling Fran Machlis about Viktor meant taking the next logical step, which was bringing in the FBI and Washington's antiterrorist police unit to protect her, Aikiko, and Meyer Waxler. That would bring in the press. Then it would only be a matter of time before the senator's relationship with Helen Silks appeared in supermarket tabloids. And could the police stop Viktor from killing? So far no police force in the world had been able to do that.

Yet by keeping quiet, wasn't Penny putting people's lives at risk? Viktor had been hired to kill Waxler. And because of Aikiko's affair with Penny, the killer was coming after them, as well. Viktor tended to hold fast to his purpose. He was also unforgiving. A few words with Warren Ganis and by now the demon knew who'd set the trap for him last night. Count on him to even the score as soon as possible.

"I just don't know how to play this damn thing," Penny said to Nickie Max. "Go official with it and the press will be all over us. Once those bastards dig their teeth into something, they won't back off. When that happens, the senator's going to be in deep shit. Anyway, who's to say the cops can handle Viktor? On the other hand, something in me says get real, pal. Call in the guys with the badges and short haircuts."

Nickie Max held his finger on a black key. "Damned if you do, damned if you don't."

Penny looked into his teacup. "So close. We came so fucking close last night."

"Close only counts in horseshoes and slow dancing."

"We chase him into the park and he disappears right in front of us. Swallowed up by a few thousand people. Jesus, I mean, we get Ganis to point him out, to identify him by name. We're maybe ten feet away, and we still don't fucking whack the guy."

Nickie said, "And let me be the first to tell you that Ganis won't be on our side in this thing. The man's probably worried shitless about Viktor and he ain't gonna want to talk to nobody, especially to cops. You sic the law on him and know what he's gonna say? He's gonna say 'Viktor who?' Be your word against his. And he's a very heavy dude, don't forget. Something else, too. No offense, but you got a thing going with his wife and this is gonna make you look bad when you go up against him, know what I'm saying? This thing with Viktor ain't that easy to figure."

Viktor. After losing him in the crowd every sound in the park fed Penny's anger. A child's laughter, a lone saxophonist near the lake, a man calling a woman's name, the pounding of conga drums, the scraping of roller skate wheels against cement. All of it stirred up Penny's rage to a dangerously murderous level. He'd ended up hyperventilating, leaning against a tree and breathing like a race horse. Not from running. But from nerves.

It was Murphy's Law all the way. Whatever could go wrong, did. Aikiko showed up at the wrong time. Crowds in the park. Crowds going in and out of the museum. And when Penny and Nickie hustled over to the sleazy hotel on 41st and Eighth Avenue, where Viktor was staying, they'd found the door to his room wide open. He'd had visitors.

Junkies, Penny figured. They'd left the walls and floor behind, but not much else. All personal property, clothing, food had disappeared. In the search for the price of a fix a thin mattress had been dragged out into the urine-smelling hallway and slashed open. Even the threadbare carpet had been partially rolled back.

In the end, it had all worked out to Viktor's advantage. The room now contained nothing to indicate he'd ever been there. At the reception desk Penny learned that Viktor had registered under the name George Yee. That was all the demon had to give the management. A name and twenty-five dollars a night in advance.

In the music room Penny said, "If Aikiko had left when I told her to instead of hanging around to pack a bag, we might have nailed the son of a bitch. As soon as Poltava saw her, it was all over."

"Come on, man. She feels bad enough, okay? These things happen, what can I tell you. Still want me to pick her up at the gallery?"

Penny sipped cold tea. "Yeah. I'll be with the senator tonight. We've got three parties and two receptions, and I don't know when we're getting back. You and Bob Hutchings take care of things here until I get back. Viktor's out there somewhere, and sooner or later we're going to hear from him."

The intercom buzzed. Penny walked across a hand-made hemp rug to an English-style games table, picked up the receiver, and pressed down the intercom button. "Penny." He listened, said thank you, then pressed down another button. "How're you?" he said. "Good. I'm glad to hear she's coming along fine. What's up?"

He listened, then frowned, appeared to hold his breath and finally said, "Yes, thank you, I'll do that right away. I'll get back to you later."

He slammed the phone down and said to Nickie, "Let's go."

"Go where?"

"We have to find a television set. Got to check out the news."

He jogged toward the door and when Nickie asked why the rush, Penny said, "That was Meyer Waxler on the phone. He called to tell me it's on the news."

"What's on the news?"

"Viktor," Penny said. "He's dead."

23

ALL WARFARE, WROTE Sun Tzu, is based on deception. Thus, when able to attack, appear helpless. When near, convince the enemy you are far away. Lure the enemy with a bait. Pretend disorder and destroy him. If he is stronger, avoid him. Let him believe you to be weak and thus encourage his arrogance. When he rests, torment him. If he is united, divide him. Attack where he appears unprepared. Strike when least expected.

In New York's Chinatown, Hanzo Gennai stepped from a taxi in front of the Canal Cinema shortly after 3:00 P.M. He walked to the box office, purchased a ticket from a fresh-faced young Chinese girl with luxurious hair, and entered the cool darkness of the almost empty theater.

Inside he walked to the center aisle, found the second row on his left, and sat down in the third seat. Nervously rubbing his withered left arm, he glanced around the theater. As usual, the darkness left him edgy. He'd hated it since he was a boy, when his mother had punished him by shoving Hanzo into a packing crate kept outdoors in the garden.

Frightened to the point of nausea, he would remain imprisoned in this wooden cell at his mother's pleasure, ropes tied around the crate to prevent his escaping. There were long hours without food or water, and he was often trapped in his own waste. "It's for your own good," his mother had said. He had to toughen his spirit. He had to become *bushi*, a warrior, or he could never follow his father as *Mujin*'s leader.

For Hanzo, the darkness of the Canal Cinema was especially terrifying because it also hid Viktor Poltava. The demon had made it clear there would be no repetition of last night, when he'd been betrayed by Warren Ganis. He would be watching Hanzo from the moment he entered Chinatown until after he left.

It was useless to probe the cinema's darkness for the killer. Viktor had a chameleon's talent for blending into his surroundings. What's more, any attempt by Hanzo to nose him out would be seen as an attempt to get the best of him, something Viktor disliked intensely. In a telephone call this morning, Hanzo had heard the chilling words from Viktor himself: The demon's very first order of business would be to punish Edward Penny for last night's attempt to kill him.

In the Canal Cinema all seats near Hanzo were unoccupied. Across the aisle a pair of Chinese teenagers, feet resting on seats in front of them, pointed to the screen with beer cans in their hands and commented on the action in Cantonese.

Eyes still on the screen, Hanzo leaned forward, reached beneath his seat, and pulled loose a white envelope stuck there with chewing gum. He folded the envelope in half, then once again before slipping it into an inside jacket pocket. On screen an old Shaolin monk did a double backflip over the heads of several attackers, safely landing several feet away. The Chinese teenagers approved loudly. A disgusted Hanzo rose from his seat and left the theater.

Outside he stood under the marquee, put on a pair of sunglasses and used a handkerchief to wipe perspiration from his face and neck. He was tempted to look over his shoulder, to see if Viktor was following him. A waste of time, he decided. Viktor came and went like the wind.

Hanzo wished he could stop being so fidgety. You walk around as though afraid your skull will be crushed like a leaf, his mother said. That may be true, he said, but who in his right mind can remain composed and unconcerned around the ghoulish Viktor. Mr. Poltava didn't just remind one of the devil. He was the devil himself.

In front of the Canal Cinema, Hanzo watched as a young woman in a clinging red silk dress strolled past him carrying a round-faced child in a sling. She reminded him of Asia. Reminded him that tomorrow he'd be flying home and leaving the abominable Mr. Poltava behind.

Today's meeting here in Chinatown was their first in almost two years. It would also be their last if Hanzo had his way. After today he was going to do everything in his power to avoid encountering that madman again.

Backing into the shade of the Canal Cinema marquee, Hanzo took the envelope from his pocket and unfolded it, recoiling at the sight of the chewing gum used in attaching it to the seat. Opening the envelope, he removed a picture postcard of nearby Confucius Plaza. The card also included a hand-written address on Mulberry Street, the heart of Chinatown. A key engraved with a room number was stuck to the postcard. With chewing gum, of course.

Viktor had been scheduled to give the Bellas tapes to Warren Ganis, who was to have passed them onto Hanzo. But last night's attempt on Viktor's life had put him off Mr. Ganis. The two had fallen out of love, a fact confirmed by Hanzo in a telephone call to the publisher. A despondent Ganis, barely audible over the phone, hadn't wanted to discuss the events of last night. Nevertheless, he'd found the energy to accuse Hanzo of conspiring with the Empress to kill Aikiko.

Naturally, Hanzo had denied the charge, a position which had failed to impress Warren Ganis. Sounding like a man on his death bed, the publisher had promised retaliation should any harm come to Aikiko. And in one of the more stupid acts of his existence, he admitted to having actually threatened Hanzo's mother. *Threatened the Empress*.

A smiling Hanzo had feigned indignation, then abruptly hung up and laughed until the tears flowed down his cheeks. Wouldn't it be wonderful if Ganis and his mother killed each other?

Hanzo found it odd that Aikiko's lover had attempted to kill just Viktor and not Warren Ganis. In any event, the tapes were now to be given to Hanzo and no one else. No chauffeur, no go-betweens of any kind. Hanzo was to come to Chinatown alone.

Viktor would be watching to see if Hanzo followed orders. Once burned, a suspicious Viktor was now twice shy. As he told Hanzo, "I will no longer wade in waters where I cannot see the bottom."

From the cinema Hanzo began walking east on Canal Street, passing telephone booths with pagoda roofs, street vendors selling pails of tea-soaked eggs, bakeries sweet with the smell of fried noodles dipped in honey. He smelled pink mangoes and bitter melons in the open air markets, saw old women in loose cotton shirts and baggy trousers shopping for live carp and chicken's feet, heard strains of Cantonese and Mandarin and Thai dialects. And all of it reminded him of Asia, a paradise compared to New York.

On Mulberry Street, the most populous area he'd seen in Chinatown, Hanzo turned left and walked past tea shops, restaurants, and stores selling jade and lacquered screens. After three blocks he found the address Viktor had written on the postcard. It was a run-down rooming house overlooking a fish market and a liquor store. Covering his nose with one hand, Hanzo hurried past the fish shop, and entered the rooming house. Viktor's room was at the end of a long dark corridor smelling of fish and what Hanzo recognized as *bok choy*, Chinese cabbage.

Using the key, he let himself into the room and closed the door behind him. To call Viktor's quarters small and miserable was an understatement. One bare room with a bed, cheap table, and chair. A couple of throw rugs on a floor white with age. One grimy window barred against intruders. No bathroom or cooking facilities. A single empty closet. A man living here could easily be judged to be on the edge of starvation.

Hanzo attempted to raise the window, to let some fresh air into this crypt, only to discover that the window had been nailed shut. He removed his jacket, loosened his tie, and sat down on the bed to wait for Viktor. No telling when he'd show up. Count on that suspicious bastard not only to have followed him from the cinema, but to be lurking about until convinced it was safe to come forward.

Hanzo lay back on the bed, yawned, and closed his eyes. He was bone tired. Three days in New York and he'd yet to get a decent night's sleep. He found the city's manic energy not stimu lating but disruptive. He'd also been involved in company busi ness from the moment he'd cleared American customs.

Most of his time had been spent on the Valencia Hotel deal As *Mujin*'s head of banking, Hanzo was responsible for seein that any new venture brought with it as few financial liabilities a possible. Therefore he was particularly concerned with the matte of the Valencia's back taxes and outstanding debts.

Hanzo had also taken care of some *Mujin* banking business and at least twice a day he'd spoken long distance to his mother a drain on his energy every time he'd done it. What he neede was a holiday. Perhaps a week in Hawaii with Yuriko. Life wit his wife was good again. Credit her newfound ardor to hi mother. And Viktor.

In Viktor's room Hanzo opened his eyes to see the killer star ing down at him. An unshaven Viktor in dark glasses, jeans, an running shoes. Somewhat trimmer. But still muscular and intimi dating. And with shiny facial skin around the eyes, which was s often the result of plastic surgery. Viktor also came surrounde by the usual air of menace. An uneasy Hanzo was instantl awake.

Sitting up, he swung his feet to the floor and rubbed his eyes "I didn't hear you come in. How long have I been asleep?"

Viktor smiled. "Not long. You came alone, I see. Followe my orders exactly. That is good."

"You've taken off a bit of weight." Hanzo patted his stomach "Might try doing that myself, one day."

"My new look serves a purpose. Hopefully it makes me les conspicuous. I must say the loss of a few kilos has me feelin better. For a time I thought I might end up looking like your twi brother. From a distance, I mean."

"I don't think there's any chance of people mistaking you fo me or vice versa. To start with, you have two arms, while I com up rather short in that department."

Viktor chuckled. "That's rather funny, you know. Short in th arm department. Yes, that is amusing. And quite true. Remind me of a joke I heard before I left Hong Kong, about the one legged woman who was raped because she couldn't cross her leg to save her ass."

He laughed and said to Hanzo, "Don't you think that'

funny?" Hanzo said yes, saying it without conviction, then quickly adding that he didn't want to be rude but he had important appointments this afternoon, and he'd appreciate it if Viktor gave him the tapes so that he could be on his way.

Viktor said, "Of course." With Hanzo watching he crouched and thumbed open the locks on one of two suitcases he'd placed beside the bed. Reaching inside, he took out what appeared to be a long, thick rope. One end had been fashioned into a noose. "Women's hair," Viktor said. "Makes the very best rope."

Rising to his feet, he slung the rope over one shoulder. Then reaching into a back pocket, he took out a cassette and tossed it on the bed. It landed on the pillow just out of Hanzo's reach.

Viktor said, "That's one." He put his hand behind his back, saying, "Let's see what else I have for you." Hanzo leaned toward the pillow, right arm outstretched for the cassette, his back to Viktor.

A very quick Viktor yanked the hair-rope from his shoulder and tossed the noose over Hanzo's neck. In seconds he'd tightened the noose to cut off any outcry. When the banker clawed at the rope with his one good hand, Viktor pulled back hard. The banker flew off the bed, dropping to the floor like a stone.

Lying on his back, a gagging Hanzo rolled from side to side in agony, his face darkening as he struggled to breathe. Viktor bent down, flipped Hanzo on his stomach, and placed a knee between his shoulder blades, pushing him into the floor. And again he tightened the noose.

Hanzo's eyes bulged; his tongue hung out of his mouth. His face was discolored and there was drool on his chin. Viktor smiled. And suddenly loosened the noose. Leaning close to Hanzo's ear, he whispered, *"Aikuchi.* That is you, isn't it?"

Hanzo said, "Please, please . . ."

Viktor tightened the rope and pushed down with his knee.

Hanzo said, "Yes, yes. I am *Aikuchi.* Please let me up. Please . . ."

Viktor loosened the noose. "What did you do with the copies you made of the Coveyduck material?"

Hanzo managed to claw a few hairs from the rope. "Sent them to Washington. Penny. Waxler. Sent to them."

"Did you now? Well, all things considered, that makes sense. And when did you send the copies to Washington?"

"Yesterday. Please, I can't breathe."

"You're quite easy to figure out, you know. I guessed you'd send something to the Jew. After all, Waxler is a journalist and spends his life crying out for public attention. As for Penny, he does work for a senator, and we know how troublesome they can be when they put their little minds to it. I suppose I'll have to go to Washington and clean up behind you, as usual. Your mother wouldn't want those copies in the wrong hands. And you really do hate your mother, don't you?"

Hanzo said, "Yes. I hate her."

Viktor sighed. "Well, that certainly gives you and dear Papa something to talk about. You'll be seeing him soon. I don't think he much cared for your mother, either. My regards to your father, by the way."

Pushing down with his knee, Viktor pulled back on the noose with all his strength and choked Hanzo to death. Then, removing the noose, he folded the rope neatly and returned it to the suitcase. Next, he stripped Hanzo of his clothes and jewelry and pulled his naked corpse to the center of the room.

Reaching into the suitcase, Viktor removed a small ax and stood over Hanzo. He pulled the dead man's withered left arm away from the body, then raised the ax high and brought it down, cutting into Hanzo's flesh with a powerful stroke. Two more strokes and the arm was severed cleanly from the body at the shoulder.

In four strokes he chopped off the right arm at the elbow, then wrapped the severed parts in a black plastic garbage bag. After rolling up the bag, he placed it in the suitcase. Then carefully avoiding the bleeding stumps, Viktor lifted Hanzo's corpse, dragged it across the room, and placed it on the bed.

Viktor now opened the second suitcase and removed clothing he'd purchased from a nearby thrift shop—shirt, trousers, shorts, black cotton socks—and carefully dressed Hanzo. The chosen attire wasn't exactly Saville Row, but Hanzo was unlikely to complain about being out of fashion.

Next Viktor took Hanzo's wallet, watch, and rings and put them in the suitcase with the severed arms and bloodied ax. Then, using his belt knife, he cut the labels from the banker's suit, shirt and underwear. After carefully folding each piece of apparel, he placed it in the empty suitcase which had contained the old clothes. Shoes and socks followed. The suitcase was then closed and locked.

Viktor planned a second visit to a Chinatown thrift shop, a different shop this time, where he would sell this suitcase and its contents. He didn't need the money. But he couldn't think of a quicker and more efficient way to dispose of Hanzo's clothing.

There was a bit of Hanzo's blood on Viktor's hands. Since he couldn't very well leave the room to use the communal bath at the other end of the hall, he washed the blood away with most of a quart bottle of Perrier water. The rest of the water was used to wash down a quick snack of rice cakes hastily eaten while sitting on the edge of the bed, back to Hanzo's corpse.

Then Viktor took a metal box from the first suitcase, opened it carefully, and dug his fingers into the gray puttylike substance inside. It was C-4, plastic explosives. After prying off an orange-sized lump, he placed the box on the bed, got down on his knees, and attached the plastic beneath the bed. From the same suitcase he removed a timer and fuse, connected both to the plastic, then set the timer.

Working faster now, he rose to his feet and placed more plastic along with a fuse and timer, at the base of the wall near the barred window. Then it was back to the suitcase to remove three false passports. One went in Hanzo's pocket. A second was tucked under the pillow. The third was shoved under the mattress.

Reaching behind his back, Viktor removed the Steyr GB. The Austrian pistol had been a trusted companion, but it would have to be sacrificed. He shoved it beneath Hanzo's body.

Finished, Viktor looked around. The stage was set. Now all he needed was an audience. He felt rather pleased with himself. But the timers were ticking away and he couldn't stand around admiring his work indefinitely.

One final glance at the room and he nodded. Nothing left behind. Then he reached into the first suitcase and removed a thick glass vial containing a light blue liquid. Walking to the bed, he looked down at Hanzo. Farewell, Hidden Sword. Carefully uncapping the vial, Viktor poured the contents, prussic acid, over the dead banker's face. As always, he found the smell unpleasant, which was why he preferred working with acid near the end of an operation.

When the tube was empty he stepped back from the bed and

watched the hissing liquid eat away the banker's flesh. Recapping the vial, he dropped it into the open suitcase, took a hand grenade from the suitcase, and closed it. Then, suitcases in hand, he walked to the door, opened it, and set both suitcases in the hallway.

He looked left and right. The hallway was empty.

He pulled the pin from the twelve-second grenade, rolled it under the bed, and closed the door. Then he picked up his suitcases and raced down the hallway and up the staircase to the third floor.

He had reached the fourth-floor landing when he heard the first explosion. Seconds later there was a second and louder explosion. Viktor continued heading toward the roof.

24

Washington, D.C.

August, 1985

AT 10:30 P.M. Edward Penny walked into Fran Machlis's huge, vaulted kitchen and told Nickie Max the senator wanted him out of her house by tomorrow evening.

As she put it, the news of Viktor Poltava's death in a New York Chinatown explosion two days ago signaled emancipation for harassed senators. She'd already had Penny dismiss the other security guards with the exception of Bob Hutchings and Nickie Max. One week's pay and see you later. The state of siege at *Casa Machlis* was over.

From now on only one security man around the house or office at all times, she said, except in case of a dire emergency. Hutchings had been given a couple of days off. Penny and Nickie Max could hold the fort alone. Thank Mr. Maximillian for her, but after tonight his services would no longer be required.

One thing more: She was seriously thinking about bringing back the doors, hedges, and plants she'd removed at Penny's suggestion. The house just didn't feel right without them.

Hutchings wasn't exactly out of the woods, either. His em
ployment was to be considered a trial period. Why? Because Fran
Machlis wasn't entirely convinced he'd licked his drinking prob
lem. Penny had disagreed. Everything was a day-to-day fight
with alcoholics, but Hutchings seemed to be winning. Fran
Machlis had said, "I'm in no mood to discuss it. Either you carry
out my orders, or I'll find someone who will."

Tonight she'd been even bitchier. Cranky, quick-tempered
and snarling like a pit bull. No wonder she'd bounced Nickie
Max. Which bothered Penny, because he definitely didn't want
him to go. Penny and the senator's life could depend on Nickie's
being close at hand.

In the kitchen Nickie sat in a hand-made cane chair cleaning
pieces of the Beretta now spread before him on a knotted pine
table. "We got us a problem," he said. "You want me to stay and
we both know why. On the other hand, this ain't my house and it
ain't your house, so I guess I'm outta here. Never pays to argue
with women. They got half the money and all the pussy in the
world."

Penny stared at his reflection in a bronze pot dangling from a
circular rack over Nickie Max's head. *You want me to stay and
we both know why. We know Viktor's still alive. The FBI, CIA,
New York, and Washington antiterrorist units don't know, but we
do.*

Penny sat down across from Nickie Max, removed the *tanto*
from his wrist, and placed it on the table. Then he stretched out
his legs and put his hands behind his head. He was still wearing
his tuxedo minus the jacket. Looking spiffy, as his dad used to
say, in a red bow tie, white shirt, gold cufflinks, cummerbund,
black pants. All dressed up with no place to go.

Fran Machlis had changed her mind about attending tonight's
reception for the Nigerian ambassador. She was also foregoing
parties at the Swiss and Bolivian embassies. In place of socializ
ing, she and Aikiko were in the library discussing Coveyduck's
unfinished book on *Mujin*. Edward Penny and Meyer Waxler had
received copies in the mail yesterday. From *Aikuchi*.

There'd been no covering letter explaining the unfinished
manuscript and the notes that came with it. No explanation had
been necessary. The book was extraordinary. Penny had read it all

n one sitting. When and if it ever got published, *Mujin* was going to end up hurting very badly.

Penny felt the book should be sent to Coveyduck's English publisher. Ethically it was the only way to go. Even Meyer Waxler agreed they owed this to Coveyduck, though he was anxous to cut a deal to run a chapter or two before publication.

Fran Machlis, however, smelled headlines. She was, after all, running for reelection. She said, "I'll read it and then we'll discuss where it goes."

Penny said, "The book was sent to me. Where it goes will be my decision."

That was when Fran Machlis pulled rank and said, "You work for me, meaning I and I alone have the last word on this material."

Penny said, "I just stopped working for you. I'm taking the book and I'm walking." It had ended up with her apologizing and him agreeing to stay. After what she'd done for him, Penny owed her that much. "I've been under a strain with this Poltava business," she said. All she asked was that Penny let her study the book, make notes, and ask Aikiko a few questions.

In the kitchen Nickie Max said, "Did you tell her why you thought Viktor was still alive?"

"I did indeed," Penny said. "I said he was as tricky as they come. I told her the man is a goddamn weasel. He throws dust in your eyes. Gets you looking in the wrong direction, then sticks it to you. I've studied his file until I can recite it from memory."

"What about New York? You mention us seeing Viktor here?"

"No. She's convinced he's dead, so I decided that part of my little story would be a waste of time. Hell, they're all saying he's dead. FBI, New York cops, the whole goddamn world. I also told Aikiko to say nothing. Far as the senator's concerned, Aikiko's big problem is her marriage and her show next week."

Nickie said, "You got to admit he made it look good."

"If you're talking about Viktor, he gets a ten for artistry in bullshit."

"Phony passports. The Austrian piece that's his favorite. And everybody knows terrorists are always blowing themselves up. Didn't some radicals accidentally trash a house in New York a few years back?"

"That they did. But they were amateurs. Viktor isn't. The man is as smart as they come. He gives us this little explosion which kills three people, sends eight others to the hospital, and leave behind a corpse which can only be identified from some very obvious evidence."

"It be's that way sometimes," Nickie Max said. "Hey, in Nam I worked with some of the best in the business, guys who could blow the dick off a parakeet and not ruffle its feathers. But I go to tell you even they made mistakes. Except in that line of work you only make one mistake. What I'm saying is, is there any chance that Viktor really did blow himself up?"

Penny shook his head. "I don't think so. I made some calls and the interesting thing is what wasn't found at the scene—Viktor's arms. That bothers me. I don't know why, but it fucking bothers me. Something else they didn't find, too. Viktor's bel knife. His favorite weapon, according to his file. Stop and think they didn't find the man's favorite weapon."

Nickie said, "Maybe it was destroyed. It can happen, believe me. Maybe the same thing happened to the arms. Maybe the knife and the arms just haven't turned up."

"That's where working for a senator comes in. You got clout up the ass. I've spoken to the New York City bomb squad every day since this thing happened, and they tell me they've gone over everything with a fine tooth comb. Guess what? No knife. They also say the arms were taken off very, very cleanly. Too cleanly for an explosion. Ends of the bone were too smooth. More like they'd been sliced off, one guy told me. Like I said, this bother the shit out of me."

Penny shook his head. "New York cops ain't got a clue, man. They're saying it might have something to do with a Chinatown drug war or it might be political."

Nickie pointed to the table. "Stripped the Browning and the .38 for you. Want me to clean them?"

Penny turned to look at a cabinet with shelves of brightly colored antique plates and teapots. "No. I'll do it myself. The senator's very testy tonight. Very testy. Makes you wonder what they're up to on Capitol Hill."

"Your tax dollars at work. She still in the library?"

"Yeah. Her and Aikiko. Tomorrow I want you to make copies of Coveyduck's book. Let's just have a backup in case something happens. First thing we do is get you a room somewhere. Don't worry about money. My salary should be enough to keep us both going for a little while."

Nickie sipped from a Coors, leaving oily fingerprints on the can. "I'm always worried about money, my man. Flat-ass broke at the moment. My little hustle with Iggy and Ganis is gone. Maybe I can hit up Ganis for a loan. Fucking guy hasn't stopped calling here. Calls nine, ten times a day. Your lady avoids him like he's got the clap. Guess he can't take a hint."

"Him and Helen Silks," Penny said. "She's hot to see the senator." He pointed to a cabinet with shelves of antique plates and teapots. "Fran Machlis tells me she started collecting them sometime last year. European, Chinese, Japanese. Some of them came from Helen Silks. I understand Miss Silks is a very generous lady."

"You'd be generous, too, if you had a pipeline to *Mujin*'s money."

"Guess so. Hell, if I were the Empress I might even buy you a present."

"Shit, I don't want much. Just a bigger dick and smaller feet."

Penny smiled. "You got it, hot lips. Christ, I did everything but stamp my feet and hold my breath to get her not to kick you out. She's making one hell of a mistake dumping her security. Viktor's out there. Man, I know the guy's out there."

Nickie Max brought the Coors to his mouth, swallowed twice, and looked at the can. "That's the way of the world, my man. Cops, soldiers, rowdy types like you and me. Nobody loves us 'til the crunch comes, 'til the assholes of this world start climbing through the window. That's when the people who think their shit don't stink, they throw a few bucks in our face and say, hey dickhead, go out and bleed for me, and while you're at it maybe you can die for me as well."

Penny picked up an oily rag, held it in two fingers before letting it fall to the table. "We drown ourselves to save drowning men. That's you and me, old buddy. Along with all the other poor bastards who got their butts shot off for the good of humanity."

He turned to see Fran Machlis walk into the kitchen. Talk about looking worried. He'd never seen her this tense. Penny stood up. What the hell was making her so uncomfortable?

The front doorbell rang. Deep chimes, which resounde throughout the ground floor for several seconds. The sound mad Fran Machlis flinch. Both hands went to her heart.

Penny said, "What's wrong?"

"It's Helen. She's just driven up to the house."

"She's what? Don't tell me. Now I know why you're so strun; out."

"Edward, please. She called about an hour ago and said sh was leaving for Tokyo tonight. She—she wanted to come by an pick up some things. She insisted on—"

"What things? What are you talking about?"

"She wants her presents back. All the things she gave me— she wants them back."

Nickie Max said, "Jesus," started to chuckle, then abruptl stopped.

Penny said, "I don't believe it. She actually said that?"

More chimes.

Fran Machlis said, "Edward, I have to let her in. I though with your being here there wouldn't be any harm in seeing her. mean, she's not going to stay. She'll just pick up her gifts an leave. Please, please don't give me a hard time on this. Just g along with me until it's over. That's all I ask. Please."

Penny threw up his hands. "Christ, I know she's pissed be cause you're ducking her, but this is ridiculous. Okay, okay. Let' get her inside before anyone sees her. But she picks up her stuf and she's gone. No private moments, no being alone with her Any letters? Anything in writing?"

"I may be a fool, but I'm not a complete fool. There is noth ing in writing. Absolutely nothing." She looked at Nickie Max who stared intently at the trigger guard in his hand before blow ing away a speck of imaginary dust.

"Which reminds me. The servants. Where are they?"

"Upstairs. I ordered them to stay there until I tell them t come down."

Penny nodded. "And you didn't tell me about your frien Helen dropping by because you knew what I'd say."

"Edward, please. I'm already very upset over this thing. I'm asking you to see me through it, that's all. Just do that for me please."

"What the hell. Let's get it over with." Penny thought, lady you may be a good senator but when it comes to Helen Silks you definitely have a bad case of the simples. The more he thought about it, the angrier he became. He looked at a grinning Nickie Max. Nothing profound there. All Nickie did was flick his eyebrows up and down á la Groucho Marx.

Fran Machlis turned and hurried from the kitchen.

Penny delayed following her only long enough to whisper to Nickie Max, "Don't say a word. Not a word."

Nickie Max concentrated on running an oil-stained rag through the Beretta's barrel. "Me?" He shook his head slowly. "What the fuck could I possibly say?"

In the living room Penny watched Helen Silks lay folded black satin sheets on top of a cardboard box containing books and a Philippine drum. Then she took a blue Chinese ginger jar from a granite coffee table and carefully placed it on the sheets. Once the petite Silks looked up, caught him staring, and quickly lowered her head, half hiding her face behind shoulder-length blond hair.

Her glances at Fran Machlis, however, were different. Longer and more frequent, for one thing. At one point she flashed the senator a small smile which Fran Machlis, chain-smoking in a textile-swathed chair, pretended she didn't see. Aikiko had appeared in the doorway, felt the tension, and without a word returned to the library. Penny thought, everybody in here has his bow strung too tight. And that includes me.

The packing was just about finished. Two cardboard boxes of gifts, along with a Chinese storage jar and a Louis XIV giltwood mirror, rested near a split staircase leading to the foyer. Edward Penny watched as Helen Silks, crouched over one box with a flat Chinese flower dish in her hands, looked across the room at Fran Machlis again. There was a touching sadness in her gaze, and Penny remembered that with lovers the hardest thing of all was to forget.

He walked over to the granite coffee table, picked up Silks's car keys which lay beside her purse, and put them in his pocket. Then he walked to the stairs, lifted up the mirror with both hands, and said, "I'll take this out to the car."

Both women were staring at each other. Penny didn't exist for either one of them.

He decided to leave them alone for as long as it would take him to walk to the car and back. What the hell could go wrong in two minutes or less? *A mighty pain to love it is and 'tis a pain that pain to miss.*

Outside in the sultry heat Penny carefully stepped down the porch stairs and onto the circular gravel driveway. He gripped the mirror tightly, thinking if he broke this sucker it would take a lot more than seven years to pay it off. And all because Helen Silks giveth and Helen Silks taketh away.

He looked up at the night sky. A half moon, half hidden by black clouds, was giving some light but not much. Thank God for the newly installed porch and garden lights.

Silks's car was a beige BMW with white sidewalls and a sun roof. La-di-da. With the Empress picking up the tab, the lesbyterian, as Nickie Max called Helen Silks, could afford to go first class.

Penny opened a back door of the BMW and set the mirror down on the seat. Then he took the car keys from his pocket, walked around to the trunk, and opened it. Nothing much here. Just a spare tire, a tire iron and an inexpensive looking suitcase. There would be room for the boxes. Everything else would have to go in the back seat.

Might as well get Nickie Max to help carry out the rest of the stuff. Do it all in one trip and say sayonara to Helen Silks.

He was about to walk away from the car and return to the house when something in the trunk stopped him dead in his tracks. A pair of men's shoes. Resting on top of the suitcase. What the hell was Helen Silks doing with a pair of men's shoes?

He picked up the shoes and looked at them in the moonlight. Nothing special. Black with brown laces and a bit worse for wear. And they definitely clashed with the pink jumpsuit Helen Silks was wearing tonight. Maybe the last guy to rent the car had left them behind.

Maybe.

He dropped the shoes on the driveway and peered into the trunk. And when he found the three dried seeds near the suitcase a horrible truth flashed into his mind.

The suitcase was unlocked. Penny, his heart racing, opened it

Inside he found a pair of men's jeans, running shoes, a denim jacket, and two plain white shirts.

He also found a leopard-skin loincloth and a Japanese demon mask made of heavy cloth. And hidden beneath the clothing were two boxes, a metal one and a smaller one carved out of redwood. A small plastic bag of dried food was in the pocket of the denim jacket.

Penny squeezed the car keys, painfully gouging the metal tips into the palm of his hand. Then he began to shiver in the hot night. *Viktor was here. And Penny was unarmed.*

He had to get to the house and warn the others. Do it quietly.

He looked around for a weapon. The tire iron, for sure. Maybe Viktor had a gun or a knife in the suitcase. Penny quickly searched it, tossing clothing and shoes on the driveway. And finding nothing. He picked up the metal box. Locked. *Fuck me.*

A frantic Penny dropped the metal box and reached for the small wooden box. Unlocked. Maybe he could get lucky. He dried his perspiring hands on his cummerbund and opened it. Nothing. Fucking worse than nothing. Just a round lump of some kind, solid gold or maybe gold-plated.

Suddenly his hands began to shake so badly he almost dropped the lump. *He was holding Viktor's grandmother's heart.*

"What are you doing?" Penny almost leaped out of his skin. It was Helen Silks, yelling from the front porch. Silhouetted against the light from the house. Freaking out. Screaming at the top of her lungs. "Goddamn you, get away from there! Get away!"

Turning, she ran back into the foyer. "He's looking into the trunk! Viktor, he's looking into the trunk!"

And then, as Penny watched, the entire house went dark.

25

VIKTOR ONCE ASKED Helen Silks why she allowed herself to be used for the greater glory of *Mujin*. "I do it for the fun and the money," she said. "And when it stops being fun, I'll keep on doing it for the money."

She'd certainly earned whatever she'd been paid for helping Viktor in France a few weeks ago. Having earlier insinuated herself into Serge Coutain's circles during one of his many trips to Asia, Helen Silks had no trouble getting invited to the Frenchman's Deauville horse farm. After all, hadn't she become an enthusiastic participant in the sex life of Coutain's chief architect and his wife?

Which qualified her to be one of Viktor's most effective Trojan horses.

She'd driven onto Coutain's horse farm with Viktor in the trunk, stepping from the car wearing extremely provocative clothing. Her small, firm breasts, completely visible beneath a see-through blouse, had been flashpoints of a sort. The guards had been beside themselves with lust. The power of tits never ceased to amaze Viktor.

Neither of the three guards had seen him make his way into

the barn and find a hiding place in the hayloft. Passion could only destroy the untrained mind.

Viktor now counted on Fran Machlis's mind being destroyed by her passion for Helen Silks, thus enabling him to kill Edward Penny and Warren Ganis's wife.

Exactly five minutes after Helen Silks entered Fran Machlis's home to reclaim her gifts, Viktor crept from the rented BMW, crouched in the driveway, and looked around in the darkness. Satisfied he hadn't been seen, he raced across the lawn and into the garden. He wore black; his face was covered by a black ski mask. A black bag hung from one shoulder. The hair rope was wrapped around his waist.

At the arbor he stopped to hunker down in the shadows. Silks had now been in the house for almost six minutes.

Penny, of course, would be predictable. Ever the faithful watchdog, he would stay close to Silks. His duty, as he saw it, would be to preserve the senator's morals, to forestall any unruly behavior. This would leave Maximillian isolated and easier to dispose of. Viktor had watched the house long enough to know there were no other guards present.

Maximillian was a professional. Under ordinary circumstances he could be relied upon to give a good account of himself. Viktor, however, was far from ordinary. As for Edward Penny, he would forever be a prisoner of their encounter in San Augustín. There should be no trouble retrieving the copy of Coveyduck's book.

Nor did Viktor anticipate the slightest difficulty in disposing of Ganis's wife and Meyer Waxler. The sole reason he didn't suppress the Jew first was that his death would have alerted Edward Penny.

Rising from the shadows of the arbor, Viktor walked toward the house, keeping the arbor between him and anyone who might be at the windows. His right hand held the belt knife.

The senator's home was quite lovely. Vaguely reminiscent of those on Hong Kong's Victoria Peak. But in the end it was simply a ripe piece of fruit waiting to be plucked. The house sat alone on a small plot of land, isolated from neighbors and prying eyes. And its sprawling confines allowed for penetration at several points. The presence of the arbor was an open invitation for villains and rogues to invade the premises at will.

It took Viktor less than three minutes to find the telephone wires and cut them. Then he made his way around back to the kitchen. Plenty of light there. Almost too much. He peeked in a window. Interesting. Mr. Maximillian was cleaning his weapon. How commendable.

Viktor worked best in darkness. Therefore he needed to get inside the kitchen to reach the fuse box. Attaching the knife to his belt, he removed the hair rope from his waist and moved toward the back door. Considerate of Maximillian to leave it open in his quest for fresh air.

Viktor was about to enter the kitchen when he stopped dead in his tracks. *Helen Silks was running through the house screaming his name. Was she insane?*

Viktor saw Maximillian stop cleaning the gun, then quickly begin to reassemble the weapon. A bloody professional. Self-preservation demanded that Viktor act immediately. He rushed through the door.

A terrified Nickie Max leaped out of his chair, knocking it over and dropping the pieces of the gun he'd been frantically reassembling. He snatched Penny's *tanto* from the table and cleared the blade from the sheath, shouting Edward Penny's name, warning him that Viktor was here in the kitchen.

A charging Viktor kicked him in the stomach with lightning speed, spinning Nickie around, knocking him across the table and sending gun parts flying to the floor. Seconds later, the hair noose was over Nickie's neck and around his throat.

Viktor yanked back with both hands, pulling Maximillian to the floor. The American, red-faced and gagging, lashed out with his legs and tried to slip his fingers under the noose. When he tried to sit up, Viktor pulled him down again.

Then Maximillian grabbed the rope and tried to pull Viktor off-balance. Viktor staggered a step or two before dropping his hips and steadying himself. And that was when an hysterical Helen Silks ran into the kitchen.

"He stole my keys," she said. She was weeping, all but incoherent and very close to losing control. "I was talking to Frances, and I never saw him leave. He took my goddamn keys!"

An enraged Viktor could hardly believe his ears. He kicked Maximillian in the head, never once looking down at him, knowing that the American was now dead or unconscious. Then he took one step toward Helen Silks. His eyes were blue ice. "You bloody cunt. You let your feeling for that old woman put my life at risk. First Warren Ganis, and now you."

"Viktor, I'm sorry."

He pulled the belt knife free and slashed her throat.

Outside in the driveway Penny took the heart from the box, then raced to the trunk and grabbed the tire iron. Seconds later he was behind the wheel, dropping the heart and tire iron on the seat beside him. Then he turned the key in the ignition, switched on the headlights, and revved the motor.

With Nickie Max's scream, all the bad memories had come back in a horrible rush. *San Augustín. Tómas. Fleur Ochoa. Oni.* Fuck up this time, and Nickie was finished. He might already be dead. The thought terrified Penny. And made him determined to kill Viktor even if it meant dying in the process.

Viktor's god was *Sun Tzu.* That was how he'd defeated Penny in San Augustín. Now it was Penny's turn to use *Sun Tzu* against the demon.

In the BMW, Penny floored the accelerator. The car wheels spun wildly, spitting gravel in all directions. As Fran Machlis called his name he gripped the wheel tightly and felt the car take off like a rocket. It flew from the driveway and landed on the front lawn. Foot on the floor, Penny sped toward the house.

He raced across the lawn, crushing wicker furniture and flattening a bird bath. Then he was in the garden, running over plants, hitting the arbor at top speed, demolishing it and braking. But not before he hit the French doors, tearing them from the hinges.

The BMW barreled into the music room, colliding with the upright piano and sending the terra-cotta animals on top of it flying around the room. As the piano sounded one long, sour note, Penny's head smashed into the windshield. Blood instantly poured down the left side of his face. Dazed, he fumbled with the door. When it opened, he fell out to the floor.

Struggling to his feet, he clung to the car door and shook his head. When Fran Machlis screamed his name Penny yelled, "Don't move! Poltava's in the house. You and Aikiko stay where you are. Don't try for the phones. He's cut the lines. Just keep quiet and stay where you are!"

Removing his tie and cummerbund, Penny dropped them at his feet. Then he took off his shirt, tore a strip from it, and folded it into a makeshift headband. When he'd tied it around his head to stop the bleeding, he reached in the car and removed the tire iron. And the gold-encased heart. Then he climbed over the wrecked piano and smashed furniture and walked into the hall.

He stood in the glare of the headlights. Time to mind-fuck the demon.

Play games with his head the way Viktor did with the rest of the world. "Poltava! Poltava! I've got something of yours. I've got your grandmother's heart. I've got your grandmother's fucking heart!"

Penny told himself not to weaken himself by thinking about Nickie. Concentrate on Viktor. On the demon. Couldn't think about Viktor having a gun, either. If he did, Penny was dead meat in this light.

Think about what was in Viktor's file. Think about his revenge against the guys involved in his grandmother's death. Think about Viktor's love for her. Play with the fucker's mind and hope it works.

Crouching, Penny placed the heart on the floor, raised the tire iron, and brought it down with all his strength. "Can you hear that, Viktor? Can you hear that, you son of a bitch?"

He hit the heart again, chipping away bits of gold. Now he gripped the tire iron with both hands and attacked the heart, cracking it in half. One half flew up, hit the wall, and bounced several feet away.

Penny, his head throbbing, crawled toward it. That was when he sensed rather than saw Viktor, sensed movement in the semi-dark corridor, then caught only a brief glimpse of the killer who charged him, screaming uncontrollably. Penny tried to get to his feet. Too late.

Viktor kicked him in the left side, cracking ribs and knocking him on his back. The tire iron went flying.

Viktor leaped on top of Penny and brought the belt knife down toward his face. Using two hands, Penny quickly caught his wrist. Viktor's strength was terrifying. They rolled left and right, as the knife was pushed closer to Penny's throat.

Breathing through clenched teeth, Viktor hissed, *"Kill you, kill you, kill you."* He smelled of pine and garlic. Hatred emanated from him in huge, hot waves.

Suddenly he put his free hand on top of the knife and pushed down with all his strength. Penny snapped his face to the left. The blade sliced into his jawbone, then became embedded in the rug. Ignoring the pain, a desperate Penny spat in Viktor's face. When the killer's head snapped back, Penny dug the fingers of one hand into his throat.

Viktor knocked the hand away and clawed for Penny's eyes. The killer's other hand fumbled for his knife, which was on the floor.

In a panic Penny kicked out wildly with both feet, scraping Viktor's shins. When the killer gave way slightly, Penny drove a knee into his stomach. Viktor rolled away and came up in a crouch. He was hurt. But he wasn't going to show it. All he wanted to do was kill the man in front of him.

The killer looked down, saw the tire iron, and picked it up.

A hand on his damaged ribs, Penny crouched and picked up Poltava's belt knife. Then he pulled off the strip of bloodied shirt. He let it fall to the rug and put his hand under it. Still crouching, he waited.

Viktor charged, tire iron raised overhead.

When he was almost on him, Penny brought his hand from beneath the bloodied shirt strip, where he'd been gripping a chunk of the grandmother's heart and tossed it into the killer's face.

Viktor hesitated, confused for the merest fraction of a second. Penny, on one knee, thrust low with the belt knife, driving it into Poltava's abdomen, quickly pulling the knife out and driving it in again.

Viktor brought the tire iron down on Penny's shoulder. The blow was not as strong as it might have been because the killer was in pain. But it was strong enough.

Penny dropped into a sitting position, his left arm paralyzed. He sat watching Viktor stagger back on his heels, then get his balance and come forward.

Penny pushed himself to his knees and looked around for another piece of heart. He saw it. At the base of the wall near the entrance to the music room. But he could only use one hand. He couldn't throw and hold the knife at the same time. *And putting the knife down would be suicide.*

Leaning against the wall for support, Penny rose and backed up until he stood over the gold chunk with its ugly gray inside. Lifting his heel, he brought it down hard, crushing the chunk into small fragments. "She was nothing," he whispered. "Just a fucking crazy woman. That's all she was."

He glanced over his shoulder, at the dark hall behind him with its sharp right turn leading to the living room. He looked back at Viktor. "She was shit. Goddamn out of her mind."

Viktor charged.

Penny turned and ran. Viktor closed in. Taking the corner with all the speed he had left, Penny stopped and quickly flattened himself against the wall. He held his breath, gripped the small belt knife, and waited.

In the darkness he counted to himself. *One, two.*

Viktor rounded the corner, rushing past Penny who quickly stepped behind him. Kicking Poltava in back of the right knee, he pushed him to the floor and into a kneeling position. Then he cut the killer's throat from ear to ear.

Epilogue

T DAWN, FOLLOWING a night of heavy typhoon rains, Reiko ennai entered the second-floor bedroom of her villa and knelt ı a large white cushion. She wore the formal pink and blue silk mono that had been her wedding dress. Her newly cut hair, dicating that she was a widow who would never remarry, was dden by a blue silken headdress.

A recently erected partition—four poles with thin white cur ins—surrounded the cushion. The polished oak floor was hid en under *tatami* and several folds of white cotton cloth, all pped by a red felt covering.

To the left of the partition Oda Shinden, the little one-eyed octor, stood hidden behind a plain white screen. Dressed en rely in white, he wore the formal samurai costume of feudal mes—a wide-shouldered, sleeveless jacket and loose-legged ousers over a kimono. In his arms he cradled an unsheathed ımurai sword with a white haft.

On the floor in front of Reiko Gennai stood a *tachi-oshiki*, a thin, wooden plate with four long legs. It held a cup of rice wine, a pair of bamboo chopsticks, and a dish containing seaweed and three slices of pickled vegetables.

Reaching to her right, she removed a coded cablegram from a low wooden table and, as her eyes shimmered behind tears, she read it for the last time. The cablegram had been sent by Viktor Poltava.

On Warren Ganis's orders I have killed your son who is Aikuchi.

Reiko Gennai touched the cablegram to a burning candle on the table, then dropped the blazing piece of paper into a small dish of unglazed pottery. Yes, I told Viktor to kill *Aikuchi*, Warren had said, but I swear I did not tell him to kill Hanzo. Viktor obviously misunderstood something I said.

Fools and cowards resorted to lies, and Warren was both. Of course, he wanted to get his own back. Reiko Gennai's attempt to kill Aikiko was all the reason he needed. Poltava hadn't needed a reason, but then he never did.

Reiko Gennai was now inextricably linked to the dead assassin. And those who forged this bond included the Thai police official Chakri, currently under arrest; the blind Hanako, under guard in a Bangkok hospital; the American journalist Meye Waxler. Aikiko, of course. And above all, Lord Coveyduck through his very destructive book.

Reiko Gennai found it difficult to accept Viktor's being dead. She had seen him as indestructible, a constant and enduring force. But death was a black camel which knelt at the gates of all.

Her ties to him removed any chance of government support for her actions on behalf of *Mujin*. Poltava had been the world most wanted criminal. He had committed crimes against the Japanese people. Reiko Gennai's association with him could not be dismissed as a legitimate means of protecting the Japanese business community.

For that reason alone, she would have to suffer the disgrace and humiliation of a criminal trial, the first time this had happened to a shadow ruler in *Mujin* history.

Oni had also become a millstone around the neck of Warren Ganis. The American police had questions about their relationship, about the murder of Warren's parents forty years ago, about his conduct while in the secret prison camp. It did not surprise

eiko Gennai when the Butterfield deal collapsed, with a loss to
ujin in excess of forty million American dollars.

Warren's days of usefulness to the company were over.

As were Reiko Gennai's. For as Tetsu Okuhara told her, when
e American killed *Oni,* he killed you as well.

In consigning her to oblivion, Tetsu Okuhara, the new presi-
nt of *Mujin,* had been nothing less than brutal. She no longer
ad a place at the company, he said. Her failure to suppress the
oveyduck book was inexcusable. She'd had unlimited power;
erefore, the current disgrace and dishonor must be hers.

She must bear the responsibility for investigations of *Mujin* by
overnments and journalists in America, England, and Europe.

Okuhara said, "Age has only diminished your knowledge and
creased your faults. The shame you have brought on *Mujin* will
long remembered. No man fears you. You are now despised."

It was Oda Shinden who reminded a despondent Reiko Gennai
at there was a solution to her problems. And that was to re-
ember that she was samurai, a very special class of human
ing. There was only one answer, one way out of this dilemma.

He said, "You must erase this shame from *Mujin,* from your
mily, from the Gennais to whom you are joined by marriage.
ou must choose the response of a samurai." He waited for her
action.

And when he saw that she understood, when he saw her nod
agreement, he said, "If you will grant me the privilege, I will
your *kaishaku,* your assistant."

She nodded once more. And with a smile began her plans for
ppuku, ritual suicide.

In the second-floor bedroom, Reiko Gennai bowed her head
d whispered, "I realize that my failure could have been more
verely punished. I am grateful for the opportunity to carry out
y own death and thereby save my honor."

From behind the white screen, Oda Shinden said, "This is a
tting day for you to die. The sun has begun to rise and the gods
e waiting to greet you. I trust that all will go smoothly for you
this auspicious day."

"There is that matter regarding my son."

"I have taken care of it."

"I thank you." She bowed her head, then repeated, "I thank
ou."

As she slowly ate the pickled vegetables, Oda Shinden spo
softly. "Yours will be a worthwhile death. In sacrificing your li
for an ideal, you will find a sense of joyful fulfillment. You w
be remembered for having retained your honor and dignity. Wh
you do can only be done by one of great determination. You a
truly an Empress."

Reiko Gennai brought the rice wine to her lips and took tw
sips, waited, then sipped twice more. Four swallows. The wor
for *four* and death were pronounced the same, *shi*.

Then she looked at the window, at a sky streaked with the go
and red of a new dawn, and at the same time her hand went to th
small table, to a white-handled knife wrapped in tissue paper a
resting on a white wooden tray.

It was then that Oda Shinden stepped from behind the whi
screen, sword raised high in the position demanded for executi
those of noble rank. Her reaching for the knife had been th
agreed upon signal. And he, in a show of great mercy, was to a
before she cut her own flesh.

Reiko Gennai had been promised that she would suffer
pain.

Nor did she, for Oda Shinden beheaded her with a sing
stroke.

New York

The morning of the next day Warren Ganis lay naked on a foa
rubber mattress in his private gymnasium. His eyes were clos
as Zasshi, the old blind masseur, placed a small metal tube on h
back, inserted a golden needle, then pushed it through the tu
and into his oiled flesh.

Ganis sighed with pleasure. These sessions with Zasshi we
the one thing that kept him from going insane. Since Aikiko le
there had been little to look forward to. The sole cause for rejoi
ing had been Viktor's demise at the hands of the man who
stolen Ganis's wife. With *Oni* in the ground, it was now possib
to sleep more soundly at night.

The press had turned Edward Penny into a demigod. It had y
to link him to Aikiko, but that was only a matter of time. H
wasn't one of Ganis's favorite people, but he had to give the ma
credit. You had to wonder how many other men could ha

triumphed over Viktor, with Viktor's own knife, no less.

Ganis, meanwhile, was up to his hips in lawyers doing their best to stave off judges, federal prosecuting attorneys, congressional investigatory committees, FBI agents, not to mention Connecticut police inquiring into the murder of his parents some forty years ago. All of this was hell on his very delicate stomach and wasn't doing much for his blood pressure, either. Zasshi with his magic touch was worth his weight in gold.

Aikiko. Ganis would never stop trying to get her back. There was no Viktor to worry about, and the Empress had her hands full trying to survive under Tetsu Okuhara, *Mujin*'s new president. Okuhara was a hard-ass and as tough as they come. Life with him was going to be very different than it had been under Yasuda and Reiko Gennai.

Ganis found him to be a cold fish, very unemotional. Count on that bastard to run a very tight ship. It just might mean the end to the shadow ruler system at *Mujin*. Or at least a temporary halt to it because *Mujin,* when you came right down to it, was goddamn eternal.

Like Japan, the company had survived wars, famine, flood, earthquakes, anything God and man could do to it. Ganis would offer odds that *Mujin* would outlive the current crisis. It wouldn't be easy, but he saw it happening.

Meanwhile forget about any female calling the shots with Okuhara. If Reiko Gennai couldn't pussy-whip that bozo, no woman in this world could.

On the floor of his gymnasium Ganis found himself drifting off to sleep as Zasshi continued inserting gold and silver needles in his flesh. The one thought on his mind, beside his own survival, was getting Aikiko back. He'd never let that Penny fellow have her. If it was necessary to have him "suppressed," as Viktor used to say, so be it. Aikiko would never belong to another man while Ganis lived.

He fell asleep thinking of ways to get his wife back. He never saw Zasshi remove the needles, then reinsert them in Ganis's flesh. But in a different sequence.

When one of the Haitian servants came to escort the blind masseur down to a waiting taxi, as was customary when the session ended, there was nothing out of order in the gymnasium. As usual, Warren Ganis lay quietly on the mattress, his pink, fleshy body covered by a sheet. And as usual, he was not to be disturbed for at least half an hour.

In the taxi returning him to his New Jersey home, Zasshi wondered how Oda Shinden was faring under the new regime at *Mujin*. The blind man smiled. Twin brothers with only a single eye between them.

Zasshi had been born blind; Oda, more fortunate, had come into the world with a single eye. Both owed much to a strong father, a samurai, who had refused to allow either to vegetate, who had pushed both into achieving all they could. It was he who had reminded them that one eye was better than ten tongues, and one hand was better than ten eyes.

Thanks to their father, both brothers had learned to use their hands quite well.

When Zasshi next spoke to his brother it would be good to talk about their father, the old warrior, as Oda used to call him. First, of course, he would tell his brother that Warren Ganis was dead. Zasshi had killed him at Oda's request, not the first time he had served his older brother in such fashion.

To a western medical examiner the cause of the publisher's death would be an apparent heart attack, occurring approximately twenty minutes after Zasshi had left him sleeping in his private gymnasium.

This was one consequence of using the acupuncture needles in improper order. But who was to know this except Zasshi and his brother Oda and the old warrior who had taught them both?

Washington, D.C.

That evening Edward Penny and Nickie Max stood in the lobby of the Brussell Gallery, eyeing a well-dressed African with tribal slash marks on his face as he left carrying one of Aikiko's framed watercolors. Penny's left arm was in a sling, and there was a fresh scar on his forehead, which Aikiko and Fran Machlis had said was quite becoming.

Nickie wore dark glasses and leaned on a cane. The kick in the head by Poltava had left him with double vision, a hairline skull fracture, and had affected his coordination. Nothing permanent, but meanwhile he didn't feel like turning cartwheels down the street.

He said to Penny, "I think you're hooked up with the right woman. This art thing of hers seems to be paying off. Her stuff's selling like hotcakes. All you got to do is sit home and help her count the money."

"You don't know the half of it. Two gallery owners are trying to steal her away from here. They're offering her big bucks just to sign up, and they're promising her the moon."

"Think it has anything to do with all the publicity she got about Viktor coming to kill her?"

Penny stepped back to let a dumpy, blue-haired lady in running shoes push through to the souvenir counter. "The publicity didn't hurt. Sure you don't want to hang around for a few more days? Everybody loves you in this town."

Nickie shook his head. "Not as much as they love you. Shit, you're Captain Midnight and Superman and Dwight Gooden all rolled up into one. Press just loves to write about you. Anyway, I got to get back to my kids. Thank the senator for offering me a job. I appreciate it, but I got people depending on me. Wanna get back and take care of them."

"You know she was under a strain the night she kicked you out. She still hasn't stopped feeling guilty about you almost getting killed. You have a job with her anytime you want it. If she hasn't got a spot for you, she'll find you one with somebody else."

"Was it her idea or yours, her picking up the tab for my medical bills? Not that I mind, but if I'm gonna chap my lips kissing ass, I want to know whose buns are in my face."

"Hers. What do I care if you live or die?"

Nickie nodded his head. "Figures."

"She really wants you to stay, but if you insist on being a schmuck and leaving, she's also picking up the tab for your ticket back to Bangkok."

Nickie Max grinned. "Shit, man, she's got my vote."

"She'll twist and shout when she hears the news." Penny reached inside his jacket, took out an envelope, and handed it to Nickie. "A little going away present from me. I was hoping I wouldn't have to give it to you, but seeing as how you refuse to hang around and bask in your newfound fame, take this and be on your way."

"What is it?"

"Results of your last visit to the doctor. You're pregnant. Wh
don't you open the damn thing and stop bothering me?"

Nickie Max placed his cane under one arm, opened the enve
lope, and removed a check. He stared at it for a long time befor
saying, "Jesus."

He looked at Penny. "You didn't have to do this."

"You didn't have to come back for me in San Augustín, e
ther."

Nickie Max looked at the check. It was made out to him fc
over three-hundred-and-eighty-thousand dollars. And it was cer
tified. *Certified with his name on it.*

Penny said, "It's half the reward money for Viktor. Coutain'
family and Molsheim's people. Almost four-million francs. Jus
under eight-hundred-thousand in real money."

"Eddie, look—"

"I keep reminding myself that nobody calls me Eddie bu
you."

"I know, I know. Listen, you got a partner. You got a busines
in France."

"Georges says if I don't split the reward with you, I'm
Communist faggot."

"Look, you took out Viktor. I was lying on the fucking floo
dead to the world."

Penny said, *"We* took him out. *We.* You bought me a fev
more seconds and you kept him in the kitchen long enough fc
him to whack Helen Silks, who is now in no position to g
blabbing about her relationship with the senator. You probabl
stopped him from getting to Aikiko. Nickie, cut the shit. Take th
money and give it to your wife's relatives."

Nickie's eyebrows went up. "What wife?"

They both laughed. Then Nickie said, It's going great wit
you and Aikiko, right? Penny admitted it was. Nickie waited
Finally, Penny said, the past is the past. She's cut all ties wit
Mujin.

"I've been watching her," he said. "She hasn't contacted any
body and nobody's contacted her, and what more can I tell you
We're getting our own place just off the Mall. She's still lookin
around for a studio, though. Right now she's working out of th
gallery. When the show's over, we're going to France for a cou
ple of weeks. I need time for my shoulder to heal, and I want t

get away from the press and film producers and the whole damn circus. That's why I wanted you to stay and keep an eye on the senator until I get back."

She trusts you, Penny said. Her investigation of *Mujin* promises to be hot stuff when it goes public. So far the senator had managed to keep most of her plans for going after *Mujin* top secret, but who knew how long that was going to last. With Penny gone, she'd feel better with Nickie Max around.

Nickie looked at the check. He grinned. "You're a silver-tongued devil, you know that? But only 'til you two get back. After that, I'm outta here. And don't try to talk me into staying."

Penny grinned. "Me? Talk Nicholas Alonzo Forrester Maximillian into doing something he doesn't want to do?"

"Fucking right, you would. What's up? Who you looking at?"

Penny moved closer to Nickie Max and stared over his shoulder. "Looking at an art lover. Campbell Espry. The fat-faced little fuck who put those black kids on me. The soup man himself."

Nickie turned. "The dude with the travel agency who's still big on the spy business. He was running Aikiko for the guy at *Mujin*."

"Running Aikiko for Tetsu Okuhara, *Mujin*'s new president. That's the one. What's he doing here?"

"Look at him. He's just picking up a painting somebody left for him at the souvenir counter. Ain't he entitled to buy like the rest of us?"

"Maybe. But if you ask me, the only difference between him and a bucket of shit is the bucket."

"Didn't you just tell me Aikiko ain't been near any of those people?"

Penny nodded thoughtfully. "So far."

"Hey, you got a good thing going with her. Don't spoil it. If she's straight with you, that's all that matters."

Penny watched Campbell Espry leave the gallery. "You're right. That's all that matters."

In the back seat of the taxi cruising down the Mall, Campbell Espry made a mental note to get in touch with his broker first thing in the morning regarding some Ohio municipal bonds recommended to him in the gallery tonight by a congressional assistant with excellent SEC ties. Espry, a small fortyish man with wobbling jowls and somber demeanor, loved money. A great deal of his time was spent cooking up schemes to get it.

The travel agency was a nice cut-out, but it damn sure wasn't making him rich. And he wasn't getting enough special work from "The Company" to allow him to live in the style to which he would dearly love to become accustomed.

His problem lay in an inability to pass up anything smelling like a good deal. So far this year he'd lost over seventeen-thousand dollars in assorted get-rich schemes ranging from gun running to shopping malls in inner city neighborhoods. One of these days he was going to learn to quit while he was ahead.

Anyone else with an ounce of sense would have stayed far away from *Mujin,* what with all of these investigations going on and reporters kicking over rocks and looking for dirt. Any dirt. God forbid they came across those nigger kids he used to try and shake up Penny. They'd gotten their butts kicked and were still pissed about it.

The press and the investigators hadn't found Campbell Espry yet, but give the fuckers time. They'd already tied August Carliner in to this thing and the ex-secretary of state was losing clients right and left. Espry had better start holding onto his pennies, because good lawyers didn't work cheap.

Which was why he still continued to toil for *Mujin* even after the shit had hit the fan in very big blobs.

He looked at the wrapped painting sitting on the taxi floor. Five-thousand dollars. Money he didn't have. Money someone else put up. Someone who wanted this particular painting in the worst way. Espry wondered why.

Shit, he knew why.

The cab slowed down before stopping on the south side of the Mall at Independence Avenue and Eighth Street. Espry paid the driver, a thin, black man with Rastafarian curls, and got out.

He left the door open for the next passenger, a small Japanese man in a dark suit and tie. As the cab pulled away, Espry watched it disappear in traffic, then he stuck up his arm and flagged another cab. It didn't seem to bother him that he had left the painting in the first cab.

•   •   •

n the back seat of the first cab the small Japanese unwrapped the
painting left behind by Espry, turned it around, and peeled a
white envelope from the back. Opening the envelope, he removed several sheets of paper and, with the aid of a pen flashlight, began reading secret information on Senator Machlis's
investigation into *Mujin*.

He showed no emotion as he read, though he did nod once or
twice when he came across items referring to the strategy the
American government intended to employ against the company in
court.

When he finished, he put the papers back in the envelope and
slipped the envelope inside his jacket. Ganis was dead, but his
wife was now serving *Mujin* in his place. Whether she acted
because she feared Okuhara or out of loyalty to Japan was of no
consequence in the long run.

Mujin's survival was all that mattered.